The Arrangement

The Arrangement

A NOVEL

Sarah Dunn

Little, Brown and Company
New York Boston London

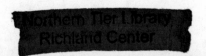

Copyright © 2017 by Sarah Dunn

Hachette Book Group supports the right to free expression and the value of copyright. The purpose of copyright is to encourage writers and artists to produce the creative works that enrich our culture.

The scanning, uploading, and distribution of this book without permission is a theft of the author's intellectual property. If you would like permission to use material from the book (other than for review purposes), please contact permissions@hbgusa.com. Thank you for your support of the author's rights.

Little, Brown and Company
Hachette Book Group
1290 Avenue of the Americas, New York, NY 10104
littlebrown.com

First Edition: March 2017

Little, Brown and Company is a division of Hachette Book Group, Inc. The Little, Brown name and logo are trademarks of Hachette Book Group, Inc.

The publisher is not responsible for websites (or their content) that are not owned by the publisher.

The Hachette Speakers Bureau provides a wide range of authors for speaking events. To find out more, go to hachettespeakersbureau.com or call (866) 376-6591.

ISBN 978-0-316-01359-8 (hardcover) / 978-0-316-44046-2 (Canada)
LCCN 2016948902

10 9 8 7 6 5 4 3 2 1

LSC-C

Printed in the United States of America

For Peter,
the only arrangement
I'll ever need

Really to sin you have to be serious about it.
—Henrik Ibsen, *Peer Gynt*

The Arrangement

One

You people with your "evolved" marriages, the ones with the fifty-fifty housework and shared earning power, the ones who tell each other everything, always, and don't believe in secrets? Does that describe your marriage? Show of hands? I have a question for you: How's that working out for you in the bedroom?

—Constance Waverly
The Be Gathering, Taos, New Mexico

After it was over, all of it, Lucy found herself making the point again and again that it had been a mutual decision. To her aunt Nancy, who was disgusted by the entire business and decided to pretend it never happened. To her sister, Anna, who was fascinated and demanded all the details. To the ladies of Beekman — the quiet few who envied her freedom and her daring, and the bigger, more vocal contingent who would have nothing more to do with her, who wanted her to Stay Away from Their Husbands — Lucy always said it had been a fully conscious and completely mutual decision. Nobody believed her, of course. These things are never mutual. One person always wants it more than the other, one of you is keeping a secret, somebody has a plan. But Lucy always said this about the Arrangement: it was a mutual decision, she and Owen both went into it with eyes wide open, and it had brought certain unfortunate things to light.

It was a Saturday evening early that July. The leaves were bright green and the fireflies were out in force. Lucy and her old friend Victoria were in Lucy's kitchen prepping food for the grill while their husbands were out on the deck drinking wine, but it could have just as easily been the other way around. Beekman was a town where men cooked at dinner parties. The men of Beekman not only cooked, they made things like pickles and cheese and beer and sauerkraut. They ground their own spices to rub on their pork tenderloins and made their own mayonnaise, just to see if it was worth it (it wasn't). Even inside Lucy's head it sounded affected and awful, worse in a lot of ways than the Brooklyn so many of them had lived in before, the Brooklyn they'd either been priced out of or willingly fled, the Brooklyn that Victoria and Thom still called home.

Victoria was painfully thin, and her skin was pale and already crepey under her blue eyes. She teetered around on her trademark vintage heels, which made her look like she might trip and fall straight into late middle age. Thom, with his wild dark curls and two-day stubble that sparkled with flecks of gray, still looked good.

"I called Frank the other day to see if he wanted to go hear this new band with us," Thom said to Owen—Thom and Victoria still had new bands they went to see, even though they had a five-year-old—"and he couldn't, because he was going out to Hoboken to learn Japanese rope tying."

"All I heard was 'Japanese rope tying,'" Lucy said as she pushed the screen door open with the plate of cheese and grapes she was carrying.

Victoria followed with two bottles of wine. "Oh my God, Thom, are you telling him about Frank and Jim?"

"Frank and Jim?" Lucy asked.

"You met them at our wedding."

"Your fabulous gay friends."

"They're a little less fabulous these days," said Victoria. "They got married and had two kids and moved to the suburbs."

"They're still pretty fabulous," said Thom.

"I just mean they're not jetting off to Milan for the weekend anymore. They coach peewee soccer together instead."

"That's sweet," said Lucy.

"Yeah, it is sweet," said Thom. "What they have is sweet."

Victoria looked across the table at her husband and rolled her eyes.

"What?" Thom said to her. "What did I say?"

"Thom is a little obsessed with this 'arrangement' Frank and Jim have."

"I wouldn't call it obsessed," said Thom. "Okay, yes, I am a little obsessed. I just find it fascinating."

"Tell us," said Owen.

Thom reached for the wine and refilled glasses as he spoke. "Okay, so, they've been married for about six years. They have two little girls, a cozy house in Larchmont, and a place up in Vermont. Frank is a stay-at-home dad, while Jim commutes into the city every day. Frank is the president of the PTA, Jim is a deacon in their church. It's like a fifties marriage, really. Dinner is on the table every night, they argue about how much money Frank spends and whether the girls should be forced to learn Mandarin or take violin lessons—"

Victoria cut him off and said, "Except..."

"Except they're both allowed to sleep with other people."

"You mean they're swingers?" asked Lucy.

"I don't know the terminology," said Thom. "They call it an open marriage."

"Swinging implies, I think, participation," said Victoria. "Like, watching each other do it or swapping or something. An open marriage is more, um, furtive?"

"Frank told me they don't talk about it," said Thom. "He said they each give each other a realm of privacy. He says it works out great."

"We saw them a few weeks ago. They're happy. The girls are happy. They're the most stable couple we know."

"How can that be stable?" asked Lucy.

"They've got rules," said Thom. "They don't let things get emotional. I think they're only allowed to sleep with a given person a certain number of times. And some people are off-limits. Exes, mutual friends, coworkers, like that. 'Out of town' seems to be a bit of a free-for-all. The whole thing is pretty clearly hammered out."

"Like Elton John and his husband," said Victoria.

"That was a threesome in a paddling pool filled with olive oil," Lucy pointed out.

Owen lifted his wineglass. *"Allegedly."*

"You gotta hand it to gay men," Thom said. "They've cracked the code."

"Yeah," said Lucy. "I bet their kids don't destroy their furniture either. Or throw up in the middle of the night."

"They get all this"—and here Thom gestured big, taking in the entire scene: the house, the yard, the wine, the friends, the coziness of domesticity, and the comfort of long, familiar love—"and sex too."

"Hey," Lucy said. "I've known Victoria for a long time. You get sex."

"Not the kind of sex those guys get."

"He's right," said Victoria. "He doesn't."

"We have sex," said Thom.

"But it's always with each other," Victoria said, laughing. She and Thom clinked glasses and kissed.

The deck extended out from the house, resting on boulders and who knew what else. The bleached wooden planks were beginning to show signs of rot, and there were three areas that sagged if you walked over them. Owen would tell male dinner guests from the city that the deck had "at least two, maybe three winters to go before we have to replace it," and they would sip their beers and nod, a khaki-clad conspiracy of cluelessness. Still, Lucy found herself thinking, the backyard *was* beautiful. An acre of rolling grass rose to a jagged (and thus authentic) rock wall, likely erected by cow farmers over a hundred years ago. In Lucy's mind, the stones held back the dense woods, offering both protection and temptation. It was one of the reasons they'd bought the house.

"Can you please start the coals, Owen?" Lucy said.

"It's too early."

"It's not too early."

"What's the rush? We're conversing. Have some cheese."

Lucy reached for one of the cheeses, a Rogue River Blue that

Thom and Victoria had brought that clocked in at thirteen bucks for a quarter of a pound. Lucy had taken it out of the paper and was reminded of her life in New York, her life before Beekman, a life of paying fifty-two dollars a pound for Oregon cheese.

"It works for them for one reason," said Owen. "There are no women involved. They're not married to women, and they don't step out of their marriage and have sex with women. There's no craziness. Sex can be just sex."

"I can have sex be just sex. I used to be able to, at least," said Victoria. "When I was younger."

"Me too," said Lucy.

"I think it's a huge myth that women can't have meaningless sex," said Victoria. "You should see these millennials in my office. All they do is have sex, all the time. The girls, the guys. They're not worried about getting AIDS or getting pregnant or being called a slut. They're all vociferously opposed to slut-shaming in any form."

"Slut-shaming?" Owen asked, rotating the cheese plate and slicing off a hunk of Jasper Hill cheddar.

"Yeah," said Victoria. "It's a thing."

"How many people did you have sex with before you got married?" Victoria asked Lucy.

"I'm not drunk enough to answer that question at a dinner party."

"This isn't a dinner party," said Victoria. "It's the four of us having dinner on your deck because you couldn't get a babysitter. How is Wyatt, by the way."

"Wyatt is Wyatt," said Lucy. "He's in our bed with the iPad while we violate all the rules of good parenting."

"Is he still…" Victoria wrinkled her brow with sympathy.

"It's not going away, Victoria. Wyatt is who he is," said Lucy. "How is Flannery?"

"Fine," said Victoria. "Good."

"He got into St. Ann's," said Thom.

"Have you cut his hair yet?" Owen asked.

"Nope," said Victoria.

"You gotta cut that kid's hair," said Owen. "We put your holiday card on the fridge and Wyatt would not believe me when I said Flannery was a boy. He kept laughing every time I said it."

"We're your friends," said Lucy. "We wouldn't bring it up otherwise."

"I love Flannery's hair," said Victoria.

"I'm starting to think we should cut it," said Thom.

"We're not going to cut it."

"He has a girl's name and girl's hair," said Lucy. "Don't you think that's gonna be hard for him?"

"Nobody ever forgets him," said Victoria. "It's his thing."

"It's your thing," said Thom.

"It's my thing that is now his thing and that's how motherhood works."

"Could you please start the coals, honey?" Lucy asked.

"The coals heat up very fast."

"People come to our house for dinner, they want to eat before eleven o'clock at night. It makes it hard to sleep."

"I'm the grill master. I know my coals," Owen said.

Lucy pointed at Victoria and said, "You are my witness. I am on record as saying that we should have started the coals already."

"The coals take ten minutes to heat up, tops," Owen said.

"That is not true, but I'm silent on this subject from here on out," Lucy said, and then she reached across the table and helped herself to more wine.

"You want the truth?" Lucy said, leaning against the avocado-colored kitchen cabinet. Lucy and Owen had planned on installing new cabinets since the day they set eyes on the house. Instead, they'd pretended for each other that they'd grown used to them.

"Yes," Victoria said.

"I'll only say if you will too."

"I'll say, I don't mind," said Victoria. She was dressing the salad while Lucy watched. "Fourteen."

"That's a good number," said Lucy.

"I feel pretty happy with it," said Victoria.

Lucy pointed both of her thumbs at herself and announced, "Twenty-seven."

"Twenty-seven?" said Victoria. "Seriously?"

"I was a bit promiscuous. In college," said Lucy. "And after college."

"She whored it up, my wife did," said Owen, who was kneeling in front of his wine fridge and studying the bottles.

"Don't slut-shame me," said Lucy.

"No slut-shaming!" agreed Victoria. "What about you, Owen? How many women did you sleep with before you met dear Lucy here."

"I don't know," said Owen, getting to his feet with two bottles of Ridge zinfandel.

"You don't know?" said Victoria.

"Nope," said Owen. "No idea."

"It was a lot," said Lucy. "*A lot* a lot."

"Yeah," said Victoria. "Thom too."

"I think I'll start the coals."

"I'm not sure it's safe for you to be around fire, honey."

"I'll help him."

"Great," said Victoria. "Now they'll both go up in flames."

Everyone loved Owen's marinade. There were lots and lots of compliments on the marinade as they sat on the deck and ate dinner with linen napkins and the Laguiole steak knives with rosewood handles Lucy's cousin had given them as a wedding present. God, men and their marinades, thought Lucy. You'd think they'd figured out how to split the atom

11

when all they did was put some Worcestershire and soy sauce into a Ziploc bag.

"I'm at the age when women start to go crazy," said Victoria. "My girlfriends are all going nuts. If their husbands knew half of what was going on, their heads would never stop spinning."

"Why?" Owen asked. "What's going on?"

"I can't tell you. This is a secret all of us are keeping from all of you."

"Give us one example," said Owen.

"Okay, I have a friend, who I will not name, who is married," said Victoria. "And she makes out with people."

"What do you mean?"

"Like at a bar, she'll make out with someone," said Victoria. "She does it at least once a week."

"Who goes to bars?" asked Lucy. "Who has time for things like that?"

"She makes the time," said Victoria.

"Do I know her?"

"I can't tell you."

"That means I know her."

"You do."

"Spill it."

"Perfect Jen."

"Perfect Jen makes out with strangers at bars?"

"She does."

"Who is Perfect Jen?" Owen asked.

"This annoying mother I used to know when Wyatt was little," explained Lucy. "She made her own organic baby food and she ate it herself for dinner every night so she could stay super-skinny."

"I shouldn't have told you who it was, but I did it to make a very particular point," Victoria said, "which is that this woman who we know and who appears to be happy and perfect and has two kids and seems normal—"

"She's not normal—"

"She's reasonably normal on the surface," Victoria said. "This semi-normal woman is, in fact, like a grenade with the pin pulled out."

"Do you think she'd make out with me?" asked Owen.

"Probably! She probably would! She's not picky."

"I read somewhere that women tend to have affairs before their children are born, and men have them after," Owen said. "Men are like, My work here is done."

"Then it's too late for us," Lucy said to Victoria.

"But not for us!" Thom said to Owen.

Owen opened another bottle of wine.

There was no coffee served that night. Nobody asked for it, and Lucy didn't offer any. Caffeine seemed altogether beside the point. Instead, Owen brought out a bottle of locally made bourbon after the last bite of steak was eaten and the marinade was commented upon one final time, and even though the bourbon tasted like tree bark, everybody just kept on drinking.

"Suppose I found out that Thom cheated on me on a business trip," Victoria said. "He had a one-night stand, met someone at his hotel bar and slept with her. Everyone would understand if I kicked him out of the house or even filed for divorce, but if I told people I *let* him have sex with women on his business trips, that we had *an arrangement,* I'd be a social pariah."

"How is it that as a culture we've decided that it's completely rational to break up a nuclear family because one of the parents has sex with somebody else, even if it's only one time, or a minor fling, or whatever," Thom said, "but it's shameful and perverted to make some temporary accommodations inside a marriage so all parties can get their needs met while doing their primary job, which is staying together and raising their kids as an intact family unit?"

"I'm not arguing with you," said Owen.

"Marriage is about kids," said Thom. "It's about having kids and raising them together and not leaving them no matter what." He gestured toward his wife. "Both of our parents got divorced while we were young and it was the single biggest force that shaped our lives."

"Yeah, but I'm not sure marriage should be like dating," said Lucy. "Where you're always looking for someone to hook up with."

"Not looking for it, necessarily. Just, not having to shut it down if it happens," said Victoria. "Being able to feel like a sexual person walking through the world again."

"I barely feel like a sexual person when I'm actually having sex," Lucy said, and then she laughed at her own joke.

"It's almost over for us, Lucy," Victoria said. "I have a friend, she's ten years older than I am, and she says it's like one day, everything changes. It's like someone flips a switch."

"That's really depressing," said Lucy.

"The other day, I was dropping Flannery off at Life Drawing, and a kid in his class asked me if I was his grandmother."

"No way."

"It's true," said Victoria. "And let me tell you, you don't bounce back from that one overnight. You stop thinking you've got all the time in the world pretty quick."

"Are those crickets?" Thom asked.

"They're frogs," said Lucy.

"They're really loud."

"They croak until they find a mate for the night, and then they shut up," explained Owen. "If you wake up in the middle of the night, there are four sad horny frogs still out there croaking."

"I can't believe you live someplace that has frogs," said Victoria.

"We also have chickens," said Lucy.

"I saw your chickens on Facebook," Victoria said. "I refuse to discuss them. You have gone full-on *Green Acres* on me and I'm not sure how much longer we can be friends."

"I'll send you home with some eggs," said Lucy.

"I won't take them. That would only encourage you."

"I need something. And Thom needs something. We're both tired of this persistent, I don't know…low-grade dissatisfaction with life, I guess," Victoria said. "Do you know how often we have sex?"

"Never," said Thom as he served himself a narrow slice of the fruit tart Victoria had picked up at Pain Quotidien that morning.

"Not *never* never," said Victoria. "But it might as well be never."

"And the weird thing is, we're both fine with it," said Thom. "That's the scariest part."

"We can feel ourselves slipping into that kind of stale marriage where you are both fine not having sex, letting that part of you sort of wither up and die, and as we talked about it we realized we didn't want that, but we didn't want to split up either."

"This is officially the strangest conversation that has ever taken place on our deck," said Owen.

"I don't get it," said Lucy. "Do you still love each other?"

"Yes!" said Thom.

"Of course we do."

"Then why are you even talking about this?"

"Let me try to explain," said Victoria. She took a big, dramatic pause and then reached over and held on to Thom's hand. "I want to grow old with this man. I love him, and he loves me. He's my best friend and my favorite person in the world and the only person I want sleeping in my bed with me at night. I want to go on vacations together and have a life together and have Flannery come home with his kids at Christmas when we're seventy. I just don't, at the moment and, if I'm totally honest, for a while now, really, feel like having sex with him."

"Maybe it's your hormones," Lucy said helpfully. "Maybe you need a patch or something."

"Our therapist has ruled that out."

"You've talked about this with a therapist?" said Lucy.

"He's a bit unconventional, but he's interested in finding ways to make long-term marriages work," said Thom. "Marriages where you don't have to disown a big part of yourself in order to stay in the relationship."

"My father cheated on my mother for their entire marriage," said Victoria. "It completely destroyed her. I don't want that for myself. I don't want to give up all my power."

"This is the way nobody gets hurt. Not Victoria or me, not Flannery."

"Has it started yet?" Lucy asked. "Do you guys both have other people on the side?"

"It hasn't started yet," Victoria said. "But we're doing it."

"We are," said Thom.

"Wow," said Lucy. "Just, wow."

Two

When people ask me, "What is the best predictor of long-term success in a marriage?" I always have the same answer: "A mutual respect for suffering." Nobody likes that answer.

—Constance Waverly
Huffington Post

W hy is there poop on the wall again?" Lucy yelled.

She didn't expect an answer. She just wanted the universe to hear her. To hear that this was her life, a life of discovering poop on the wall. Again.

Because, really, is there any good answer to that question? Why was there poop on the wall? Because Lucy was a mommy. Because she had a five-year-old son with some challenges. Just because, really. Because, full stop.

Actually, not full stop. This is why there was poop on the wall: Because sometimes, when Wyatt went to the bathroom, he accidentally got some poop on his hand. And then he did what he considered the most efficient thing. He wiped his hand on the wall next to the toilet. Apparently, with his sensory issues, having poop on his hand was the equivalent of a neurotypical person having, say, acid on his hand. *Think about it,* Wyatt's occupational therapist had said to Lucy. *If you had acid on your hand, your brain might stop working normally. You might forget what your mother had told you a million times. You'd get rid of it the quickest way possible.*

Which was all well and good, but for some reason, Wyatt never thought to tell her about it when it happened, so she was frequently *surprised* to find poop on the wall. She would sit down, intent on enjoying a rare moment of solitude, trying to eke out the most possible enjoyment she could get from a few minutes alone on the toilet, armed with a *Real Simple* or a Pottery Barn catalog or the free local newspaper, grabbing the tiniest of tiny pleasures for herself, a pleasure so tiny even calling it a pleasure was pathetic, and she would turn her head and find herself staring at a smear of drying-out shit.

Shoes that tied were the first thing to go.

Lucy needed shoes she could put on without using her hands, with a writhing, screaming, occasionally biting child in her arms, shoes she could tip up with her toes and slide her feet into without so much as bending a knee. Flip-flops when at all possible, clogs or Merrells the rest of the time.

Then it was earrings. Earrings were so long gone, the holes in her ears had closed up. Next it was eyeliner, then mascara, then returning phone calls, then going to the dentist, then looking in a full-length mirror before she left the house, then lip gloss, unless she found some in the bottom of her purse while she was stopped at a red light. There was more, of course. Pedicures, thank-you notes, RSVPs, Christmas cards, flossing, stretching, remembering birthdays, exfoliation. Basically, Lucy was down to nothing but deodorant, toothpaste, and a pony-tail five days out of seven. She was lucky she was thin and had cheekbones and good skin.

Lucy had planned to move to Chicago after college, because that was where her friends were all headed, but her father had pronounced in that way of his, "If you're going to move to Chicago, you might as well move to New York."

It was good advice. The only time to move to New York City is when you're fresh out of college, unless you happen to be rich. If you're rich, you can move to New York whenever you want.

Lucy could still remember the moment she met Owen like it was yesterday. It was one of those disgusting East Coast summer days, where everyone was sweating and midtown Manhattan was perversely heaped with piles of garbage everywhere you looked. Lucy had just turned twenty-six and she'd gotten an interview for the job of her dreams. She arrived at Rockefeller

Center on time, but there was a hang-up at security and her pass wasn't there. She waited. And she waited some more.

By the time she finally got into the elevator, it was two minutes to one. The elevator was slow and hot and seemed to stop on every floor. Lucy was sweating—a combination of nervous sweat and residual city sweat—and she kept looking up at the elevator numbers and then down at her watch. All of a sudden, she felt a strong, cool breeze coming from her right. She turned her head and saw a tall man in a gray suit fanning her with the Metro section of his *New York Times*. He fanned her, wordlessly, while the elevator made its way up the next eighteen floors.

"Don't worry," the man said to Lucy as she stepped out of the elevator. "Whatever you're doing, you're going to be great."

Lucy got the job.

She started out as a junior line producer for a morning network news show. It was a great job, but it was challenging. It wasn't just making the trains run on time, it was making the trains run on time in a world where there were no tracks, no trains, no trial runs, no do-overs, and no excuses. She remembered the time she was covering a protest against the war in Iraq and one of the lazier grips told her he couldn't manage the setup she wanted because the power cord couldn't reach the outlet. "*Anything* can reach *anywhere*," Lucy pronounced, and she marched across the street and bought three extension cords. Her boss, witness to this all, immediately gave her a promotion and a raise.

She lived in a world of concrete, solvable problems: Get a camera and the weatherman and a backup power source to a safe-but-seemingly-dangerous spot to cover the hurricane. It was difficult, it was stressful, and it was prestigious and relatively well paying, but it wasn't particularly creative. Lucy thought about that, often, after she quit her job and moved up to Beekman. If she had been a writer or an artist, a photographer or a filmmaker or a poet, perhaps she could have found a way to wrestle some meaning out of the pockets of free time allotted to her. She could have pretended to write a screenplay in the spare room, could have joined the glassblowing collective, could have carried around a notebook and written down all of her interesting thoughts. Instead she had entered a world of problems that didn't play to her strengths. She wasn't the least bit tidy and she could find no satisfaction in housework. And then there was Wyatt, her lovable, impossible, unsolvable cipher.

Owen never forgot her face. That's what he always said, how he explained it, how it was that he spotted her two years later, sitting at a bar on the Lower East Side.

"You were sweating in an elevator at Thirty Rock two summers ago," Owen said to her. "I fanned you with my *New York Times*."

"That was you?" said Lucy.

"It was me," he said. "I'm Owen."

"I'm Lucy," she said.

"Hey, dude," Lucy's date, a hipster with a beard so long he looked like a lumberjack who'd gotten lost, said to Owen. "Uncool."

"I hear you," Owen said to the guy. "And I get where you're coming from. But I've been looking for this girl for the past two years, and unless you two are married or she's carrying your baby, I'm giving her my phone number."

Owen and Lucy had been together ever since.

"Hey, Claire, can I stop by later and snag a few of Augie's Ritalin?" asked Sunny Bang.

They were at summer-school drop-off, and the kids who qualified for the program—kids who either needed extra help or could benefit from some genius-type enrichment—were already inside the school. A few of the moms always hung around at the bottom of the concrete steps to chat, and today Lucy was one of them.

"What?" asked Claire.

"Just five. I have to do my taxes and you know I can't focus."

"It's July."

"I got an extension. Please. Three, even; three would probably be enough."

"Are you being serious right now?"

"Yes," said Sunny Bang. "At least, I thought I was."

Claire folded her arms across her chest and said, "The answer is no."

"Why not?"

"Why not? Because I'm not going to let you borrow and consume my teenage son's *prescription medication*."

"Oh."

"There is a cop *right over there*."

There was a Beekman cop, sitting in his police car out in the parking lot in front of the school, drinking coffee and doing paperwork. Ever since Sandy Hook, the local cops had spent their downtime near the school, parked in plain sight.

"This is not a crime. It is one mother asking to borrow something from another mother at drop-off," said Sunny Bang. Then she said loudly, in the direction of the police car, "I would also like to stop by your home to pick up any fall hand-me-downs you might have lying around."

"I'm going to pretend we never had this conversation," said Claire.

"She's a little uptight today," said Sunny Bang after Claire got into her minivan and drove off. "I should have just made an excuse to go over there and palmed a few."

"What do you need Ritalin for?" Lucy asked.

"What don't I need it for?" Sunny Bang said. "I take one, I can do two weeks' worth of bullshit mommy tasks in a single day. I'm like a whirlwind. Totally focused and totally energized. And Augie's got the good stuff. It's slow release. It lasts for twelve hours, and you don't feel like eating for two days."

"That sounds a lot like speed," said Lucy.

"It's better than speed," said Sunny Bang. "I can't wait until Tobias is old enough to get a prescription that I won't ever let him use."

Sunny Bang was one of only three Asian American women who lived full-time in Beekman, and it was a sad fact of their lives that they were all mistaken for one another again and again and again. They were addressed by the wrong name in the grocery store, at the club pool, at school functions, at Christmas parties, in parking lots, and at the farmers' market. It took the average new Beekmanite sixteen months to be able to reliably tell them apart, and a few of the more disengaged husbands never did manage it. Andrew Callahan was always trying to cover for himself by saying, "I'm sorry! I'm sorry! Don't get mad at me, Sunny, I used to only date Asian women!"

"How was your weekend?" Sunny asked.

"Honestly?" said Lucy. "It was weird."

"How so?"

"These old friends of ours from Brooklyn came by for dinner Saturday night. They told us they have an open marriage. We spent the whole night talking about it."

"Were they trying to get you to"—and here Sunny did a hand motion to indicate sex—"with them?"

"I don't think so," said Lucy. "God, I hope not. That thought never even entered my mind."

"I bet they were," said Sunny Bang. "I bet they were just trying to feel you out."

"Well, if they were, it didn't work."

"Maybe that's what all those idiots are doing in Brooklyn. Having sex with each other's spouses. Otherwise, why would you still live there? Why would you live in Brooklyn when you could live here?"

This was a common refrain for the residents of Beekman. *How come I never heard about this place before? How come everyone doesn't want to live here?* They hadn't just fled the city because they couldn't afford it anymore, although that was true for a lot of them. They hadn't been forced to do that dreaded thing, *move to the suburbs*. Beekman wasn't the suburbs. It wasn't Dobbs Ferry, it wasn't Mamaroneck, it wasn't New Jersey, it wasn't Connecticut. Every house was on at least two acres of land, you could commute into Grand Central on Metro-North, and yet there was not a Wall Street asshole in sight—how was that possible? It was twenty-five minutes to the nearest Starbucks. And nobody went to Starbucks! Starbucks had become a thing of the past, like a rotary phone or a VCR. Beekman attracted the kind of people who didn't want shopping malls or Starbucks or a keeping-up-with-the-Joneses mentality, and they'd found it. They had found someplace they believed, truly believed, to be inestimably better.

"That was weird, the other night," Lucy said to Owen.

They were in the living room, sitting on the couch. Lucy's feet were tucked under Owen's legs.

"You mean when we woke up and Wyatt was standing at the foot of the bed staring at us?"

"Well, yes, that was weird, but I'm talking about the conversation with Thom and Victoria."

"Oh. Right."

"Do you think they were hitting on us?"

"Thom and Victoria?"

"I told Sunny Bang about it and she thought maybe they were trying to swing with us or something."

Owen started to laugh. "Like the four of us all together in one big pile, or like tradesies?"

"I don't know," said Lucy. "It's just strange that they told us about it, that's all, don't you think?"

"If we ever did something like that, rule number one would be we tell no one."

"Rule number two," said Lucy, "would be no falling in love."

"I think we should write these down," Owen joked. "Let me go get a pen."

Owen headed to the kitchen.

"Rule number one: No one can ever know," Lucy called to him.

"No one!" Owen yelled. "I'm with you on that."

"There is no Fight Club!"

"There is no Fight Club!"

Owen came back into the living room carrying a legal pad and an orange Sharpie.

"Rule number two: No falling in love," said Lucy.

"I'm writing it down," said Owen.

"And underline it."

"Rule number three: Condoms at all times," said Owen.

"We should buy a huge box of condoms at Sam's Club, so many that they're impossible to count so neither of us would know how much sex the other person was having."

"We're not buying Sam's Club condoms," said Owen. "Their trash bags don't even work."

"I know you hate it when I buy those bags, but they are practically free and you get a million of them."

"Just, sidebar, and for the millionth time, could you please stop buying those trash bags?"

"Okay," said Lucy. She sighed a big sigh. "It will be painful, but I'll stop."

"Rule number four: No Sam's Club trash bags or condoms," Owen said.

"Rule number five: Whoever breaks rule number one, two, three, or four wins full custody of Wyatt."

"That's awful," said Owen.

"He's been driving me nuts all afternoon."

As if on cue, Wyatt walked into the living room. He spotted the orange Sharpie in Owen's hand and stated, "I want the pen."

"No pens, Wyatt," said Lucy.

"I want the pen."

"How about a crayon, bud?" Owen said. "Or a colored pencil?"

"I want the pen!" Wyatt screamed.

"Oh, just give him the pen," Lucy said.

"You sure?" said Owen.

"No writing on the house, Wyatt," said Lucy.

"Okay," said Wyatt.

"Not on the walls and not on the furniture," said Lucy.

"Okay."

"Do you promise?"

"I promise."

Wyatt took the pen and headed upstairs to write on the walls or on the furniture.

"We really shouldn't do that," said Owen.

"I know," said Lucy. "I just can't face a two-hour meltdown over a Sharpie. Our house looks like crap anyway."

"I'll get another pen," said Owen. "Where were we?"

"I can't remember," said Lucy. "I was looking at myself in the mirror this morning and thinking about what Victoria said. I think I'm nearing the end of my window."

"Your window?"

"The window wherein people other than the man I'm married to will be willing to have sex with me without, I don't know, being financially compensated in some way."

"You're crazy."

"Which brings us to this: no prostitutes."

"Of course not," said Owen.

"Seriously. Write that down."

"No prostitutes."

"Because it's skeevy and we can't afford it."

"I've got a rule," said Owen. "No sexting inside the house."

"I wouldn't want to sext, period," said Lucy. "Would I have to do that?"

"I don't know how things work these days," said Owen. "But if you want to sext, you have to sit outside. That's my rule."

"You know what would be brilliant?" said Lucy. "I think there should be a time limit."

"What do you mean?"

"I think it should start and then it should stop. We both agree on an end date, and then when it's over, it's over. Boom."

"That's sort of genius," said Owen. "It'd be like a *rumspringa*."

"And we'd have to promise to actually end it. No more contact. Of any sort. With any of our, uh, our, uh —"

"Sex partners?"

"SPs for short."

"How long, do you think?"

"Long enough that we can make something happen, but not so long that it becomes the new normal."

"Six months?"

"Six months. And we can't have sex with anyone we know," said Lucy.

"What do you mean?" said Owen. "We have to find complete strangers?"

"No, I mean you can track down old girlfriends or whatever, or people in the city, but you can't have sex with anyone in Beekman. Not with our crowd. I don't want to be sitting at a dinner party and wondering if you're sleeping with any of the women at the table."

"Okay, that's fair," said Owen.

"What about talking about it? With each other, I mean."

"Would you want to talk about it?"

Lucy thought for a moment. "No. I wouldn't want to know anything."

Owen wrote down *No talking about it*.

"I'd want to be completely in the dark," said Lucy.

"No asking about it, then."

"No looking too happy," said Lucy. "No swanning around

the house with a big smile on your face. No whistling while you get dressed in the morning."

"No snooping," said Owen. "We accept that we each have a realm of privacy. Our computers, our cell phones, our credit card bills. So with no snooping there can be no hiding of things, and no lying."

"No leaving," said Lucy.

"No leaving," Owen agreed. "And no falling in love."

"You already wrote that down."

"I'm writing it down again," said Owen. "We're joking about this, right?"

"Yes," said Lucy. She laughed. "Yes, we're joking. We're not insane."

"That's what I thought."

Wyatt picked that moment to walk into the living room. He had orange Sharpie scribbled all over his face.

"I'm a largemouth bass," Wyatt announced, and then he strode purposefully into the playroom.

Downtown Beekman was pretty Norman Rockwell–y, really, with its sidewalks a stone's throw from front porches, and houses separated by thirty feet of driveway or grass. Main Street itself was both quaint and a bit pathetic. Beekman had never really caught on as a Hudson Valley tourist destination. It was missing the artsy tone of Beacon, the hippie flavor of Woodstock, the crunchy rock-climbing vibe of New Paltz, the ritzy country flair of Rhinebeck. Still, it had its charms.

Owen wandered into a quirky store on Main Street, looking for something to send to his mother for her birthday. Owen's mother wouldn't stand for something Amazoned to her with a click of a button. She wanted something that was purchased and wrapped and mailed to her with as much hassle as humanly possible.

The store was small, with an industrial/artisanal feeling, bars of brown soap stacked on old metal shelving, a soy fig candle burning, various odds and ends encased in muslin.

"It's truffled honey," a voice said. "Taste it."

Owen looked over and saw an attractive blond woman who had just come out of the back. She was wearing a peasant blouse and jeans.

"It's nice," said Owen. It was weird-tasting honey.

"It's *amazing*. The truffles are flown in from Italy and the honey is hyper-local. If you live in Beekman, you have *seen* the bees that make this honey. We sell out of this the minute we get it in the store. Smell it." The woman waved the little jar of honey under his nose. It smelled like honey that had been filtered through a very clean person's sweat sock.

"What do you do with it?" Owen asked.

She looked at him. "What do *I* do with it?" She laughed a hearty laugh. "This is a family store, my friend."

Is she coming on to me? Owen thought. *I think she is. Who is she?*

"It will end your allergies forever," she said. "And the truffles are an aphrodisiac."

"Sex without sneezing," said Owen.

She laughed like this was very funny.

"This place is great," he said.

"Thank you. It's my baby."

"It's your store?"

"It is. I am the proprietress." She did a little curtsy, and he tried not to look at her boobs. "I'm glad you like it."

"I've been in Beekman for five years, but I've never been in here before."

"You are not a good local shopper!" She hit him playfully on the arm. "That's what we do around here. We shop local!"

"You're right, I'm not a good…local shopper. I'll do better."

"You promise? Because it's not just me. We're not going to have a thriving Main Street if the rich weekenders don't buy things once in a while."

"I'm not rich. And I'm not a weekender anymore," said Owen. "I live here full-time."

"That's how we get you," she said. "You buy a weekend house and two years later you're living in it. You either lost your job or had a baby. I've seen it a million times. I'm Izzy, by the way."

"I'm Owen."

"Izzy and Owen," she said. She got a faraway look on her face. "That would be a great title for a children's book."

"Oh yeah?"

"It should be about the unlikely friendship between a mouse and a, uh, crocodile."

"A penguin and a hippo," he said.

"A mouse and a hippo!" she said.

"Yes, that sounds about right," he said.

"We should write it together!"

"Yeah. That's a great idea," Owen said, thinking, *No, it's not a great idea.*

"It *is* a great idea. This is how things happen. The universe likes to make things happen."

She had this kind of twitchy way of smiling and moving her shoulders, twitchy but in a good way, like a kitten or a stripper. Her bare shoulders and her long neck kept on moving, moving the entire time she was talking to him, and it took Owen a while to realize she was dancing to the music that was thrumming softly through the store. She also had a half smile that, when you looked into her eyes, you could have sworn was a full smile. Her eyes were bright blue.

"So," he said. "I'll, uh, take the honey."

"Fabulous!" she said. "It'll be thirty-eight dollars. Cash'll save you the sales tax," she said. And she winked.

"No spitting, Wyatt. You know that."

Wyatt was angry at Lucy, but she had no idea why.

Sometimes it was clear why he was mad: You didn't let him have a second helping of ice cream. You took away the iPad. But then there were days like this one, days where everything was fine, and nothing unusual had happened, when, on a dime, Wyatt turned on his mother.

Wyatt spit at her.

"That's one," said Lucy.

He spit at her again.

"No spitting, Wyatt. If I make it to three, you're getting a time-out."

He spit in her direction, ineffectively, and the spit dribbled off his chin and landed on his shirt.

"Okay, that's two. Let's go find something to do" — *Redirect,* the therapists loved to say, although it felt like giving him a reward for bad behavior, especially when she was already at two. "Do you want to play a game with Mama? Let's see what's in the playroom."

Wyatt narrowed his eyes, and a look of what seemed to Lucy to be pure hate crossed over his face, a look so primitive and raw it always took Lucy's breath away.

He stepped toward her, looked her in the eyes, and spit again, this time in her face.

"That's it, Wyatt. That's three. Upstairs. Time-out."

Wyatt took off like a shot.

"Do not run away from me, Wyatt! Time-out!"

Wyatt darted into the playroom. The layout of the downstairs was such that you could run in a circle, a big circle, from the kitchen through the playroom and the foyer, through the living room, and back to the kitchen again. Catching Wyatt when he settled on this path was nearly impossible. You had to outwit him. You had to hide in a nook or behind a door and then pop out and grab him when he passed by, all of which he found unbearably exciting.

Lucy did just that. She hid behind an old wingback chair and then grabbed Wyatt's arm when he ran past her.

"Walk!"

Wyatt went noodle-y. Lucy was afraid she was going to pull his arm out of its socket, like one of those awful nannies you were always hearing about in the city.

"Feet on the floor, Wyatt. Walk!"

Lucy did a hold one of his therapists had taught her, kind of one hand dug into his armpit and the other on his upper arm, and he slowly got to his feet. His other arm was completely free, though, and he used it to scratch her as they walked up the stairs.

"I hate you."

"That hurts my feelings, Wyatt."

"I'm going to kill you, Mama. I hate you. I'm going to kill you!"

Wyatt's time-outs used to be in a chair like normal time-outs. But Wyatt would not stay in the chair. No matter what Lucy and Owen said or did, Wyatt would not stay put in the chair. So the only answer Lucy could come up with was to hold him in the chair, grab his wrists, and sit behind him, basically making herself into a human straitjacket. And he would struggle and bite and yell and sob and spit and pinch and scream, driving himself into deeper and deeper hysterics. Lucy had had bruises up and down her arms and scratches all over her hands ever since he was old enough to walk.

How do you discipline a child like this? It felt impossible. It was impossible.

"I can't wait for you to die, Mama," Wyatt yelled through the closed door once she got him into his bedroom.

"I'll be sad when I die," said Lucy calmly. "Dying is a very sad thing."

"I can't wait for you to die, Mama."

"That hurts my feelings, Wyatt."

"I can't *wait* for you to die. And when it's your *funeral*, I'm going to have a big party, and I'm going to make a *cake*, and it's gonna say *Ding-dong, the witch is dead*. And I *hope* that *hurts* your *feelings!*"

That's actually pretty creative, Lucy thought. *That's an interesting and original use of language.*

"You're in a time-out, Wyatt. And the timer doesn't start until you're calm."

"I'm *calm!* I hate you, Mama! I can't wait for you to be dead! Dead as a doornail!"

Lucy slumped down on the floor in the hallway, her left hand on the doorknob to keep Wyatt from getting out.

Behavior is communication. That was one of the first things the therapists had told them about Wyatt. Over the years, Owen and Lucy had repeated that phrase to each other hundreds of times—when Wyatt was arching his back and spitting, when he poured water onto her computer keyboard, when he shattered the fake Tiffany lampshade at that Applebee's. *It means he's having trouble with this transition. It means he's overstimulated by the noise in the restaurant. It means he's frustrated because he can't catch the ball. It means he feels out of control around other children. It means his brain doesn't work the way everyone else's does. It means he's tired. It means he's hungry. It means he's scared or confused or excited or worried or anxious or angry or sad.*

Lucy's arms were scratched and bloody. Wyatt was pulling on the doorknob with all of his might. She closed her eyes and held on.

From age two until just about age four, Wyatt did not sleep. It wasn't a question of not sleeping through the night—he flat-out didn't sleep. He napped a little, in fits and starts, on the bus to and from his special preschool, sometimes falling asleep on the couch when he got home or in his car seat on his way to one of his therapies, but at night, he did not sleep. He couldn't sleep. It was as if sleep were beyond him, and sleep had no connection to tiredness.

Lucy and Owen took turns staying up with him, sometimes alternating nights, sometimes splitting them in half. They felt like they'd aged fifteen years in just under three. They both nearly lost their minds.

Just when they thought things were starting to get better, when Wyatt had finally found some sort of rhythm, he woke up in the middle of the night and, for the first time in his life, he did not cry or bang his head or scream bloody murder. Instead, he figured out how to climb out of his crib. He made his way down the stairs, unlocked the front door, and walked down the long stone driveway to the mailbox. He was obsessed with the mailbox at the time, something to do with *Blue's Clues,* and he enjoyed putting the red flag up and then down and then up and then down, flapping his hands each time he put it up again like a penguin trying to fly.

Around two a.m., a middle-aged man coming home from a bar drove by and saw this: a little boy, barefoot, in Spider-Man pajamas, standing on a large flat rock next to a black mailbox. The man was drunk, and he had done a fair amount of cocaine. He was afraid to call the police. He was afraid to be seen drunk and high with a little boy in Spider-Man pajamas on a dark road in the middle of the night. He kept driving. When he finally called the police, he couldn't remember the name of the street or the number of the house, just that it was a black mailbox and the house was set far back from the road.

What do you do? Years without sleep? Years of waking up in a blind panic with each creak of the house? Four years of crying every day? And watching yourself and your spouse slowly fall apart before your eyes. And that's after the regular-new-parent no sleep, regular-new-parent nights with midnight feedings and diaper changes and fevers and coughs and croup. Maybe they were better now, but still, sometimes Lucy worried.

A volunteer firefighter had driven by and found Wyatt, shivering, still playing with the mailbox. He'd brought him home. It was a close call.

They installed sliding locks up high on the insides of the doors the next day, and Wyatt went back to not sleeping.

*   *   *

"I've changed my mind," said Lucy.

It was dark, and Owen and Lucy were in bed. Lucy was wide awake and staring up at the ceiling.

"About what?"

"The list. The open-marriage thing. I think I want to do it."

"What? Are you being serious?"

"Yeah."

"That's crazy, Lucy."

"I'm not so sure it is."

"You said it was crazy, remember?" said Owen. "That was your word."

"Well, I think I've changed my mind."

"You *think* you've changed your mind, or you've changed your mind?"

"I've changed it. I want to do it."

"No, Lucy," said Owen.

"Is that a real no?"

"Yes," said Owen.

"Your voice went up at the end of that yes," Lucy pointed out. "That means you're not sure it's a real no."

"Well, it's a real no until we discuss it," said Owen. "And I mean, really discuss it. Like, a paid professional should probably be involved in the discussion. A marriage counselor or something."

"No." Lucy sat up. She pulled her knees into her chest and wrapped her arms around her legs. "That's just it. I don't want to discuss it. I don't want to spend two years talking about whether or not this is a good idea. I think that would be profoundly destabilizing, actually."

"And you don't think both of us fucking strangers for six months would be a bit destabilizing?"

"It might be," said Lucy. "But honestly, Owen? I don't think it will be. And I don't think you think it will be either."

"I don't know what I think."

"We made the list of rules. That was the discussion. It's either a yes or a no. It's like we're on a nuclear submarine, and it only happens if we both turn our keys."

"And you're turning your key."

"But only if you will. This is not me announcing that I'm going to go run around and cheat on you. I'm saying let's both do it, and let's swear to keep our mouths shut about it for the rest of our lives. Let's decide right now, and then not another single word about it, ever," said Lucy.

"How much wine did you have tonight?"

"One glass. Maybe two, but that was hours ago. In no way am I drunk."

Owen sat up and leaned against the headboard and looked at his wife. "I'm just trying to process this."

"We stick to rules," said Lucy. "Especially the end date. Six months from tomorrow."

"I need to know you're one hundred percent serious, Lucy."

"I am," said Lucy.

Owen would never know why he said yes, beyond the stupid reasons, beyond the "my wife is going to let me sleep with other women" reasons—but he did. She leaned over and kissed him, a kiss filled with meaning and love and a little bit of danger, but still it was the kiss of the person he'd been kissing now for years and years and years. *Maybe that's why I said yes,* he'd think to himself later. *Maybe it's as simple as that.*

"I know this is weird, but I think we should shake on it," he said.

"This is it," Lucy said while they were shaking hands and looking into each other's eyes. "This is done. We've made the deal. Now, not another word about it."

Three

Schopenhauer rather famously said, we forfeit three-fourths of ourselves in order to be like other people.

—Constance Waverly
Esalen Institute, spring 2015

T he *Titanic* was unsinkable!" said Wyatt.

"Yes, that's what they called it," Owen said.

It was the next morning. Owen was shaving, and Wyatt had followed him into the bathroom so he could flick his fingers under the faucet while the water was running.

"The *Titanic* was unsinkable! It was the unsinkable ship!" Wyatt said again.

"But what happened to it?"

"It sank! The *Titanic* sank in the middle of the North Atlantic Ocean!"

"Yes, it did."

"Over two hundred *thousand* people died in the freezing water."

"I think that's not the right number, Wyatt."

"Over two hundred *thousand* people died in the freezing, freezing water," said Wyatt. He had both of his hands under the running water now, flicking them with excitement. Owen filled the toothbrush holder with water so he could clean his blade.

"We might have to ask Siri about that number, Wyatt."

"The *Titanic* was unsinkable!"

"We're unsinkable," said Owen, wiping his face dry with a towel.

"If our house got a hole in the side, and water poured in, our habitat would be destroyed!"

"But that's not going to happen, Wyatt."

"Our habitat would be completely, completely destroyed!"

*   *   *

Did last night really happen? Owen thought as he was driving to work. *Was that whole thing my imagination, or did that really just happen?*

1. They were both sober.

2. Everything was written down, first in orange Sharpie and then with an ordinary black pen.

3. They'd shaken hands on it.

He had six months! Six whole months! The only time he'd even allowed himself to imagine being in a situation like this was when he occasionally daydreamed about Lucy's death. In his defense, it was always a quick and painless one. It was like, dead Lucy, sadness, poor Wyatt, must be strong for Wyatt, a dismal six to twelve months, the worst six to twelve months of his life, and then sex with new women. Owen never even entertained the idea of a divorce. It just never struck him that he and Lucy would end their marriage. Her death, that he could imagine. Aneurysm, plane crash, blood clot from a long plane trip that slowly worked its way up to her brain, spinal meningitis diagnosed two days too late—those things he could picture. Divorce, no way.

But this? This he never would have imagined in, as Wyatt would say, a million gazillion years.

I could fuck any of the men in this place, Lucy thought as she sipped her latte.

Correction: *I'm* allowed *to fuck any of the men in this place.* Whether or not she could was a different question. Whether she could figure out a way to make it happen—that was yet to be determined. Even when she was single, Lucy had never thought things like that. In fact, she'd always been a little surprised when someone wanted to have sex with her. She'd slept around, yes, but most of it took place during a five-year period when she was working through the most painful issues of her childhood; at least, that's how she thought about it now. Even when she was going home with just about whoever asked, she was always on the lookout for a boyfriend, a partner, a husband, a father-to-be of her children-to-come. But now she had that. She had found the perfect husband, the perfect father, and he loved her.

Back then, she would never have given a second glance to what she saw before her now. She was in a coffee shop three towns away from Beekman. It seemed like a safe distance; she was unlikely to run into anyone she knew.

Exhibit A: Salt-and-pepper hair, bushy eyebrows, glasses. Intelligent-looking, but that could be the glasses talking. But—he was tiny. Lucy was not planning to be picky, but she did not want to have sex with a tiny little teeny-tiny man.

Exhibit B: Close-cropped salt-and-pepper hair, scruffy beard, a white Wilco T-shirt, paint-splattered brown pants, broad chest, looked like he might smell like turpentine or furniture oil.

Exhibit C: Salt-and-pepper hair. (Why were all the men here so old? Lucy needed to find a different coffee shop! Somehow she'd stumbled onto a place filled with unemployed middle-aged white men, all of them nursing two-dollar cups of coffee while they pretended to do important things on their laptops. They were like ants. First you noticed one or two, but then when you really looked, you realized the place was crawling with them.)

There was a thing, she found. Once her antennae were back up (and they'd been down now for years, for *years*), Lucy started noticing men who had their antennae up. It was like a whole world of signs and signals had been floating right past her—lingering looks, secret smiles, eyes moving up and down, wineglasses lifted in solidarity, charged conversations in bookstores. It was like an energy field, and some people were aware of it and some people weren't. Lucy had been walking around with fifteen extra pounds on her, wearing bulky sweaters with things like foxes on them, obsessed with her son and his challenges, completely oblivious to the thick ever-present sexual haze that was in the air. Lucy had turned herself off—in defense of love and marriage and family and community—and now that she had finally turned herself back on, she had no idea what would happen.

Exhibit C smiled at her. She smiled back.

Gordon Allen, Beekman's only billionaire, was in his backyard, hitting golf balls into the Hudson River. The sky was turning pink and the wispy clouds were both purple and gold, and Gordon was thinking that his swing was looking better than it had been in years. It helped, having a driving range just a few steps off his lower back deck. It made it easier to hit golf balls than to not hit golf balls. Gordon had had his landscape architect construct him a little hideaway so boaters couldn't see him and report him to whomever you would report someone who was driving silicone golf balls into Robert Kennedy Jr.'s precious protected Hudson River. Surely it was less than legal. Surely Bobby would have something sanctimonious to say about this, Gordon thought as he watched another one of his golf balls sail through the sky and plop into the river.

One of his idiot grown sons had bought him some biodegradable fish-friendly golf balls as a somewhat pointed gift the previous Christmas, but Gordon didn't like them. The *thwack* didn't feel as satisfying and they didn't fly nearly as far. So he kept them on hand, in a bucket inside the hideaway, but the balls Gordon drove into the river were brand-new Titleist Pro V1xs he bought by the pallet.

"Goddamn it, Gordon!"

He shanked it.

"What now?"

"One of your bees stung me again!"

He looked over and saw Kelly, his wife, sitting up on her pool chaise, pressing an icy pink drink to the inside of her perfect thigh. She was topless, but he barely noticed.

"How do you know it was one of mine?"

"Well, I don't know," said Kelly. "Maybe because you decided to put half a million bees in our backyard. I'm *guessing* it was one of yours."

"I don't have that many bees, Kelly."

Gordon did have that many bees. He had ten hives, and each hive hosted between sixty thousand and eighty thousand bees, at least during the summer, according to his bee guy. His bee guy was named Dirk and he looked like some kind of prophet. He was bald with an almost comically huge red beard, and he always wore sandals, some kind of fair-trade eyesores made from old tires pulled out of an open-air landfill by AIDS orphans or one-legged land-mine victims—Dirk had told Gordon the sob story of his footwear once but Gordon had forgotten the particulars.

"Do you know how much those bees save us in real estate taxes every year?"

"I don't care! I don't care, Gordon! We're rich! I'm sick of being stung by a bee every time I walk out my front door."

"You always want me to be more concerned about the environment. I'm single-handedly battling colony collapse! Dirk says I'm doing God's work with those bees. He's going to nominate me for an environmental award."

"You hit sixty brand-new golf balls into the Hudson River every day, Gordon. No one's giving you an environmental award."

Gordon lined up his shoulders, straightened his left arm, and swung. The ball floated like it had wings and then dropped into the river about ten yards shy of the tugboat he was aiming for. "Touché," he said to Kelly.

Every time Gordon looked at Kelly these days he was struck by the same thought. *What in God's name was I thinking?* A man of his age, a three-time loser, a goddamn billionaire (twelve billion is where *Forbes* had pegged him last March, and they weren't far off, no siree!), marrying a cocktail waitress less than half his age and not insisting on a prenup? It boggled the mind! It was one of the great mysteries of Gordon's life. He peed a good five or six times each night these days, and every time he woke up thinking the same thought: *Fuck, I have to goddamn pee again and why didn't I make Kelly sign a goddamn prenup?*

She wasn't even pregnant when he married her! That at least would have made some sense. A tearful, knocked-up young girlfriend, a sentimental rush to do the right thing. But Kelly got pregnant on their honeymoon. Gordon had had a paternity test done, secretly, all men in his position did that, it was practically included in the price when you sprung for the presidential birthing suite at Lenox Hill—but there was only a 1 in 11,200,247 chance that Rocco had been sired by someone other than him.

Rocco was the only reason Gordon lived in Beekman. After Rocco arrived, Gordon had become obsessed with solving the problem of where to raise him. He didn't like his options. It was live with either the rich assholes in Connecticut, the rich assholes in the Hamptons, or the slightly less rich assholes up in northern Westchester.

Finally he sat down with the Best Real Estate Agent on the East Coast and said exactly that. He needed to live near the city and he didn't like his options. There had to be another choice.

The agent had had him sit back in his chair and close his eyes and told him to describe exactly what he was looking for. To imagine he could have every last thing he wanted. He told Gordon to dream out loud. It sounded a little airy-fairy to Gordon, but he decided what the heck and went with it.

He started by saying he wanted to live someplace where there were ordinary people.

("How ordinary?" the Best Real Estate Agent prompted.)

People who lived contentedly in houses with four bedrooms. People who paid strangers to mow their lawns but looked at the lawn-mowing bills and thoughtfully considered both the economics and family-time trade-offs of buying mowers and doing it themselves the next summer. Some millionaires, that was fine, and impossible to avoid these days, really. But: Churches. Bake sales. Soccer games. A place where kids built forts out of sticks they found in their backyards. Rock collections. Snowball fights. Sledding! Cheerful, chubby stay-at-home moms who believed in raising their own kids and giving back to the community. A picturesque main street with no chain stores or homeless people. And not New Jersey. He wasn't going to live in New Jersey.

("That's it?")

A Fourth of July parade with people waving those little American flags. Trick-or-treating. Kids who believed in Santa longer than you thought humanly possible. A scenic, manageable, non-Hamptons-like commute to the city. Mostly Caucasian. Mostly Protestant. Some solid, salt-of-the-earth Catholics, that was fine. A public school he could feel good about putting his son in, at least until fourth or fifth grade. A view of the ocean, or anyway a view of some water. But not a lake. Lakes creeped Gordon out.

("Is that it?" the Best Real Estate Agent asked him one last time.)

Gordon thought for a moment.

"I like trees."

Owen had taken Wyatt shopping at GroceryLand. It was one of the things Owen and Lucy tried to do with Wyatt at least once a week, to pique his interest in different types of food. So far, it hadn't worked.

"Hey! You're Owen."

"Yeah," said Owen. "Hi, uh—"

"Izzy. Izzy of 'Izzy and Owen.' Remember? The mouse and the hippo!"

"Of course."

"And who is this young man?"

"This is Wyatt."

Izzy crouched low and met Wyatt's eyes. "Hi, Wyatt," she said. "I'm Izzy."

Wyatt didn't say anything and looked down at his shoes.

"You are a handsome little boy. Are you helping your daddy do his grocery shopping?"

"We're buying banana yogurt," said Wyatt.

"I love banana yogurt!" said Izzy. "Banana yogurt is my absolute favorite!"

"We're buying it all," said Wyatt matter-of-factly. "We're buying all the banana yogurt in the store."

It was true. There were twenty-three banana yogurts in their grocery cart. La Yogurt brand banana yogurt was one of the five foods Wyatt would eat. And it was hard to find. So when they found it, they bought them all.

"Oh no. So none for me?"

"Nope."

"Not even one?"

"Sorry, Charlie."

"But I love banana yogurt," she said.

"We're buying it all," said Wyatt. "Sorry, Charlie."

Izzy stood back up and turned to Owen. "Oh my God, he's gorgeous!"

"Thank you."

"He looks just like you."

"No one ever says that."

"It's true! He has your eyes. And I'm serious about the children's book," said Izzy. "Give me your e-mail. We'll just send a document back and forth while we work on it. It'll be fun."

She pulled a crinkly receipt out of her purse and Owen

found himself writing his e-mail address on it while Wyatt looked at him out of the side of his eye.

In the parking lot, Owen was loading groceries into the back of the car when Izzy drove by in a black pickup truck. She rolled down her window.

"Izzy and Owen!" she shouted, and then she drove off.

"Izzy and Owen!" Wyatt said as Owen strapped him into his seat. "Izzy and Owen! Izzy and Owen!"

That was one of the things Wyatt did: he repeated what he heard. It was called scripting. His brain was filled with scripts, scripts from months ago, scripts from videos he'd seen on YouTube, from cartoons he'd stopped watching years ago.

So when Wyatt repeated "Izzy and Owen!" on the drive home, Owen had no idea how long he would keep it up.

"Izzy and Owen! Izzy and Owen! Izzy and Owen!"

Lucy was taking a shower, washing her hair with a cheap drug-store shampoo that smelled like strawberries. It was that chemical strawberry scent that smelled stronger than the juiciest of strawberries, and it brought to mind something Lucy hadn't thought about in years.

It was before she had Wyatt, long before Beekman, back when she and Owen were still living on the Upper West Side and trying desperately to have a baby. She had just come from work and she was waiting in line at the Gourmet Garage when she overheard a woman in front of her talking into her phone.

"I don't know, really," the woman had said. "I just want something *juicy* in my life."

Lucy remembered it like it was yesterday. Juicy? Who thinks things like that? Who has the luxury of juicy?

What Lucy had wanted while she was standing in line at the Gourmet Garage was this: A baby. A child of her own. Her egg,

Owen's sperm, her womb, period. Or, rather, no period—every time her period arrived, it felt like a knife to her heart. They had done three rounds of IVF—three was all they could responsibly afford—and Lucy had found out that morning that the third one hadn't worked. And she'd burst into tears again, right there in line. She hated that woman, the juicy woman, because she was standing in line with her two adorable kids climbing up her legs, complaining into her cell phone about wanting something juicy in her life.

But now it was many years later, and Lucy had gotten what she wanted: a child. They'd left the city so they could afford a decent house. She and Owen had a happy marriage. She had close friends, a nice community.

But she did not have juicy. She was a lifetime away from juicy, she was miles, light-years, eons away from juicy, and now it seemed that juicy was what she wanted.

Lucy remembered her lowest point in what felt like years full of low points, infertility-wise. She'd just gotten her period, two weeks after yet another costly and painful medical procedure— although by no means the costliest and most painful she would endure—and she'd been sobbing off and on for forty-eight hours.

She was in bed, watching a segment on *Sixty Minutes* about the genocide in the Ivory Coast. Apparently, the rebels would come into a village and go from home to home forcing fathers to have sex with their daughters in full view of the rest of the family, on threat of death. Once rumors of this spread, village men wisely decided to switch huts with each other at night, so they wouldn't be made to have sex with their own daughters in front of their own wives and sons. Still, the whole thing was incredibly horrific and grim and as the segment unfolded, Lucy felt for a moment that it put her situation in perspective. *Face it,* she said to herself, *things could be worse. You have food and clean water, a loving husband and air-conditioning*—air-conditioning was one of Lucy's all-time-favorite things—*and no one is breaking into your hut, raping you, and killing your family.*

Then the story homed in on a thirteen-year-old girl who had been forced to have sex with a neighbor who was pretending to be her father and then made to watch as both of her brothers were killed. Next, she was abducted and taken to the rebels' camp deep in the jungle and held as a sex slave, being forced to have sex with up to thirty men in one day. After about six months, she managed to escape and make her way to a refugee camp. It was at the refugee camp, in front of the rolling cameras, that she discovered she was four months pregnant, carrying a rebel-rapist's child.

And Lucy thought: *How come everybody can get pregnant except for me?*

That's infertility. It takes over.

Every woman Lucy saw on the street back then was pregnant or pushing a stroller; every old friend who called out of the blue was announcing a new baby. Facebook was impossible. The holidays were impossible. Everything hurt, time was running out, what were they going to do, how much would they be willing to spend, would they consider adoption—they would, of course they would, they'd agreed at the beginning, back when it first looked like there might be a problem, but both of them secretly believed that there wasn't, wouldn't be, a *big* problem—but as each try failed, even talking about it had become dangerous emotional ground for them to tread.

IVF was all numbers. She and Owen finally scraped together enough money for a fourth round. Only five eggs were retrieved. Four were good on day three, two were good on day five, both were implanted. Two weeks later, a ten p.m. phone call from Dr. Hamilton.

"Congratulations," he'd said. "You're pregnant."

Owen parked his car on a short residential street near the river and walked the seven blocks to the address Izzy had sent him. He was not entirely sure what was going on.

After their chance meeting at GroceryLand, Izzy had e-mailed him and suggested he stop by so they could talk about *Izzy and Owen,* their children's book about the unlikely friendship between a mouse and a hippo. She said she already had a few preliminary thoughts she wanted to run by him. She ended with a ;*, which he looked up online and found meant a wink and a kiss. Early afternoon, flirty woman's house, e-mail winks and kisses—was it possible she actually intended to write a children's book with him? That made no sense! No sense whatsoever.

Had he implied he was a writer of some sort? Had he suggested he fancied himself an illustrator? Or said he worked in publishing? Or proclaimed a love of children's literature? No! None of those things. Owen's mind circled back through his two encounters with Izzy to see if there was anything to hang this children's-book idea on, any logical reason why she would have invited him, alone, to her house at two o'clock on a Thursday afternoon. There wasn't. But this didn't make much sense either. And before the Arrangement, he would have ignored it altogether. But now, well, he was curious, if nothing else.

He rang the doorbell. He forced himself not to look up and down the street like a prospective adulterer and instead tried to stand up straight, like an aspiring children's-book author, like a man who had absolutely nothing to hide.

Izzy opened the door and smiled at him. It was a wicked, sexy half smile that reminded him of the Ellen Barkin of fifteen years ago.

"Well, hello there," she said.

"Just so you know, my wife and I have an open marriage," said Owen.

Izzy started to laugh.

"What?" said Owen.

"You're in my bed. You already slept with me. You don't need to lie to me now."

"I'm not lying, I swear—"

"Don't talk," said Izzy. "Just lie there and be all quiet and pretty."

Owen suddenly felt self-conscious. He pulled the sheet up to his chest and stared at the chandelier hanging over the bed. Lucy would kill for a chandelier like that.

"Okay, you can talk," said Izzy. "Explain yourself."

"My wife and I have a good marriage, we're happy, and we love each other, but we've decided to sort of give each other a free pass for a couple of months to bypass any midlife crises or things like that. Like the way the Amish kids get a *rumspringa* when they turn eighteen."

Izzy nodded her head slowly, like she was taking it all in, like she was thoughtfully processing what he had just said, and then she burst out laughing.

"Oh God, I'm sorry, I'm just thinking of all the things my idiot husband must have said to the women he fucked while he was married to me," she said. "I can't imagine it. He probably told people I was okay with it."

"No, we do, we have an open arrangement."

"Will she sign a note to that effect? 'Dear Izzy: You hereby have my permission to fuck my husband, signed'—what is her name?"

"Lucy."

"Lucy." Izzy narrowed her eyes. "She's not the Lucy with the frizzy black hair who wears the overalls with homemade patches on them, is she?"

"Different Lucy."

"Good," said Izzy. "I couldn't quite see you with a woman who patches her own overalls. There are so many things wrong with that Lucy, I might actually feel bad about fucking her husband."

"I'm telling you, you don't need to feel bad. This is allowed."

"You're not getting it. I wouldn't feel bad even if it *wasn't* allowed. This is me, not feeling bad. I, Izzy Radford, no longer feel bad about fucking other women's husbands. Excuse me, but I'm going to drink to that."

She reached over and grabbed her goblet from the nightstand and took a healthy swig of what Owen would come to think of as her house wine, a thick buttery chardonnay that came in a jumbo-size bottle.

"I have lost my faith in the sisterhood of women."

"Why? What happened?"

"My best friend slept with Christopher."

"Christopher..."

"My ex-husband. But we were very much married at the time. My yoga teacher Ilianna slept with him too. She spent a weekend with him in a bed-and-breakfast in Woodstock. Christopher claimed he was in Oregon at the time."

"How do you know about all this?"

"Oh, I figured it out eventually," she said. "I downloaded keystroke spy software onto his computer and tracked his car and his cell phone, I found a secret credit card he had with a bunch of motel charges, and when I had enough detail, I confronted him with it. And he spilled his guts. Told me things I didn't even have a clue about from years ago. I filed for divorce the next day."

"So, uh, we good?" Owen said to Izzy. He had already grabbed his coat and was just about to let himself out. He was eager to check his phone—something he felt would be rude to do in Izzy's presence—and see if something terrible had happened to Lucy or Wyatt while he'd been committing adultery. Even though, he told himself, it wasn't technically adultery.

And the truth was, he was a little bit afraid of Izzy. But he liked her spirit. She was who she was. The ultimate no-bullshit woman. She was erotically adventurous and, from what he could tell, temperamentally the opposite of his wife. She was a good choice, arrangement-wise.

"We're good," said Izzy, "as long as we're going to do this again sometime soon."

"We are," said Owen. "I mean, I'd like to very much. I'll text you."

"Do that."

When Owen walked through the front door, he was immediately accosted by Wyatt, who was bouncing up and down on his toes with excitement and twisting a string of Mardi Gras beads around his neck.

"Dada, Dada, I gotta tell you something," Wyatt said. "Guess what?"

"What, Wyatt?"

"Mr. Lowell is now *Mrs. Lowell!*"

"What?" said Owen.

"Yes," said Wyatt. "Mr. Lowell is now *Mrs. Lowell.*"

"No way," said Owen.

"Mr. Lowell is now *Mrs. Lowell.*"

"Does that blow your mind?" Owen said.

"Yes." Wyatt laughed like this was the funniest thing he'd ever heard. "He was a boy but now he's a girl!"

"Let me put down my stuff and you can tell me about it," Owen said. He slipped out of his coat and set a bottle of wine on the kitchen counter while Wyatt walked over to the table and started to play with his beads. Wyatt played with his beads when he was excited, or when he was stressed, or when he was happy.

"Dada, Dada, I gotta tell you something."

"What?"

"Mr. Lowell is now *Mrs. Lowell!*"

"You told me that already," said Owen. "What do you think about it?"

"Mr. Lowell is now *Mrs. Lowell!*" Wyatt repeated. "He started out as a boy but now he's a girl!"

Wyatt was shaking his Mardi Gras beads frantically on the kitchen table. His face was about six inches away from the beads, and he was staring at them with wide-open eyes while he spoke.

"How did he do that?" said Owen.

"I don't know! He started out as a boy but now he's a girl. He wears dresses!"

"He wears dresses to school?" said Owen.

"Yes. Mr. Lowell is now Mrs. Lowell and he wears dresses to school! And he's going to use the *ladies' restroom!*"

"He is? How do you know that?"

"He told the class he's going to use the *ladies' restroom*. And that it's *totally normal*. Mr. Lowell is now Mrs. Lowell and he wears dresses now and even ladies' underpants!"

"Well, that sounds kind of silly," said Owen. "Do you think it's silly?"

"It's super-silly!"

"Do people usually go from being a boy to being a girl?"

"No, because it's very hard to do."

"Yes, it is."

"It's very, very hard to do but it's *totally normal*."

"You're right, Wyatt."

"You have to take *special medicine* to turn from a boy to a girl and it's very, very hard to do."

Owen looked over at Lucy, who'd been watching the whole thing from the doorway, and shrugged his shoulders. At least the kid had his facts straight.

"Guess what, Dada? Mr. Lowell is now *Mrs.* Lowell!"

"I know, Wyatt. You told me that already. What color dress did Mrs. Lowell wear today?"

"It was green. It was a green dress and he had on ladies' underpants because he's now *Mrs. Lowell*."

"Is that okay with you, Wyatt? That he's now Mrs. Lowell?"

"Yes, Mr. Lowell is now *Mrs.* Lowell."

"Did Mr. Lowell tell the class he was wearing ladies' underpants?" Lucy finally asked. She couldn't help herself. It seemed like a little more information than was called for, frankly.

"No."

"Who told you that?"

"Brannon did! Brannon said that Mrs. Lowell was wearing ladies' underpants! And probably a bra!" Wyatt started talking in circles again, this time about bras and ladies' underpants, while he stimmed with his beads and laughed and laughed.

Lucy had given Owen a heads-up, of course. Owen was driving home from Izzy's when Lucy called him. He'd felt a flash of guilt and then what could only be called confusion when he saw his wife's picture show up on his phone.

"Wyatt has something big to tell you when you get home," Lucy said. "I think you should be prepared."

"What is it?"

"You know Mr. Lowell?"

"Wyatt's teacher?"

"Yes," said Lucy.

"What about him?"

"He's turning into a woman."

"What?"

"He's transitioning. He's becoming a woman. He started wearing a dress to school this week. And Wyatt's going to want to tell you the second you walk through the door, and I thought you should have a bit of a warning."

"Are you serious?"

"I am."

"That's insane."

"Well, yeah," said Lucy. "Act like it's normal around Wyatt. That's what I've been doing."

"Okay. Wow."

"Yeah. See you soon," said Lucy. "Don't forget the wine, please."

"Already got it."

That Monday, Mr. Lowell had come to school wearing a long, tasteful gray skirt, but for some reason nobody thought anything of it. It was so long and so gray it almost passed for a pair of trousers, that was all anyone could remember. On Tuesday, he wore a dress and a pair of low heels. Eyebrows were raised, to say the least, and the teachers began to talk among themselves, but Mrs. G., the principal, was off the grid in Tulum for a yoga retreat that week and no one knew quite what to do. Some said that on Wednesday he added makeup; others insisted he'd been wearing makeup on Tuesday as well. Thursday morning, he walked into the kindergarten classroom wearing a dress, high heels, full makeup, fake lashes, and a blond wig. He wrote his new name on the whiteboard and explained to his students that he was now a woman. The fourth-grade teacher, a strict Baptist, tracked down Mrs. G. in Tulum, and she took an early, angry flight home.

"Wyatt's got enough to deal with," said Lucy. "How's he going to get his head around this?"

"The way he gets his head around anything," said Owen. "He'll think about it for a month or two, talk in circles about it, and then move on to the next thing he wants to understand, like how astronauts go poop in outer space."

"At least he has a sense of humor," said Lucy. "That's very unusual, you know, for kids like Wyatt. At least he knows when something is funny."

"You're his mom," said Owen. "Of course he has a sense of humor."

"Awww," said Lucy. "That little shit Brannon is the one who taught him the word *fucker*."

"He was going to learn that one sooner or later."

"I know."

"I think it's going to be good for this place," said Owen. "We have to hope people will accept Wyatt for who he is and not expect him to be like everybody else. Maybe this whole Mrs. Lowell thing will be a blessing in disguise."

"Well, the ladies of Beekman are going nuts about it," said Lucy. "My phone blew up from all the texts flying this afternoon. Is it okay if I go to the school-board meeting next week?"

"Of course. Go ahead," said Owen. "I love you."

"I love you too."

◈

"You realize your wife is an idiot," Izzy said to Owen after they'd had sex the next day.

Owen had come back for seconds. He hadn't planned on it, not exactly, not right away, but Izzy had sent him a text around noon, nearly all emoticons. He had to hunt for his reading glasses in order to see the text clearly. Rumpled bed, fireworks, hands folded in prayer, winky eye, winky eye, dancing bear, and then *two o'clock* with a long row of question marks after it.

"Actually, Lucy's a lot smarter than I am," said Owen.

"Well, you're an idiot too," said Izzy. "You're both morons if you think this is going to work. This is a divorce you guys are looking at. This is a divorce in slow motion."

"We're trying to avoid getting a divorce."

"Well, you're going about it the wrong way."

"What would be the right way?"

"You really want to know?" Izzy said.

"Sure."

Izzy climbed back on top of him and started grinding herself against him, trying to see if he was good for another go.

"Only. Have sex. With *each other*," she said, and then she started to laugh like a mental patient.

Izzy was like that. She was a different world. Not a better

world, not a kinder or gentler one, but a different one. Owen had read somewhere that the brain needs novelty. Novelty is what keeps the neurons from dying. Novelty makes new connections; it rewires things, it repairs, it renews. Drive a different route to work, the article suggested. Order something new from your favorite restaurant. *Have sex with someone who's the polar opposite of your wife.*

The best word to describe how Izzy fucked was *angrily*. She was explosive and hungry and passionate and crazy and would allow more or less anything to penetrate her anywhere. Owen had gone out and gotten himself some strange—but it turned out to be pretty strange strange. Izzy asked to be tied up, she liked to bite, she begged to be spanked, and she had a sex-toy collection that was truly astonishing. One time, Owen opened up her dishwasher, and there were two gigantic rubber penises in the silverware compartment. *What the hell is going on around here?* he wondered, but then he chose to put it out of his mind.

Another thing: Izzy was highly orgasmic. She came, a lot. Many, many, many times. Izzy came so much and so often that it was, paradoxically, difficult to satisfy her, to *completely* satisfy her—it was like trying to fill a bucket that had a hole on the bottom. No matter what Owen gave her, it was never enough.

Owen had gotten so used to his hands being guided away by Lucy, with her "Not tonight" and "Please no, not there," her distinctly unsexy desire to keep her T-shirt on during sex (he'd put his foot down on that one, thankfully), that for a while the sheer pleasure of being able to do anything he wanted to do was enough. Like a kid in a candy store, really, that's how he felt. *I can do this! And I can do this! I can put this in here! I can touch that! I can look at this with the lights on!*

And the pictures. Good God, the pictures. After his second time with Izzy, a seemingly unending stream of pornographic selfies popped up on his screen, to the point where Owen's once rather cozy relationship with his cell phone was forever changed. He'd type in his password and see he had four new texts and then be like, *Whah?* She really didn't have a good eye, Izzy. She didn't seem to know the difference between a sexy picture and an alarming one. It didn't help that she held her iPhone at strange angles, and always a little too close, so that he often had to spend a good fifteen seconds figuring out which way was up and, occasionally, what exactly he was looking at. Once, while he was giving Wyatt a bath, he glanced at his phone and saw what he thought was an extreme close-up of Izzy's vagina. It turned out to be a picture she'd found online of one of those wrinkly hairless cats.

Owen tried to get her to stop with the pictures.

"You mean because of your wife who knows we're sleeping together and is fine with it? You're worried she's going to see something on your phone?"

"Yeah. It doesn't mean she needs to see any of that. Plus, my kid plays with my phone."

"So password-block your texts."

"I don't know how to do that. And even if I did, I don't want to have to type in a password every time I get a text. It's not efficient. Just, do you mind stopping?"

"I thought you liked my pictures."

"I do like them. It's just—you send a lot of them. And maybe it would be better if we just toned that part of things down for a while."

"Whatever."

Four

The only virtue of a marriage based purely on love is the expediency of a divorce based on hate.

—Constance Waverly
The Waverly Report

The tot park was one of the things real estate agents made a point of showing to prospective home buyers on sunny days, when it was filled with nice-seeming moms chatting on park benches while their toddlers poured sand out of plastic dump trucks and took turns swinging on the swings. A lot of moms in Beekman spent a lot of hours at the tot park. Each spring it was replenished with a batch of new mommies, exhausted and half brain-dead, wondering what their lives had become.

Lucy and Sunny Bang were sitting next to each other on a park bench in the sun.

"I feel so bad for Arlen," said Sunny Bang.

"Who's Arlen?" Lucy asked.

"Eric Lowell's wife," said Sunny. "I wonder how she's handling all this. She's had a really hard life."

"Hard how?"

"One of her parents murdered her sister."

"*What?*"

"It was a long time ago. Her sister disappeared and the whole town looked for her for days and then they found her body in this pond behind their house. Apparently everybody knew it was one of the parents but nobody could prove anything."

"That's horrible."

"I know, right? And Arlen and Eric still live in the house she grew up in. Can you imagine? She looks out on that pond every day. And now her husband is turning into a woman. I'd be like, Are you fucking kidding me, God?"

"Why didn't they search the pond right away?" asked Lucy. "I mean, isn't that the first place you'd look?"

Lucy had to run across the tot park to wrangle Wyatt away from a scooter that had caught his eye while another kid was riding on it. After about ten minutes of redirection, she got him settled on an empty swing. She walked back to the bench. Sunny eyed her intensely as she approached.

"Why are you so skinny?" Sunny Bang asked.

"I'm not skinny," said Lucy, sitting back down next to her.

Sunny Bang squinted. "You've lost like, what, eight pounds?"

"Eleven," said Lucy, "but who's counting."

"How? I need to know."

"I have no idea," said Lucy. "I haven't been hungry so I haven't been eating."

"I don't believe you," Sunny Bang said. "If it's pills, I demand some."

"I haven't been hungry lately. I can't explain it."

"Maybe you have a tapeworm," said Sunny Bang. "I know this guy who went to Africa, and he got these parasites in his skin, and they put slabs of bacon all over him and the worms came out and ate the bacon and then they ripped the bacon off like a Band-Aid. And the worms got pulled out of him like strands of spaghetti."

"You *know* this person?"

"Friend of a friend," said Sunny Bang. "You ruin all my stories. TOBIAS, GIVE LOUISA A TURN ON THE SPRINGY ZEBRA. YOU'VE BEEN ON LONG ENOUGH. Maybe you have cancer."

"Thanks, Sunny. Thanks for that."

"Sudden unexplained weight loss. It's a symptom. TOBIAS, GET OFF THE ZEBRA RIGHT THIS SECOND! OFF! NOW!"

"I cut out carbs," Lucy said. "Carbs and sugar. All the whites."

"You are lying to your friend," Sunny Bang pronounced. "You are a lying woman talking!"

"I'm not," said Lucy.

Sunny Bang narrowed her already narrow Korean eyes.

"Oh my God, I can't believe it," said Sunny Bang.

"What?"

"I know what's going on with you."

"What are you talking about?"

"Do not tell me what I'm thinking right now is true."

"I don't know what you're thinking, Sunny."

"You know exactly what I'm thinking."

"Do I look like I'm having sex with strange men?"

"Yes, actually, you do. You got super-skinny quickly and you're wearing lip gloss."

"This is Carmex."

Lucy had to tell someone. Otherwise she was going to explode. It had been just over a month since the Conversation and Lucy hadn't said a word to anybody. (Lucy found herself thinking about all of this in formal, capitalized phrases: the Dinner Party, the Conversation, the Arrangement, the Rules.) And Sunny Bang was a lot of things—unapologetic discipliner of other people's children, wearer of kneesocks when kneesocks were not called for—but she was trustworthy. And she was fiercely loyal. She was Lucy's best friend in Beekman. And she could keep her mouth shut.

"Can you keep a secret?" Lucy asked.

"You know I can."

"You can't tell anyone what I'm about to tell you. *Anyone*."

"I swear I won't. Not even Jake."

"Normally I would let you tell Jake, but you can't on this one, you have to promise."

"I promise. I swear."

"We are," Lucy said. She lowered her voice as low as it could go. "Doing it. The thing."

Sunny Bang stared at Lucy for a second and then bent down and put her head between her knees like a passenger waiting for the airplane to crash. "Oh my God," she whispered. "Oh my God, oh my God, oh my God."

"Sunny," Lucy said through a forced smile, "the ladies are watching you."

"This is nuts! You guys are crazy!"

"Sit up, Sunny," said Lucy, still smiling. "People are staring."

"It's easy to lose weight because you get to have sex with strangers. It's the best diet ever."

"I'm not having sex with strangers. I haven't done anything."

"But you *can*," said Sunny Bang. "That's enough motivation. I haven't even shaved my legs since my sister-in-law's wedding, and that was in April."

"That can't be true," said Lucy. "You've been to the pool."

"I don't shave for that pool. TOBIAS, STOP THROWING SAND OR WE ARE GOING HOME RIGHT THIS SECOND.

"Is Owen sleeping with anyone?" Sunny asked.

"I have no idea."

"Yes, you do," said Sunny. "You do have an idea."

"We agreed not to talk about it."

"Even if you aren't talking about it, you must have an inkling."

Lucy did, in fact, have an inkling.

Lucy had been cooking dinner, a real dinner, which happened less often than she'd have liked. Wyatt ate his five foods and his five foods only, and as he got older Lucy found it depressing to cook entire meals she knew he wouldn't even try, and she didn't attempt recipes that might smell up the house in a strange way and set him off on a sensory panic attack. But this was Marcella Hazan's lemon-up-the-butt chicken, the easiest and tastiest roast chicken in the world, and she'd made it before and Wyatt didn't mind the smell.

Owen came home early, and Lucy's hand was, in fact, up the chicken's butt trying to wedge the second of the two "rather small" lemons Marcella insisted you could fit up there, the one that always rolled out whenever Lucy tried, when Owen gave her a kiss. Her hands were chickeny so she just stood there, motionless, arms stiff and a little out to the sides, and felt the kiss. It was a real kiss.

"I can't touch you," said Lucy. "I'm all chickeny."

"I don't care. Rub me with salmonella."

"Tempting," said Lucy, "but I can't take any more people in this house throwing up."

"I love you," said Owen.

"I love you too."

Owen went into the playroom and started playing with Wyatt. Lucy could hear them laughing. She tied the chicken's legs together with cooking twine and then used her elbow to turn on the faucet. She washed her hands. She slid the chicken into the oven and set the timer. She was getting a big bunch of elephant kale out of the refrigerator when it hit her.

He did it.

She knew it. She could feel it.

When?

That week? That day? That afternoon?

Where? Who?

Lucy felt faint. She leaned against the butcher-block island and took a few deep breaths. It's not that she hadn't thought he would do it—she was always pretty sure he was going to do *something*—but here, faced with the reality…she took another deep breath.

My husband is having sex with another woman. And I'm letting him! I told him he could! I said, "Go right ahead"! What is wrong with me? Have I lost my mind?

Then she washed the kale. She dried it with a paper towel. She placed it on the cutting board. She reached for a knife.

She felt an odd sense of calm descend on her while she went to work on the kale. The good thing about kale is it needs a lot of chopping. It was ideal for a situation like this. Chopping kale had become a certain kind of American housewife's version of chopping wood, carrying water. Something you did, and then you did again, and then you did again. Chopping kale, for women like Lucy, never stopped.

How did she feel? Surprised, really. Surprised that this was her life. Surprised that something so fundamental had changed and yet it felt like nothing had changed. A little scared. Less curious than she'd thought she'd be. But still a little curious.

Can I handle this?

She heard Wyatt in the playroom telling Owen his knock-knock joke about the interrupting monkey.

Is this a bad idea?

Maybe. Who knows? This is crazy. What's done is done.

Lucy kept chopping the kale.

"I'm pretty sure he's done it."

"Really?" said Sunny Bang. "What makes you say that?"

"Oh, he just seems happier. A little peppier. And he wants to spend all this time with Wyatt. He'll play the beaver game for two hours on a Saturday morning without complaining. It's like this thick fog he had over his head has finally lifted."

"The beaver game?"

"Wyatt's the beaver, Owen's the zookeeper, and a bunch of imaginary kids come visit the zoo, including a character named Stinky who takes off his pants in the middle of the field trip and has to go sit alone on the bus as a punishment. Wyatt would play it all day if he could."

"That's very inventive," said Sunny. "Tobias just plays Minecraft."

"It's the exact same script, every single time. If you try to change one word, Wyatt goes completely batshit."

"A friend of mine once flew on a private jet with Bill Gates, and she said he had a blanket over his head and was rocking back and forth the whole time. Wyatt's gonna be just fine."

They both looked over at Wyatt. He was dangling on one of the swings, with his belly in the sling part, trailing his fingers meditatively in the sand.

"So, what do you think Owen is doing?"

"I don't know. Maybe seeing an old girlfriend. Maybe he found someone online. It's possible he tried it once, and it made him appreciate what he has. Or maybe it's still going on. Either way, it's like he's seeing his life a little more. Even me."

"Are you going to ask him about it?"

"I don't want to know."

"I'd be so curious," said Sunny Bang. "I'd be tracking his every movement."

"I thought I'd be jealous, or at least curious, but I feel this strange sort of calm. And, honestly, it's nice to see him happy. I know that sounds weird, but it's true."

"What about you?"

"If something happens, it happens. I feel better just thinking that I could if I wanted to."

"You should go on Facebook and message all of your old boyfriends. When they ask you how married life is, just type in '*Eh*, dot-dot-dot, *you know*, dot-dot-dot.' That's the code."

"I don't want to have sex with any of my old boyfriends."

"There's a website, you know. For married people who want to have affairs. You could try that. I'll send you the link."

"How do you know about it?"

"Everybody knows about it," said Sunny. "It's like Match.com for married people."

"I don't want to mess with someone else's marriage. That just seems wrong."

"Well, you have to do something."

"Actually, I don't think I do," said Lucy. "Thinking I could feels like enough. Thinking I have the option feels like it's enough. I feel like a completely different person already and nothing's even happened."

Sunny just looked at Lucy for a moment. She had an expression on her face like she was about to say something meaningful, something profound, something that might permanently alter the course of events. Then she started screaming. "THAT'S IT, TOBIAS! WE'RE GOING HOME RIGHT THIS SECOND! I TOLD YOU

NOT TO THROW SAND! SAY YOU'RE SORRY TO HUDSON AND GET IN THE CAR!"

It was funny that Lucy realized Owen had actually gone through with it because of the kiss. The Marcella Hazan Chicken Kiss, is how she would forever think of it. It was a good kiss, a real one, one she felt all the way through her body. It had been a long time since she'd been kissed like that. A very long time. *Marriage changes the kissing,* Lucy found herself thinking later. *Why is that?* The kissing had almost stopped. And when it did happen, it felt different than it used to. It felt— well, *weird* wasn't quite the right word, but it was the closest one Lucy could come up with. Kissing without all the fireworks that used to be there; it was a strange activity.

Marriage doesn't hurt the cuddling or even change the sex all that much, but it does do something very bad to kissing, Lucy thought. *It does. And it's a shame.*

Five

Too often, a harmonious relationship is like a beautiful yacht tied up alongside a dock. Everything looks dreamy, but eventually you have to sail out into the open ocean.

—Constance Waverly

The Beekman elementary school's auditorium was filled to overflowing. Lucy was sitting up front, next to Claire, who always got to these things an hour early and saved seats for people she liked. Signs on the doors read PARENTS ONLY! and all but the nuttiest of the attachment-theory adherents had obeyed. Other than a four-year-old who was lolling long-limbed on his mother's lap, breastfeeding out of sheer boredom, there wasn't a kid in sight who was old enough to understand what was going on.

The meeting had begun with a welcome from Mrs. G., sunburned from her recent truncated vacation in Tulum and sitting behind a long table flanked by Emma, the school psychologist, and a pale, balding man in a three-piece suit. Mrs. G. droned on for a good twenty minutes about courage and respectfulness and dignity and honesty, pointing to the words painted on banners that hung over the bleachers and addressing the roomful of agitated parents as if they were half-witted seven-year-olds.

Next, the man in the three-piece suit, who turned out to be the school district's lawyer, reeled off statements about employee discrimination and hostile work environments. He said that Mrs. Lowell was now a member of a protected class and that parents and the school staff had to honor her right to change genders. Parents were asked to instruct their children to refrain from making jokes, comments, slurs, or aspersions of any kind about Mrs. Lowell, in person or on social media. When he was done, he slid the microphone across the table to Emma, who perkily announced plans for biweekly discussion groups for parents and interested students and encouraged anyone who needed additional resources to e-mail her night or day. By the time the floor was open for public discussion and a microphone on a stand positioned down front by a heavyset middle-schooler, the grinding wheels of public school bureaucracy had just about sucked the life out of the one thing every last person in town had been talking about for days.

A rangy brunette wearing dark brown cords and a fluttery white top came up to the microphone. She adjusted the mic so she wouldn't have to slouch, tossed her lank brown hair to one side, and slowly surveyed the crowd.

"Wow. *Wow*. Okay. Hi! For those who don't know me…my name is Susan Howard." Was it just Lucy, or had Susan paused for a murmur of acknowledgment that hadn't come? "First, let me just say, it is an honor to be addressing you tonight. My husband, Rowan, and I feel so, so grateful for the hard work you, the people of Beekman, have done to build this community.

"A tiny bit about me. I'm a poet, a deacon at St. Andrews right across the street, and a stay-at-home mother to three utterly amazing kids. And I'm afraid I plead guilty to being one of the progressive parents Karl was just talking about. Hi, Karl!" Susan waved at Karl, a jowly fourth-generation Beekmanite who had opened the public-comments portion of the meeting by reading a stinging indictment of the newcomers who were trying to impose socialist values on this all-American town.

Lucy nudged Claire and whispered, "Since when is Susan a *poet*?" Claire just rolled her eyes.

"I completely understand why Mrs. Lowell's brave personal journey has been so controversial. I get it. I *do*. But the truth is, some people are born inside the wrong bodies and they know it from a very young age. And when their cries aren't heard, when society makes it impossible for them to be who they really are, the result is depression, anxiety, and suicide. Statistically, ten percent of the children of the people in this room are transgender but are too frightened to say anything about it."

Ten percent? Lucy thought. *That's not possible.*

"Every child in this school has had a wonderful kindergarten experience in Mrs. Lowell's class. And now they have an opportunity to watch her as she becomes who she truly *is.* Which is, really, all we want for our children anyway, isn't it? To become who they really are, whether straight or gay or bisexual or transgender or gender-neutral."

Lucy heard someone in the back of the auditorium say, "What the hell is gender-neutral?"

"And who better than Mrs. Lowell to normalize something that is *completely normal?* Next it might be your child. It might be my child. But this is not going away. And I think that the bravery Mrs. Lowell has shown should be applauded and recognized. She is our Rosa Parks, and kudos to her for refusing to sit in the back of the bus."

"Thank you, Mrs. Howard," said Mrs. G.

There was a smattering of applause—Lucy noticed that Susan was in no hurry to return to her seat—and then whispers as a tall, thin man in a cashmere sweater, pressed blue jeans, and Gucci loafers approached the microphone.

"Who is that?" Lucy asked Claire.

"Gordon Allen. The billionaire. He's got a kid in Mr. Lowell's class."

"Are you serious? Which kid?"

"Rocco."

"Rocco's father is Gordon Allen?"

"I can't believe you're just finding this out now," Claire whispered.

"I've been a little distracted lately."

"I'll say," said Claire.

"This is not acceptable," said Gordon. "He needs to go."

The school district's lawyer leaned forward and spoke. "I

respectfully remind you that in the context of this public forum, we are using Mrs. Lowell's preferred form of address. The pronoun should be *she*."

"Forgive me." Gordon folded his arms across his chest and said, "*It* needs to go."

The room erupted. It wasn't altogether clear to Lucy who was on what side of things at this point. Most, she hoped, objected to Gordon's use of the word *it*. Some were clearly thrilled.

Mrs. G. pounded her gavel and shouted, "Order! Order!"

"You can't control what I say. I know you'd like to. But I can use the pronoun of my choice, the pronoun that members of this community have been using to address Mr. Lowell for fifteen years."

The lawyer leaned into the microphone. "I would like it on the record that the Beekman school district does not support this position, but according to our bylaws, the gentleman is entitled to have his voice heard. You may continue."

"This is not San Francisco," Gordon said. "It's not New York City. It isn't Brooklyn, no matter how many of you hippies wish it were. Beekman is a small town. We came here for a reason. And part of it was not to force our children to witness men changing into women before their very eyes."

A few *Woo-hoo*s, along with scattered hisses. Lucy craned her neck to see who was doing what and her eyes fell on Sunny Bang, who was standing in the back of the room with her hands on her hips, hissing for all she was worth.

"This is a civil rights issue," the school psychologist said. "We're here to help the members of the community adjust to this new reality."

"I want to know when traumatizing a roomful of kindergarteners became a civil right."

"Transgenderism may be difficult for some people to understand," Emma said, "but it is a fact of life."

"It's not a fact of *my* life," said Gordon. "It's not a fact of anyone I know's life."

A voice called out, "Well, you know one now, Gordon. And so does your son."

"I want it out of the classroom."

The room went crazy. The lines were becoming plain. Most of the old-time Beekmanites whooped whenever Gordon said *it*, while the former city folk either hissed or shouted "Shame!" at him. Gordon didn't appear to care.

"The law is clear on this point," the school district's lawyer said. "This is not a reason for termination."

"You're wrong. The law is not at all clear on this point. And do you know how I know that? This is my lawyer. His name is Hugh Willix. You might want to get to know him because you're going to be spending a lot of time with him, time I'll be paying him six hundred dollars an hour for. Hugh likes to rack up those six-hundred-dollar hours, don't you, Hugh?"

Hugh nodded, but to Lucy he didn't seem overly happy to be a prop in Gordon's little show.

"Hugh has got three kids in private school," Gordon said. "Turns out, he's smarter than I am."

Hugh looked down and shook his head.

"I moved my family to Beekman because I wanted to believe in public education again," said Gordon. "I wanted to believe in *America* again, frankly, if that isn't too patriotic. Well, one thing I know about America is that the public has a voice. And you, all of you, sitting up there on the stage, are here at the pleasure of the people. We pay your salaries and we can hire and fire you. The school board is elected and can be recalled. The administration can be replaced.

"Either the drag queen goes, or you'll be seeing me in court."

Gordon Allen didn't typically take an interest in local affairs. He viewed Beekman as his own personal Brigadoon, completely removed from reality, which for Gordon meant from global finance, George Soros versus the Koch brothers, the nonstop flickering of his Bloomberg terminal, the price of gold, the boneheaded mistakes the Republicans in Congress kept making, the browning of America, the dangers posed by artificial intelligence, and his own creeping mortality. If you'd asked him a month earlier, he would have said he'd be more likely to go to the moon than show up at a local school-board meeting.

But an incident earlier that week had changed everything.

He had been in the kitchen making himself a protein shake when Kelly and Rocco and one of the nannies came home from soccer.

"Hey, champ. How was the game?"

"I didn't score any goals."

"You gotta score goals, buddy! That's the whole point of soccer. Otherwise you're just a schmuck running up and down a field," said Gordon. He ruffled his son's hair and was struck by how silky and perfect his blond curls were, like he had spent the afternoon at the salon. "Did your team win?"

"Everybody won," said Rocco.

"It was a tie?"

"I don't know."

"Were the scores the same?"

"We're not allowed to keep score."

Gordon turned to Kelly. "They're not allowed to *keep score?*"

"It's like this everywhere," said Kelly. "You can't get away from this stuff, Gordy. You know that."

Gordon turned to Rocco, who had begun to suck on a yogurt stick like it was a clarinet. "How are your grades?"

"He's in kindergarten," said Kelly. "They don't give them grades."

"Tell his teacher we want grades," Gordon said to Kelly. "I want to know where he is in the class, because if he's not at the top of it in this place, something's really wrong."

"They color things and sit on alphabet mats. How can anyone be at the top of that?"

"Trust me, there's a kid at the top of that class, and the

teacher sure as hell knows who it is. I want to hear that it's Rocco."

Kelly rolled her eyes.

"My teacher wears dresses to school," Rocco volunteered.

"Good for her," said Gordon. "That's nice. I like it when women wear dresses."

"Yeah, I guess," said Rocco. He slurped down the last of his snack, and his yogurt clarinet went limp in his hand. "But he's a boy."

"What the *fuck!*"

Gordon was in the great room, pacing up and down in front of the fireplace, which was blazing even though it was unseasonably warm outside. Gordon kept the temperature in the house low so he could enjoy a fire twelve months out of the year. He loved his fireplace. It was an exact replica of the fireplace in the lobby of the Ahwahnee lodge at Yosemite, and it could burn logs that were twelve feet long. It could, and it did.

"Calm down, Gordon. You're going to have a heart attack and we're an hour from a halfway-decent hospital."

"Goddamn it, Kelly, why didn't you tell me about this?"

"Because I knew you'd have this reaction," Kelly said. "And I didn't want to deal with it. There's nothing we can do about it and it's not that big of a deal."

"It sure as fuck is a big deal! If the goddamn kindergarten teacher is going to chop his dick off? I'd call that a big fucking deal!"

"He's not gonna do it in the classroom, Gordon. The surgery isn't until the summer."

"Oh, well, that makes it better," Gordon said. He was stalking around like a madman. "He's gonna have a dick under his dress all year and then chop it off in July. That'll make for an interesting what-I-did-last-summer essay, don't you think?"

"Teachers don't write those essays, Gordon."

"I can't believe you didn't tell me this, Kelly. This is

unacceptable. I would have pulled Rocco straight out of that school and you know it."

"Well, I'm sorry. He's already been exposed. I think making too big of a deal about it around Rocco would be counterproductive at this point, but what do I know?" Kelly said. "Good night. I'm going to my room."

Lucy would love this, Owen thought as he trudged up the narrow staircase of Izzy's basement. He was carrying a rusty old air-conditioning unit, the kind he hadn't owned since college, and it had to weigh seventy pounds. He could already tell that this little task of Izzy's was going to be more difficult than she had let on. *If Lucy saw me doing this,* Owen thought as he took another shaky step, *she'd never stop cracking up.*

Owen had dropped by Izzy's for a quickie, twenty minutes of what turned out to be exceptionally hot and sweaty sex. He was sitting on the foot of the bed, pulling on his khakis, trying to think of what he needed to pick up at GroceryLand and whether there was enough wine in the house, when he heard Izzy sigh loudly.

"That was amazing," he said.

"Um-hmm," said Izzy.

"Look at you," he said. "You're dripping with sweat."

"This isn't from the sex," Izzy pointed out. "It's a million degrees in here. My window unit is shot."

"Oh yeah?"

"I've got a spare one down in the basement," said Izzy.

Could I ever tell Lucy about this? Owen thought as he braced his lower back against the handrail and tried to catch his breath. Was this the kind of story he could tell his wife: that the woman he was sleeping with had him hauling an old air-conditioning unit up two flights of stairs and installing it in a window?

Owen didn't even do this sort of thing in his own house. He paid a guy named Larry to do it. Lucy made a list of things that in a perfect world her husband would do, and then Owen called Larry and paid him to do it. And if Owen could have figured out how to get Larry over to Izzy's, he would have. But unfortunately, in the course of the past few years, Larry had become something of a family friend. He also was not an idiot. *The penis is an interesting organ,* Owen thought as he shuffled along the landing and then paused for a moment before starting up the second flight of stairs. *The penis truly has a mind of its own.*

"Lift with your knees, not with your back," Izzy called from the kitchen. She was standing naked in front of the open refrigerator, drinking white wine from a half-empty bottle.

Helpful, Owen thought. *Very helpful.*

"Jesus fucking Christ!" Owen yelled.

"What the hell is going on up there, Owen?"

"Jesus fucking Christ!" Owen yelled again.

Owen could hear Izzy's footsteps hurrying up the staircase.

"Holy shit," said Owen.

"What happened?"

"Holy shit!"

"Where's my air conditioner?"

"It fell out the window."

"Are you serious?"

"I almost lost a finger," said Owen. "This finger right here was almost ripped off of my hand."

"If you didn't know how to install an air conditioner, you should just have told me."

"I did tell you. I said exactly that. And then you said it was easy and that your idiot husband Christopher did it every year."

"You're right. You did tell me that," said Izzy. "My bad."

"Do you have a first-aid kit?" Owen asked. He looked down

at the gash in his finger. It was bleeding profusely. He tried not to think of all the rust that encrusted the old AC, the one that was now outside in pieces on the lawn. Rust caused tetanus, right? Jesus. Jesus! "I need some Neosporin."

"I'll see what I can dig up," Izzy said. She looked out the window at the air conditioner, which had flattened one of her boxwoods. "I can't believe you did that."

"Can we take a moment and be grateful it didn't hit anybody?"

"No. No, we can't."

"It could have killed somebody. Or a dog or a cat or something. It fell two stories down."

"I'm not grateful for this. I can't afford to be doing things like buying new air conditioners, Owen. I live on a fixed income. It's called alimony, and it's shit."

"I can't turn back time, Izzy. I apologize for not making my inability to install an air conditioner clearer to you at the onset."

"I'm perimenopausal, Owen."

"What does that mean?"

"It means," Izzy said, "I get hot."

Six

It is true that in the natural world, there is one foolproof way to revive a flagging libido—find a new partner.

—Constance Waverly
The Indigo Initiative

T he Waldmans' outdoor wood-fired Japanese soaking tub had achieved almost mythical status in Beekman, even though the Waldmans had moved away long ago, the tub itself had fallen into disrepair, and the house was now owned by wealthy retirees who spent their winters in Palm Springs. Still, the tub lived on in the communal mommy-memory of the town, passed down from woman to woman on park benches at the tot park, over bottles of wine at the Cutting Room, alternately chilling and thrilling, scandalous and intriguing.

What had happened was this. Some number of years earlier, a local attorney named Elliot Waldman had installed a hand-made wood-fired Japanese soaking tub in the woods behind his home. Elliot had built it himself—he was that kind of guy, very handy, always finding plans for things on the Internet and then building them for less than seventy-five bucks. The sprawling Waldman property also boasted a saggy, stained yurt and a lethal-looking tree house that Elliot's wife forbade their three children to use.

The soaking tub sat six people comfortably and eight or even nine if everyone was willing to be ever so slightly pressed up against one another. And sitting in the middle of the woods in a tub of hot water drinking wine while snowflakes floated down all around you, or looking up at the stars while passing around a glass pipe, turned out to be just about as much fun as anyone had managed to have in Beekman in a very, *very* long time.

There was still a debate about whether swimsuits were worn in the tub. Some said yes, others whispered no. Some claimed suits were wriggled out of, or people forgot them altogether, quite possibly on purpose. But swimsuits or no, the tub was filled with drunk and/or high, slippery-wet mommies and daddies pressed up against one another in the pitch-dark, deep in the woods.

Late the following summer, the divorces started. Only two of the original hot-tub buddies still lived in town, now married to each other, and they were looked upon with suspicion by the Long-Memory Mommies, the ones who knew which young mothers of current pre-Ks used to be nannies in the employ of their now-husbands, who knew which man used to live with his ex-wife in a house presently owned by a new couple running in their set, who knew where all of the bodies were buried.

The lasting impact of the Waldmans' soaking tub was this: the young mothers of Beekman were fundamentally conservative, not in their politics, but in their behavior. They did not flirt with one another's husbands. Cleavage was suspect. Bikinis worn to the club pool were analyzed and then texted about. Sometimes even photographed if it was possible to do it discreetly (and it was). Lingering hugs, drunken conversations that took place in corners of rooms at Beekman parties and lasted ten minutes too long—all of that was frowned upon.

And the wives—well, they looked out for each other. So when Claire Chase and her son Blake were driving through the parking lot at Home Depot, and she spotted Owen, she made a mental note of it.

Something about it struck her as off. It was the middle of the workday, for one thing, and Owen had a large window-unit air conditioner wedged into the top of a shopping cart and was walking rapidly toward his Subaru. Once there, he popped the back open and began an awkward dance of trying to get the air conditioner from cart to car. For reasons she was unable to fathom, Claire did not stop her car, roll down her window, and say hello.

A few minutes later, it hit her: *Owen and Lucy have central air.*

Saturday-morning soccer was an exercise in futility, but Lucy and Owen kept signing Wyatt up for it every year. They wanted him to have the experience of playing a team sport.

That Saturday, Lucy and Wyatt showed up to the game twenty minutes late because Wyatt had refused to get into the car. Finally, Lucy bribed him with five—yes, five—Hershey's kisses. *He'll burn the sugar off on the soccer field,* Lucy thought when she gave them to him. Wyatt could be a tough negotiator when he sensed he had the upper hand.

"Go on," Lucy said to him when they got to the field. "Your team is in the yellow. Go and have fun. Remember, no hands on the ball!"

Wyatt wandered off slowly in the direction of the scrum of kids chasing the ball just as Sunny Bang sidled up to Lucy and said quietly, "Yo."

"Hey, Sunny."

"I've found someone for you."

"A babysitter?" Lucy was always looking for new babysitters. Wyatt chewed through them. They'd babysit once, and then become mysteriously, perpetually unavailable.

"No, you idiot," said Sunny Bang. "A guy for you to have sex with."

"Sunny—"

"GO, TOBIAS!" Sunny shouted. "GO, TOBITO-BAMBITO! GO! KICK IT! KICK IT! GOOD TRY! GOOD TRY, BABY!"

"Well, you're not making any progress on your own," said Sunny. She turned away from the soccer field and stared intently at Lucy's face. "Unless you are and just aren't telling me about it, in which case I will be extremely mad at you. But also proud of you. I'll be equal parts mad and proud."

"I haven't done anything."

"But you're pretty sure Owen has. *Is.*"

"I'm pretty sure. Basically, I'm sure."

"But you haven't asked."

"We don't talk about it. Asking is against the rules."

"The rules! I love it," said Sunny. "You do realize this whole thing is completely insane, right?"

"Nothing bad has happened."

"Yet," added Sunny Bang. "Nothing bad has happened *yet*."

Lucy couldn't help herself. She was curious. "So, is he, like, a guy from that affair website you told me about?"

"No. He's just a guy I know. I went to college with his sister. He lives in the city."

"How do you know he'll have sex with me?"

"Trust me, he'll sleep with anyone," said Sunny. "Plus, you're gorgeous. Anyone would sleep with you."

Lucy rolled her eyes. "What's wrong with him, besides the fact that he'll apparently sleep with anyone?"

"Nothing."

"Sunny…"

"Okay," said Sunny Bang. "He's not what you'd consider classically good-looking."

"Here we go," said Lucy.

"But you know how those not-super-great-looking guys can hit their early forties and develop some character in their faces and become sort of appealing? That's him. And he works out. He goes to the gym. His body is pretty decent from what I could tell."

"When did you see him last?"

"At his sister's second wedding last Saturday. It was at some rent-a-loft in Tribeca," Sunny said. "GO, TOBIAS! YOU GOT IT! YOU GOT THIS ONE, BABY! GOOD EFFORT!"

"And you talked to him? About me?"

"I didn't use your name. But I told him about you. I explained your situation."

"You just said you had a married friend who was looking to have meaningless sex with someone and he was like, Sign me up?"

"What part of this don't you understand?"

"Just, who would say yes to that sort of thing?"

"Um, a man?"

Lucy looked over at Wyatt. He was dressed in his soccer uniform, everything except the long yellow socks, which were a truly vile wool-polyester blend that he refused to wear because they itched. He was alone, far away from the action, flicking the flag that marked a corner of the field while he flapped his hands and bounced up and down on the balls of his feet. *At least he's on the field,* Lucy thought. *At least he's having fun.*

"Is he repulsive or something?"

"No. Not even a little bit. I promise you. He's got a weird sexy thing going. He once slept with Helena Bonham Carter."

"Really?"

"It was a while ago. But yes. It happened. It is verifiable. I have it from multiple sources. ETHAN, I SEE YOU! STOP PICKING YOUR NOSE!"

"Sunny, that's not even your kid!"

"So?"

"You can't yell at other people's kids!"

"Of course I can. People don't yell at other people's kids enough as far as I'm concerned. ETHAN, COME OVER HERE FOR A WET WIPE RIGHT THIS SECOND."

Sunny started to fish around in her enormous purse for a wipe for the nose-picker. "He's not looking for anything serious. He just got a divorce. I think his ex did a number on him. They have two preteenish girls together, and they share custody."

"Why'd they get a divorce?"

"Unclear," said Sunny. "But I can make a few calls if you want."

"Please don't."

"I'm just saying, he seems perfect for this scenario," said Sunny.

"Perfect how, exactly?"

"Well, he's not going to slit your throat in a motel room somewhere. Call me crazy, but I consider that a major plus," said Sunny. "And he's smart and he's funny and he's a good guy. He lives in the city, so no one in town will find out. And he won't screw up your entire life."

"It just feels, I don't know, not like me," said Lucy. "But thanks for thinking about me. Thanks for trying to be my pimp."

"The clock is ticking," Sunny said, and then she lowered her voice. "And you need to get your dick wet."

"Jesus, Sunny."

"I expressed my opposition to this entire experiment, but now that it's actually happening, it's not fair that Owen is running around having sex with strangers and you aren't," Sunny Bang said. Parents of the opposing team cheered poor-sportsmanship-ly when the ball rolled slowly past Beekman's goalie and made its way into the side of the net.

"You know me," Sunny Bang said. "I'm all about fair."

Claire watched Sunny Bang and Lucy's little confab from about twenty yards down the sideline while she pretended to be paying attention to the soccer game and typing important things into her phone. Normally, Sunny and Lucy would have waved her over and had her join their conversation, but there was almost a bubble around the two of them, the way they were talking to each other so quietly and intently. *Something's going on,* Claire thought. *I wonder what it is?*

It wasn't until the game was finally over, and Lucy was loading up her car, that Claire found an opening. "I saw Owen on the other side of the river yesterday afternoon," Claire said.

"Oh yeah? He didn't mention it."

"I don't think he saw me," said Claire. "He was at Home Depot."

Lucy looked like she was barely listening. She was wrestling with Wyatt, trying to get him into his car seat.

"You have to be strapped in, honey," Lucy said to Wyatt. "It's not safe."

"I don't want to be safe!"

Wyatt was arching his back as hard as he could and Lucy was pushing him into the car seat, trying to get the straps buckled across his chest.

"He was buying an air conditioner," Claire continued. "Owen was. One of those window units. Like we all had in college!"

"Sorry, Claire, I can't talk, I've gotta handle my kid."

"Of course," Claire said. "Blake used to hate his car seat too. It's very normal."

Just then, Wyatt yelled, "I hate you, Mama!" and spit in Lucy's face.

Lucy calmly wiped the saliva off her face and went back to wrestling her son. Claire hurried across the parking lot and slipped behind the wheel of her black BMW X5, completely speechless.

There existed a general consensus among the married women of Beekman that husbands were useless. Not that any of the ladies wanted to be husbandless—not quite, not yet, probably never—but if you gathered two or more around a bottle of wine, the complaints would begin pouring out, first a trickle and then a flood.

Andrew showed up forty-five minutes late to his daughter's third birthday party. Jake gave Sunny premium cable for her thirty-sixth birthday present and then canceled it eight months later. Rowan had been promising to set up the wireless printer/copier/scanner for six months, and the box was still unopened on the floor in the corner of the kitchen because Susan wanted to see how many times he could walk past it without either putting it away, returning it, or setting it up. So far, he'd done it at least ten times a day for a hundred and fifty days, which meant, conservatively, fifteen hundred times and counting. Edmund had so completely worn down Claire with his chronic forgetfulness and ineptitude that he had been given only one—one!—domestic responsibility, scooping out the cat box, *and yet he failed to do it!* Unless Claire nagged him! Which her therapist told her not to do under any circumstances! *Just wait and watch,* her therapist had said. *You're overfunctioning,* her therapist pointed out. *It makes him underfunction.* Which meant the cat pissed all over the house, and Claire suspected her husband was trying to drive her slowly insane.

And in a life of niggling mommy minutiae—of finding the Batman sippy cup and the *other* pair of purple tights, of pulling out splinters and searching for ticks, of signing up for the book fair and then remembering that you'd already signed up for the book fair, of putting quarters in lunch boxes and scheduling trips to the dentist—the fact that their husbands had morphed into endless open loops, like three-fer federal employees you could never fire, like bathroom doors that had swelled while you weren't paying attention, bathroom doors that you couldn't shut but you couldn't fix and you couldn't replace, bathroom doors you were stuck with until you *physically moved out of the house,* well—

"Hey, honey, can you make sure you take the recycling down tonight? The guy comes tomorrow and if it's not there, he knocks on the door and complains."

"Gotta go," Owen said into the phone. "Gettin' chored by the wife."

Owen hung up. Lucy just looked at him.

"What?" Owen asked.

"Do you have any idea how much I hate that word?"

"What word?"

"*Choring.* Getting *chored.* You and Scott's shorthand for when your wives ask you to do something."

"It's just a word. It doesn't mean anything."

"But it does. It does mean something," said Lucy. "First of all, it is contemptuous of me. Me asking you nicely to do something you've promised to do, promised over and over and over to do and still haven't done, is not me assigning you a chore. And somehow now, every last thing I ask you to do is me choring you. Like you're a kid and I'm the mom. These are not chores, Owen. These are things adults do to keep a household running."

"It's just a word," said Owen. "Don't overreact."

"Well, since I'm choring you anyway, can I ask when you plan to deal with the situation in the garage?"

"I'm gonna take care of it."

"When?"

"When I have the time."

"It's going to start to snow in a few months, and we're not going to be able to fit our cars into the garage unless you clear it out."

"I'm aware that the garage needs to be cleared out before it snows. But it's September."

"Can I put a date on the calendar when it will be done, so I won't have to think about it anymore?"

"You can put anything on the calendar you want."

Lucy just looked at him.

"And I can't control what you choose to think about," said Owen. "I don't have that particular magical power."

"If I put a date on the calendar, will you promise to do it by that day so I can stop thinking about it and I won't have to nag you about it anymore?"

"All I can promise is what I've already said," said Owen. "I intend to do it when I have the time."

"Are we really going to fight about this?"

"I'd prefer not to."

"I need to understand why you are doing this to me!"

"Because I don't want to do it right now! I will do it,

eventually, but it falls under the category of 'things I'd really rather not do.' And like many things you don't want to do, you don't just wake up on a beautiful Sunday like today and decide to ruin it by doing something you don't want to do."

"I don't want to be a nag. That's not who I want to be. This isn't fun for me, Owen."

"Then stop nagging me! I said I'll do it."

Lucy just looked at him. She took a deep breath.

"We could not park our cars in the garage last winter, Owen. Because you didn't make the space for us to. You promised me you would, and yet you didn't. You promised me again and again. I had to scrape snow and ice off the car over and over and over again, all winter long. So I'm not being crazy worrying that you will not complete this task."

"Enough!" shouted Owen. "Enough!"

Why did my husband buy an air conditioner at Home Depot? Lucy thought for the thousandth time since Claire had oh so carefully let her know. Obviously, he bought it for some person he was seeing. There was no other logical conclusion. But still— an air conditioner? The Arrangement had only been going for six weeks and Owen was involved with someone to the degree that he was *buying them an air conditioner and transporting it to their home?* Who on earth was this person? And what the hell was going on between them?

Lucy slowly walked up the stairs and lay down on the bed, on top of the comforter. Her shoes were still on, and she looked down at her feet, at her sad Merrells, black potato shoes, the shoes of resignation and defeat. She reached over to her night-stand and picked up her phone.

"Sunny?"

"Yeah?"

"I'm in," said Lucy.

"Are you serious?"

"I am," said Lucy. "Set it up."

Seven

Constance Waverly: Someone needs to admit that this is almost impossible.

Charlie Rose: And when you say "this," I take it you mean, um, you mean—

Waverly: Lifelong, sexually satisfying, non-deadening, non-soul-killing marriage—

Rose: Right, yes, but this is not new, people have been talking about this since the seventies.

Waverly: The seventies might as well be ancient history, Charlie. We're talking almost fifty years ago.

Rose: And the French, uh, the French have been making accommodations in their marriages, the Europeans—

Waverly: I'd like to talk about here and now, Charlie. I think someone needs to start the conversation again.

Rose: And you think that that person is you.

Waverly: Well, I think it should be someone who's not a pervy, out-there, free-love weirdo.

—Constance Waverly
Charlie Rose

It's so romantic," said Sunny Bang.

Lucy, Sunny Bang, and Claire were having ladies' night cocktails at the Cutting Room. Lucy thought it was hilarious that Beekman had a bar named the Cutting Room—like they were filmmakers grabbing a drink after a long day in the editing suite instead of three stay-at-home moms who'd miraculously been allowed out of the house at seven thirty on a Tuesday night.

"It's completely insane," said Claire.

"It's somewhere between romantic and insane," said Lucy. "It's somewhere in there."

The news had just broken that Arlen Lowell was going to stay with her husband. Her now-wife. They were to be the two Mrs. Lowells.

"And it's not just that they're not splitting up," said Sunny Bang. "They're staying happily, committedly, romantically married."

"I don't get it," said Claire. "Is Arlen becoming a lesbian?"

"I think we've entered the zone beyond labels, Claire," said Sunny Bang.

"This is the weirdest part of this whole thing," said Lucy. "I mean, can you imagine? What would you do if Jake came home and told you he wanted to become a woman?"

"It's more likely that I'd tell him I wanted to become a man," said Sunny Bang. "That's the more probable scenario."

"Yeah, okay, whatever, Sunny," said Claire. Sunny Bang never missed an opportunity to shock. "What would Jake do if you told him you wanted to become a man?"

"Honestly?" said Sunny Bang. She looked up in the air and appeared to give the question some serious thought. "I think he'd have a pretty major problem with it."

"Exactly."

"But who knows what goes on between people. Love is a strange thing."

⤞✦⤝

Arlen and Eric Lowell's house did not look out on the pond where Arlen's sister's body was found.

The pond in question was behind the house next door, a fact that had been more or less lost by the town gossips over the years. The pond was down in a little hollow, and it was impossible to see it from the Lowell property, especially now that the underbrush in the woods between the houses hadn't been properly cut back in decades.

Arlen was seven years old when Rose disappeared. After a frantic search that brought out the entire township of Beekman, Rose was discovered in the murky pond behind their next-door neighbor's house. She could have wandered into the pond, of course, although Rose was not known to wander off. *Not known to wander off,* Arlen could imagine the police writing in their little notebooks. There was a rock wall that separated the two properties, one of those ancient walls that was really nothing more than a row of loose stones heaped there by the farmers who had cleared the land sometime in the 1800s. How did she get over the wall? But there were two places where the stones had tumbled, two places where a three-year-old could conceivably have passed through, although she hadn't left any traces. *Not a trace near the rough rock wall, not a hair, not a scrape.* Still, it was at least a possibility. Rose was only three, she couldn't swim, and that particular pond had a way of sucking hard at one's feet. And a person can drown in two inches of water. But still: It's always the parents, right?

Both of Arlen's parents lived under a cloud of suspicion for the rest of their lives, and yet they chose to remain in Beekman. Theories abounded—the crazy mother did it, the drunken father did it, they did it together, the father did it and the mother helped him cover it up, although this last theory was hardest to believe, because by the time Rose died, Arlen's parents weren't even attempting to hide their contempt for each other. In the end, nothing was proven, no evidence was found, and no charges were ever filed.

The result was that the good people of Beekman had been feeling sorry for Arlen her entire life. They bought her presents at Christmas, they remembered her birthday, they gave her hand-me-downs, they checked up on her. They were thrilled when her father died of cirrhosis at forty-seven and positively gleeful when her mother was institutionalized in the late 1970s, although she was let out later, back when releasing the crazies was the popular thing to do.

Arlen never went to college. It just wasn't in the cards. She married Eric when she was twenty, and they had had two kids, a boy and a girl. Once her kids got to junior high, Arlen took a job at a shelter for women who were victims of domestic abuse. Over the years, she'd done just about everything at that place that you could imagine, from cleaning the toilets to hauling sheets to the Laundromat to offering unofficial life-coaching sessions to the women and scrounging up books and craft supplies for the kids. Man, the things she'd seen.

The things she'd seen! So much pain and suffering. Those beautiful women, heartbroken and lost and scared, often with nothing more than the clothes on their backs, afraid for themselves, terrified for their kids. And the little kids! They broke your heart. One time she walked in with a small stuffed owl she'd gotten for opening a checking account, and a little girl had looked up at her and said, "Is that for me?" Working at the shelter had, more than anything else, shaped the philosophy of Arlen's adult life, which was, in a nutshell: *If this is my biggest problem…*

*   *   *

It was Christmas Eve two years earlier. Arlen's mother had refused to come home for the holidays, nearly breaking the burly nursing-home attendant's jaw when he tried to force her into Arlen's car. The Lowells' daughter couldn't travel because she was on probation, and their son was going skiing with a girlfriend in Nevada, so Christmas was going to be just Arlen and Eric. Which was nice, really. Arlen liked to spend time alone with her husband, which was more than most women at her stage of life could say. She liked to sit across the kitchen table from him and tell him stories about the women in the shelter and pick his brain for advice. Arlen started a lot of conversations at the shelter with her trademark phrase "Now, I don't mean to should on you, but I'm gonna go ahead and do it if you'll let me," and she got a lot of her best suggestions from Eric. "Where the mind goes, the behind follows" is what she said when she talked to a woman who seemed to be thinking too often or too fondly about her ex. Arlen liked a good folksy saying. She collected them like cats.

Arlen was doing the dishes, looking out the window to her backyard, reminding herself to fill the bird feeders and put out a Christmas bonus for the mailman. Eric had strung the lights on the juniper tree like he did every year, even though the tree kept getting taller, and Arlen knew the day would come when it wouldn't be safe for him to string the lights on it anymore, and the thought made her suddenly sad. *Enjoy the lights right now,* she told herself. *Don't worry about somedays and might-happens.*

Eric cleared his throat and said her name. Arlen turned around.

He was wearing a red dress. Heels, wig, and makeup. Fake eyelashes, even, it looked like to Arlen, though she was standing at the sink a good fifteen feet away from him. *My husband is wearing fake eyelashes.* For some reason, the eyelashes were what told her that this wasn't a joke. The eyelashes told her this was very serious indeed.

Eric stood there, silently, looking at Arlen's face, a million thoughts in each one's head, not a word spoken, the weight of the moment and the years of their lives running together in a blur, and then he started to cry.

Arlen looked at him and thought: *If this is my biggest problem…*

"Hi," said Lucy. "I'm, uh, Lucy."

"And I'm Ben. Come on in."

Sunny was right, Lucy thought. He wasn't classically good-looking, but he had something. A quality.

"What a great place," Lucy said.

"Thank you," said Ben. "I don't own it. I wish I did."

"This is a cool neighborhood," said Lucy.

"Yeah," said Ben. "Although an old lady got shot on the corner last week. We're at that tipping point, half artisanal coffee bars, half stray bullets. A good time to buy."

"The perfect time to buy," said Lucy.

He walked over to the bookshelf and turned on some music. He was wearing 501s and a waffle-weave shirt that clung to him just enough that you could tell what was underneath. His stomach was perfectly flat. It just went straight down into his jeans at a 180-degree angle. *I'm treating him like a piece of meat*, Lucy thought. Well, that's what this was supposed to be, right? Lucy and her piece of meat.

"Can I get you something to drink?" Ben asked. "I've got some wine."

"Wine is good."

"Sunny said white. Is that right?"

"It is. Thank you."

He went to work opening the wine while Lucy tried to think of something to say.

"So, your sister went to college with Sunny Bang?"

"She did. Sunny used to come to our house for Thanksgiving every year because it was too far for her to fly home."

"I can't even imagine Sunny Bang in college."

"That's funny," he said. "You call her Sunny Bang?"

"Yeah. We all do. I don't know why," said Lucy. "If she's not in the room, she's always Sunny Bang."

Ben handed her a glass of wine. She took a big sip.

"So," said Lucy.

"So," said Ben.

Lucy took another sip of wine. "Um, this is nice. This wine. I like it."

"Good."

He leaned in and started with her neck. Not kissing it, exactly. More like smelling it. Really softly. Really, really nicely.

Lucy put her wineglass down.

"That was…" Lucy said.

"That was what?"

"That was really, really"—Lucy searched her brain for a better word but only one would fit, and so she said it—"weird."

Ben started to laugh.

"The sex was, I mean, new, and good, but mostly it's just incredibly weird to be here, doing this. With you."

"I was married for thirteen years. I think I understand."

"Can I ask you something? How is it that I could just walk into your apartment and drink three sips of wine and then you had sex with me?"

"What do you mean?"

"It was like being in a porn movie. Is this what people do now? Is this how people behave?"

"I got the sense, in the kitchen, that too much talking was going to freak you out. And we both seemed pretty clear on why you were here. So I rolled the dice."

Lucy looked at him. "I bet you have *a lot* of sex."

Ben just smiled a self-deprecating smile.

"Do you have a girlfriend?"

"Nope. Not at the moment," said Ben. "I date a lot, I guess. People fix me up."

"You get around," said Lucy.

He smiled. "I get around."

"Well, um," Lucy said. "Thanks?"

Ben just laughed at that.

"I kind of feel like I should shake your hand," said Lucy. "Or leave some money on the nightstand."

"So, what do you think?" he said. "You want to try this again sometime?"

"I don't know. Maybe. Probably," Lucy said. And then she blushed and said, "Yes."

"No more playdates with Blake," Owen announced the moment Lucy walked through the front door.

Owen was reading a thick paperback in the red chair when Lucy got home from her day in the city. Her sex day. He had a bottle of wine by his side and looked a little bedraggled from his time with Wyatt and Blake.

"Why, what happened?" Lucy asked.

"Well, apparently his house is bigger than ours," Owen said. "And his parents' cars are nicer. And he has three cars and we only have two. And why do we only have two cars? And why are they so messy?"

"He always says that," said Lucy.

Lucy went to grab a wineglass.

"Blake also is very concerned about how clean our house is," Owen called.

"Tell him to join the club."

"Apparently his mother puts the laundry away right when it comes out of the dryer. She folds it as she takes it out of the dryer so nothing gets wrinkled, and then she puts it into everyone's drawers. And she vacuums the entire house every day, which is why he has to put away all of his toys right after he plays with them. And he also helps her with the laundry, because he likes to put his clothes away into his drawers neatly."

"None of this is news to me," said Lucy. "Blake has told me all this before."

"And then every five minutes, he walked up to me and said, 'Um, excuse me, Mr. McIntire? I found another Cheerio on your couch.' And then he'd hand it to me. And stand there, with his hands on his hips, judging me. After the third one, I just started popping them in my mouth. I'd say, 'Thank you, Blake, I'm very hungry.' 'Why, thank you, Blake, this is a tasty snack.'"

Lucy laughed. "Why does Claire vacuum their entire house every day?" she asked. "That's what I want to know. Half the women who live up here are wasting their whole lives on complete bullshit."

"Their house does sound very clean and nice," said Owen.

"Well, I'm not standing between you and the vacuum," said Lucy.

"He's obsessed with his EpiPen. I took him outside and he started screaming, 'Where is my EpiPen! I need my EpiPen!' I'm like, 'What happened? Did something happen?' And no, he just really, *really* wanted his EpiPen."

"Claire told me if Blake gets stung by a bee, he could drop dead in thirty seconds."

"That's not possible. Nobody dies from bee stings like that."

"Something happened when he was a baby," said Lucy. "He got stung and ended up in the ICU at Mount Sinai for over a month."

"Really?"

"Yeah."

"That's horrible," said Owen. "I hereby retract the neurotic EpiPen obsession from my list of complaints about Blake. But the rest still stands."

Owen snuggled up to her. "I'm starting to understand why you've been losing your mind," Owen said. He put his arm around her waist and kissed her on the neck. "How was the city?"

"It was good," said Lucy. "I had a nice day."

"I'm glad."

Owen slid his hand onto Lucy's hip.

"Did you close the chickens in?" she asked.

"I forgot. I'll do it."

"No, no," said Lucy. "I'll go."

One of the only times Lucy noticed the stars these days was when she went out to close the door to the chicken coop. Which was one reason they'd lost so many chickens—a chicken door should be shut tight long before it's dark enough to see the stars; the predators prowled around at dusk, and a chicken coop with a dozen chickens nestled side by side up on their roost was like a drive-through fast-food joint to them. One time, Owen went in to lock up the chickens and a possum was up on the roost with its teeth buried in the neck of a buff Polish chicken named Cacciatore. Owen battled the possum with a metal snow shovel for about ten minutes until it finally sauntered out of the chicken coop and slunk back into the woods. Lucy drove Cacciatore to the friendly local veterinarian's house, and, two hundred and fifty dollars later, she was fine.

The inside of the chicken coop smelled much better than you'd think. It was a nice earthy smell, and not at all like chicken poop, believe it or not. Lucy went inside and counted the chickens. Eleven, still. She stroked each chicken along the back as she counted it. Kiev, Nugget, Curry, Marsala, Fat White, Fat Black, Ugly Chicken, Crazy Chicken, Cacciatore, Tikka, and Gluten-Free Patty. She had raised them all inside the basement from the time they were two days old and she had violated the most basic rule of chicken-raising. Don't name them, everyone said. Don't do it. You'll regret it if you do.

Lucy had named them. And she didn't regret it.

Eight

If you're content not having sex with your partner, that's fine. But you might want to consider the following fact. Most people are having sex with *somebody*.

—Constance Waverly
The Waverly Report

Four years earlier, when the twins finally made the jump from half-day preschool to full-day kindergarten, just after baby Charlotte turned one, Susan Howard realized she and her husband, Rowan, were no longer having sex.

It was their anniversary. They went out to sushi for dinner, stopped by the country club for dessert and more drinks, and yet they still made it back home by eleven. They usually got home late from nights out, around one or even two, but those were nights out with other couples, dinner parties and party-parties, Beekman parties where the good red wine never stopped flowing. But Rowan, when forced to pay the restaurant's markup for a bottle of wine and twelve dollars for each drink, drank less than usual. And the two of them, without the distraction of the twins or baby Charlotte or the buzz of a party whirling around them, didn't have that much to say to each other. It was difficult for Susan to sit across the table from Rowan and keep herself from reminding him of things he needed to do—get the minivan inspected, pour the fifty-pound bag of salt crystals into the water purifier, stick the tall orange reflector sticks into the driveway before the ground froze. But she didn't. She kept her mouth shut. She smiled and tried to be interesting and engaging and entertaining and fun. She scrounged around inside her brain to come up with things to talk about that weren't about the twins, that weren't about baby Charlotte, that weren't mommy nonsense.

When they got into bed, Susan realized her heart was pounding. She could feel it in her fingertips, the blood pulsing. She wasn't drunk enough to pretend it wasn't happening, she wasn't sleepy enough to fall asleep. *It's our anniversary,* she thought. *You have to have sex on your anniversary, right? Something is really, really wrong if you don't.*

We've stopped having sex. When did we stop having sex?

For a long time, Susan had welcomed the reprieve from any sexual demands. She was exhausted. She was overwhelmed. She had other things to worry about. Sex was like the can of baking powder she kept on a high shelf in her pantry, something she didn't need *right now* but that she knew she could get her hands on without too much trouble. "Marriage isn't about sex," Susan's mother had told her when she was growing up. "Passion fades," her mother had said. That, and "Men don't like to have fat wives."

So Susan did not let herself get fat, and she didn't worry about fading passion, and she channeled her energy into her volunteer work and into breastfeeding her kids longer than most women considered either necessary or normal. But once the sex thing became an issue in her head, it was just about all she could think about. After trying to initiate sex a bunch of times—bona fide humiliations, every last one of them—she more or less forced Rowan to go see a therapist, Dr. Weinberg, who specialized, according to his website, in sex.

"Do you remember that commercial for Dunkin' Donuts? With that old guy who woke up early every morning and said, 'Time to make the doughnuts'? He was dragging himself around, saying, 'Time to make the doughnuts, time to make the doughnuts'?" Susan asked Dr. Weinberg at their first joint therapy session. "Seriously, do you remember?"

"I do remember that commercial," the doctor said finally.

"Okay, well, that's how Rowan makes me feel about wanting to have sex. Any time the idea of sex comes up, it's like there's a thought bubble over his head that says, 'Time to make the doughnuts.'"

"Because you're putting a lot of pressure on me," said Rowan. "You don't see it, Susan, but you are."

"What pressure?"

"All of it! The new lingerie. Every time I get into bed I feel like I'm disappointing you."

"You *are* disappointing me! This is a really messed-up situation, Rowan. I don't see why you don't see it!"

"I do see it. I'm here, right? I'm willing to work on it. I want to fix it."

"Are you gay, Rowan? If you're gay, just tell me."

"I'm not gay."

"Do you think he's gay, Dr. Weinberg?"

"No, I don't."

It seemed rather unusual for a shrink to say something that definitively, but Susan liked it. *He must be pretty sure,* she thought, *to put it that plainly.* Dr. Weinberg had had three sessions with Rowan on his own. Who knows what he might have teased out in those hundred and fifty minutes? Perhaps Rowan had revealed a very deep, very symbolic, profoundly heterosexual dream.

"Okay," Susan said. She scooched a bit on the couch, turned her body toward her husband, and looked him directly in the eyes. "Are you having an affair?"

"No! Jesus, Susan. No."

"Just tell me if you are," she said. "It's okay to tell me. Honestly, at this point I'd rather know."

"I'm not! I swear," said Rowan. "Are you having an affair?"

"Of course not."

"I love you. I love our family. I want us to work."

"I do too," said Susan.

Rowan took Susan's hand in his. He turned to Dr. Weinberg and said, "What are we supposed to do?"

First, Dr. Weinberg insisted they move Charlotte out of their room and install a lock on their bedroom door to keep the twins at bay. This was almost more than Susan could handle, losing Charlotte, locking the boys out; it felt cruel and dangerous. ("What if there's a fire? What if there's a fire and we're asleep and they can't get in?") But Dr. Weinberg wouldn't bend—getting the eighteen-month-old out of the marital bed and making sure the door would lock was nonnegotiable. "It might be enough," Dr. Weinberg said at the end of that first session. "Quite often, that's enough."

It wasn't, though. It wasn't enough.

And thus was ushered in a particularly grim phase of their marriage, the Working on Sex phase. They saw Dr. Weinberg every Thursday night, and at the end of each session he sent them off with homework to complete by the following week. They bought scented massage oils, they slept naked, they forced themselves to cuddle and kiss and give each other long-drawn-out nonsexual massages. Susan was encouraged to masturbate. Rowan was told in no uncertain terms not to. They wrote down their fantasies and then read them to each other while Dr. Weinberg looked on from the comfort of his Eames chair. They held hands when they didn't want to, they made out in a movie theater, groping each other like teenagers. Only that was the thing—the groping didn't feel teenager-ish, the groping felt forced, staged, awkward, and distinctly unsexy. Working on sex, it turned out, was worse than not having sex.

Through it all, Susan could feel how difficult, how truly unpleasant, this was for Rowan. It always came down to one thing: The pressure! He couldn't take it! And the more Rowan couldn't take the pressure, the angrier Susan got. *He's really fucked up,* Susan thought. That's all there was to it. And if Susan had been a different woman, a woman with a baseline of instinctual health, she probably would have cut her losses right then. But—the kids. The life. The friends. Beekman.

It started as an innocent experiment in reverse psychology. Susan sat Rowan down after the kids were in bed one night and told him that she wanted to stop Working on Sex. She wanted to stop seeing Dr. Weinberg and maybe use the money they saved for a date night every few weeks if that sounded good to him, but no pressure. She'd decided that she was okay, she was happy, and things were good the way things were. They were both tired, the twins were still a handful, Charlotte was still in diapers, and his job put him under a lot of pressure. They loved each other, they had a life together, and the sex would eventually sort itself out.

Two more years passed.

Ten days after the meeting in the school auditorium, Colleen Lowell was relieved of her position as the kindergarten teacher of the Beekman elementary school and placed on paid leave.

The administration pulled Mrs. Gibson away from one of the first-grade classes and placed her in the kindergarten spot and then blended half of the first-graders with the second-graders, going from four classrooms down to three. Of course, this had the effect of angering even more parents, the parents of the first- and second-graders who were now in classes with higher pupil counts, the second-graders sitting side by side with the first-graders, with all the parents comparing notes, trying to figure out if they'd put the smartest first-graders in with the second-graders or if it was truly random, as Mrs. G. insisted over and over again.

The school board had finally settled on the excuse of gross insubordination, based on the fact that Mrs. Lowell hadn't informed the principal or the superintendent of her plans before commencing her transition. She was tenured, though, and continued to receive full pay while on leave, and since there was only one elementary school in the Beekman Unified School District, there was no other school in which to place her.

The local Catholic school was oversubscribed by ten o'clock the morning after the initial public hearing as a small but significant group of Beekman parents rushed to pull their kids out of the public school. The Archdiocese of New York trucked in mobile classrooms and placed them in rows on the big, flat lawn in front of Beekman's beautiful two-hundred-year-old Catholic church, creating an eyesore and sparking a new round of contentious municipal-zoning hearings. Before long, parents who had never set foot in a church were listening to their children saying Hail Marys at the dinner table and then again while they knelt beside their beds each night. *A little religion never hurt anybody,* these parents would say to themselves and then try not to think about whether or not that statement was actually technically true.

It was Susan Howard who came up with the idea for Colleen Lowell's silent protest. She didn't want Colleen, in particular, and the subject of transgenderism, in general, to disappear from the "Beekman dialogue," and so she persuaded Colleen to take up residence during school hours on the bench in front of the Country Crock, so no one in town would be able to ignore this colossal injustice! Colleen was dressed to the nines every day, looking like she was either on her way to a cocktail party (all black, wearing statement necklaces) or doing duty as mother of the bride (pastels, with the pearls she'd bought herself as a present for coming out). Her wife, Arlen, joined her whenever she wasn't working at the shelter or visiting her mother at the retirement home, and the two would hold hands, scratch dog bellies, and chat with friendly passersby.

For the first time in my life, I'm glad my parents are dead, Lucy thought.

Lucy was on Metro-North, heading south, heading toward Ben, and for some reason she found herself thinking about her parents.

Her mother had died when Lucy was three years old. She'd

pulled over to help a stranded motorist along the small stretch of highway she used as a shortcut to and from Lucy's ballet class, from exit 18 to exit 19. Lucy was in the back of the car and her mother had gotten out to talk to the stranger, who had run out of gas, when she was clipped by a drunk driver and then flattened by an eighteen-wheeler. Lucy had overheard one of the EMTs use those exact words, *clipped* and *flattened,* and they were not words her three-year-old mind could forget.

Her mother, driving her home from ballet. Her mother, stopping to help a stranger.

Her father was a famous scholar, tenured young at a small Midwestern liberal arts college, and everything about that suited him. He never remarried, and Lucy and her older sister, Anna, grew up like feral cats. Every year, he hired graduate students to help with household tasks like shopping and organizing, cleaning and cooking, always women, always B-plus students who were thrilled to get to spend so much time in his orbit even if it meant scrubbing his toilets and changing his sheets. Not the superstars, never the superstars, and never, not once, a man. That was the lowest thing you could be in the world Lucy's father had made for himself: a woman who was not a superstar. A woman who changed the sheets.

He was warm, though. He was kind and he was loving and mostly, well, he was around. He was *there,* literally, spending nearly all of his time inside the house—a stately Victorian with a wraparound porch and a widow's walk even though it was fifteen hundred miles to the nearest ocean. He held office hours in the parlor and did his reading in his study, and twice a week he walked the three blocks to campus and gave a lecture to two hundred and fifty students who treated him like a god. Other than that, he brought the college to him, hosting potluck dinners several nights a week with his grad students, and Thursday sherry hours, a tip of the hat to the four years he'd spent at Oxford in the sixties.

Lucy's father wasn't good with things like remembering to sign permission slips and buying hair bows and putting on tights, but he had a lap he would let her sit on for hours, both of them reading, in front of the fire. That's what Lucy thought of when she thought of life after her mother died, reading on her father's lap and, later, curled up next to him on his ancient Chesterfield couch, the one with the silver duct tape slapped over the cracking parts.

He died quickly, of pancreatic cancer, when Lucy was four months pregnant with Wyatt. His life's great work was a European history textbook that was still popular, one that had been in use for three decades and was now digitized and enhanced and changed around a bit every few years by the publisher to ensure continuing sales. Inheriting her share of its copyright was like being gifted with a very small and yet extremely reliable money machine. It generated enough revenue that Lucy didn't have to feel guilty about not working. It paid for Wyatt's extra therapies, the special horseback riding and the vision therapy, the ones that weren't covered by the generosity of the taxpayers of New York State. Not riches, not by a long shot, but breathing room.

Lucy's therapist, back when she had one, during the worst six months of her infertility treatments, had commended her on her resilience. There she was, saddled with a dead mother and an extremely traditional, intellectual father, and yet: A good marriage, a satisfying career. No addictions or phobias or neuroses to speak of. A desire for children so strong that she was willing to go through a great deal of pain and disappointment and expense in order to have one of her own.

But Lucy was unmothered, as unmothered as it was possible to be, and the thing that therapist never told her, the six-months you're-so-very-resilient therapist, was that it was hard to be a mother when you had never been mothered yourself. Your children's needs remind you of your needs. Their pain reminds you of your pain. All of it reminds you of how bad it felt, how hard it was, how much you wanted and needed and didn't get.

It's very hard.

The elevator opened and Lucy stepped into the hall. Ben was standing in his doorway, smiling a small yet undeniable smile. Lucy walked toward him, knowing what was next, knowing exactly why she was there, again, ready this time, ready to lose herself in whatever was to come.

Ben put her purse on the table and locked the door behind her. Then he took her by the shoulders and turned her away from him. He pressed her against the wall, pulled her hair up with one hand, and kissed the nape of her neck.

This.

The kisses did not stop. She felt his body, solid, behind her. She closed her eyes.

This.

He pulled her skirt up. He slipped his hand between her legs, and she gasped.

This. This. This.

Nine

If your wife, approaching midlife, found herself vivified by a passing infidelity, if after years of quiet desperation she woke up one morning and felt glad to be on this planet, if she once again felt the wind on her cheek, on what rational basis would you object?

—Constance Waverly
The Man Summit, New York City

Gordon Allen was pretending to be sick.

He'd chosen this day carefully, with the strategic help of a flotilla of attorneys. He needed a day when Rocco would be home from school. He needed his wife, Kelly, and Judith Ann, their weekday daytime nanny, both in the same room at the same time. He could have done it on a weekend, but the weekend nannies were Jamaican and Hispanic. Maybe one was Guatemalan. Hell, he didn't know; he didn't even know their names. But Judith Ann was British, middle-aged and dignified, and she would do well during a deposition if it ever came to that. So he'd been hanging around the house all day, feigning illness, waiting for an opportunity.

Kelly doesn't spend a goddamn second with our son, Gordon thought, and not for the first time. All day long he had been lurking around the house in his forest-green bathrobe, peeking around corners, trying to catch Kelly and Rocco together and, by extension, Judith Ann, because Judith Ann never let Rocco out of her sight.

Finally, around three thirty in the afternoon, Kelly wandered into the kitchen wearing her yoga pants and happened upon Judith Ann giving Rocco his afternoon snack. Gordon watched from the hallway as Kelly poured herself a big glass of wine and sat down at the kitchen counter.

Gordon tightened the sash on his bathrobe and ambled into the kitchen, coughing for effect. He had a thick stack of papers tucked under his arm. He went to the fridge and poured himself a glass of orange juice.

"Hi, Rocco."

"Hi, Daddy."

"I can't get too close to you because I'm sick."

"Okay."

"Hi, Gordon," said Kelly.

"Oh. Kelly. Glad you're here. I need a signature," Gordon said oh so casually. He slid the stack of papers along the smooth, cold marble and handed her a pen.

"What is this?"

"It's something the lawyers drew up. It's about our estate. Sign right here."

It's about our estate. That's what the lawyers said he should say. That, and nothing more. And all within earshot of Judith Ann.

"I'll do it later."

"It'll take two seconds. I told Hugh I'd get these back to him by tomorrow."

"I want to read it first," said Kelly. "I don't believe in just signing things."

"There's nothing to believe in. Part of our life is signing a lot of documents. You've seen me do it a million times," Gordon said. He chuckled. "If I read everything I signed, I'd never have a second to do anything else."

"Just put them on my desk," Kelly said. "I'm trying to spend some time with our son."

Foiled!

Gordon walked upstairs to Kelly's "office"—it was decorated like Marie Antoinette's sitting room, all mirrors and gilt and washed-out pastels, completely out of keeping with the rustic Adirondack style Gordon had insisted on for the rest of the house—and did his best to gather his thoughts.

His plan had been this: Have Kelly sign the papers, and then, seemingly as an afterthought, ask Judith Ann to sign as a witness. And then messenger the papers to his lawyers so they could be filed with the court. Simple!

Gordon sat down on a tufted silk chaise longue and fanned through the pages of the document. It was, technically, a postnuptial agreement. It provided a huge trust for Rocco, the interest on which, should his parents' marriage end, his mother would be entitled to for her lifetime, unless and until she elected to remarry. Gordon didn't want to give Kelly money—certainly not the amount of money he would have to give her if they were to divorce—but more important, he didn't want another man married to Kelly and raising his son.

The agreement wouldn't stand up in court, of course, not if things got that far, but at least it would be something. That's what his lawyers told him. They wanted to get Kelly's signature on *something*, anything, some sort of agreement, no matter how legally suspect, just so they'd have something to fight with if it ever came to that.

And, Gordon thought, it was increasingly looking like it might come to that. Kelly had started sleeping in what she was now referring to as her room, a majestic guest suite that was equidistant from the master suite and Rocco's bedroom. She claimed Gordon's snoring and his peeing and his phone pinging kept her up all night. It was true Gordon snored loudly and he peed about eight times every night and his phone pinged if something major was happening in the markets overseas, but all of his other wives had been able to tolerate it! They hadn't complained! They'd all slept next to him!

Well, they had until the end, really. Until the very end.

Lucy had started to worry about how she was going to keep seeing Ben regularly. There were only so many excuses she could make for her new trips into the city. Even with the Arrangement it wasn't going to be simple—the trip to Brooklyn was a trek, and not a simple one, and she had responsibilities. She had a spectrum-y five-year-old, for God's sake!

Perhaps she'd made a mistake not finding someone closer to home, like the married dentist in Rye she'd stumbled upon online who was looking for discreet, no-strings lunchtime fun.

She was searching for a packet of taco seasoning in the pantry when an idea hit her.

"I think I know what I want to do," she called out.

"What?" asked Owen. "I can't hear you."

"I mean about the thing," Lucy said. She walked out of the pantry carrying a bunch of spice jars, chili powder and onion flakes and cumin. She'd make her own taco seasoning. "I've decided what I want to do about our arrangement."

"I thought we weren't supposed to talk about it."

"Well, this part we can talk about," said Lucy.

"Okay," said Owen. "Shoot."

"I want to start taking French lessons in the city one night a week, like I used to do before we met. So I can feel like myself again. More like myself."

"And?"

"That's it," said Lucy. "Sometimes I might have dinner with a friend or do a little shopping too. But you'll have to take care of Wyatt and get him fed and to bed and everything. I want to be off duty."

"I think that sounds good," said Owen. "You love French."

"I miss it," said Lucy. "I miss having something going on in my brain."

"I think we still have a box of your old French stuff in the attic. Those flash cards you used to make and some other things. I'll get it down for you."

"That would be great."

Lucy walked back into the pantry, looking for nothing, but her heart was beating fast and loud and she needed a second to regroup. She was not going to take French lessons. But the imaginary French lessons would make it possible for her to see Ben once a week, and it would save her from having to come up with a new lie every time. And lies were okay, according to the rules, if they were used to spare the other person's feelings. Her husband didn't need to know that French lessons meant Ben.

Owen called to her, "I have two questions."

"Shoot."

"Does your class have to be at night," he asked, "and does it have to be in the city?"

Lucy walked over to the sink with a can of black beans and a bag of yellow rice.

"If I take a class during the day, there'll be sick days and parent-teacher conference days and fall break, and I won't be able to count on it. And I want to go to the Alliance Française like I used to, not some dopey place up here with a bunch of retired old ladies planning a week in Provence. All I'm asking is that you be in charge of Wyatt, on your own, one night a week."

"Okay," said Owen. "Sounds fair enough."

Lucy turned on the faucet and measured out the water for the rice.

"I looked online this afternoon," she said casually. "New classes start up in a few days."

Owen and Lucy had bought their house in Beekman before they had Wyatt, back when they both had well-paying jobs, during what would turn out to be a blink-and-you-missed-it substantial dip in the price of real estate in Beekman. They couldn't afford to buy what they wanted in the city and suspected that might remain true no matter what imaginary unending upward trajectory their careers took, so they did that odd Manhattanite thing of continuing to pay rent on an apartment that would serve as their primary residence while purchasing a house they would make use of only on the weekends and holidays.

For a long time, Owen and Lucy were weekenders—a different species, it turned out, than full-timers, but at that point they had no idea of the extent of the difference. They didn't know a soul in town for the first few years, and that's the way they liked it. They didn't even like to have houseguests. In the summer, they fell asleep in the hammock and grilled expensive cuts of meat; they watched the fireflies and made love on floors in partially furnished rooms. In the winter they read book after book after book in front of the fireplace; they watched more snow fall than seemed possible, and they let the soup simmer all afternoon. Lucy planted peonies and daffodils in the fall, and she ran fishing line through the leaves of the tiny Japanese maple to startle any deer who tried to eat it. Owen bought a chain saw, snowshoes, a used kayak, and a telescope.

Even cleaning the gutters was romantic, with Lucy holding the ladder up to the second floor, and Owen, terrified, bravely aiming the leaf blower. Think of the money they'd just saved! There was a bumper crop of acorns their first fall, and Lucy collected them and put them in a big basket. She wanted to have a home filled with interesting rocks, pinecones and pussy willows and artfully twisted driftwood. She built a small cairn out of river rocks on the kitchen windowsill, and just looking at it made her calm, just looking at it made her workday life in the city feel a million miles away.

A few weeks after Wyatt was born, Owen was unexpectedly laid off from his marketing job. Some back-of-the-envelope math made it clear that with their new baby plus two residences and minus one paycheck, the money they had was not going to cut it. The logic was simple: Move to Beekman. Owen could find a job outside the city, in Westchester perhaps, or figure out a way to work from home. If necessary, he could do the hour-long commute into Grand Central. They would move into their sweet little house and begin the next part of their life, the easy, slow-paced, family-friendly part. Lucy could put in a vegetable garden. They could get a dog.

People often asked her if she was sad she'd left New York City, and when they did, she always told them the same story. In the story, which was true, she was riding in a cab, headed up Madison Avenue, on the way to have lunch with a friend. She saw a bunch of private-school kids playing on a side street that had been closed off to traffic for their recess. They were just running in circles on the asphalt, these kids! Not even with a ball! They weren't allowed to use a ball because it might break somebody's window. And those were the rich kids! Those were the kids whose parents were paying forty grand a year for elementary school!

And I realized I didn't want that, she would always say. *I didn't want that life at all. I didn't want my tombstone to read, "She somehow managed to scrape together enough money to raise her family in New York City." I wanted trees and air and rocks and hammocks. Fireflies and thick books and snow days.*

The truth was, Lucy could barely remember those early years in Beekman, because they were also the early years with Wyatt. A few things stood out, mainly a six-month or so period where it seemed likely that Wyatt might in fact be a genius. When he was sixteen months old, he could stack his wooden alphabet blocks eighteen blocks high. He would reach up and carefully, carefully balance them, with a look of total focus on his little round face. It was like a party trick—it *was* a party trick, actually; Lucy would put a pile of blocks in front of Wyatt whenever people came to the house just so she could witness their stunned reactions. And he taught himself the letters of the alphabet in two weeks, using a toy keyboard that made sounds when he pressed the buttons. When she told her sister, Anna, about it during one of their phone calls, Anna said, "Do yourself a favor. Don't repeat that to any of the mothers in town if you want to have any friends."

But he was also banging his head against the wall. And he wanted to do nothing except watch the washing machine—he would watch the soap and the water sloshing around inside the front-loading washing machine for hours if they'd let him, and sometimes they let him. At some point, he stopped sleeping more or less entirely. And Lucy's head, what was left of it, was filled with the escalating beat of *Something is wrong, something is wrong, something is wrong.*

The artful stacks of river rocks and the bowls of acorns and the ornamental deer antlers were long gone, tossed in the garbage once Wyatt discovered just how easily they could be weaponized. Lucy didn't have time to put fishing wire on the tiny maple anymore, the optimism to keep planting things, or the energy to weed. She was left with a house with black Sharpie on the walls, Cheerios and red-wine stains on the couch, and a huge brown splotch on the kitchen ceiling just below the upstairs bathroom because Wyatt had left a faucet running while they went to OT. And the last book Lucy had read she couldn't remember, and hadn't finished.

Lucy was alone in Ben's bed, looking around the room, trying to take everything in. She'd been to his place three times now, and up until this exact moment she wouldn't have been able to tell you what color the walls were painted, or if he had rugs, or lamps, or art, or books. But now: beige walls, oriental rugs, groovy lamps, and lots of books. Not much in the way of art, however. Some framed…things. He wasn't arty. That was okay.

The main thing Lucy noticed was that his apartment was very neat and tidy. That's something you paid attention to after you'd been married for a while, how neat people were, because it was the kind of characteristic that never changed, no matter how much you wanted it to. Owen wasn't neat, but neither, to be fair, was Lucy. They were both basically slobs. Slobs who fought their slobbiness and didn't always win.

"I still don't understand why you said yes to this," Lucy said when Ben came back from the bathroom.

"Aren't you happy I did?"

"That's not the point," said Lucy. "Who *are* you? What kind of person would say yes to this?"

"Pretty much all heterosexual men."

"Men," said Lucy. "What is wrong with you?"

"There's a lot wrong with us," he said. "Honestly, I thought it was a little strange when Sunny brought it up.

I wasn't completely sure I was going to go through with it. But then, when you walked in, you were so nervous and fragile and beautiful, I just thought, *I'll do this lady a solid and fuck her brains out.*"

"You didn't fuck my brains out," said Lucy.

"I didn't?"

"Last I checked, I still had my brains."

Ben grabbed one of Lucy's ankles with each hand.

"And she throws down the gauntlet."

Lucy was still breathing heavily when she asked Ben, "Did you really have sex with Helena Bonham Carter?"

"That's what you say? That's all you have to say to me after all that?"

"I can't help it. I'm a curious person."

"Who told you I slept with her?"

"Who do you think?"

"How does Sunny Bang know I had sex with Helena Bonham Carter?" said Ben. "Look at me. I'm calling her Sunny Bang now too."

"She said you met her at an Italian villa where you were staying with some mutual friends and you had sex with her one night in a swimming pool."

"That is true."

"Are you serious?"

"I am."

"Was it amazing?"

"Honestly, I couldn't really say. It was a lot of my head going, *I'm having sex with Helena Bonham Carter. I am. I actually am. Right now. I'm having sex with Helena Bonham Carter.*"

"So then what happened?"

"It was her last night," said Ben. "She was flying back to London to shoot a movie the next day."

"That is so cool," said Lucy.

"It was pretty cool," said Ben. "It's safe to say it was the coolest thing I've ever done. I also had sex with a bank teller once, but that was considerably less cool."

Lucy got out of bed and looked around on the floor for her underwear. "So, this might sound kind of weird, but is there a day of the week that would work better for you than other days, for this, if we're going to keep doing this?"

"Thursdays," Ben said, after thinking for a second. "Thursdays would be good."

It was after nine o'clock before Lucy was on the train, heading back to her real life, staring out at the bright lights reflecting off the black of the Hudson River. She'd told Owen she was having dinner with Aly again, that Aly was going through a bad breakup, so he was home with Wyatt.

She couldn't stop smiling.

When did I stop feeling like this? Lucy wondered. It had been a very, very long time since she felt like this.

It really wasn't the sex. Or it wasn't *just* the sex. It was, well, feeling like the best version of herself, the version she used to be a long time ago. Only back when she was that version of herself, she hadn't appreciated it. She didn't know it was something that would go away, that would disappear so slowly and yet so quickly she wouldn't even notice it was gone until it was too late. Maybe it was just youth, but it seemed like more than that. This is how Ben made her feel: completely adorable. That was the word. Lucy felt adorable. When did she stop feeling like this? What happened to her? Where did it all go?

One of the results of turning yourself invisible was that the moment somebody actually paid attention to you, the minute somebody actually looked into your eyes for three seconds too long or touched your arm a few too many times or sent you a mildly flirty e-mail, you thought you were in love with him. It didn't take much.

And, to be fair, Ben was doing more to her than that. A lot more.

It was like she had turned her dimmer switch way, way down, and now it was up, and she was herself again for the first time in a very long time.

Anyhow, whatever it was, Lucy couldn't stop smiling.

And her pretend French class started up next week. On Thursday.

Ten

As the Lord Buddha famously said, "Life is suffering."
Part of the problem, okay, a big huge part of the problem,
is when you expect that it is the job of your life partner to
rid your life of suffering.

—Constance Waverly
The Waverly Report

Izzy's fat, neurotic, semi-invalid cat was asleep on Owen's blazer. Owen could hear Izzy walking around upstairs, singing the opening bars of a song he couldn't quite put his finger on. He was trying to nudge the cat onto the floor when Izzy slinked down the stairs in a flimsy silk robe, belting out the refrain of "Blue Bayou."

"You have a great voice," Owen said when she finished.

"I know," said Izzy. "You don't have to tell me that. I used to be a singer."

"Really?"

"Yep," she said. "I used to sing at Eighty-Eights in the city."

Owen was surprised. "You used to sing at Eighty-Eights? Are you serious? That place was amazing."

"Yeah, well," said Izzy. She sighed theatrically and leaned against the door frame, her right thigh peeking through the slit in her robe. "What can I say? It was another life."

Owen knew there were a million questions he should ask her, out of basic human courtesy more than anything else, but really what he wanted to do was retrieve his blazer from under her fat orange cat and get back to the office before anyone noticed he was missing.

"Can you help me with…" He motioned to the cat and his jacket.

"Buttons!" Izzy yelled. "Buttons, down! Off the chair!"

Buttons swiveled his neck and stared at Owen, pissed off. Izzy finally scooped him up with both hands and held him like a baby. He seemed to like that.

"Oh, I forgot to tell you before," said Izzy. "I bumped into your wife this morning."

"What are you talking about?"

"Don't get crazy," said Izzy. "It was nothing. She was at GroceryLand."

"You told me you and Lucy had never met."

"I don't *know* her. I saw a woman buying fourteen banana yogurts."

"That doesn't mean it was Lucy."

"Owen, come on. Nobody buys fourteen banana yogurts at GroceryLand," said Izzy. "Besides, I've seen her picture on your Facebook page."

"Oh."

"She seemed nice."

"How do you mean?"

"She was nice to the checkout lady. They talked about chickens. Apparently Lucy is having a big problem with a rooster. And the checkout lady knows a guy who takes roosters."

"You were behind her in line?" said Owen.

"It just worked out that way, I swear," said Izzy. "I didn't know you had chickens."

"We have chickens."

"How many?"

"A lot," said Owen. "Too many. I think about fourteen."

"Can you bring me some eggs next time you come over?"

Owen tried to sweep the cat hair off his blazer. "Can you do me a favor and stay away from Lucy?"

"What are you talking about? I am staying away from her. I saw her at GroceryLand. It's a public place."

"One of the things we're trying to do with this is not humiliate each other. And I think, if she knew that you and I were doing this and she didn't know you, but you *knew* and knew her, it would—"

"You guys and your rules." Izzy laughed. "You still think you can get out of this thing with no consequences."

"Not no consequences necessarily," said Owen. "I'm just trying to be respectful, okay?"

"Yes, that was very respectful of your wife," Izzy said, gesturing up the stairs to her bedroom. "What you just did to me."

Owen worked two towns away from Beekman, inside an old industrial loft that had been turned into an open-plan office space and housed several unrelated small companies.

For a long time, Owen was a respected and well-compensated executive at a large marketing firm on Madison Avenue. He'd liked his job and had climbed the ladder both quickly and graciously. By the time he was thirty, he had a few small, prestigious luxury brands and three major book publishers in his portfolio, and he would have been content to keep it more or less like that until he retired. People liked him. They liked working with him, they liked talking to him, they liked going out to lunch with him.

He should have known change was a-brewing when people started to refer to his department as Old Marketing, as opposed to New Marketing, but he hadn't really paid much attention to it. And then, out of the blue, the asteroid hit the U.S. economy in 2008, and by the time the dust settled, Owen's whole world had changed. The prestigious, high-profile books Owen knew how to market were being tossed like greased watermelons into that spring-break swimming pool known as social media. Marketing efforts for the luxury goods he knew how to position were scaled back, and executives soon decided they could handle their needs in-house. When things finally started to normalize, the consensus seemed to be that Owen was too old to market, or to understand the market, or to change with the times. His social media presence consisted of Facebook posts of his kid saying funny things. Somebody had moved his cheese. His cheese was gone, and he couldn't find it.

After nearly a year out of work, Owen managed to find a job as a corporate recruiter. In his best moments, he thought of it as marketing people to jobs and jobs to people, but really it was just spending a lot of time on the phone and on the Internet tracking down individuals through their LinkedIn profiles and trying to wrestle their cell phone numbers out of them so he could hound them into changing jobs so he could earn his split of 15 percent of their first year's salary.

Owen had developed something of a specialty, matching medical professionals to new opportunities, and he'd even begun to contemplate leaving the small firm he worked for and setting up his own shop. The thought of it was depressing, though. The thought that this was his forever job, that this was his legacy, was almost too much to bear. He wasn't interested enough in money for its own sake. If he had been, he could have embraced the entrepreneurial aspect of starting his own recruiting company; he could spend time implementing systems and motivating his employees, maximizing profits and expanding into new markets, but instead, well, instead—

"I wanted to reach out to you to see if you are interested in a new opportunity—

"And if I may, can I ask, what is your current salary?

"Would you be willing to relocate for the right opportunity? What about Danbury, Connecticut?

"I see. Well, yes, Danbury isn't for everyone—

"Can I ask you, do you know of anyone, perhaps an individual not as senior as yourself, who might be interested in a new opportunity in your field that might involve relocating?

"Yes, well, thank you for your time. Is it okay if I reach out to you in the future if I find any opportunities in your field that would meet both your salary and relocation targets?"

It was either that, or this:

"You'll show up tomorrow for the interview? It's at Mount Sinai. It's at three o'clock. Can I confirm with them that you'll be there at three?

"And you know where you're going. I sent you an e-mail yesterday with the details—

"I'll send you the e-mail again right now. There. You should have it. Do you have it?

"All right, one last thing. You haven't been returning their calls, and it's made them nervous, and they've expressed concern to me that you aren't interested in the position. I'd like you to take down this number and call them right when we hang up the phone. Do you have a pen and paper handy? Okay, I'll hold."

Good God, this job! It was like babysitting. And these were well-compensated medical professionals. Specialty nurses who made six figures a year. Lab technicians, radiology profession-als, diagnostic sonographers. Even doctors!

"Okay, now call and confirm that you will be there at three tomorrow. Can you do that right after we hang up? Great. And I'll be following up with them in five minutes to confirm that you've reached out to them."

Now imagine having those two conversations over and over again, day after day, for the rest of your life.

You might want to have sex with strangers too.

It was at the behest of Hugh Willix, his personal attorney, that Gordon snuck into Kelly's office while she was off at yoga to see if she had signed the papers.

"They're not here," Gordon said into his phone while he was creeping around.

"What do you mean?" asked Hugh.

"They're not on her desk where I put them. I can't find them."

"Look for them."

"I looked. I'm looking. I've looked everywhere."

"Maybe she signed them and put them somewhere in your office."

"I don't think so. If she did, she didn't mention it."

"Shit," said Hugh. "Tell me again exactly what you said to her."

"I said what you told me to say," said Gordon. "I said I wanted her to sign some papers about our estate. Nothing more."

"And now you can't find the papers."

"No," said Gordon. "Should I ask her where they are?"

"No. Don't do anything," Hugh said. "Let me think on this a bit."

"Let me think on this a bit" meant at least three billable hours, which would cost Gordon eighteen hundred dollars, but Gordon was not in the mood to pick nits.

"Why do you need to think?"

"If she took them to an attorney, we could have a situation on our hands."

"Kelly wouldn't do that," said Gordon. "She wouldn't even know how to find a lawyer."

"You'd be surprised."

Kelly had, in fact, done just that.

"So, your husband asked you to sign these papers, and you told him you wanted to read them first, but instead you brought them here."

"Yes," said Kelly. "I just want to know what I'm being asked to sign."

"That's wise," said one of the two lawyers she was facing. "You're a smart woman."

"I don't want to sign something I don't understand."

"Of course," he said. "Now, before we go any further, tell us what you know about your prenup."

"I don't have a prenup."

"I mean your and Gordon Allen's prenuptial agreement. Do you know what it contains, in broad strokes?"

"Gordon and I don't have a prenup."

The young lawyer looked over at Lawyer Number Two, who had been furtively zipping through his BlackBerry under the conference table and totally silent up until he heard this.

"You don't have a prenup," said Lawyer Number Two.

"No."

"You never signed a prenup?" Lawyer Number Two was clearly taking over.

"No."

"Gordon Allen and his attorneys never asked you to sign a prenuptial agreement of any kind?"

"Nope," said Kelly. "Am I not being clear?"

"How is that possible?" Lawyer Number One asked Lawyer Number Two. "The guy's gotta be worth ten billion dollars. That's legal malpractice."

"We got married pretty impulsively," Kelly said.

"What do you mean, 'impulsively'?"

"Well, we dated for a while, and then he got a divorce from Elaine—it wasn't my fault, she's a major-league bitch—and the day the divorce was final we flew to Vegas."

"And in Vegas…"

"We got married."

"You got *legally* married."

"Yes. Legally married. Is there another kind?"

"Was Gordon Allen compos mentis at the time?"

"What does that mean?"

"Was he in his right mind? Does he have Alzheimer's? A history of cognitive difficulties of any kind?"

"We've been married for over six years," Kelly said. "If Gordon was out of his mind, I'm pretty sure I'd know."

It was, in hindsight, a freakish stroke of luck that Kelly was halfway through Philippa Gregory's novel *The Other Boleyn Girl* when she first met Gordon Allen. Kelly was not what you would call a reader. She'd dropped out of high school in eleventh grade and could count the books she'd read since then on one hand. But Kelly picked up the book in a nail salon during a French pedicure and found herself turning pages, so she'd slipped it into her purse on her way out.

Gordon Allen was stuck in Key West because his yacht needed

a two-and-three-eighths-inch bilge strainer that no one had in stock in the entire Western Hemisphere, apparently, and he was alone in the Screaming Lobster at three in the afternoon because he was mad at his wife, Elaine, and at her bitchy friend Coco and at Zeek, the faggoty hairdresser Elaine insisted on shipping down with them each winter to the Caymans. The Screaming Lobster was dark as night and smelled like booze and fries and fish. The decor—dark wood and droopy fishing nets, rusty anchors and weathered wooden mermaids—matched his mood.

"Hi, I'm Kelly and I'm going to be your server," said Kelly.

"I'm Gordon."

"What can I get you, Gordon?"

"What's good?"

"It's all good," Kelly said with a smile.

"Is it, now."

When Kelly came back with his Glenlivet, Gordon didn't waste any time. "I just got off my yacht."

"Oh yeah? Everybody in this place just got off a yacht."

"I'll bet mine's the biggest."

"That's what they all say," said Kelly.

After two hours and six scotches, Gordon left Kelly a thousand-dollar tip and a business card with a phone number scrawled on the back. This was not the first time something like this had happened to Kelly. Waiting tables at the Screaming Lobster was about two inches shy of prostitution, at least for a girl with a face and a body like Kelly's.

When she got back to her apartment, Kelly popped open one of her roommate's Coronas and sat down in front of her computer. She Googled the name on the business card, out of curiosity more than anything.

Gordon Allen. Sixty-two. Real estate developer. Prominent Republican donor. Outspoken conservative. Anti-environmentalist. Racist. Fascist. Bigot.

Net worth?

Twelve billion dollars.

*   *   *

Refusing to have sexual intercourse with Gordon Allen before their wedding night turned out to be easier than Kelly could have ever imagined.

For one thing, Kelly had a boyfriend at the time. His name was Renaldo, and he worked as a day-hire deckhand who dealt drugs in international waters. He was Argentinean, and he was extremely popular with the ladies, because he had an unending supply of Xanax and Vicodin and Klonopin and Oxy, as well as ones for the super-old gals like Darvocet and Seconal. He even had fen-phen! It would put a hole in your heart, but it kept the weight off! Whether he made the ladies happy in other ways was not something Kelly chose to waste her time thinking about. She and Renaldo knew they had no real future together, but they dug each other and they *got* each other.

Gordon didn't know a thing about Renaldo, of course. Gordon would have had a major problem with Renaldo.

Kelly had had a few rich old boyfriends, but she didn't have anything to show for it. Well, that wasn't true; she had some things. Gifts. Little presents she kept hidden under her mattress. Her jewels. A Cartier watch. Things she held on to, thinking someday she might be forced to sell them. She didn't want to be one of those strippers who waited too long to go to nursing school. At some point, the world was going to stop putting twenties in your G-string and start tossing quarters instead. Best to plan ahead.

It started out as something of an experiment. Like Anne Boleyn, Kelly slowly ceded her married lover territory, and with each new drawing and redrawing of the borders, he was permitted to explore new undiscovered terrain. She said she was shy. She respected the institution of marriage. She was not that kind of girl.

It was a long-drawn-out, Oscar-worthy cocktease. And it worked.

"I'm filing for divorce."

"Not because of me, I hope," said Kelly.

"Of course because of you," said Gordon. "I'm in love with you."

"Don't say that, Gordy," said Kelly. "You're a married man."

"Not for long."

❧

Owen brought home pizza for dinner, and the two of them ate off paper plates at the kitchen island with paper towels for napkins.

"I think I might have found someone to take Randall off our hands," said Lucy.

"Oh yeah?"

"There's a guy up here who loves roosters."

"Does he eat them?"

"At this point, I don't really care. But no. Apparently he just likes to rescue roosters. I'm sure he's a very normal and well-adjusted individual."

"Does he have a farm or something?"

"I would assume so. I hope they aren't living in his house. Anyhow, I got his number."

"Do you think you-know-who will be upset?" Owen gestured toward Wyatt, who had already eaten and was wandering around, wordlessly, looking both focused and confused.

"Upset would be good," said Lucy. "Upset would show awareness of feelings, and empathy, even."

"You're right, he will not be upset," said Owen. "Maybe we can try to make him upset. Take him on the trip to give away Randall. We could all stand there and cry."

"I'm not sure that's the best idea," said Lucy. "Anyhow, I was reading about this online. The problem with Randall is, he thinks we're chickens."

"What do you mean?"

"Because we raised him the way we did, in the house. And because we let him roam around outside near us. He thinks we're his, uh"—Lucy glanced over at Wyatt, who was pacing in and out of the kitchen, touching the sides of the door frame with his fingertips each time he passed through, muttering to himself—"ladies."

"He thinks we're his ladies?"

"Yes, he does. That's why he's charging us all the time. The other day, he chased me around the car. I had to dive into the passenger seat."

"Are you serious?"

"Yeah," said Lucy. "And I've been using the umbrella and poking it at him, and then opening it up to scare him, but it's starting not to work. He's not afraid of the umbrella anymore. He's trying to make the umbrella his lady too. Plus he's having his way with all of the chickens too much, I think. I think they're getting tired of it."

"Is that even possible for a chicken?"

"If you watch them, they're like, *Dude, get* off *me*."

"So what do you want to do?"

"I want to give him to the rooster guy," said Lucy. "Apparently the minute you're scared of your rooster, you need to get rid of him."

"Let's do it," said Owen.

"Oh, and honey?"

"Yeah?"

"You're covered in cat hair," said Lucy.

"What? I am? I don't think this is from a cat—"

"Honey." Lucy picked a piece of orange cat hair off his blazer and held it up. "This is a cat hair. And we don't have a cat."

Owen just sat there, half guilty, half caught, a little confused. Lucy stared him straight in the eye for a moment that felt like it went on forever.

"Do us both a favor," she finally said, "and put a lint roller in the glove compartment. Hey, Wyatt, bath time. Upstairs."

❧❦❧

Well, it's official. She knows.

Owen was wrapping the leftover pizza in foil. *My wife knows I'm sleeping with a woman who has a cat.* In a way, it was good. In a way, it was proof that the Arrangement was working, that it wasn't just a weird dream he'd had, and that Lucy wasn't going to snap at some point and act like the whole thing hadn't been essentially her idea. He had fought the urge to check in with Lucy on more than one occasion. He had forced himself not to ask, *Are we really doing this? Is the deal still on?* Or maybe just two words, followed by a question mark dangling up in the air: *Fight Club?*

Because Owen was pretty sure Lucy wasn't doing anything. Not 100 percent sure, but, say, 95 percent sure. From what he could determine, she was as busy as ever with her usual mom stuff, taking Wyatt to soccer practice and horseback riding and birthday parties, and whenever he glanced over her shoulder at her computer screen she was on Etsy or Instagram or Pinterest, just the way she always had been. And she still lost her phone at least once a day. Completely lost it. It would show up several hours later under the front seat of the car, or in a laundry basket, or on a shelf in the pantry, or in the back pocket of a pair of jeans she'd slipped out of and then kicked under the bed. *If she had something going on, she'd be much more attached to her phone,* Owen thought.

But mostly, well, it was a feeling. Owen felt like he would *know,* he felt like he would be able to sense it if Lucy was sleeping with somebody else. He was okay with it if it happened. That was the deal, and he was fine with their agreement, he was cool with her taking advantage of it. On some level, he liked to think, he even *wanted* her to take advantage of it, so she didn't end up feeling like she'd missed out—but he didn't think she had done anything yet.

Yet.

Eleven

How many times have you heard a woman say that her idea of foreplay is watching her husband do the dishes? How about changing diapers, scrubbing the toilets, vacuuming the floor? Are you getting excited, ladies? Feeling a little tingle down there? Today's marrieds have been told so often that a man folding the laundry constitutes foreplay that both parties are shocked when it doesn't actually work.

—Constance Waverly
Women and Power, New York City

I'm not going to caulk your tub, Izzy."

Owen and Izzy were in bed, watching the ceiling fan as it made slow, lazy, a bit wobbly rotations.

"Why not?"

"Because I don't know how to caulk a bathtub. I am not a handyman. Nor am I a plumber. I'm not even handy around my own house."

"The guy at Home Depot said it was easy," said Izzy.

"Then you do it."

"You know I'm very sensitive around chemicals," said Izzy. "It's a small space. I'll pass out."

"Then it sounds like you have a problem," said Owen. "You should probably figure it out. But I am not going to caulk your bathtub, I don't care how easy the Home Depot guy said it was."

"Well, how would you get your tub caulked if you needed it done? The one at your house."

"I'd call a guy," said Owen. "I'd pick up the phone and call someone who knew how to caulk a tub."

"The Home Depot guy said that would be very expensive and it was super-easy to do this kind of repair by yourself."

"I've got an idea," said Owen. He was out of the bed now and pulling on his boxers. "Why don't you try fucking the Home Depot guy. Why don't you get him over here. He seems to know an awful lot about DIY home repair."

"All right," said Izzy. "Forget I said anything."

"This is not what I signed up for, Izzy."

"What do you mean?"

"I mean, I have a wife for this. Her name is Lucy and she nags me about things like caulking the bathtub."

"Maybe she nags you because you're over here fucking me instead of doing the stuff you've told her you'll do."

"Are you serious right now?"

"I'm just saying, as an outside observer of your marriage, you seem to have it pretty good."

"Yeah, well, trust me," said Owen. He buckled his belt and noticed it was in yet another notch. His belly had just about disappeared. "You don't know everything."

How had this happened? How had he ended up with a girl-friend who was worse than his wife? Izzy was beginning to make Lucy look like a paragon of sweetness and sanity, and if it weren't for the — Owen was going to be honest with himself, he prided himself on unwavering honesty *to himself* — if it weren't for the ease and simplicity of their encounters, the fact that he could send Izzy a text and she would tape a handwritten *Back in fifteen minutes* sign to the window of her store and zip around the corner to her house and somehow be in a different slutty lingerie getup every time, that she was kinky and wild and most of all *game,* Owen would consider calling the whole thing off.

But, alas, he was not stupid. Izzy was a rare find for a man in his situation, and he was wise enough to realize it. But he didn't need to pretend that it was more than it actually was.

When Owen got back to the office, he found himself staring at the calendar hanging over his desk. It was already October. He and Lucy were three months into the Arrangement. Three months in, three months left. The halfway point, almost exactly. Thus far, he had confined himself to just Izzy. To be fair, Izzy had been about all that he could take — but he had, he believed, shown admirable restraint.

Still, it didn't seem smart to limit himself to just Izzy. The whole point of this thing, he told himself, was to explore his options, to partake of life's sexual buffet. He scrolled through his contacts on his phone, looking for inspiration.

Cassie Lambert.

She was an old colleague who'd known him back when he was still a rising star, during the heyday of his Madison Avenue career. They'd once had…an encounter.

He fired off a quick, friendly e-mail. Cassie e-mailed back two minutes later. By the end of the day, they'd arranged to meet for a drink at the Campbell Apartment the following week to catch up.

Gordon was lying on the couch in front of the fire with his laptop balanced on his chest, his eyes at half-mast, and his enormous Bose headphones covering his ears and a good portion of his skull.

He was watching Simka.

She was Polish, she spoke very softly, and the first time he saw her, she folded towels. She was completely clothed. You couldn't even see her face, not even much of her body—although she did have an impressive bust, quite impressive, quite, *quite* impressive—but she whispered and folded towels and licked her lips and sometimes tapped her manicured fingernails on the table. And for some unknown reason, listening to it gave him goose bumps. Mostly on his head, sometimes down his spine, occasionally all over. And it wasn't just him, it was clearly a whole thing, these ASMR videos, and while he knew he could Google *ASMR* and find out in about five seconds what exactly was happening to him when his beautiful blond Polish girlfriend folded towels and crinkled paper and tapped her nails and licked her lips, Gordon didn't want to know. He didn't want to risk breaking the spell.

It was so relaxing. It was *so* relaxing. And it was Gordon's secret place.

Kelly grabbed his feet and shook them hard.

"If you want to watch a woman fold towels, Manuela's in the laundry room," said Kelly. "I'm sure she'd whisper things to you if you paid her extra."

Gordon snapped his laptop shut and swung his legs off the couch and sat up. Kelly and her yoga instructor/only friend in Beekman, Jamie, were standing there, wearing bright stretchy clothes, both covered in a sheen of sweat.

"I'd understand it more if she was at least naked while she did it," Kelly said to Jamie. "At least that would be normal. Kind of normal. Weird, but normal."

Spending time watching Simka online was one of Gordon's last remaining pleasures in life, and Kelly treated it like it was some sort of perversion. Well, it wasn't a perversion. It was just odd. He didn't know why he liked it but he did, and by the looks of the number of views on YouTube, so did millions of other people. Perfectly normal people, probably. Some of them had to be normal.

Still, Gordon could appreciate the fact that people might think it was weird, and so he liked to keep it private, which was why he didn't like Kelly yapping about it in front of Jamie. He was a public person! The last thing he needed was some dippy yoga twit telling one of the lefty journalists who was always sniffing around that Gordon Allen was into some bizarre towel-folding fetish.

"You really should throw away that sweater," Kelly said to him on her way to the kitchen. "People your age can't really pull off yellow."

This is what he was up against. Kelly had no tenderness for him anymore. Had she ever? Gordon wondered. It was not something Gordon liked to think about. He'd been in such a froth during their courtship he could barely remember who he'd thought Kelly actually *was*. That's not true. He did remember. Gordon had thought Kelly was a sweet, genuine, Catholic virgin who fell deeply in love with him against her will and did not want to break up his marriage to Elaine. Was it possible he'd been that wrong?

All he wanted now was tenderness. Not even sex, not that much, not the way he used to. He wanted a woman who would lie next to him in bed and stroke his head gently until he drifted off to sleep and be there when he woke up in the middle of the night terrified because his heart had skipped too many beats or his next breath didn't want to come. He wanted softness, compassion, a cool silky hand to reach out and touch his forehead in the middle of the day to check if he was running a fever, to see if he felt flushed.

Instead, he had Kelly. And her contempt for him, and for their life together, and even for Beekman did nothing but grow. At this point, Gordon had settled on one objective, and that was to keep his son Rocco in his home, with him, raised under his own roof, for as long as humanly possible. And if that meant putting up with Kelly, and a life without tenderness, so be it.

Gordon had other kids, of course. His two grown sons were completely awful, a pair of rich, entitled assholes devoid of drive and character in equal measure, and his daughter, well, she was a lost soul who'd built her entire life around rejecting everything Gordon stood for.

Gordon had been busy building his empire while the three of them were growing up; he'd been traveling constantly, having affairs, divorcing or being divorced by their respective mothers—but still. They'd had every opportunity. They'd gone to the best schools. They'd seen and done and tasted and experienced more things by the age of eighteen than most people had in five lifetimes, everything from the Super Bowl to the aurora borealis, sleeping at the White House and being backstage with the Rolling Stones. What's more, they'd been surrounded by kids who had every opportunity, and the truth was, their friends were awful too, hateful entitled little rich pricks. "Every opportunity" was not all it was cracked up to be.

Gordon and his daughter, Violet, were estranged. That was the word, *estranged*. She refused to talk to him or see him or answer his e-mails or come to visit. Even when he'd had his heart scare all those years ago, back when he was still married to Elaine, Violet refused to come see him in the hospital. He'd written her out of his will and then written her back in two weeks later, and then out again and then in. And then out. And then in.

Violet owned and ran a trendy dry-goods store up in Woodstock, Vermont, and drank, according to his private investigator, two and a half bottles of red wine every night. ("What the hell is a trendy dry good?" Gordon had asked his private investigator when he phoned in his report. Even though they weren't on speaking terms, he liked to keep up with her goings-on. His investigator sent him a large box of items purchased from Violet's store: a tea towel with a quote attributed to somebody named Margot Tenenbaum, a pair of hand-felted bedroom slippers priced at a hundred and sixty-five dollars, some wooden whirligigs and yoyos and slingshots, Bazooka gum and Charleston Chews, a flannel bathrobe, seed packets sporting sketches of lumpy purple tomatoes and warty hook-necked gourds, and a sack of pinto beans.)

His two sons lived in Hollywood. They'd started a production company called Two Rich Guys Productions.

"Help me out with this, you two," Gordon said to them every Thanksgiving. "What exactly have you done in your life to earn the label *rich?*"

"It's supposed to be ironic," one of them always said.

"It's moronic," said Gordon. "It's not ironic, it's moronic," he said, laughing at this joke.

Gordon stayed fit just to spite them. Whenever they came to visit, Gordon would stride into the living room to greet them wearing his sweat suit, with a damp towel around his neck, slurping a repulsive-looking green juice out of a tall clear glass. *I'm not going anywhere,* he all but shouted.

But whether he was alive or dead, this was the truth: You got to a certain point, wealth-wise, and it was impossible to keep your kids from being rich too. You made decisions when they were young for certain sentimental and tax avoidance reasons, you moved money in your children's direction during your various acrimonious divorces in order to keep it from your hateful ex-wives, and then when they were forty and hadn't worked an honest day in their lives, you had only yourself to blame.

Rocco was born early in the morning of March 21, the first day of spring, and while Gordon was not generally one to think in either symbolic or poetic terms, with this he couldn't help himself. Rocco was a fresh start, a new beginning, a fierce purple crocus pushing up against the winter's dirty snow.

Gordon just wanted one of his kids not to be a total shit. Was that too much to ask?

The papers. God knew what she'd done with them.

"I've figured out what you are," Lucy said to Ben.

"What's that?"

"You're the great evener-outer," said Lucy. "No matter what Owen gets up to during our six months, I'll have had you, even if we stop this today, even if this is all it is, this will even it out. In my head at least. In our marriage, in my head, I'll be fine."

"That is quite a compliment."

"It is. You should take it as one."

"What do you think your husband is doing?"

"He's having sex with a woman who has an orange cat," said Lucy. "And he may or may not have bought her an air conditioner at Home Depot."

"Explain, please."

"Well, it's possible that the cat lady and the air-conditioner recipient are two different people. I don't know."

"Does it bother you?"

"I do my best not to think about it," said Lucy. "And that, by the way, is one of the strangest things about this whole arrangement. When you stop and think about what your spouse would actually do. For example, I'm doing exactly what I *would* do, but not what Owen would think I would do."

"What do you mean, you're doing what you would do?"

"I mean *this*," Lucy said, gesturing big, somehow taking in Ben and the bed and the sex they'd been having with one swoop. "Falling into something that's delicious and life-affirming and, most important, temporary. You're like…" Lucy thought for a second, and then it came to her. "You're like the junior year abroad of marriage."

"What does that mean?"

"When I went to Barcelona for my junior year, I remember worrying that all of my friends were going to have an amazing time at school and I would be left out when I got back. Instead I had this once-in-a-lifetime experience, truly the time of my life, and when I went back to campus, *nothing* had changed. Not one thing. It was like an episode of *The Twilight Zone*."

"What does your husband think you're doing?"

"Owen?" said Lucy. "He thinks I'm taking French lessons."

As she walked down the hallway to the elevator, Lucy called over her shoulder, "Don't let me fall in love with you."

"Don't worry," said Ben. "That will not happen."

Lucy pushed the elevator button and looked back at him. He was standing in the doorway, leaning against the frame, wearing a button-down shirt and boxer briefs. "Because that would be the fly in the ointment," she called.

"There is no fly here," Ben said, "only ointment."

Lucy stepped into the elevator, smiling. The doors started to close, and she heard Ben calling after her.

"Only ointment!"

Lucy had been trying to avoid having any big, private conversations with Sunny Bang for what seemed like forever. It was hard, but so far she'd managed it by canceling on two ladies' nights at the last minute and pretending to be in a big rush whenever they bumped into each other at the school. Still, Sunny Bang was pretty much everywhere any kids were, and Lucy finally found herself standing next to her at a child's birthday party, out of earshot of the other mothers, at the indoor bouncy-house place with the MRSA and the bad pizza.

"So," Sunny said.

"So."

"How've you been?"

"Good. Busy. Things have been crazy."

"Yeah?"

"Yeah."

"Did you ever get in touch with Ben?"

Lucy took a breath and then nodded.

"And?"

"I think maybe it's best if we don't talk about it," said Lucy.

"Okay," said Sunny Bang.

"Yeah."

"But you're not mad at me," said Sunny.

"Why would I be mad?"

"I just mean, I didn't steer you wrong or anything."

"You did not," Lucy said—and then a smile came over her face, one of those smiles that is lit from within—"steer me wrong."

"Oh my God, you did it! What the hell? Why didn't you call me?"

"I think we shouldn't talk about it, Sunny."

"You're right," said Sunny Bang.

"Let's pretend it never happened."

"Okay, but stop smiling. You're freaking me out."

"I'm not smiling."

"You're smiling with your eyes," said Sunny Bang. "Stop eye-smiling!"

Lucy didn't say anything.

"I can't believe I made this happen," said Sunny Bang. "Please don't ruin your perfect life, Lucy. I'll never forgive myself."

"No one," said Lucy, "is ruining anything."

The Campbell Apartment was tucked away upstairs in Grand Central Station, and you had to know where it was to find it. Owen always thought that it struck the perfect note between business and sex. If you walked in at six o'clock on a weeknight, you'd swear that half the people there were going to close a deal and the other half were about to get laid.

"You're married," Cassie said.

"I know," Owen said. "But do you remember that party? That was twelve years ago. And I still think about it."

"I was drunk. Sometimes I do things like that when I'm drunk. It doesn't mean I'm going to go fuck somebody else's husband."

Owen tiptoed onto delicate ground.

"I don't usually tell people this, but Lucy and I have sort of an arrangement," said Owen.

"What are you talking about?"

"We have an arrangement. And not *sort of*. It's real. It's confidential, though. I'd appreciate it if you didn't repeat it."

"Are you serious?" said Cassie.

"I am serious. We're happy, and we love each other, but we're giving each other a free pass for a few months. Like Amish kids. It's a *rumspringa*, but for marriage."

"Ugh," said Cassie. "I thought you were one of the good guys."

"I am one of the good guys," said Owen. "It was my wife's idea."

"There's no way that's true."

"It's a hundred percent true."

"So you're saying you're allowed to hook up with me. And you want to hook up with me. That's what this drink is all about."

"I wanted to see you," said Owen. "I've always liked you. But yes to the other parts too."

"Interesting," said Cassie. "Very interesting."

"It is interesting," said Owen.

"I'm going to go to the restroom," said Cassie.

"Okay," said Owen. "Do you want me to…" Owen gestured toward the restroom.

"Follow me into the bathroom?" Cassie laughed at him, a little meanly. "No. I've gotta pee."

Owen had been thinking about Cassie Lambert for years and years, idly, not obsessing really but occasionally brightening his day by remembering the way she managed to press her boobs up against him any chance she got. Any time he saw her someplace socially—at a party, or a lecture, or out for drinks—she always gave him a kiss on the lips and a double-boob hug. A real two-boober, as Owen and his friend Scott liked to call it. Those hugs that make married men think about their friends' boobs. And their friends' wives' boobs. And then there was that night at a Christmas party that Lucy had been too tired to attend, long before they were even engaged, when Owen had gotten so hopelessly drunk he had to sleep it off on a couch in the host's study. He had a vague, fuzzy memory of following Cassie down a long narrow hallway and into the laundry room and kissing her. He'd snapped out of it before things progressed too far, his muddled head filled with thoughts of Lucy. "God, I'd kill my own mother for this laundry room," Owen remembered

Cassie saying at one point during the proceedings, so it's possible she hadn't been as enraptured as he'd thought.

Cassie came back from the restroom and slid into her chair. "I thought about it, and my answer is no."

"Fair enough," said Owen. He took a big sip of his bourbon. "Can I ask why?"

"No good can come of it," said Cassie. "And the bad parts won't be that interesting."

"Well, I have to disagree with you on that," Owen said. He felt ridiculous the moment the words were out of his mouth. He used to be smoother than this.

"Besides," Cassie said, "I've got a boyfriend."

"You do?" Owen said. He was surprised. Cassie Lambert was famous for never, ever having a boyfriend. This state of affairs had persisted for so long that Owen, like every other person in Cassie's life, figured something pretty major was wrong with her, something was broken deep, deep down inside, in a secret place unreachable by traditional psychotherapy.

"I do," Cassie said. She took a smug sip of her wine. "His name is Philip, and he's perfect."

Owen was not what you would consider a goal-oriented person, but he did have one overarching aim in life. He did not want to be like his father.

Owen's father was a real bastard, that was the truth, a drunk and a gambler and most likely a cheater, although Owen never knew that for a fact.

"He goes to Vegas, without his wife, for five days every month," Lucy would point out. Owen's stock response—"He likes to gamble"—sounded more and more lame each time he said it.

Healy McIntire owned a small manufacturing company, Healy's Safes, which had been started by Owen's grandfather. Healy sat in a small, windowless office with fake wood paneling behind a metal desk with a fifth of rye and a pistol in a drawer, across from a tattered green velour couch "for my VIP clients." They made safes—home safes, gun safes, and jewelry safes. ("So your wife won't lose sleep and you won't lose your shirt!") It was a job a drunk could do.

In the mid-1980s they made the leap into home vaults (though never bomb shelters, which Owen and his two brothers regretted). It turned out that the same people willing to pay upwards of five thousand dollars for a safe also wanted to buy American, which minimized competition from cheap foreign knockoffs. The company was steadily profitable, but when Healy announced his retirement—the cake at his party was in the shape of a safe—Owen was secretly thrilled that his brothers stepped in to run the business. He could continue nurturing his big-city dreams. He wasn't like his father. Or his mother, for that matter.

Back when Owen was in high school he fell in love with Valium. One day after track practice he went home to find the house unoccupied. He nonchalantly climbed the stairs, swung open the medicine cabinet in his parents' bathroom—noting, for the first time, the strangeness of the two sinks, side by side, as if his miserable parents would enjoy brushing their teeth together—and opened the bottle of Valium as gingerly as if he'd been defusing a bomb. The pill was blue. He popped it onto his tongue, cupped his hands under the icy water, and within minutes—safely in his room, on his bed—he was under the spell of a floaty bliss that spiraled into a nap that pulled him down with soft hands; it was like the entire universe was giving him a hug.

He managed to steal about twelve more before the bottle of pills disappeared from the medicine cabinet. He searched for it too. But the theft of the blue pills, and then the vanishing of the blue-pill bottle, was never discussed. Over the years, whenever he came home to visit, Owen would check the medicine cabinet. There were always pills—blood pressure pills, unused antibiotics, blood thinners, the growing cache of small orange pill bottles that are part of the aging American's arsenal—but never again anything like Valium. Had she stopped taking them? Or was it possible his mother was hiding her downers from her youngest son twenty-five years after he'd stolen his last little blue pill?

It's possible the pills explained everything. The fuzzy, there-but-not-there feeling Owen associated with his mother. His midnight thoughts of *Why does she put up with him?* and *Why doesn't this all come crashing down?* His dad, drunk, selling safes. His mother perpetually tranquilized. His father was a problem, for sure, but his mother never even knew who Owen was.

That was one of the things he loved about Lucy from the beginning. She *saw* him. She wanted to know every part of him. She was naturally curious and loved to talk and she asked him question after question. They'd been seeing each other for just two weeks when they spent their first weekend in bed, talking and watching old movies and having sex again and again and again. They were near the end of *North by Northwest* when it hit them: *If we don't see Mount Rushmore now, when will we ever see it? Not until we're seventy!*

They rented a car the following Friday and headed west, laughing and talking the entire way. They pitched a tent in hidden spots to save money on hotels and were woken up, twice, by nice farmers offering them breakfast and warm showers.

"I was a little worried it would be disappointing," Lucy had said when they were finally staring up at the looming stone faces.

"Me too."

"But," she'd said, turning to him and smiling a big smile, "it's so much fucking cooler than I ever expected."

When Owen found himself thinking about the early days with Lucy, the early years with Lucy, one thing stood out above all others: They had been really in love.

"I love your bathtub," said Lucy. "New York City apartments never have tubs two people can fit in."

Lucy and Ben were in his bathtub together. The faucet jutted out from the side of the tub, so both of them were able to lean back and stretch out their legs. Lucy's feet were on Ben's chest, and he was casually sucking her little toe.

"This is on the list of things that stop but that shouldn't stop when you've been with a person for a long time," said Lucy. "Taking long bubble baths together and toe-sucking."

"I sucked my wife's toes until the bitter end."

"You lie."

Ben popped Lucy's toe out of his mouth and said, "You're right. The toe-sucking stopped. To be fair to me, though, she went through a long clogs-without-socks phase."

"It's weird," said Lucy. "You go through your life, and you think it's going to be this one thing, that everything is all figured out. I'm surprising myself, I guess."

"What do you mean?" said Ben. "With this?"

"Yes. Look at me. I'm taking a bath with a man I barely know. And the woman whose toes you used to suck? I don't even know her name."

"Her name is—"

"No!" Lucy cut him off. "I don't want to know it."

"Fair enough."

"The weirdest part is that when I go home, nothing has changed. Owen is there, Wyatt is there, and there's lots of talk about the *Titanic* sinking. Or poisonous snakes. Or how to escape from quicksand. And the only thing that's different is, I feel a little happier. A little lighter inside. A little like I have a secret, but that it's okay to have this secret. I really can't describe it."

"So what about when it's over," said Ben. "When the six months end."

"But, see, that's the genius of all of this. It *is* going to end. And I'm pretty sure I'm going to be fine."

Ben kissed the sole of her foot. "What if I'm not fine?"

"Are you being serious?"

"I'm not *not* being serious."

Lucy laughed at that. "How many women are you going out with between now and when I show up next Thursday?"

"Three," said Ben.

"Three?" This seemed, to Lucy, a little excessive.

"But two are Tinder Trash, and one is a blind date arranged by my former sister-in-law, I'm pretty sure as a way to punish me."

"How long have you been divorced?" asked Lucy.

"Just over two years."

"And you've got three dates lined up this week? Forgive me," said Lucy, "if I don't worry about you just yet."

Gordon was strolling on his treadmill at a speed of 3.2 miles per hour, gazing out at the Hudson River, counting bald eagles. He'd been walking for just under fifteen minutes and already the count stood at three.

Gordon had named his estate the Eagle's Perch. He'd designed it himself. Lots of wealthy people claim they designed their own houses, but Gordon drew his on actual paper. He drew it and then paid a firm to "translate the renderings into 'architectural-speak,'" as they said. Meaning put in the outlets and measure the doors, stuff like that. But the house was his baby, it was his creation, and he loved it.

The day he'd closed on the land, he'd driven out from the city and stood on the edge of the cliff where he'd eventually build the house. It was February, and the Hudson was frozen over. Massive sheets of ice had shifted around like tectonic plates, crashing into one another, pushing one another straight out of the water, looking like a classroom model of how the Rocky Mountains had been formed. A bald eagle soared over Gordon's head, blessing him, Gordon believed, and then landed on the tallest crest of ice and stayed there, motionless, until Gordon finally got too cold and went back to his car.

Gordon's cell phone rang. He slowed the treadmill down to 2.6 and picked it up.

"Anything?" Hugh asked, without preliminaries.

"No," said Gordon. "I told you, they're not here. But I'm not sure why it's such a big problem."

"Well, the only real danger, I'd say, is that if lawyers examine those documents they'll know what you want. We'd have given them our playbook, so to speak."

"Are you fucking the fuck serious right now?"

"I'm not telling you anything you don't know, Gordon."

"What I want to know is why I'm in this situation. I want to know why my attorney let this happen to me."

"Because I didn't think you would give the papers to her. I didn't think you would leave them alone in her possession. Honestly, Gordon, the thought didn't cross my mind."

"Well, you're my attorney. I pay for thoughts to cross your mind."

"You're right. I should have made myself clearer."

"What do we do now?"

"Now? We sit tight."

Owen and Izzy were upstairs at her house when they heard heavy footsteps down below.

"What is that?" Owen asked.

"Shush," Izzy said. "Someone's down there. A burglar."

"It's three o'clock in the afternoon," said Owen.

"It's those druggie kids," Izzy whispered. "Those high-schoolers who keep breaking into houses during the day and stealing drugs from people's medicine cabinets."

Well, they've come to the right place, Owen thought. Izzy's medicine cabinet was a sight to behold. He'd opened it one afternoon looking for some Advil for his back and saw nothing but orange pharmaceutical bottles with red and yellow warning stickers all over them.

Owen looked around Izzy's bedroom for some sort of weapon. A baseball bat? Isn't that what he was supposed to carry in this situation? But he couldn't find anything, not even a tennis racket or a golf club. He finally picked up a spindly, straight-back chair with a woven cane seat. He held it up to his chest, legs pointed forward. It was half weapon, half shield.

"Be careful," said Izzy.

"Stay there," he said. "I'll be right back."

Owen was slowly tiptoeing down the stairs, chair braced in front of his torso, trying to avoid the steps he knew were squeaky, when he heard Izzy's voice booming out from behind him: "What the fuck?"

A guy Owen had never seen before was standing in the middle of Izzy's living room trying to make off with the antique writing desk that usually sat between Izzy's two front windows.

"You can't just walk into my house and steal things, Christopher," she said.

"I'm not stealing anything," said Christopher. "This is my great-grandfather's desk."

"You asshole. I can't believe you broke into my house. That's it, I'm calling the police."

"Who are you?" Christopher asked.

"This is a guy I'm fucking," Izzy said. "His name is Owen. He's one of the many, *many* men who's been fucking your ex-wife."

Owen just stood at the bottom of the staircase. He finally thought to put down the chair/weapon.

"Please, Izzy. It's my great-grandfather's desk. I want to give it to Jason's son. I want to keep it in the family."

"Sorry, my friend, you lost it in the settlement."

"I didn't lose it, I just didn't want to fight over it, because you were in such a state I knew it would cost us another twenty thousand dollars in legal bills. My lawyer advised me to wait until you calmed down and then to ask you for it, since it's a family heirloom."

"Well, your lawyer screwed you," said Izzy. "Because you're not taking that desk."

"Izzy."

"Besides, why did you break in here? If you were going to ask me for it nicely."

"Because I didn't think you'd be reasonable. I'm sorry, I made a bad call. I'm willing to pay you for it, Izzy. It's important to me."

"You'll give me actual money for it?"

"I will," said Christopher. "Name a reasonable price."

"A gazillion dollars? How does that sound?"

"Jesus, Izzy—"

Izzy picked up the phone and dialed and then said, "Hello, yes, my name is Izzy Radford and I have an intruder in my home."

"Hang up the phone, Izzy," Christopher said.

"Fifty-five Riverview Lane," Izzy said.

"Hang up the phone, I'm leaving—"

"Describe him?" Izzy said. "He's five foot eight, he's wearing a green windbreaker, and he has a potbelly. Oh, and he's about to start losing his hair."

"He's leaving," said Owen. "Hang up the phone, Izzy. I'm escorting him out."

Owen opened up the front door and followed Christopher onto the porch. Christopher took two steps down to the sidewalk and then turned around and looked up at Owen.

"I don't know you, dude. And believe me, I don't care what's going on with you and Izzy. But here's a friendly heads-up. She's five kinds of crazy."

Lucy was naked and lying in Ben's bed, gazing out the window at the top of a chestnut tree. It was simple, now, getting to Ben's every Thursday, claiming French lessons, and Lucy found herself looking forward to Thursdays the way you'd look forward to a day at the spa. Or maybe a little more. Maybe just a little bit more.

Ben was running his fingers from her neck to her waist to her hip in a deliciously slow, postcoital figure eight.

"Sometimes I think, *This could really be something,*" said Ben.

Lucy's heart rose and sank at the same time.

"I know what you mean," she finally said.

"Do you?" said Ben. "I guess I'm asking, is it just me?"

"It's not just you," Lucy said.

Even saying that was farther than Lucy wanted to allow herself to go. Already, this conversation was bigger than any infidelity. *No falling in love.*

This is not love, Lucy said to herself. *I'm in love with my husband. I'm temporarily infatuated with Ben.*

"I think about you when you're not here," he said. "Like, the other night, I was making dinner and I wanted to tell you something. I don't even remember what I wanted to tell you, but I had to fight the urge to pick up the phone."

"You could have texted me."

"I guess I don't know the rules," said Ben.

"The rules are, you can text me," said Lucy.

"Okay."

Ben was quiet for a moment, and then he rolled over on his back and looked up at the ceiling.

"Can I text you constantly?"

Lucy stayed at Ben's apartment fifteen minutes later than usual that night, and by the time she made it to Grand Central, she'd missed the ten o'clock train. She wandered around inside the station aimlessly, wishing she were still in bed with Ben, wishing she had timed things better so she didn't have to waste an entire hour in the city and not be touching and talking to Ben.

She got on the next train early, took a seat by the window, and stared out at the rusty brown wall.

I've finally got juicy, she thought. *That's what this is. It's just perfectly, unbelievably, stupendously juicy.*

"Look at you. You are smiling out the window at nothing, like a woman in love."

Lucy looked up and saw Andrew Callahan standing in the aisle, suit rumpled from a long day at work, tie rakishly askew.

"Hi, Andrew."

"Lucy," he said. "What are you so goddamn happy about?"

"I just had a good day, that's all," said Lucy.

"Mind if I sit?"

Please no.

"Of course not," said Lucy. "I'd like it."

Andrew had a bottle of good red wine he'd picked up in Grand Central, and he even had two small stemless wineglasses in his briefcase. He was gallant, Andrew Callahan was, and a happy, carefree, almost gleeful drinker, and he always made a point of having enough booze to share.

"Cheers," he said after he'd uncorked the wine and poured.

"Cheers," said Lucy.

"I wish my wife smiled like you when she was heading home to me," said Andrew. "I wish she had that look on her face."

"Your wife is a very happy woman."

"Listen to me, Lucy," Andrew said. He put his arm on the back of the seat and leaned in and lowered his otherwise booming voice. "You gotta help me with this one thing that's been bothering me."

"What?"

"Okay. The other day I came home, and Margaret was trying to open this box, this, like, big huge cardboard box her mother had sent her. And she had a box cutter in one hand, and there were packing peanuts flying out all over the place, and she was saying, 'Fuck this shit! Fuck this fucking shit! I can't take this goddamn fucking shit anymore!'"

"What did you do?" asked Lucy.

"I pretended I didn't see it. I just tiptoed back into the garage and hid in there for ten minutes," said Andrew. "Do you think she should be on a pill for that kind of thing?"

"I don't know," said Lucy. "Sometimes being a mom of little kids is hard."

"Yeah, I can see that, I guess," he said.

"Is she like that all the time?"

"No! That's what was so weird about it. Otherwise she's pretty normal. It was like a weird window into her that made me think, um, my wife might be batshit crazy."

"Margaret is not crazy," said Lucy. "She probably just had a bad day."

"Yeah, maybe," Andrew said. "What are you doing on this late train?"

"I had French class. I take French. On Thursday nights."

"Ah," Andrew said, nodding his head knowingly.

"Ah what?"

"That's why you look so happy," said Andrew. "Owen's finally letting you out of the house."

Twelve

All paradises fail.

—Constance Waverly

Owen and Lucy had gotten married inside the basilica on the college campus where Lucy's father taught. It was a huge wedding, and not at all what Lucy would have wanted if she had stopped for even a minute to ask herself what she actually wanted. But she was working for the *Today* show at that point, up at four a.m. just about every day, and she and Owen lived half a continent away from where they were having their wedding. Lots of women get married before they really know themselves, but Lucy didn't have a mother to impose her own taste on the affair, and her father had no taste to speak of. If it had been up to him, he would have walked Lucy down the aisle wearing green wool pants that bagged at the knees and his lucky houndstooth jacket.

Instead of a mother, Lucy had Olive Steppenfeld. Olive was earning her PhD in medieval studies, and she was toiling away on a dissertation entitled "These Boots Are Made for Walking: The Unencumbered Wench Takes Flight — Medieval Woman on Foot to Canterbury." She'd been working for Lucy's father for years, running his household, balancing his checkbook, coordinating his calendar, and he'd handed her his youngest daughter's wedding-planning responsibilities as a reward for her overall competence and attention to detail. Olive had a blank check, a disengaged bride hundreds of miles away, and the gut sense of a thirty-eight-year-old Midwestern spinster that she would never get the chance to plan the wedding she'd been dreaming of all her life. It stands as a credit to Olive's formidable life force that she went ahead and ran with it.

To this day, all Lucy could remember was the initial phone

call, when Olive had said to her, "The chapel is so brooding and dark, and it's going to be October, I'm thinking red roses."

"Red roses would be good," Lucy said.

"Red roses, excellent," Olive said, the way you say something when you're writing it down.

"What color are your bridesmaids going to be wearing?" Olive asked. "I was thinking maybe jewel tones."

"I'm not having bridesmaids. I'm keeping this simple. My sister is going to be my maid of honor. You can talk to her about the color of her dress."

"Okay, I'll get in touch with her," Olive said, and then she made a sound like she was writing something down on a list. "A few of the faculty members who work with your father have little girls. They are *dying* to be flower girls. Can I say yes on your behalf?"

"Of course," Lucy said, and then she had to hang up because they were two minutes to live, and there was a gray-haired man walking slowly back and forth behind the news correspondent holding a big sign that said STOP THE FLUORIDE CONSPIRACY.

The first, and only, clue to what lay ahead was the invitation. Lucy didn't see it until her friend Aly called her.

"Are you serious with this thing?"

"What thing?" Lucy had asked.

"The invitation to your wedding."

"I haven't seen it."

"You haven't *seen it?*" And with this Aly started laughing—cackling, really—through the phone.

*The honour of thy presence is hereby
requested at the marriage of
Lady Lucy Miranda Ringwald
and
Sir Owen Jeffrey McIntire
on the eleventh of October in the year
of Our Lord two thousand and nine*

at half past the sixth hour in the eventide
in the Basilica of Our Most Benevolent Lord
(Feasting and revelry to be held at the great hall until dawn

In Lucy's defense, by the time she laid eyes on the invitation, the wedding was five weeks away and she still hadn't settled on a dress. She'd been promoted again at work, she was about four months away from developing a duodenal ulcer, and she was in no position to begin to micromanage her wedding. Besides, she and her father had agreed: It was to be a typical understated, ecumenical university wedding. Olive was simply handling the details.

Lucy got dressed in her old bedroom and rode over to the church in a limo with her father. When they arrived, Lucy looked out the windshield and saw this: Two straight lines of male undergrads, armed with what appeared to be real swords, dressed in silky purple pantaloons. They were on bended knee, heads bowed, with their swords before them. When Lucy stepped out of the limo, a bugler, standing on the steps of the church, began to play reveille, and the swordsmen stood in unison and clanged the tips of their weapons overhead, making a tunnel for Lucy and her father to walk through.

Once inside the vestibule, Lucy watched through the small square window as an altar boy, dressed like he was on his way to a Renaissance fair, swung a smoking thurible down the aisle, arching it over the heads of any of the seated guests that he could reach. The church itself was filled to capacity with all of her father's grad students, both current and former, every last faculty member, as well as the college's groundskeepers, the food-service personnel, and the janitorial staff. It was true Lucy had known most of these people all of her life. She just hadn't expected to see them all at her wedding.

The flower girls, all eight of them, were wearing floor-length dresses and those pointy princess hats. Two were in ruby red, two in emerald green, two in amethyst purple, and two in sapphire blue—jewel tones; to be fair to Olive, they were all in jewel tones!—and they each had yards of tulle and shiny satin trailing along behind them. Lucy's sister, Anna, was waiting for her at the end of the aisle wearing a tasteful knee-length dress of deep blue and looking deeply apologetic. (Later, at the reception, Anna told Lucy, "By the time I saw the whole setup, it was too late. I tried to make the flower girls take off those crazy hats but they all started crying.")

"I'm going to kill Olive," Lucy whispered to Owen when she finally made it to the altar, where he was standing.

"Just breathe," said Owen. "I'm in love with you, and we're getting married."

The bagpipes kicked in when they stepped out of the church. Olive had always wanted bagpipes at her wedding, and doggone it, she had made it happen. She'd found a bagpipers' club a few counties over and promised them dinner at the reception and as much alcohol as they could drink. The sound filled the campus and made it all the way to Main Street. The locals thought the police commissioner had died, and more than one called the police station to inquire about it.

The flower girls were jubilant. The flower girls had never had a better day in their entire lives.

Now it was nine years later, and it was their anniversary. Owen had made reservations at an expensive Italian restaurant, he had lined up the sitter, and he had brought home a dozen red roses. Red roses were their anniversary joke, but Lucy still loved them. She couldn't hold Olive Steppenfeld's lunacy against red roses forever.

"You look beautiful tonight," Owen said to her once they sat down.

"Thank you."

"I like your new hair," said Owen.

"I did this two weeks ago, you know."

"Did I forget to say something about it?"

"Yes," said Lucy. "But that's okay."

"Happy anniversary."

"Happy anniversary."

"Is it weird that when I think of our wedding day, all I can remember are bagpipes?"

Owen's phone buzzed. He glanced at it and then flipped it over.

"I wonder how Olive is doing?" he said.

"Last I heard, she was co-chairperson of Dad's old department."

"Good for her."

"I still want to kill her," said Lucy. "I would kill her if I thought I could get away with it."

"She meant well," said Owen.

"No, she didn't."

"You're right. She didn't mean well," Owen admitted. "But I do believe she couldn't help herself."

Owen's phone buzzed again. He glanced at it, and then flipped it over again.

"Tell her to stop texting you," said Lucy. "For the next two hours. So we can have a nice dinner together."

"If I do that," Owen said, "it might not have the intended effect."

Lucy looked across the table at Owen.

"Give me your phone," said Lucy.

"Lucy—"

"Trust me on this."

Owen handed Lucy his phone. She hunched over it and hammered out a text with her thumbs.

"What did you say?" asked Owen when she gave him back his phone.

"I said, 'This is Owen's wife, Lucy. If you call or text or e-mail my husband in the next four hours, I'm going to flush his phone down the toilet.'"

"Nice," said Owen.

"I just want her to know that I know," said Lucy.

"I've told her all about it," said Owen. "She knows you know."

"Yeah, but I want her to *know* that I know."

"I'm feeling happier," said Lucy.

"I am too," said Owen.

"It's weird, right?"

"Yes, but we're not supposed to talk about it."

"I know," said Lucy. "But we could talk in general terms. Just for tonight."

"Okay."

"But only very general."

"I'll go first," Owen said. "I feel like I'm choosing you. Like when we were first dating. Like, 'I pick…you.'"

"I feel not trapped. Not that you were trapping me. I don't mean that—"

"Like *life* was trapping you—"

"Exactly."

"It's like I'm not in a submarine anymore," said Owen. "Like I'm walking around on the deck of a sailboat with the wind in my hair."

"I think I'm less depressed," said Lucy.

"You seem less depressed. You seem better."

"I feel better," said Lucy. "I feel more like me. It's hard to explain."

"You don't have to explain it," said Owen. "I get it. I do."

Earlier that evening, before the babysitter arrived, Owen found himself standing alone in the mudroom, chatting with Wyatt through the closed bathroom door.

"You know, buddy, you're old enough to poop alone," he'd pointed out.

"I don't like to poop alone!"

"Fine," said Owen. "Tell me something that happened today at school, then."

Lucy's handbag was dangling from one of the hooks by the back door. It was a brown canvas messenger bag, aggressively unstylish, with a big flap that snapped closed on the front. Lucy had never been one for fancy purses, which was just as well, Owen thought, because they couldn't afford them.

It wasn't that he was suspicious. Not exactly. And, to be fair, Lucy was allowed to do what she wanted to do. That was their deal, that was the Arrangement, and Owen intended to honor it.

But still, a small part of him had started to wonder.

He unsnapped the flap and peeked inside.

He saw a teal-colored book, a paperback, with *Allons-y!* printed on the broken spine. He wasn't sure what he'd expected to find, but the sight of a beat-up French textbook was enough to make his entire body suddenly relax.

"Look, Dada!"

The bathroom door swung open. Wyatt was standing in front of the toilet with his pants around his ankles, staring into the toilet bowl.

"It's a big one," said Wyatt proudly. "It's a very big poop."

"Is it possible we've cracked the code of married life?" said Lucy.

"It feels kind of like we did."

"What if this is the secret? What if it's like *The Secret*, but for marriage."

"We'll have to write a book about it."

"We'll be rich *and* happy," said Lucy. "We can start giving seminars to help people we don't know."

"People will want to do yoga and eat clean foods and come to us for marital wisdom," said Owen.

"You'll have to learn yoga," said Lucy.

"I want a gong. A big gong."

"I'll grow my hair long and wear big turquoise rings."

"I'll wear nothing but floppy cream-colored drawstring

pants made from hemp," said Owen. "Those pants that make people think, *Does he have anything on under those things? Because he seems really free and easy.*"

"We're gonna be friends with Deepak Chopra."

"Is Deepak into this?" asked Owen.

"I think once he sees what we're doing and how well it works and how evolved we've become, he'll be on board," Lucy said. "I think Deepak is pretty flexible. He's ushering in the new global consciousness and maybe this is part of it."

"Nonattachment."

"Nonduality."

"This is total nonattachment and nonduality."

"I'm not sure I understand what nonduality is."

"Nobody does," said Owen. "That's part of it. It can't be understood with the mind."

"Maybe we should go the other direction, be normal," Owen said. They were deep into their second bottle of wine, finishing up the main course.

"What do you mean?"

"That could be our hook. Like, be super-ordinary and straight and clean-cut. Like Mormons, but with the Arrangement."

"I think Mormons invented the Arrangement."

"You know what I mean. We should look like we work for the CIA. It would seem less threatening that way."

"So I don't get to wear big rings?"

"No. And I have to wear underwear and no floppy pants."

"Can we still go to Costa Rica?"

"No," said Owen. "It'll have to be places like St. Louis."

"That doesn't sound fun. If I'm going to be a life guru, I don't want to do it in St. Louis."

"Right. Screw St. Louis!"

"Screw St. Louis!"

"I love you," said Lucy.

"I love you too."

"I think I even love you more these days," said Lucy.

"That's how I feel too."

"And the stuff with Wyatt doesn't upset me as much," said Lucy. "He is who he is."

"Truer words were never spoken," said Owen.

"He had a two-hour playdate with Blake on Friday and they actually played together," said Lucy. "They even took turns at Candy Land. They've been working on it at school."

"At Candy Land?"

"Taking turns. It went really well until Blake got the gingerbread man and flipped the board and Wyatt punched him in the side of the head."

"What's wrong with the gingerbread man?" asked Owen.

"You have to go back pretty close to the beginning."

"Why is Wyatt friends with that kid?"

"Because we're friends with Claire and Edmund."

"I don't like them all that much," said Owen.

"Me neither."

"I say we can do without them."

"You know what?"

"What?"

"I have this overwhelming urge to have sex with you *right now*," said Lucy.

"Check, please."

Lucy frequently found herself thinking back to that night. She and Owen had come home, paid the babysitter, and fallen straight into bed. Nobody checked e-mail, neither of them flossed. They still had passion; it hadn't gone anywhere, just maybe underground for a bit, but here it was, evidence of who they were together, what they had with each other.

She thought about Ben in the middle of it, that was true, but only for a fleeting moment. She didn't think about what Owen was doing or who he was doing it with, only that she hoped he was happy. She hoped he was getting what he needed.

They were three months in. Three months down, three to go. Everything was working out just the way they'd planned. Better, even. It was like this haze that had covered them for years now had not only started to lift but had actually burned off, and the day ahead promised nothing but blue sky and sunlight glittering off an open sea. It's not that Lucy woke up each morning with a huge smile on her face, but she no longer woke up consumed with dread. And from what Lucy could tell, Air-Conditioner Cat-Hair Lady didn't seem like much of a threat to their marriage.

Later, of course, Lucy wondered what would have happened if they had just stopped. If, in the middle of the night, she had reached over and touched Owen's shoulder. If she had shaken him, gently, until he woke up. If she had softly said, *Honey?*

If they had just stopped.

Thirteen

Thirty-five years ago, I attended a talk on marriage by M. Scott Peck, the author of the blockbuster *The Road Less Traveled*. He said the only reason to get married was for the friction. Everyone in the packed lecture hall laughed. Nothing I've seen or experienced since has proven him wrong.

—Constance Waverly
WaverlyRadio podcast #63

Gordon Allen's lap pool was enclosed inside a large outbuilding that Gordon had had built for just that purpose. The pool was forty meters long, fresh water, and chlorine-free, and it was maintained at such a careful pH balance that it was home to three turtles (Reagan, Nixon, and Goldwater) and a couple of large, slow-moving fish.

About six months after construction was completed, Gordon lost interest in swimming in the pool, although he still liked to give tours of it to guests. He liked to wow them with the turtles. Kelly hated the pool, and Rocco was uninterested in it, so Gordon had more or less given Dirk the bee guy the run of the place. It would help, come winter, simply to have somewhere warm to shower. And Dirk loved it. When he did his laps each day, the Republican turtles swam right alongside him like old friends. *This is what a few billion dollars feels like,* Dirk always found himself thinking. *And I'm the one enjoying it.*

Dirk let himself in through the side door that opened onto the changing room. He put on his bathing suit and took a quick shower. The guy who took care of the pool, Gordon's turtle guy, had told him to shower before he got in, and there was a special kind of soap and shampoo there just for that purpose.

When he opened the door to the pool area, he realized something was off. The lights were on, and Gordon Allen's wife—Kimmy? Carrie?—was in the pool, naked, floating on her back.

"Oh, sorry—" Dirk turned away from her. "I didn't know anyone was here."

"No worries," she said.

"I'll just grab my stuff and take off," said Dirk.

"No, don't go, I was just getting out."

"Still, I'll wait outside till you're done," said Dirk.

"Don't be crazy," she said. She climbed slowly out of the pool and picked up a flimsy robe and tied the sash around her waist.

"Gordon told me you never use the pool."

"I don't, usually," she said. "But I thought today I'd give it a try."

"How was it?"

"Not great," she said. "The fish and the turtles creep me out."

"They're the best part."

"Now you sound just like Gordon," she said.

She walked over to the little sitting area off to the side of the pool and opened the refrigerator.

"Have a quick drink with me," she said. "You must get bored out there in the woods all the time."

"Okay," he said. "I guess I can do that."

She handed him a beer and took one for herself too.

"Can I ask you something? Do you get stung by your bees?"

"It happens," said Dirk. "Not often. And it doesn't bother me very much."

"I get stung all the time," she said. "I keep begging Gordon to get rid of the bees, but he won't listen to me. Maybe you could talk to him."

"Well, I can't argue in favor of getting rid of the bees, because then I would be out of a job," said Dirk. "And a place to live. So you'll have to handle that one on your own."

"He doesn't listen to me. He doesn't care if I get stung."

"I use tea tree oil," said Dirk. "I'm pretty sure that's what keeps the bees off me. I can bring you some if you want."

"I'd like that."

"I gotta warn you, it doesn't smell great."

"Honestly, I don't care at this point," she said. "Gordon told me you live inside a school bus."

"That's right."

"Is it yellow?"

"It is. I might paint it, I just haven't gotten a chance to do it yet."

She wrinkled her nose. "Do you drive it around town?"

Dirk laughed.

"Right now, it's technically broken down. I'm trying to see if I can make it through the winter in it. I'm weatherizing it, and I just put in a rocket stove. Your husband's finding me a snowmobile so I can get in and out when the weather's bad."

"I'd like to see it sometime," she said.

"I'll have you and Gordon out soon," said Dirk.

She looked him in the eye. "I'd like to see it by myself."

Dirk nodded slowly. "Yeah, I'll have you and Gordon out sometime," he said. "I think Rocco would get a kick out of it too."

Dirk was that rare type of person who could pinpoint the moment everything, *everything*, in his life changed.

It all began with a blind date.

"Make yourself comfortable," his date said when he arrived at her apartment, "I'm almost ready."

Dirk sat down heavily on her couch and leaned back and put his feet on the Lucite coffee table. He pulled out his phone and checked his e-mail.

"I'll be just a minute," she called from the other room.

Her name was Melody and she was his boss's wife's niece. He could tell by the look on her face when she opened the door that she had been prepped for the sight of him. Dirk was not the blind date you wanted to see through the peephole of your apartment door. He was, at that time in his life, over three hundred pounds, covered in freckles, and going bald in a weird way. But Dirk was a banker—a *big banker*—and it didn't take much imagination to piece together the conversations that went on between the married women who fixed him up and the single women who agreed to go out with him. They knew what *big banker* meant. It meant managing director. It meant hedge fund. It meant all the things in life that these kinds of women wanted, and if Dirk was three hundred–plus pounds of lumpy, pale freckled flesh, at least he wasn't seventy. At least he didn't have ex-wives and grown children, a bum prostate and a nine o'clock bedtime. And the right woman could put him on a diet and encourage him to shave his head.

Melody was taking a long time to get ready. Dirk swiped right on twenty pieces of Tinder Trash for later in the evening and then slipped his phone in his pocket. He stood up and went over to the bookshelf and examined the titles. A mix of college paperbacks, cookbooks written by television personalities, and hardcover bestsellers. He'd seen worse. He turned back to the couch and that's when he saw it.

A dog.

A tiny one. White as a snowball.

Motionless, with its neck at a weird angle.

Oh, shit.

Dirk poked it with his index finger.

Still warm.

But dead. Dead in that way dead things are—clearly, undeniably dead.

Dirk panicked. He'd killed the dog. He'd thought it was, well, not a pillow, but maybe a part of a pillow; there were a lot of freaking pillows on that couch, and some fluffy ones, fluffy with scraggly Mongolian fur, and anyone could have made a mistake like this, and it wasn't his fault, he was a big guy, and weren't little dogs supposed to yap when strangers came by, maybe the dog was dead before he got there—*Unlikely, Dirk, unlikely!*—and Melody was his boss's wife's niece! And Dirk had just sat on her dog!

Almost without thinking, Dirk picked up the dog and slipped it into the silver umbrella stand by the front door, then quietly let himself out.

He hailed a cab and headed straight to JFK. He looked at the departures board, starting with the *As*, and settled on Aruba. It wasn't until he reached the ticket counter that he realized he didn't have his passport. His passport, along with everything else he owned, was inside his loft in Tribeca. He knew if he went home to get it, he'd stay there.

He went back to the departures board.

Bozeman. Bozeman sounded good.

He was done with New York City, done with dating women who had small dogs and umbrella stands. He'd been that guy, the fat banker whose expensive tie slithered over his belly all day because it couldn't find a good resting spot. The guy who looked fifty at thirty and would probably die of heart failure before his sixtieth birthday. He'd never quit his job, not officially; he just disappeared. He knew that accidentally killing a teacup poodle was not a fireable offense, not when he brought in over four million dollars a year for the firm, but what the whole thing had given him was clarity. Clarity was a commodity that had been in short supply for Dirk for pretty much all of his life, and when it came, it came big.

He stumbled upon a worn copy of Helen and Scott Nearing's old homesteading bible *The Good Life* at a used bookstore and fell in love with it. There were newer books, of course, and the Internet — people all over the Internet were talking about this stuff, permaculture and tiny houses, leaving the rat race and living the simple life — but it was the Nearings' book he kept on his nightstand at whatever motel he happened to be staying at, it was the Nearings' book he read cover to cover.

After playing pool with a guy in a bar in Butte who'd been living inside a refurbished school bus for three years, Dirk began to develop his plan. He liked the idea of starting with a school bus. Dirk could afford to do things differently — he had money in the bank, he could buy himself whatever he needed, really, within reason — but he was, fundamentally, a man who liked a challenge. So he bought an old bus at an auction for six thousand dollars, listed the seats on Craigslist, and sold them to the owner of a drive-in movie theater for the labor it took to pull them out. Then he hit the road.

His plan was to head to Maine and try to replicate the Nearings' homesteading experiment as closely as possible. He'd live in the bus, teach himself to farm, eventually build himself a little cabin off the grid. He wanted to do as much with his hands as possible, with his hands and with his brains, mostly to see if it could still be done.

He was driving through the Hudson Valley when his bus broke down for the third time. He happened to pick up the local paper and noticed a small ad in the back.

Beekeeper Wanted. No experience necessary.

Kelly stalked back to the house from the pool in a pissy mood.

It was like she was in prison! Even that idiot beekeeper wouldn't lay a finger on her. And she'd all but offered herself up to him. And not even "all but." It was like…it was like she was Gordon Allen's *property,* and no one would dare to get near her. Certainly nobody on his payroll, and everyone Kelly encountered was on Gordon's payroll in one way or another.

A week earlier, Kelly had looked up Renaldo. Good old Renaldo. It had been over six years, and he had never been an e-mail type of guy, but she finally tracked him down through a bartender/coke addict she was friends with on Facebook. Renaldo was still living in the Keys, still unmarried, still casually dealing drugs and napping in hammocks, living the life of a man who'd figured the whole thing out. But for some reason, he seemed less than interested in flying in to visit her, living it up in a five-star hotel in Manhattan for a week or so, all paid for by her.

When she pressed him, he admitted he was involved with someone. He said, in that formal way of his, the way of a lothario for whom English is a second language, "The truth is, Kelly, I have met someone."

"I don't mind, Renaldo. You know that."

"Yes, but I must tell you, Kelly, I am in love."

"You're *in love?*"

"She is my perfect woman. I wish you could meet—"

Kelly hung up the phone.

It was well past two o'clock in the morning when Owen's cell phone started vibrating on top of his nightstand. Lucy finally jabbed him in the kidney with a pointy knee, waking him from a dead sleep.

"Hello," he mumbled into the phone.

"I'm sorry for calling so late."

It was Izzy.

"You can't do this," Owen whispered. "You can't call me like this."

"I know," said Izzy. "I'm sorry, but it's an emergency."

"What kind of emergency?"

"I can't tell you over the phone. I just need you to come here right now. You know I wouldn't call you like this if it wasn't important."

"It's the middle of the goddamn night."

"This is really serious. Just come, please."

Owen hung up the phone. Lucy had rolled over and watched the back of his head throughout the entire conversation.

"I'm sorry," he said. He got up and pulled on yesterday's jeans, which he'd left in a heap on the floor by the bed. "I've got to, uh. It's um, it's sort of an emergency."

Owen had the look on his face that he had a lot these days, half apology and half nonapology. Half this-is-what-we-get. Half this-is-what-we-agreed-upon. Half you-had-to-know-things-like-this-could-happen, things like your husband being called away in the middle of the night to deal with something, and someone, you know nothing about. "I can't say much more about it."

"Go," said Lucy. "Just go."

Beekman was incredibly dark at night. There were no street-lights, and people kept their houses dark. Owen parked his car halfway down the block from Izzy's and walked to her front door, tripping twice on the uneven sidewalk. Before he had a chance to knock, the door swung open.

"Thank God you're here," Izzy said.

"What happened? What's the matter?"

"Come in."

Owen went in and looked around. He didn't see any emergency.

"What's going on?" he said.

"I'm gonna burn the desk."

"The what?"

"The desk. Christopher's great-grandfather's desk. And I need your help."

"You got me out of bed for this?"

"Yes, I apologize for that, but I need your help."

"You can't call me up in the middle of the night and tell me it's an emergency, Izzy. I have a—"

"A wife and a kid and a home and a life, I know all that. You and your happily married wife named Lucy with her stupid chickens."

"How much have you had to drink?"

"Not much. One bottle."

"A regular bottle or a big bottle?"

"A regular bottle," said Izzy.

"Izzy…"

"Okay, it was a big bottle! I was upset! Stop judging me!"

Owen knew Izzy well enough by now to understand that she kept her daytime-drinking tally separate from her night-time drinking. Not that she tallied anything, not really. She just considered the daytime to be a different day than the nighttime. So *one big bottle* meant, at a minimum, a daytime regular bottle plus a nighttime big bottle. Which explained a few things, Owen thought, as he watched Izzy lurching around her living room. It was the first time he'd seen her lurch.

"I'm not judging you," said Owen. "I just like to know what I'm dealing with."

"What is that supposed to mean?"

"Nothing. It doesn't mean anything."

"Christopher coming by the other day was very upsetting to me. I thought you'd understand. I'm sorry if I was wrong."

"I do understand," said Owen. "I just don't think this is the way to handle it."

"Well, then, go home to your wife. I'll do it by myself."

"If you burn it, it's done," said Owen. "Why don't you just enjoy having something he wants for a while."

"He'll just steal it like he tried to do the other day. He'll come by when I'm not home and take it."

"Change the locks. I'll find someone to do it for you. I'll get it done tomorrow."

Izzy just stood there.

"You're going to set your house on fire, Izzy. You are in no condition to handle matches and lighter fluid. Come on upstairs, I'll put you into bed."

Izzy stood there and appeared to think about it. She swayed a little to the left and grabbed the back of a tattered wingback chair, steadying herself, although just barely.

"Give me the lighter fluid," said Owen. "I'll help you up the stairs."

"I need you to hold me."

"I can't carry you up the stairs, Izzy," said Owen. "I'll kill us both."

"No, I mean tonight. I need you to stay. I don't ever ask for anything like this, but tonight I need it."

"I'll stay with you," said Owen.

*   *   *

Owen jolted awake deep into the night. He was in Izzy's bed. He was tangled up in a linen sheet, drenched in a clammy sweat, possessed by a single terrifying thought.

What if Izzy got pregnant?

They were using condoms, yes, but using condoms the way Owen suspected most people did, meaning less than perfectly and not all the time. Owen and Lucy had had such a difficult time conceiving children, they had spent so many thousands of dollars they didn't have in order to create Wyatt in a petri dish and have him implanted in Lucy's belly, that there was a small part of Owen that didn't actually *believe* that sex caused babies, and that small part occasionally overruled his more rational side when it came time to put on a condom when he was naked with Izzy and she was doing something crazy. He wasn't proud of it. He had promised Lucy condoms, promised them as part of their agreement, and here he was, in this most primal and fundamental way, failing her. In the way that could cause her the most harm, the most pain, that could put her most in jeopardy.

"I'm not going on the pill," Izzy said to him when he brought it up the next morning.

"Why not?"

"Oh, I don't know, Owen," she said. "Maybe because I don't want to put pig hormones into my body?"

"Is that what the pill is made out of?" Owen asked. "That doesn't sound right, Izzy."

"They have to get the hormones somewhere, right? And whatever kind of strange hormones they are, I don't want them in my body."

"Okay, but what about the other thing. A whatchamacallit. We can put two men on goal."

"A diaphragm? You want me to get a *diaphragm?*" The word *diaphragm* struck Owen like a Ziploc bag full of cold pudding.

It felt strange and truly surprising. *How is it that I'm talking to this woman who's not my wife about getting a diaphragm? When did this become my reality?*

"I want you to get something, to go to the doctor and get something, yes. If we're going to keep doing this."

"I haven't been to the gynecologist in ages," said Izzy. "I don't think I can even get pregnant. Although I'm so bloated these days I look pregnant." She paused and stared at Owen. "This is where you're supposed to say I don't look the least bit pregnant."

"Don't change the subject, Izzy. I'm serious about this. I want you to go to the doctor."

"Okay, fine," she said. She wiggled her shoulders a bit theatrically. "I'll make an appointment."

❧

"Tell me something about your life upstate," said Ben.

Lucy had come to Brooklyn early that day, and they'd already had sex twice, and now they were both lying on their sides, looking at each other's faces.

"It's too boring to talk about," said Lucy.

"Just one thing. Anything."

"Let me think," said Lucy. Finally she said, "I have chickens."

"You have chickens?"

"I do."

"Explain, please."

"Last winter I was drinking perhaps a little too much wine in front of the fireplace and I ended up ordering fifteen baby chicks online."

"Fifteen?"

"That was the smallest amount they'd sell you," said Lucy. "I went to the wrong website. I went to one meant for chicken farmers, not housewives looking for a new hobby. And then when the box came, there were nineteen in there," said Lucy.

"They give you extra. They call them packing peanuts. And I did not know that at the time."

"You have *nineteen* chickens?"

"I started out with nineteen chickens," said Lucy. "I currently have eleven."

"You eat your chickens?"

"Nope," Lucy said. "Just the eggs."

"Okay, I'll bite. What happened to the missing eight chickens?"

Lucy sucked her teeth and said, "They died while under my care."

"How did they die?"

"This is not a good conversation to have with anyone who's never had chickens."

"No, no," said Ben. "Keep going. I'm fascinated."

"First of all, chickens look for ways to die," said Lucy. "You know how people always get upset about chickens being kept in those little cages on factory farms? Well, those are the lucky chickens. You take those chickens out of their cages and put them anywhere near the natural world and they will die horrible, gruesome, violent deaths."

"Give me an example."

"Okay, so one morning I go out to the chicken coop, and there's a dead chicken inside. It's missing its head. Its head has just disappeared."

"What happened to it?"

"I had to go online to find out," said Lucy. "Apparently, a raccoon ripped it off and ate it. Raccoons do that. If a chicken gets too close to a spot with chicken wire, a raccoon will reach his hand in and rip off its head."

"That's horrible."

"I know. So what you do is, you make the coop more secure, you figure out what happened, and things go well for a while and then one night, a chicken vanishes."

"Just—disappears," said Ben.

"Exactly. And then the next night, another one goes. And the next night, another. And every day you try to figure out what is happening, you look for holes and you take pictures of the carcasses and post them online for chicken people to make sense of. If you can find them. The carcasses, I mean. It's easy to find the online chicken people."

"If you can find them?"

"Sometimes they're dragged off into the woods. Sometimes they're eaten in the coop or in the run."

"This whole thing sounds horrible," Ben said, laughing. "You should be in jail."

"I know!"

"Really. I should report you to the authorities."

"And sometimes, it remains a mystery," Lucy went on. "You plug some little hole someplace and the carnage stops, but you never really know what caused it."

"My sister would love you," Ben said. "You're living her dream life."

"You have a sister?"

"I have a sister and two brothers. What about you?"

"Just a sister. She's a lawyer. She lives in San Francisco."

"Are you youngest or oldest?"

"Youngest. You?"

"Oldest."

"Look at us," said Lucy. "First-date talk."

"Yeah," said Ben. "So, tell me, Miss Lucy. Where did you grow up?"

For the first stretch of their life together, Owen and Lucy visited Owen's family once a year, at Thanksgiving. They flew to Colorado and slept on a pull-out couch in a room that doubled as the TV room and they carried their toiletries in and out of the bathroom because there was no counter space or drawer space or even so much as a bit of an unclaimed shelf on which they could place them. The house was overrun by Owen's extended family, his two brothers and their wives and kids, who'd arrived early and claimed all the spare bedrooms, a pattern that started when Owen and Lucy were not yet married and then perpetuated itself year after year with no apparent option for renegotiation. Still, they came every year, and they tried not to talk about politics, or guns, or religion, and if you'd asked either of them, they would have agreed that it would continue like that more or less forever.

But things changed when Wyatt was two. The visit had been four days of misery, with Wyatt completely off the chain, overstimulated by his seven loud, hyperactive, proudly unvaccinated cousins (the entire Colorado clan was opposed to vaccinations, in some weird strain of Republicanism they linked with their love of the Second Amendment and desire for freedom from the federal government). Lucy had pleaded with Owen to go home early, or at least check them into a hotel, but Owen had refused, worried that either option would damage his mother's feelings beyond repair. Wyatt became more and more unglued—he would not sleep, he did not eat, and Owen's mother insisted on taking pictures of him without switching off the flash, even though every time it went off, it sent him into another round of hysterics. On the flight back, Wyatt had gotten so completely out of control that the plane had to land. Owen and Lucy rented a car and drove the rest of the way home.

A week later, Owen got a long, handwritten letter from his mother stating in no uncertain terms that there was nothing wrong with Wyatt, he was just in his terrible twos, and the real problem was that Lucy refused to discipline him. And then she suggested that he and Lucy might have made a mistake when they opted to have Wyatt vaccinated, because, well, there had been links. And she had warned Lucy about them, remember?

Lucy found the letter a few months later, tucked into the nest of junk inside Owen's nightstand, and she exploded. (*Why didn't I throw away the letter?* Owen thought a million times. *I should have burned the letter.*) But what was done was done. And their yearly trip to Colorado to see his family was no longer in the cards.

"They can come here," Lucy suggested coolly whenever the topic came up. "We have a spare room. Your father is retired, and fortunately for them, your parents don't have an autistic child. They're welcome to visit us whenever they want." But as she aged, Owen's mother was beset by neuroses and maladies that served her most basic desires — she wanted to sleep in her own bed, be matriarch in her own house, cook her own holiday meals. Earlier that year, when Owen pressed her to come visit, she'd claimed her doctor told her it was no longer safe for her to fly.

It was weird, the thought of facing life without any real connection to extended family. And Beekman felt like roots, in a weird way. It was probably why both he and Lucy were not just drawn to Beekman, but committed to staying there. Beekman felt like a place your kids could come back to. Or, in the case of Wyatt, a place your kid would be okay if he never actually left.

What was going to happen to Wyatt? It was a thought that struck Owen a lot, most often late at night. What happens to these kids? Once, when Wyatt was in preschool, all the kids and their parents went on a field trip to a farm that was a boarding school for autistic teenagers and, it turned out, a permanent residence for autistic adults. They trained dogs there, the bomb-sniffing and seeing-eye kind, and they ran an organic farm, which required a lot of labor. ("When you don't use pesticides, somebody has to pick the slugs off the lettuce," Owen overheard one parent say.)

The day of the field trip was almost impossibly beautiful, blue skies with puffy white clouds, the grass springtime green, baby sheep scampering in the fields, and Owen tried to be optimistic. There were two-story dormitories scattered across the property, connected with winding paths painted different colors. *This wouldn't be so bad,* Owen tried to make himself believe. A life filled with well-behaved dogs and frolicking sheep and puffy clouds and organic tomatoes? Harvard might be out of the question—okay, Harvard was out of the question—but was this kind of life really so bad?

On the ride home, Wyatt fell asleep in his car seat.

"That was kind of nice," said Owen.

Lucy didn't respond.

"I mean, it was a nice place," he said. "It wouldn't be the worst thing in the world, I mean, if things ever came to that."

"That's not going to happen to Wyatt," Lucy said.

"I'm just saying," said Owen. "It's nice to know places like that exist."

"I suppose it is," said Lucy. "But that place has nothing to do with our son."

❧

The weekend nanny whose name Gordon could never remember was standing by the front door, helping Rocco put on his coat. They were heading out for a walk.

"Tell the nanny not to let Rocco go near Fang," Gordon said to Kelly.

"Maria. No Fang! No Fang *por* Rocco! Not safe. *Muy dangeroso.*"

"Okay, Miss Kelly," Maria said. "Okay, no Fang."

Fang, the Allens' new Doberman puppy, was outside, tied to a hundred-yard zip line that zigzagged through the trees. The dog practically lost his mind each time an acorn fell or a squirrel scurried by or a bird flew overhead. Fang was not yet trained, not by any stretch of the imagination, although he was getting better at waiting to attack the dog guy until the dog guy was wearing the protective suit. Other than that, they hadn't seen much progress. The next step was to send Fang away to Texas for six months to be trained in a controlled setting. The promise was, when he came back, he'd be the world's best guard dog and yet gentle as a dove.

"Enjoy your walk, sweetie," Kelly said to Rocco, and she tightened his scarf. Once the front door closed, she walked over to the couch and dramatically flopped down on it, groaning a big groan.

"God, I'm so bored."

This was Kelly's latest refrain. She'd just come back from Vegas, loaded down with shopping bags—that's why Kelly went to Vegas, she went there to shop, whereas Gordon's other wives had disappeared for weeks to Paris or Milan. It took him a while to realize Kelly's shopping trips to Vegas weren't signs of her thriftiness, or even of what Gordon thought of as her fundamental Americanness, but were in fact disturbing reminders that deep down, she was tacky and cheap. She'd put on a silver lamé minidress to go out to dinner with Jamie the yoga instructor and when Gordon told her, "You can't wear that kind of dress around here," she'd said, "Okay, Grandpa."

Grandpa! The disrespect! The disrespect was mounting!

"This place is so boring. There are no movie theaters. There's nowhere to shop."

"Go to the city if you want to shop. And we have a movie theater in the house."

"That's not the point," said Kelly. "I'm talking about Beekman."

"Why don't you volunteer at the school," said Gordon. "I read in the paper that a bunch of the mothers get together to cook hot lunches twice a week. That would be fun."

Gordon loved stuff like that. The women cooking the hot lunches. Volunteering their time, banding together, driving to the local big-box club to buy massive blocks of cheese and bags of baby carrots that were as big as actual babies. It was also a PTA fund-raiser—they charged five bucks for each lunch, and each lunch couldn't have cost more than twenty-five cents. Hot lunch, cooked by an army of mommy volunteers raising money to do things like buy books for the school library and new equipment for the gym. And zero tax dollars involved! That was the America Gordon wanted to live in.

"With those busybody nobodies? No, thank you."

"This is a community," said Gordon. "That's part of what we do. We give back."

"You want me to be the lunch lady? And wear a hairnet? That's what you want me to do for fun?"

"Okay, maybe not the hot lunches. But you could join a club or something."

"Join a club? Am I in junior high? I don't want to join a club. I want some kind of a life. I want to move back to the city."

"Only animals raise their kids in New York City," said Gordon without even looking up from his computer screen.

"Someplace else, then," Kelly said, giving up easily.

"Like where."

"South Beach."

"*South* Beach? Are you kidding me?"

"There's lots of art there. Culture. Good food."

"I'm not raising my son in South Beach," said Gordon. "Besides, I have to be near the city for my work. You know that."

"Okay, the Hamptons, then. We could live there year-round. They have excellent schools."

The last time Gordon had been in the Hamptons, Alec Baldwin had walked up to him at a farm stand and yelled at him about climate change. He accused him of being a climate-change denier, spitting it out like it was worse than being a Holocaust denier, and Gordon had said, "I *am* a climate-change denier. I deny climate change. I don't think it's happening. I don't think the planet is getting hotter because of what man does or does not do. I am pro-fracking, pro–fossil fuels, pro-pipelines, pro-jobs, pro-America, pro-freedom. Drill, baby, drill, Alec! Drill, baby, drill!"

Gordon loved it, of course, and he dined out on that story for years, but he didn't want to live in a place where there were people richer than him, more famous than him, who hated him and weren't afraid to show it. Maybe twenty years ago, he would have been up for a dustup with a celebrity or a liberal billionaire every time he walked out the front door, but now he was getting tired. Gordon liked being the biggest fish.

"I'm not gonna live in the Hamptons, Kelly. We've been over this a million times."

"Well, I'm going crazy, Gordon," Kelly said, sitting up. "I'm thirty-one years old. I don't want to count bald eagles and watch YouTube videos of a woman folding towels for the rest of my life."

Enough with the mocking of Simka! Simka was one of the last legitimate pleasures in his life! Plus she didn't just fold towels! She collected greeting cards and fancy journals and old library books and tapped her fingers on them while she talked quietly about them! And wrapping paper!

"You have a six-year-old son," Gordon reminded her. "You could try spending some time with him. Why didn't you go on his walk with him if you have nothing else to do? Lots of mothers find their children fascinating."

Kelly rolled her eyes at him. *His wife rolled her eyes at him!* What was next? Giving him the finger? Gordon had to get things back under control. He had to. He could feel his control slipping away. The postnup! The missing fucking postnup! How was it that a man of his age and experience, a three-time loser in the marriage game, a goddamn *billionaire,* had married a woman less than half his age and hadn't insisted on a prenup? It was one of the great mysteries of Gordon's life, really.

"You can go to the city whenever you want. You have a car and driver at your disposal. You want a different car? I'll buy you a different car. You don't like Bo? I'll get you a different driver."

"Bo's fine," said Kelly.

"You can do whatever you want, whenever you want. Don't

talk to me about bored. Look at this place. You live like the goddamn queen of England."

Kelly flopped back down.

"I bet she's bored too."

❧❦❧

Lucy was putting Wyatt to bed. He had a pretty elaborate bedtime ritual at this point, stuffed animals in a long row down the side of the bed, each in its proper place, various sound machines plugged in and humming at just the right frequencies, and a special weighted blanket that provided proprioceptive input to help him calm down.

"Remembering people's birthdays is an excellent way to make friends," said Wyatt.

"That's true," Lucy said.

"You can give them a phone call," said Wyatt. "You can give people a phone call on their birthdays and it's an excellent way to make friends."

"Do you want to call someone on their birthday?"

"Yes."

"Who do you want to call?"

Wyatt's face went completely blank. He looked up at the ceiling, like he was stumped by the question.

"Remembering people's birthdays is an excellent way to make friends," he finally said. "And you can say something nice about their clothes. Saying something nice about people's clothes is an excellent way to make new friends."

"Do you want back scratches tonight?"

"Of course I do."

Wyatt rolled over, and Lucy started to scratch his back.

I have a crush on Ben, Lucy thought for the first time.

It was weird, how the Arrangement had made all of this happen backwards. For the first few times, the sex with Ben was just what it was supposed to be: Meaningless sex. Surprising, satisfying, a bit educational, delicious — all of those things too — but essentially meaningless.

But lately, things had changed. She was walking around with a goofy smile on her face all the time, not because of the sex, but because of Ben. She thought about him constantly. She dreamed about him, happy dreams, dreams where the rest of her life didn't exist. They'd started texting each other, not a lot, just a bit, but they'd gotten into the habit of saying good night every night. *Good night. Kiss. Sleep tight. Kisses back.* And her heart jumped every time.

This is why people have affairs, Lucy thought. *This feeling, this one right here.*

No wonder. No fucking wonder.

Fourteen

Lust is energetically expensive. It consumes time and resources. It impairs judgment. From an evolutionary point
of view, once the desired number of children are born,
there is no advantage in feeling lust for your spouse.

—Constance Waverly

Choke me."

"Excuse me?"

"I want you to choke me," said Izzy.

Owen was, at that moment, in his favorite sexual position, the one that most closely resembled taking a nap. He was on his back, with Izzy straddling him and doing the lion's share of the work. Izzy occasionally used Owen almost like a prop, just like one of the countless dusty sex toys she pulled out from under her bed ("One sec, gotta go wash this bad boy off").

"Put your hands around my neck and sorta strangle me."

"Izzy—"

"Please?"

"I don't want to do that."

"Just enough to cut the air off for a little bit. It'll make me come hard."

"Are you serious?" Owen had stopped moving altogether, but Izzy continued to move her hips in a tantalizing way, like an ocean swell slapping against the hull of a boat.

"You've never heard of this?"

"I've heard of it," said Owen. "I just don't want to hurt you."

"You won't hurt me," said Izzy. "I've done it a thousand times."

A thousand times? Owen thought. *That can't be true. That simply cannot be true.*

"I'm not sure I'm comfortable with this, Izzy."

"Just do it."

Izzy was in a weird mood this afternoon, that was for sure. She'd greeted him at the door already semi-drunk, although it was not even one o'clock. Apparently, she'd just received an unexpected property-tax bill from five years back. Apparently, it was Christopher's fault, but getting him to pay it was going to involve lawyers, and Izzy didn't know if she could go through that again. Apparently, this was never going to end. She wasn't a poster child for divorce, Izzy wasn't, that's for sure.

When else am I going to get the chance to choke a woman while I fuck her? Owen thought. Probably never. And, on some level — he knew this sounded weird but it felt, at the time, nonetheless true — it seemed like the gentlemanly thing to do.

Owen put his hands around Izzy's neck and squeezed a little and then paused.

"Shouldn't we have a signal or a safe word or something so I know when to stop?"

"Be quiet. You're making this not sexy."

"Okay."

He tightened his hands around her neck again and squeezed.

"Harder."

Owen squeezed harder.

"Better. Now do it even harder, and fuck me hard at the same time," said Izzy.

Owen obeyed. He felt a surge of energy at the base of his back, like a ball of molten lava, and it seemed to radiate up his spine and out through all of his limbs. Izzy's neck was small, birdlike even, and he enjoyed the feeling of having his hands encircling it. *I'm choking her,* he thought. *I'm cutting off her air supply. This is weird. Weird, but cool.*

Izzy started to come — he could feel it, he could always feel it, but he could tell this was a big one, not one of her run-of-the-mill, six-times-a-session orgasms — and so he kept going, choking her and fucking her and feeling her body shiver and shake and throb. Finally, he took his hands from her throat. She flopped down on his chest with a *thwack,* her face in the pillow next to his head.

She was completely still. She did not appear to be breathing. It felt like she weighed two hundred pounds. Two hundred pounds of deadweight. *Oh my God,* Owen thought. *I've killed her.* Bits of his life flashed past his eyes—Lucy, Wyatt, happiness, this stupid experiment—as he carefully rolled her off of him. He slapped her cheek. Nothing. He slapped her harder and yelled her name. *How soon do I dial 911? Do I give her mouth-to-mouth? Should I stabilize her neck?*

Finally he remembered the sternum rub, an old fraternity trick they used to do when someone passed out in college. He knelt on the bed next to her and rubbed his knuckles up and down Izzy's sternum, hard and fast.

"Ow!" Izzy yelled. She sat up and shook her head, pissed off and a bit stunned. "Why the hell did you do that?"

"That was amazing," Izzy said. "Amazing, amazing. I'm still shaking. Look, my knees are shaking. I can barely walk."

"I'm glad you enjoyed it," said Owen. "But I can promise you one thing. I'm never, ever doing that again."

"Why the hell not?"

"Because I thought I killed you!" said Owen. "I thought you were dead! I thought I was going to spend the rest of my life in prison!"

"I passed out. That's what happens when you do that the right way. I thought you knew that."

"You didn't pass out, Izzy. You flatlined. You stopped breathing."

"I did not stop breathing."

"Yes, you did."

"I passed out. You still breathe when you pass out."

"You. Stopped. Breathing."

"You're being a hysteric."

"I don't care what I'm being," said Owen. "That was a first and last time for that particular stunt. Deal with it."

"You're such a pussy."

"And please stop calling me that," said Owen. He was standing at the foot of the bed, pulling on his jeans.

"It's a real boner-killer, right?" said Izzy. "That's what Christopher always said."

For the first time since the relationship began, Owen found himself thinking about breaking things off early with Izzy. Early, meaning before the Arrangement officially ran its course. Between her attempt to burn her ex-husband's great-grandfather's desk and that afternoon's choking episode, Owen couldn't fight the thought: *Maybe I've ridden this particular train as far as I want to ride it.*

But could he just sit Izzy down and tell her that he and Lucy were ending the Arrangement early and therefore he would not be having sex with her anymore? Or bringing her fresh eggs? Or performing any of the small duties around her house that she had queued up for him the moment he rolled off her, it was starting to seem, every time he stopped by, even for the quickest of quickies? That day it had been: Open the jar of roasted red peppers on the kitchen counter, change the lightbulb in the stairwell, and see if he could figure out what was up with the powder-room toilet, and did he think she really needed to call a plumber or could she maybe fix it herself. Oh, and drop off her plastic shopping bags filled with plastic shopping bags at GroceryLand, since he was headed there anyway and they had that big recycling box out front.

His girlfriend was choring him! It hit him when he was walking across the GroceryLand parking lot carrying Izzy's three enormous bags full of bags under his arm. The air-conditioner installation, the bathtub-caulking fiasco, all that time he spent inspecting her drains and creeping around in her dank basement, flipping switches on her fuse box while she yelled down at him, "No, not that one! Try the next one!"

"Owen!"

Susan Howard was standing behind a portable table covered

with baked goods. Three fourth-grade boys were off to the side, wearing soccer uniforms, taking turns punching each other as hard as they could.

"Soccer bake sale? Yum," Owen called to her. "Put something good aside for me, I'll hit you on my way out."

Susan vacated her post and made a beeline for Owen.

"Please don't tell me you and Lucy use plastic grocery bags," said Susan.

"We don't."

"Owen."

Owen was, in fact, at that very moment shoving Izzy's enormous collection of plastic grocery bags into the recycling box in front of GroceryLand. The box in question had a very small opening, and Izzy's bags of plastic bags had each been knotted tightly shut and were the size and shape of large human heads. Owen had ripped the first one open and was squishing handful after handful of ancient, balled-up plastic into the recycling bin as fast as he could.

"We just...sometimes I guess a few end up in our house and we save them until we have enough to recycle. This is, like, two years' worth."

"I have to lecture you."

"Please don't, Susan. I can't handle it today."

"They are *so bad.* Not a little bit bad. *So* bad. And I know you think by putting them in that recycling bin, you're doing a good thing and helping the planet, but you're not."

"I'm not?"

"When people like you and Lucy—smart, educated consumers—choose to use plastic, it just perpetuates the entire system. It makes the checkout people feel less bad just shoving plastic down the planet's throat."

"I don't think you can blame the checkout ladies at Grocery-Land for plastic bags—"

"Of course I can! They shouldn't even *offer* plastic. Plastic should be kept in a locked room in the back of the store, and if you ask for plastic, you should have to wait for them to find the key."

"I think they'd lose their jobs pretty quickly if they did that."

"I'm going to send you a link to a video."

"Please don't, Susan."

"It's that huge floating island of garbage that's out in the middle of the Pacific Ocean. This young woman gets in the middle of it in her kayak and it's nothing but plastic water bottles and plastic shopping bags and dead fish as far as the eye can see. She just floats there and weeps."

"I look forward to it," said Owen.

"Don't be sarcastic. Watch it," said Susan. She grasped him by both shoulders and looked into his eyes. "It will change you. Hey, Rowan, lecture Owen about plastic grocery bags. He won't listen to me."

Susan's husband, Rowan, walked over from the ATM vestibule. Their youngest kid, Charlotte, was climbing on Rowan's head and shoulders like a monkey, and Rowan was wearing a long red skirt.

"Dude," Owen said.

"What do you think?" Rowan said, doing a twirl.

"Great, right?" said Susan. "We're raising awareness."

"Susan won't let me put on a pair of pants until Colleen Lowell gets her job back."

"Oh yeah?"

"I'm kinda diggin' it," said Rowan. "You've got all this room down there, things can breathe, move around—"

Susan cut Rowan off. "Tell Owen how bad plastic bags are."

"They're really bad," Rowan said.

"Sometimes we forget to bring our canvas bags, I guess," said Owen. The plastic bags were balled up like snowballs and several of them were, for some reason, damp. It was hard to push more than two or three through the slot at one time no matter how hard he tried. "We've got a bunch in the house, but it's easy to walk out the door and forget them."

"Keep them in your trunk!" Susan said. "When you unload the car, bring them right back. That way you'll always have them."

"Good tip," said Owen.

Charlotte rappelled down Rowan's left arm and disappeared under his skirt.

"Seriously, Owen, it's pretty important," said Rowan.

"Yeah, you know, when you have a kid like Wyatt, sometimes things fall through the cracks."

Owen didn't like playing the Wyatt card, but he found himself doing it more and more these days. His mother wondered why he'd been so out of touch? *Oh, you know, things with Wyatt have been a little rough lately*. His boss needed his expense report? *Wyatt's not sleeping again, Lucy and I are taking turns with him at night, I guess I've gotten a little backed up on things*. Wyatt had become his get-out-of-jail-free card, his all-purpose excuse, his reason why.

But really, it wasn't Wyatt. Not lately, not the way it used to be. Wyatt was doing better. It was hard to put a finger on just what exactly was going on with his son. It wasn't simply compliance, although that was part of it. He put up less of a fight doing the ordinary tasks of life. Getting dressed, putting his shoes on, climbing in and out of the car, brushing his teeth, going to bed. They had reinstituted the visual schedule at home, and that was probably part of it. Wyatt liked to know what was next, so Owen and Lucy Velcroed small laminated PECS cards with simple pictures and phrases—*Get dressed, Eat snack, Play game, Ride in car*—down a long grid, with the day carved into manageable half-hour units.

But then, the other day, Wyatt stole Blake's canned peaches. Blake had gone to the bathroom during snack time, and Wyatt grabbed them and ate them! This from a kid who'd consumed nothing but bananas, banana yogurt, crunchy peanut butter on saltine crackers, applesauce, and Cheerios for his entire life. And suddenly, out of the blue, he's stealing peaches! Canned peaches were now in the mix! And it was starting to feel like, well, a succession of things like that, things like canned peaches and animal crackers, eye contact and *actually playing with other kids,* actually playing, like kids do, letting the game change and *going with it* instead of rigidly sticking to a Wyatt-made plan.

"Can I make a skirt for you?" Susan asked Owen. "I got a bunch from the Salvation Army store and I'm altering them so they'll fit."

"A skirt? For me?" said Owen. "That would be a no."

"Owen."

"I love you, Susan, but no."

The pain started on his drive home, a low throbbing at the base of his spine, and by the time he pulled into the driveway, Owen could barely get out of the car.

"I have to lie down," he said to Lucy. "My back went out."

He dropped the car keys in the basket filled with shoes and crumpled to the floor in front of the staircase, still in his jacket and ancient beat-up wingtips.

"Can you make it to the couch?" she asked. "I'm trying to clean up in here."

"I can't move, Lucy. I'm in incredible pain. Can you bring me three Advil?"

"If I can find some."

The stress of almost killing Izzy was somatizing at a rapid rate. It had shot past his lower back and was starting to radiate out through his limbs. He couldn't turn his head without just about screaming.

"How long do you think this is going to last?" Lucy asked after she brought him the pills. She was standing up by his right shoulder, looking down at him, while he sipped water out of the side of his mouth and tried to swallow the Advil.

"I have no idea. It's never been this bad before. Never, ever, not even in this ballpark."

"Did you do something to yourself?"

"What do you mean?"

Lucy folded her arms across her chest and asked, "Did you physically exert yourself in some unusual way?"

"It started when I was in the car," said Owen. "My lower back seized up, and then pain started shooting down my legs. I'm lucky I made it home without driving into a ditch."

"I have French tonight," said Lucy.

Owen groaned.

"Do you think that's going to be a problem?"

"I don't know, Lucy. I can't move my body."

"I really don't want to miss class tonight," said Lucy. "We have a big test."

"I can't lift my arms, Lucy. I don't know what to tell you," said Owen.

"Should I call a sitter?"

"If I still feel like this, I'd really appreciate it if you'd stay home."

Lucy was not happy. She didn't want to stay home with Owen and his bad back. She wanted to see Ben. She needed to see Ben. She'd been looking forward to it all week.

She took Wyatt outside and zipped him up in the trampoline and left Owen alone and moaning on the kitchen floor.

"The African black mamba can sink its fangs into a grown man's face!" Wyatt yelled as he bounced around on the trampoline. He careened hard into the net and lost his footing.

"Are you okay, sweetie?"

"Yes," said Wyatt. He got back on his feet and started bouncing again. "The African black mamba can sink its fangs into a grown man's face!"

I can't come today, Lucy texted.

How come? Ben texted back.

Owen did something to his back. He doesn't want me to leave. I'm really sorry.

Could we talk, do you think?

On the phone?

Yes. If you can.

Lucy looked down at her phone. Why shouldn't she and Ben talk on the phone? That wasn't against the rules. They hadn't done it before, but there was no reason not to, at least none that Lucy could come up with at the moment.

I'll call you when I get Wyatt to bed. It'll be a while, Lucy texted.

I'll be here.

"Mama! Mama! I have something to tell you!"

Lucy looked up. Wyatt was jumping with stiff legs in the center of the trampoline.

"The African black mamba can sink its fangs into a grown man's *face!*" Wyatt said again.

"Where'd you learn that?"

"Siri showed me," said Wyatt.

"What? Why?"

"Siri showed me videos of snakes attacking humans!"

"I don't think those are good videos to watch, sweetie. They might be too scary."

"They're super-scary," said Wyatt.

He started to bounce-walk in a big circle, landing on the balls of his feet. *The autism walk,* Lucy thought for the millionth time.

"Heels down, Wyatt."

"They're super-duper scary!"

Owen found himself watching Lucy out of the side of his right eye, from his spot on the kitchen floor, while she started making dinner for Wyatt. She was clearly angry about missing French. She banged a few pots and pans around to make her point, but Owen didn't see how he had any choice. *I can't lift my arms,* he wanted to say to her yet again. *It's not my fault I have a bad back.*

Lucy was wearing workout pants, but tighter than the ones he was used to seeing her in; they looked like pants a person might actually do yoga in. From his angle on the floor, he thought her ankles were appealing, fragile and girlish. She looked good, he thought. She looked like she hadn't looked in years, sort of shiny and new. And, was it possible…was she actually wearing lipstick?

There was a time, a few years back, when Owen and Lucy had had what they forever would refer to as the Lipstick Fight.

The Lipstick Fight went like this:

Over dinner one night, when Wyatt was a toddler, Owen casually suggested it would be nice if Lucy put on some lipstick before he came home from work. He was using lipstick as sort of a signifier, but it was the thing he thought of when he thought of a woman putting some care and attention into her physical appearance.

Because this was what he came home to every night: A woman wearing saggy old workout clothes that she never worked out in, that had somehow become her pajamas and the clothes she went to the grocery store in and the clothes she wore around the house all day, with her dirty hair pulled back in a ponytail and who looked like she'd just been run over by a sedan.

"Put on lipstick" meant *Stop that. Stop looking like that. It's not fair to me. I married a beautiful woman.*

And Lucy had gone ballistic. It was one of the biggest fights of their marriage. Probably the biggest. This was before they knew Wyatt was any different from any other typical-yet-difficult little boy. He was banging his head against walls, he was not sleeping, he was darting off into the woods behind the house and hiding silently behind trees.

The terrible twos, people kept saying to Lucy. Every parent goes through it.

"Lipstick? Are you serious right now? Do you have any idea what my life is like? And you want me to put on *lipstick* before you come home?"

She'd stalked up the stairs and slammed the bathroom door. Owen sat at the table, drinking his wine, realizing he had said the wrong thing.

When Lucy came back down, she had bright red lipstick smeared all around her mouth, like a little girl who'd raided her mother's purse.

"Can I do anything else for you?" she said. "Would you like a foot massage? Shall I bake you a pie?"

And then she collapsed on the floor, sobbing, and she didn't stop for hours.

Owen took the next day off to look after Wyatt while Lucy stayed in bed with tears slowly, continuously leaking out of the corners of her eyes. He wished she had a mother he could call, a mother who would get on a plane and move in for a few months and get everything sorted out. Her mother was dead, though, and his own mother was such a distant, uninterested presence that the thought of asking her for help was essentially unimaginable. When the crying started to look like it might never stop, Owen decided to call Lucy's older sister, Anna, who had a big job and three kids of her own but who still hopped on the first flight out.

Anna stayed with them for two weeks. She looked after Wyatt, organized the house, cleaned out the pantry, opened stacks of mail, and coaxed Lucy into her first shower in weeks. Anna and Owen interviewed sitters together and eventually found a nice middle-aged woman to watch Wyatt for three hours every afternoon so Lucy could rest. Her name was Paulette and she had raised three kids. Paulette lasted a little over four months, four months before Wyatt became too much for her, which was just long enough for Lucy to get her sea legs again. When both

Owen and Anna insisted they hire someone else, Lucy refused. ("I don't work," she'd said. "I'm not going to pay someone to raise my child.")

So Lucy went back into the trenches full-time, and Wyatt got harder and more inscrutable. No lipstick was worn. And then when Wyatt was three, their pediatrician suggested they get him evaluated.

But it's back again, Owen thought. *The lipstick is back.*

Wyatt finally fell asleep at ten, and his entire dinner-calm-down-bath-time-bedtime routine had fallen on Lucy's shoulders. Owen had managed to make it up the stairs and into bed, but he'd asserted that anything more was too much for him. He texted a few people he knew in town asking if anyone had any old pain pills lying around, but nobody in Beekman wanted to give up their spare pain pills for actual physical pain, so he suffered through the evening with bourbon and Netflix.

Like he's on a goddamn vacation, Lucy thought when she walked past their bedroom on her way downstairs. *I was supposed to be with Ben, and he's drunk and watching* Game of Thrones.

Ben picked up the phone on the first ring.

"Hello."

"Hi."

"It's really you," said Ben.

"It's me."

"It's weird to hear your voice without seeing your face."

"You have a very low voice," said Lucy. "I never noticed how low it was until now."

"I can't believe we've never talked on the phone before."

"Neither can I."

"I like it."

"I do too."

"Where are you?"

"I'm sitting outside, on an Adirondack chair, wrapped in a blanket."

"Nice."

"It's cold and dark and all the stars are out. I see the Big Dipper and something that may or may not be Mars," said Lucy. "What about you?"

"I'm in bed."

"What are you wearing?"

"Me? Nothing. You?"

"Sweats and an old ski cap."

"Nice," he said, mock-sexily.

"I told you, it's freezing out here," Lucy said.

"I'm really glad you called."

"You are? I was worried it was too late."

"It could never be too late," said Ben. "We don't get to talk enough, I think."

"We don't," she said. "Sometimes I think I barely even know you."

"Well, what do you want to know? I'll tell you anything you want. I'm serious, Lucy. I've got all night."

Lucy ran into the house for some wine, and then once about an hour later to pee, but other than that, they just kept talking.

"Tell me about your marriage," Lucy finally said.

"What do you want to know?"

"What happened to it," said Lucy.

"That's a tough question," said Ben.

"Take a swing at it."

"I think life happened to my marriage," said Ben. "Or maybe marriage happened to my marriage. Something about not knowing how hard it was going to be, or not being able to accept it. Taking it for granted."

"Too vague, my friend, too vague," said Lucy.

"We met in college. I wanted to be a history professor, and she wanted to be a doctor. Mostly what we did was study together. I know that sounds weird, but it was a lot of sitting on the couch reading and taking notes with our feet in each other's laps and then having sex and then studying some more. I think if we could have gone on like that forever, things would have been different."

"Well, that's stupid," said Lucy. "Life isn't like that."

"I agree, but you don't necessarily realize that in college."

"College seems like five lifetimes ago."

"Yeah," said Ben. "Which is only one of many reasons why you shouldn't marry your college sweetheart."

"So that was the problem? You got married too early?"

"No," said Ben. "That's too easy."

"Did you fight a lot?"

"Neither of us are fighters," said Ben. "We only really disagreed about one thing."

"What?"

"She didn't want to have kids."

"And you did."

"Yep."

"That's a pretty big problem," said Lucy. "That's what most people would consider a deal-breaker."

"She told me she didn't want kids when we first met. On our first date, actually. I was nineteen. Kids were the furthest thing from my mind. And the truth is, I didn't believe her."

"Why not?"

"I guess I'd never thought that women who say they don't want kids really don't want kids. I realize now that's stupid, but at the time, it just seemed like a thing a certain kind of ambitious girl would say. For effect, I guess, or to show that she wasn't trying to trap you. I figured either it was a lie, or it would change."

"And you guys had kids."

"We did."

"So she changed her mind?"

"I don't think she ever really changed her mind," said Ben. "I won't say she had the girls against her will, but if you got her drunk enough, she might say it."

"Is she sad she had the girls? What are their names?"

"Eliza and Peggy. And no, I don't think she's sad she had them. That's not quite it."

"Send me a picture of them. Text it to me."

"Okay."

"They're adorable," Lucy said when the picture came through. "Which one is which?"

"Eliza is the oldest, with the freckles. She's twelve. Peggy is ten."

"Does your wife have freckles?"

"Ex-wife," said Ben. "And yes, she does."

"Like, freckles all over? Like Julianne Moore freckles?"

"I guess you could say she has Julianne Moore freckles."

"Interesting."

"Why is that interesting?"

"Actually, it's not interesting," said Lucy. "Sometimes I say *interesting* when things aren't in fact interesting. You should know that about me."

"Interesting," said Ben.

"Ha."

"She has one of those jobs that is all-consuming, and she loves it. She's one of the best heart surgeons in the country. In the world, actually. Heads of state fly in to be operated on by her."

"Well, now you're just making me feel bad about myself and my lack of personal achievement."

"You wanted to talk about this."

"I know," said Lucy. "Keep going."

"What else can I say? She loves her job, she's great at it, and it eats up all she has to give. And she left her husband unattended."

"That means you cheated on her," said Lucy.

"We cheated on each other."

"Who first?"

"I honestly don't know. I guess I assume it was me. But there was no 'catching anyone' or anything. She finally told me she was in love with some guy she met at the hospital and she wanted a divorce. His name was Grant. I remember I kept saying, 'Grant?' over and over again when she finally told me."

"Are they still together?"

"Who?"

"Deborah and Grant?"

"No," said Ben. "Grant is long gone. I met him once, when I dropped off the girls. He had long gray hair, pulled back in a low ponytail, and I couldn't stop thinking, *She left me for* that?"

"Was he a doctor?"

"No," said Ben. "He's a social worker in the cardiology unit. I picture him lurking around, offering solace to dying people's families and hitting on my wife."

"What happened to them?"

"I have no idea," said Ben. "I think he was just the fuse she needed to light to explode our life. In my experience, it's pretty hard to end a marriage without a third party involved. Whether the third party decides to stick around is another question entirely."

"Is she with someone now?"

"Nope. She's single, which is probably the way she wants it. She dates a bit, I think. I assume so, at least."

"Are you guys close?"

"We co-parent the girls without much disagreement," said Ben. "But other than that, no."

"Do you do holidays together?"

"No. Never. We trade off," said Ben. "It makes for some lonely Christmas mornings."

"Yeah."

"I probably would have stuck it out for the girls. I really didn't want them to go through this. I like to think I would have done that fine old-fashioned thing and waited until our youngest went off to college."

"I'm not sure that's always the best plan," said Lucy. "For the woman, at least. Deborah probably didn't want to wait that long."

Deborah the freckled, brainy, child-hating cardiothoracic surgeon. Deborah, the woman who left her husband unattended, like a bomb in a backpack in a subway station.

"The stars keep moving," said Lucy.

"Yeah?"

"I've been watching them this entire time," she said. "They move faster than you'd think."

It was well past three in the morning by the time Lucy and Ben stopped talking and she finally slipped into bed.

Owen was lying on his left side with pillows and bolsters arranged carefully around him, like a woman in her ninth month. He'd smeared himself from head to toe with a tube of Ben-Gay his mother had left behind years ago, back when they'd first moved into the house, during her one and only visit. The room smelled disgusting, a combination of Ben-Gay and bourbon and unbrushed teeth.

"Who were you talking to out there for so long?" Owen asked sleepily.

Lucy paused for a long moment and then said flatly, "My sister."

"How's she doing?" Owen mumbled.

"Fine," said Lucy. "She's doing fine."

Owen adjusted one of his pillows and winced in pain. And then he was snoring again, faster than Lucy thought humanly possible, a man completely dead to the world.

He has no fucking clue, Lucy thought. *It's now officially weird.*

And, Lucy thought, *it's becoming insulting.*

Fifteen

Have you ever known a middle-aged man who's fallen head over heels in love with a woman who's not his wife? They're pretty goddamn happy. And a brand-new one walks into my office just about every other day.

—Constance Waverly
Huffington Post

Rowan Howard was a hopeless romantic who was convinced he had married the wrong woman, which was why, periodically and yet pretty consistently throughout his marriage to Susan, he had had love affairs.

And they were love affairs, emphasis on the *love*, long-drawn-out illicit courtships, emotionally intimate, all-consuming, can't-think-about-anything-else love affairs. Most recently, Rowan had been entangled with Juliette, a married woman who'd been seated next to him at a farm-to-table fund-raising event at their local CSA. They'd both felt it immediately, an electrical current that ran between them when Rowan accidentally on purpose brushed his hand against her knee under the table, which was heaped with warty heirloom turnips and stringy grass-fed beef.

Rowan had pursued Juliette doggedly. After a flurry of e-mails, she said she'd meet him, just once, for lunch. They'd had lunch nine times, nine exquisite times, before they broke down and had guilt-filled sex, in his old beat-up Jeep Cherokee at the end of one of Beekman's famous dirt roads. The sex ended with Juliette crying softly while Rowan held her as tightly as any human being could—it was perfect. It went like that for a good nine months—sex, then crying—until Juliette finally put a stop to it. She agreed, however, to let Rowan write her a letter every week, as long as he mailed it to a post office box in a neighboring town.

Those letters! Rowan was never more himself than when he crafted those letters, and after putting the first two into the mail and being sad he wasn't able to reread them, he decided to make a copy before he mailed each one off. Rowan's love letters were very nearly works of art, he thought, and they were effective too; every couple of months, Juliette would break down and send him a text, and then she'd agree to meet him, for the very last time, at "their" place, a bed-and-breakfast with a detached cottage, deep in the woods, that, midweek, Rowan was able to rent by the day. Then it was sex, tears, and more holding, and the whole thing would start up all over again. Rowan Howard was a family man, a loving father and an upstanding local citizen, a scratch golfer and a genius with a boneless pork loin—he was famous, in Beekman, for both his golf game and his pork loin in equal measure—who just so happened to be in search of the love of his life.

Long before Juliette, and years before Susan, even, Rowan had spent his twenties in Manhattan involved in what he feared would prove to be the most passionate, intense, all-consuming love affair of his life. Her name was Marissa LeFevre, and he still woke up from a dream about her at least once a week.

Marissa was a model and a former ballerina—technically, by the time they met, at age twenty-five, she was a former model too, but Rowan discovered that it took about a decade for a woman to admit that she was no longer a model—and she worked in an art gallery in a capacity that was largely decorative. She had an epic eating disorder, but Rowan didn't figure it out for two years—not until he came home early to Entenmann's boxes, the unmistakable sound of vomiting behind a closed door. The food thing didn't alarm him. Didn't all ballerinas-turned-models do that? It was practically in the job description. And Marissa responded to his acceptance of her binging and purging with a childlike gratitude. Here she was, being seen and known and still loved. She'd send him out at midnight with lengthy lists of foods she craved, and he would buy them, even if it involved stopping at several stores. He'd hit the Gourmet Garage for the ice cream she liked, then load up on candy bars at the twenty-four-hour Duane Reade, then pop into the bodega for an assortment of Hostess treats. He was her enabler, and she was his entire world.

Then he went to Vegas for his brother's bachelor-party weekend, and Marissa swallowed a bottle of Advil and then dialed 911. You can kill yourself with Advil, Rowan learned later at the hospital, but the very choice of the drug convinced him it wasn't a serious attempt, even though Marissa spent three days in the hospital on a psychiatric hold. He loved her. He loved every last bit of her, crazy and all. And he did his best to save her. She moved back in with him, and Rowan spent the next two years treating her like a fragile, precious doll. He asked her to come home with him for Christmas, but she refused, and then she orchestrated another breakdown to prove how much she needed him not to leave. The doctors at Bellevue advised him not to have any contact with her, for her own good, and they sent her home to Iowa, to her mother and the calm of life on the plains.

By the time he met Susan, Rowan was like one of those soldiers back from the trenches in World War I, unable to reenter normal life and incapable of communicating what he'd lived through. Their first date was a setup, orchestrated by one of the nosy yentas who worked alongside him at the firm, and he went along with it more or less against his will. He sat across the table from her, and it was like he was trapped inside a glass jar. He was numb, aloof, barely reachable.

Susan hadn't noticed. Here she had the advantage of her narcissism—which was in the subclinical range, but just barely—and her laserlike focus on her life plan, which was clicking along nicely but now required a suitable man. And Rowan—tall, not bad-looking, with a decent job and all of his hair—was suitable. He was more than suitable. And she was thirty-eight.

Susan had been the engine driving their courtship, with

her optimism and determination and purposefulness, and for the most part Rowan didn't mind. He didn't believe love could conquer all anymore. He had convinced himself that there were more important things than whatever Marissa LeFevre had to offer, things like stability, sanity, warmth. He didn't exactly long for hearth and home, but it seemed preferable to a life of midnight bodega runs and biannual suicide attempts. He wanted a woman who would make a good mother. A woman who wouldn't threaten to slit her wrists to get out of going to a dinner party. He found his new role as passive participant in the unfolding of Susan's life plan refreshing. He'd been Marissa's caretaker, her mother and father and shrink and best friend, and he was tired. He had nothing left to give, and he'd stumbled upon a woman who required very little of the deepest parts of him. He didn't have to do anything, really. As long as he didn't put up a fight, Susan took care of everything.

Six months into his marriage to Susan, Rowan realized he'd made a terrible mistake. He couldn't stop thinking about Marissa. When he couldn't reach her on her cell phone, he broke down and called her mother in Iowa.

"Marissa's dead."

"Oh my God," said Rowan.

"She hung herself in the garage," Marissa's mother said. "People always want to know how she did it, so I figure I might as well tell them."

"Captain Edward Smith, wireless operator John Phillips, and Mary Smith's husband, Lucian, who would never see his unborn child alive."

Wyatt was flicking his beads on the kitchen table while Lucy, exhausted and exhilarated from the night before, was staring into her coffee cup.

Don't think. Stop thinking about it. This is an unsolvable problem, it is a riddle with no answer, it is an inverse Zen koan, one that sends the mind spinning in a million different directions instead of stilling it.

When you're with Ben, you can think about Ben. When you're with Owen or with Wyatt, think about them. It started to feel bad only when she thought more than a few months into the future, when the impossibilities started lining up like Wyatt's Matchbox cars in impossibly long, perfectly straight rows.

"Captain Edward Smith, wireless operator John Phillips, and Mary Smith's husband, Lucian, who would never see his unborn child *alive*."

"What's that, Wyatt?"

"Captain Edward Smith, wireless operator John Phillips, and Mary Smith's husband, Lucian, who would never see his unborn child *alive*."

"Who are those people?"

"People who perished in the ice-cold water of the North Atlantic Ocean."

"Oh yeah?"

"They perished in the ice-cold water of the North Atlantic Ocean."

"Do you know what *perished* means, Wyatt?"

"They perished in the ice-cold water of the North Atlantic Ocean."

"Do you know what that means?"

"Not exactly."

"It means they died."

"*Perished* means they died. *Perished* means you die."

"That's right, Wyatt. *Perished* is a long word that means die."

"Dead as a doornail in the middle of the ice-cold North Atlantic Ocean."

It's called dissociating, a part of her said later.

It was three o'clock in the morning, and Lucy was wide awake, keyed up from the sugar in one too many glasses of white wine. She remembered the word from a psychology class she took at Oberlin.

That's what this is. You've split yourself in two.

Owen's back did not get better overnight. He had to call in sick every day for a week, and Lucy's patience, which wasn't that thick to begin with, grew infinitesimally thin. He couldn't help with Wyatt, he couldn't take out the garbage, he couldn't do anything, really. All he did every day for a week was lie flat on the floor, staring up at the ceiling, and then somehow manage to drive himself to the local acupuncturist and stare down through her therapy table's doughnut hole and think about his life.

He decided he would gently ease Izzy out of the picture. He instituted Delayed Text-Response Time. He forced himself to wait three hours to respond to one of Izzy's texts. Three hours, to Izzy, was an eternity. *Hey, baby, I miss you, how is your day so far?* Smiley face, winky face, sexy bear emoticon. Twenty minutes would pass. Sexy bear, glass of wine, winky face. Twenty more minutes. Dancing poop, dancing poop. *How's it going? You okay? I'm getting worried.* Angry poop! Super-hot and angry poop! Gun aimed at head! Flames coming from a house!

One thing was clear: Izzy did not want this to stop. Whatever the two of them had together—which, at this point, was Owen canceling two out of every three meetings, and on the one he showed up for, they had a quick half hour of angry sex followed by the requisite jar-opening and dry-rot examining, laying of mousetraps and opening and then closing and then opening again of fireplace flues—she intended to keep it going as long as she possibly could.

Owen found it a little perplexing. It was not as if they had fallen in love. If anything, Izzy seemed mad at him most of the time. He wasn't sure she even liked him. She was lonely and she liked to talk, that's for sure, and he didn't think she had many friends. She didn't seem to like women very much. In fact, she enjoyed telling Owen about the women in town, the women who came into her shop, and how much she loathed them all. She was, he realized, what Lucy would call a very negative person. He couldn't figure out why it had taken him so long to see it.

"This is a hypocritical little town," Izzy said.

"What are you talking about?"

"Everybody is secretly happy that the weird man in a dress isn't teaching their kids the days of the week, but when he sits on a bench on Main Street holding hands with his wife, they all treat him like he's Rosa Parks. I watch them out my window all day long. It's like they have to kiss the ring. And he's wearing a lot of rings."

"That's a little harsh, Izz."

"There's all this sweet stuff going on on the surface around here and all sorts of dark shit brewing beneath. That's why I'm putting my house on the market. I'm getting out. I'm moving back to the city, where the dark stuff is out in the open."

Owen fought hard not to show any reaction. "You're moving to the city?" he asked. "When did you decide this?"

"Well, I had an epiphany. The last time I was in the city. I was going to the dentist."

"What kind of epiphany?" said Owen.

"I was walking up Sixth Avenue and this man came up to me and said, 'I want to take a shit on your forehead.'"

"*What?*"

"Yep," said Izzy. "I was just walking down the street, minding my own business."

"Someone really said that to you? That's insane."

"I didn't make it up. He seemed normal too. He was wearing a suit."

"A guy in a suit walked up to you and said he wanted to take a shit on your forehead?"

"I don't know how to be any clearer, Owen. But you're missing my point. My point is, everyone in Beekman wants to shit on your forehead, but nobody actually says it out loud."

"I'm sure that's not true."

"Oh, it's true. Trust me. Nothing could be truer."

"So you're really gonna move?"

"I already talked to a real estate agent," she said. She rolled over and kissed him on the cheek. "I'm sorry, sweetie, but you always knew that this was temporary."

Owen went into Izzy's bathroom to take a quick shower. Izzy kept her coffeemaker on the bathroom counter, along with a sixty-four-ounce jug of powdered creamer and a filthy spoon. ("Because I don't want to walk all the way downstairs to make my coffee in the morning.") Approximately twenty different hair-care products lined the edge of the tub, and half a dozen cardboard flats of canned cat food were stacked next to the toilet. The smell was a potent cat-food-litter-box-French-roast blend. If Owen had seen this bathroom before they'd slept together the first time, he liked to think a few alarm bells would have gone off. Whether or not he would have heeded them—that was a different question.

But none of that mattered anymore. It was like the message on the steam-crinkled Post-it note stuck to Izzy's bathroom mirror. *Everything always works out perfectly for me!*

Deus ex machina. Izzy moving away.

Everything always works out perfectly for me!

That night, after Lucy went to bed, Owen locked himself in the spare room and went online.

He had had a lot to drink. That might have been part of it, who knows. He didn't know what he was looking for exactly.

He didn't have a plan. He just knew he had a window, and he owed it to himself, to his life, and, yes, *to his marriage* to make the most of it.

He clicked around for a while, not seeing much of anything, and he was just about to give up and go to sleep when he found just the sort of thing he realized he wanted.

It was a picture, cropped artfully, so you couldn't possibly recognize the person's face. The woman in the photo was sitting back on her ankles with her knees spread, her hands mostly covering herself with what Owen felt was an endearing display of modesty. She had no top on. It was one of those pictures that was grainy enough to feel authentic, and he was reasonably sure she wasn't a prostitute or a man. There was a cell number.

He sent the woman a text.

Simka put out a brand-new ASMR video once a week. She usually put them online on Friday evening, and Gordon had begun to count on it, to count on spending his Friday night listening to the new Simka offering three or four or even five times, thumbs-upping it and making a handful of appreciative comments below, using his secret Gmail handle, Gordon726.

Yesterday, however, had been Friday, and yet there'd been no sign of Simka. Gordon spent most of the night worried, first only a bit, but by four a.m. his mind would not stop racing. Where was Simka? What happened to Simka? What if Simka was gone forever?

Then, at 7:26 a.m., his phone woke him up and told him a new video had finally landed on Simka's channel.

She looked beautiful, as usual. She was wearing her hair the way he most liked it, falling forward over both shoulders, as thick and shiny as any head of hair he'd ever seen. She had her little mischievous smile on, too, and Gordon could tell she was in a good mood. Simka was always in a good mood, but the glow around her suggested today's was a particularly good one, particularly, particularly good.

"Before I start today, I just want to take a moment to say thank you to a few of my super-special friends, I really love you and appreciate you and your comments and I love knowing you're out there, it makes me feel so happy. You are so special to me, I know you might not believe that but I really treasure my special friends, and I want to say a super-special hi to chiefogomo, exactomac, wallabiefifteen, Gordonseven-twenty-six, fariephantom—"

Gordon726!

That was him! He was Gordon726! Simka was talking to him!

Gordon clicked on the screen and listened to the beginning again, waiting to hear his name. It was like a crack in the time-space continuum, Simka whispering his name, her tongue do-ing unimaginable things to the *d* in the middle and to the *seven* and the *twenty* and the *six*. She had over two hundred thousand followers, and yet, and yet! She'd singled him out! Gordon726! Simka knew him. He was special to Simka. She loved him and appreciated him.

To be fair, Gordon knew Simka didn't *really* know him, and she didn't *really* love him, but he had the sense that she did ap-preciate him! She must have seen something in his comments that stood out to her, stood out enough for her to single him out from among her *over two hundred thousand followers*.

He started again, from the beginning.

"My mother said you're having a midlife crisis," Madison said to him the second time they met.

Her name was Madison and she was twenty-six! She'd texted him back that first night saying that she was twenty-nine, but then after they slept together she admitted she was twenty-six, in her sexy kitten voice. He never would have slept with her if he knew she was only twenty-six, but, well, at this point, he figured the damage had already been done.

"You told your mother about me?"

"I tell my mother everything."

"Did you tell her you're sleeping with me?"

Madison rolled her eyes at him.

"I don't understand that eye roll," said Owen. "Does that mean yes, you told her, or no, you didn't?"

"I tell my mom everything. She's my best friend. We text a thousand times a day."

"Are you serious?"

"Yeah," said Madison. "She said you probably don't really have an open marriage."

"Your mom said that?"

"Yeah. And she said I should just be aware of that if I'm going to spend time with you."

"Well, first of all, I do have an open marriage. That is in fact the truth."

"She said that's what you'd say," said Madison.

"I'm saying it because it's true. I have a six-month free pass."

"What happens after six months?"

"We both stop. End of the experiment. Life goes back to normal."

"I went out with this fireman who told me he and his wife were separated, and then it turned out they were still living in the same house, but he said he slept on the couch. And then his wife found his burner phone in the glove compartment and tracked me down and went batshit on me. It was awful. I was totally in love with him. I had to move back home for, like, eight months. My mom doesn't want to see me go through all that again."

"You told your mom all that?"

"My mom's not uptight about sex," said Madison.

Her mom's not uptight about sex.

"She raised me to believe that there's no such thing as a slut."

This was the problem with the millennials, in a nutshell. There still was such a thing as a slut. You could say there wasn't, but there was. For example: Madison. Madison was a slut.

"All of my friends are like me with this stuff," she said.

"How is that possible? I've never met anyone like you, ever."

"That's because you're super-old," said Madison with a smile. "So, next time, you want to do some molly?"

The world is going to hell in a handbasket, Owen thought on the drive home. It was funny, really, how doing the most transgressive thing of his entire adult life was making him feel like a real fuddy-duddy. That's how he felt, like a fuddy-duddy. And proud to be one! Proud to be a fuddy-duddy if the alternative was this, having sex with the Madisons of this world, becoming the kind of person who did this. No, he didn't want to "do some molly." He didn't even know what molly was. Something like ecstasy, only better or much, *much* worse, depending on how your Internet search went. Owen wanted to stand on his front porch and yell at the neighborhood kids. He wanted to watch Fox News and boycott things and get really scared about the direction the country was headed in.

He had a plan. He was going to fuck Madison again. No doubt. Maybe even a few more times. And he was going to keep freezing Izzy out until she got the message and left him alone or sold her house and moved away, whichever came first. Then, in a couple of weeks, he was going to sit Lucy down, tell her how much he loved her and their life and their family and the way they knew each other inside and out, the way they made love and the way they raised Wyatt, and call the whole arrangement off early. Oh, and take her to Bermuda for five days. She'd like that.

Sixteen

Change is the only constant.

— Constance Waverly, quoting Heraclitus

The Wayside was a sleazy motel, and Owen planned on doing something sleazy inside of it. It had a parking area hidden from view, and it was a place where nobody from Beekman would ever go and where out-of-towners routinely died. Well, not routinely, but twice in the time Owen had lived in Beekman, a dead body was found at the Wayside; once, a soccer mom from Westchester who'd driven north and OD'd, the other time, a gangbanger from Newburgh who'd done something unwise on the other side of the Hudson and hid out at the Wayside for three weeks. He was shot, finally, two times in the head, on a trip back from the vending machine. He never even got a chance to enjoy his orange soda and peanut M&M's, according to the local paper, which had an above-the-fold photo of the Wayside's parking lot filled with cop cars and volunteer firefighters.

"Nice," Madison said when she walked in.

"Sorry," said Owen. "I, uh, I thought since we're just going to be here for a few hours it didn't make sense to drive all the way to—"

The first two times he'd slept with Madison, Owen had picked a considerably nicer hotel, a Doubletree Inn near White Plains. They'd given him a warm chocolate chip cookie when he checked in and charged him two hundred and forty dollars for his three hours of midday extramarital bliss. It was unsustainable, spending that much on a hotel room, and Owen, after the second meeting with Madison, didn't think she'd notice the absence of soft sheets and wireless access, the fact that there wasn't a business center off the lobby or a complimentary breakfast buffet complete with a make-your-own waffle station. (She did like the warm cookie, however.) At the Doubletree, Owen had had her on the floor the first time, and then up against a window that looked out over a Bed Bath & Beyond, and finally they'd taken a shower together and washed each other all over with little tiny bars of extremely smelly soap.

"Turn the lights off," Madison said to him now. "I don't want to see any black and curlies."

Owen flipped off the lights and started to unbuckle his belt.

"Take your top off," he instructed.

Madison slouched out of her hoodie and then reached down and pulled her T-shirt over her head. She wasn't wearing a bra. Her breasts were magnificent. They defied all known laws of breast gravity.

"Now your jeans," he said.

Madison ran her hands over her breasts rather theatrically and then slowly down her stomach to her jeans. She slipped a hand inside and looked Owen directly in the eyes. Like so many of Madison's moves, it had a rehearsed quality, like she had practiced it in front of a mirror after watching a lot of porn. *Kids these days! Stop it, stop it,* he told himself, *this is not your problem!*

"Do you want me to do anything special for you?" she asked.

"Um, let me think about that," Owen said. "What kind of special?"

Suddenly, there was a pounding on the door. A real pounding.

"Is that your wife?"

"I would be truly surprised," said Owen. "Let me check."

Before he could look through the peephole he heard a familiar voice. "I know you're in there, Owen."

It was Izzy.

Of course, thought Owen.

"Let me in, Owen, or I'm gonna make a real stink."

"Just go home, Izzy," Owen said through the door. "I'll call you later."

"I'm not going anywhere."

"Well, you're not coming in here."

"Let me in or I'll do something bad to your car."

"Jesus, Izzy."

"I'll put rocks in your gas tank, Owen. I will fuck your shit up."

"Calm down, Izzy."

"I just want to talk to you. I swear."

Owen was pretty sure she wasn't joking. He didn't want anything done to his car. He slid the chain off the door and opened it.

Izzy forced her way inside.

"Oh, nice, Owen. Real nice. I wonder how Lucy's gonna feel about this."

"Who's Lucy?" Madison asked.

"Oh, shut up, you little skank," said Izzy.

"Who's Lucy?" Madison asked again. Being called a skank to her face didn't seem to faze her in the least.

"My wife."

Madison turned to Izzy and appeared genuinely perplexed. "Then who are you?"

"I'm his girlfriend," said Izzy. "And you must be the preteen with the freshly waxed undercarriage."

"Excuse me?" Madison said.

"You heard me," said Izzy.

"Where are you getting this stuff, Izzy?" asked Owen.

"Oh, you idiot," Izzy said. "I know everything. I've got you wired."

Madison pulled on her T-shirt and sweatshirt and then headed out the door.

"I'll call you," Owen said.

"Oh no, he won't," said Izzy. "Say your good-byes, sweetheart."

"Whatever, lady," Madison said. "Enjoy the rest of your life."

* * *

"You ginormous shit."

"You told me two days ago that this was temporary," said Owen. "Forget two days ago. We both always knew what this was, Izzy. You're not allowed to act like this."

"I never said that you could humiliate me," she said. "I don't remember signing off on that."

"How is this humiliating you?"

"Oh, come on, Owen. *Come on.*"

"Honestly, I have no idea what you're talking about, Izzy. You're not making any sense. I'm going out to my car now. We can talk about this later after you calm down."

"I'm not gonna calm down!"

"Well, I'm not going to talk to you until you do."

Owen grabbed his belt and his jacket and sort of skipped-slash-ran out to his car while Izzy chased him, hitting him on his back with both of her fists.

"Goddamn it, Owen! Do not run away from me! I can't believe you think this is okay! You owe me more than this, you prick! This is not okay!"

Somehow he managed to get into his car and lock the door.

He couldn't find his keys. *Please don't tell me I left them in the hotel room.* He dug around deep in his jeans pockets but they weren't there. His old barn jacket was draped over his arm, and it had a million different pockets. He started searching through them as fast as he—

Crash!

Izzy was standing by the door of her pickup truck, holding an empty wine bottle up in the air. "Get out of the car, asshole! Get out of the car or I will fuck your car up! I will fuck your life up, Owen! I'm not kidding, I will fuck your whole shitty little fake life up!"

Owen could feel the car key, but it was inside one of those strange pockets-behind-a-pocket that you had to figure out exactly how to get into—

Crash!

Izzy, it turned out, had a lot of empty wine bottles in her truck. Like a conscientious drunk, whenever her recycling bin started to fill up too fast, she tucked a few in the tiny backseat under a black contractor's bag filled with giveaways and then offloaded them at faraway places, shopping-center dumpsters and gas-station garbage cans.

"I'm not discussing this until you are calm," yelled Owen through a cracked window.

Izzy threw the bottle straight at his face. It bounced off the window and exploded on the asphalt.

Keys!

The crazier Izzy got, the calmer Owen got. It happened when he fought with Lucy too, although he and Lucy rarely fought. (They rarely fought! They had a home and a child together! Why were they doing this? *Why am I doing this?*) A rare, completely apoplectic Lucy once told him that having a real fight with him was impossible, because the madder she got, the more he started to sound like a psychiatrist addressing a woman in a straitjacket. It was impossible to get a reaction out of him. And a reaction was clearly what Izzy wanted.

Fortunately, Owen had backed his car into the parking spot, subconsciously setting himself up for a quick getaway. By the time he got the engine started, Izzy was standing directly in front of his car wielding two jumbo bottles of Chilean chardonnay like martial arts weapons. He couldn't move the car without running her over.

He began to slowly ease the car forward, all the while saying soothing things through the crack in the window. Izzy wasn't having any of it. She started banging on the hood with the wine bottles. They were thick, though, and didn't break.

As he finally managed to pull away, Owen yelled out the window, "I'm just letting you calm down! We'll talk about this later, I promise."

She launched one of the wine bottles, and it bounced off the hood of his car, denting it pretty bad.

*   *   *

Owen drove around the back roads of Beekman for a while, collecting his thoughts. He wasn't going to go home or to work, because he was afraid Izzy would track him down and go at him with the wine bottles again. Lucy was in the city seeing Dr. Hubble, their dentist, and Wyatt was with the afternoon sitter, so Owen was free and clear. He'd blocked out the afternoon for Madison, anyway.

He finally parked his car on a small private dirt road that bisected a bigger dirt road, the main dirt road, the historic one that the local dirt-road wingnuts were always going on and on about preserving. Beekman was overrun with dirt roads, and every last one of them was a money pit. Every year, potholes the size of kiddie pools materialized, and tax dollars were siphoned off to fill them in, smooth things down, regrade, and sprinkle them with nonpotable water in order to keep the dust down in the summer. It was a huge waste of money, Owen thought, but that was a position he did not mention in polite company. It was impossible to figure out who was on what side of the big dirt-road fight, and Owen found it was wisest to keep his mouth shut. It was one of those local battles with no end in sight, like the war over the occupancy permit for the Zalinskys' garden shed–turned–home office, which, depending on whom you believed, either did or did not extend two feet over the original footprint.

He stared out his window at some rolling farmland dotted with white houses with screened porches. The leaves had all turned, but he'd been so preoccupied lately he'd barely noticed. It was clear to him he had made a fundamental mistake along the way, but he wasn't quite sure what it was. He really didn't believe Izzy was in love with him. Up until today's wine-bottle-chucking fiasco, she certainly hadn't acted like a woman in love. It's possible he had underestimated his importance to her, but it was just as likely that what her ex-husband Christopher had said to him outside Izzy's house that evening not long ago was true: she was five kinds of crazy. Maybe it was as simple as that.

Should he tell Lucy about it? Did he have a responsibility to let her know what was going on, the turn things had recently taken? He didn't think he did, but he didn't want Lucy to be blindsided by some nutjob either.

Contain it, he thought. *Talk to Izzy, calm her down, figure it out.*

"God, I miss takeout," said Lucy.

She was sitting up in bed with Ben, sharing green chicken curry and *pad see ew.* It was Monday, and she and Ben were having a late lunch. When Ben texted that he had the afternoon free, Lucy arranged for an after-school babysitter and told Owen she was going to the dentist.

"They don't have takeout in Beekman?" Ben asked.

"They don't deliver. Owen and I fight over who has to go pick it up, and by the time we start to eat, it's cold and we're mad at each other."

"Why do you live there?"

"I forget. The air smells good?"

"You've got too much nature up there. It's not healthy."

"I saw a rat on the subway tracks in Grand Central on my way here," said Lucy. "It was as big as a rabbit."

"Yeah, see, that's just the right amount of nature," said Ben.

"I miss eating takeout in bed," said Lucy. "I miss having sex, ordering food, and eating it naked in bed. And drinking out of real wineglasses."

"I'll buy you some wineglasses," said Ben. "That much we can fix."

"We don't use any glass in our house."

"What do you mean?"

"Well, when my son was about two, he would pick up a glass

and ask, 'That's glass?' and if you said yes, he would hurl it to the floor and watch it shatter. He found it unbelievably exciting. Finally I got rid of all of our glasses and replaced them with plastic."

"Would he still do that?"

"Who knows? Probably not. I guess I just haven't been in the mood to find out," said Lucy. "Now he does this thing where whenever he spots a knife on the kitchen counter he picks it up and yells, 'It's *knife time!*'"

"Oh my God."

"Then, if you make the mistake of showing any reaction whatsoever, he runs away from you, brandishing the knife. I almost had a heart attack the first time it happened. He had a twelve-inch chef's knife in his hand and wouldn't stop running around the dining-room table."

"So what do you do?"

"I act like it's no big deal. I get completely relaxed and move super-slowly and say things like 'Wyatt, give Mommy the knife' until I can disarm him. I'd say I'm about two weeks away from throwing away all of our knives," said Lucy. "I'll just stick to soft foods for the next ten years. Plastic wineglasses and soft foods."

After they ate, they made love again, and then Lucy got up and started to get dressed.

"I don't want you to leave."

Lucy was buttoning her blouse, and Ben was in bed, looking at her. "I don't want to leave either. I'm not even supposed to be here today. I told Owen I was going to the dentist."

"I mean I don't want you to leave ever," Ben said. And then he smiled a smile Lucy felt like she would remember for the rest of her life.

The next morning it was raining, and the wind was blowing very hard. The tree branches were whipping around frantically, dropping their leaves the way they did some years, more or less all in a single day. Lucy was packing Wyatt's lunch, daydreaming about Ben, and wondering if the storm meant they would lose power.

"Any cavities?" Owen asked. He was at the table drinking coffee, scrolling through things on his phone.

"What?"

"At the dentist. Yesterday in the city. I thought you went to see Dr. Hubble."

"Yes, actually," said Lucy. She thought fast. "Three. I have to go in next week to get the top two filled, and then the week after for the bottom one."

More Ben, Lucy thought. *I just figured out how to get more Ben.*

"You never get cavities."

"I know. Hubble wanted to know if our water out here has fluoride in it," said Lucy. "Does it?"

"I don't see how it could," said Owen. "It's from the well."

"He said we should get fluoride drops for Wyatt," said Lucy. *My goodness, I've become a good liar.* "Otherwise he's going to end up with a million cavities."

"Isn't fluoride supposed to be bad for you?"

"What do you mean?"

"I mean bad for you. Like microwave ovens and high-voltage power lines."

Lucy looked at her husband and said, "Are you channeling Susan Howard now?"

"Is Susan into that?" asked Owen.

"Yeah. Susan goes nuts about microwaves. She once saw Claire put Tupperware into a microwave and she lectured us about breast cancer for two hours," said Lucy. "And that's when Susan stopped being invited to ladies' night."

The Beekman Café was across from the elementary school and right next to St. Andrews, an old Episcopal church with a picturesque graveyard. The little square—made up of the school, the church, the café, and a run-down, two-pump gas station—was about two miles from downtown Beekman in an area otherwise occupied by graceful old houses with mature gardens tucked behind stone fences. Every few years, a shiny-eyed newcomer would come up with plans to turn the humble café into a swank wine bar or tapas restaurant, only to be har-rumphed into silence at local planning-board meetings. And Lucy had to admit, part of what made Beekman appealing was that it was unlikely to appeal to the sort of people who couldn't imagine living more than a five-minute walk from an overpriced glass of pinot noir.

Wyatt had missed the bus that morning—it was a sock-related meltdown, the specifics of which Lucy never did figure out, but the fifth pair he tried on were apparently okay—so Lucy had to drop him off at school. It was still raining hard but the air was strangely warm, and it made Lucy feel like she might have a fever. She'd decided to put off her plan to get the winter clothes down from the attic and grab a cup of coffee in-stead. She pulled her car into the gravel parking lot in front of the Beekman Café, soaked her left Merrell in a puddle, and hurried inside.

Susan, Claire, and Sunny Bang were sitting together at a small round table, and they waved her over the minute she walked through the door.

"Lucy! We're doing a big thing at St. Andrews. The Blessing of the Animals. You guys have to come," said Claire, a mug of cappuccino curdling in front of her.

"We don't go to church," said Lucy. "We're not religious."

"This is not going to be religious," said Susan.

"It's gonna be a little bit religious," Claire corrected Susan. "It's at a church, and they're going to be blessed."

"It's an ecumenical blessing," said Susan. "It's like me saying, 'Claire, I bless you.' Is that religious?"

"If we were standing in front of the altar inside a church and you were a priest? Yes, that would be religious. I don't care. I want Louisa and Blake to start going to church anyway. I just can't get Edmund out of bed on Sundays to go."

"We're trying to raise awareness about the unresolved employment situation of Colleen Lowell," Susan said. "The men are all going to wear skirts as a show of solidarity."

"Let me grab a cup of coffee," Lucy said. "Then you can tell me all about it."

"The kids are going to walk down the aisle in a big procession, with their pets, and then Reverend Elsbith is going to bless them. The animals, and the kids too. Oh, and they're all going to be wearing only white," said Susan.

"The animals?" asked Lucy.

"The kids. We're not dressing up the animals," said Susan. "Although maybe we could put garlands around their necks or something."

"I'm not making any fucking garlands," said Sunny Bang.

"I'll make them," said Claire. "I like doing that sort of thing."

"Jesus," Sunny Bang said under her breath.

"Sunny, I'm not a moron because I like making garlands," said Claire.

"I did not say you were a moron, Claire."

"I think garlands would be nice," said Susan. "I'm going to write that down. Claire, garlands."

"Wyatt doesn't have white clothes," said Lucy. "At least, not any white pants. That much I know."

"He can borrow Louisa's white cords," said Claire.

"No, he can't," said Sunny Bang. "Tobias is wearing those cords."

"What about tights?" said Claire. "I've got a ton of Louisa's old white tights from ballet. I'm sure they'd fit Wyatt."

Lucy let herself imagine the scene, trying to get Wyatt to put on Louisa's white tights. *These women have no idea what I'm dealing with,* Lucy thought. *They have such small problems, they need to invent them.*

Lucy made a semi-apologetic face and said, "I can't really see Wyatt agreeing to put on tights."

"Forget the white clothes," Susan said. "Wyatt can wear whatever he's comfortable in. We're looking for participation, not perfection."

Claire got a look on her face. Claire was generally looking for perfection.

"I think we might have to skip the whole thing, actually," said Lucy. "Wyatt doesn't have a pet and I don't want him to feel left out."

"You can borrow the Genslers' turtle!" said Susan. "He doesn't really walk, but Wyatt can pull him in a wagon or something."

"Why aren't the Genslers bringing their own turtle?" asked Sunny Bang.

"Because they're Jewish," Susan explained. "They'll let the turtle participate for the good of the town, but they don't want their kids to go to the church."

"Do you have a wagon you could decorate?" Claire asked Lucy.

"Ah, no," said Lucy.

"I'll loan you ours," said Claire. "I'll drop it off this afternoon. And I'll put in a pair of white tights, just in case you get inspired."

"You'll have to arrange with the Genslers to pick up the turtle. He weighs about fifty pounds, but apparently he's very friendly," Susan said. She grabbed her phone. "I'm sending you their contact info right now. There. Done and dusted."

Lucy could feel the situation slipping away from her. She thought fast.

"You know what?" said Lucy. "I wasn't thinking. Wyatt will want to bring his goldfish. Someone else can have the Genslers' turtle."

"Are you sure?" said Susan. "The turtle would be pretty fun."

"Yeah, it sounds fun," said Lucy. "But Wyatt will want his fish to get the blessing. He's really into his fish."

There was a bottle of Dom Pérignon on the Allens' kitchen counter, gift-wrapped rather garishly in crispy green see-through plastic. Gordon glanced at the card. It was from a local property developer who was grateful he had taken care of the transvestite problem in the elementary school. Gordon *had* taken care of it. Gordon had arranged for the teacher to be placed on paid leave until another school could be coaxed into taking him. It had been several weeks, though, and the lady-man teacher still didn't have a job, and before long the local taxpayers were going to feel the pinch.

Gordon rubbed the starched white bow between his thumb and index finger. It made a zippy, almost crunchy sound like, well, like nothing Gordon had ever heard before.

He touched the plastic wrap, oh so gently, with just the tips of his fingers. It was exceptionally, terrifically, unbelievably crinkly.

Simka would love this, Gordon thought. *Simka would go nuts for this.*

He tucked the bottle under his arm and headed up to his study.

Seventeen

The relatively large size of the human male's testicles is often cited as proof that men are evolutionarily hard-wired for promiscuity. But it is perhaps more indicative of this: If prehistoric man, while off on a hunt, could trust his partner to keep her legs together, he wouldn't have needed all of that excess sperm to do battle inside her when he got back.

—Constance Waverly

You know the 'young' thing presses all my buttons."

After about twelve hundred texts, Owen had finally agreed to meet Izzy at her house to talk. Just to talk. They were sitting at her kitchen table, somewhat formally. Owen was drinking tea, with his legs crossed, balancing the teacup on the inside of his left ankle. Izzy was deep into her wine and possibly still drunk from the night before.

"The 'young' thing?"

"You leaving me for a younger woman," said Izzy.

"I didn't leave you for a younger woman."

"Semantics. You know what I'm talking about. And, by the way, that girl is not twenty-six."

Owen had figured out that Izzy had tapped into his communication systems. Text for sure, e-mail probably, possibly even his phone. He knew it and he knew that she knew that he knew it. He didn't see the point of bringing it up.

"How old do you think she is?"

"Nineteen," said Izzy.

"There's no way Madison is only nineteen," said Owen.

"She's *nineteen,* Owen. I found her on Facebook."

Owen's blood ran cold. Holy shit. *Holy shit! Nineteen?*

"Are you kidding me? Please tell me you're fucking with me."

"I'm not. You big perv."

"I did not know she was nineteen," said Owen. "I would never have *touched* her if I knew she was only nineteen."

"Of course you would have," said Izzy. "Any man would have."

"Not me. Never. Not ever."

"Listen, Owen, I get it. It would be easier if I didn't get it, if I could be one of those deluded women who think, *Why would anyone want to be with someone that young? What would you talk about? What would you have in common?* But I used to be that girl. Men went *crazy* for me."

"Men still go crazy for you," said Owen.

"Not in the same way." She sighed a big sigh. "Something fundamental has changed. I was so young and so beautiful."

"You're still beautiful, Izzy."

"But I used to be *beautiful*," said Izzy. "And it is extremely hard to be a woman who used to be beautiful. You cannot begin to understand it."

"You're hardly past being beautiful, Izzy. You're only thirty-four."

"I'm thirty-eight."

"So? Who cares?"

"I'm forty-two."

"You're forty-two?"

"Yeah," she said. "I lie about my age."

"You look amazing. Seriously, Jesus, Izzy, you look great."

"For my age, you mean. I look great for my age. That's the best I'll get for the rest of my life."

"You look great for any age," said Owen. "And plenty of men will go crazy for you for a very long time to come."

"But not you anymore," said Izzy.

"That's not true. But you have to get control of yourself," said Owen. "What happened yesterday is not acceptable behavior."

"I know. I got a little crazy. It won't happen again."

"Did you go see your doctor?"

"Not yet," said Izzy. "I had an appointment but I had to cancel it."

"I'm not even going to discuss having sex with you again until you see your gynecologist. I can't keep waking up in the middle of the night worrying about having a child with you. I'm putting my foot down on this one, Izzy."

"Okay." She sighed. "I'll go."

Owen had no intention of sleeping with Izzy again. Never, ever, ever. Never, ever, *ever!* But he would cross that particular bridge when he came to it.

So now Owen was lying to Lucy and lying to Izzy. Well, he wasn't exactly lying to Lucy, but he had this whole entire part of his life he couldn't talk to her about, and that felt like lying. She'd asked about the dent in the hood of the car and he'd told her it was the work of a tree branch during the storm. Even though it was the agreement they'd made, it felt strange to have all of this life in his life he couldn't talk about with her. He was used to telling Lucy everything—almost everything, anyway, 85 percent of everything—and it was only now, now that he had a completely separate life, that he realized how much he missed it.

He was ready for it all to end. As far as he was concerned, the Arrangement had run its course. He'd dropped almost twenty pounds, he felt happier with his life—his real life, his Lucy-and-Wyatt life—than he had in a long time. What he had was better than what was out there for him. He did not want to have sex in seedy motels with emotionally damaged nineteen-year-olds. He was not that guy. He didn't want to be that guy. Growing up meant saying no to some things. Life was a series of losses, some big and some small, and trying to imagine it was something else was folly.

It had actually been interesting, this whole thing. Would he recommend it? If, say, a friend of his confessed to him, out on the deck late at night over a glass of bourbon, that his marriage had gone stale, that he was feeling the icy hand of mortality gripping his shoulder, that he had started to wonder if this was all there was, would Owen tell him what he and Lucy had done? He thought about that a lot lately. Would he suggest that other couples—couples who had hit "the hump," as he liked to think of it—would he tell them to try this on for size? Try it the way he and Lucy had, with a list of rules and a cut-off date, with a steel foundation of "our family comes first and we're never getting divorced"? With an understanding that this was just a quick, temporary time-out from the boring, middle-aged, soul-killing part of married life?

That was an interesting question.

He was able to see the potential land mines. What if he had gotten addicted to the Madisons of this world? Not the nineteen-year-olds but the vast pool of millennial women who seemed to have evolved past the rest of humanity in their approach to sex so that having sex with them was like being suspended in the middle of your dirtiest dream, a dream where you're allowed to do anything you want, a dream where you never hear the word *no*.

And Izzy. Well, Izzy had turned out to be a bit of a wild card, but, and this was the important part, *he had handled it*. He had let her vent at the motel, he'd let her fly her crazy flag with her twelve hundred texts—most of them were just long strings of threatening emoticons, bombs and knives and shotguns and dead people—and then he'd let her connect and feel understood and cared for over tea at her house. Just talking to Izzy honestly about her fears about aging was probably more of a genuine connection than she'd had with anyone in years. That, plus being calm and cool when she showed up at the motel, using his Wyatt-whispering skills, the blanket of other-worldly calm that he wrapped around himself whenever Wyatt launched into one of his freak-outs—the combination of the two were like cutting just the right wire in a mixed-up jumble and managing to defuse a nuclear bomb. If he had met Izzy when he was twenty-five, God knows what would have happened. He'd be either dead or married to her.

But with age came wisdom. He was much more able to negotiate the female psyche at this point, undoubtedly because he'd been with Lucy for so long. And all of Izzy's dire warnings—that this was just a divorce in slow motion—had turned out not to be true. In fact, he could feel that he was going to be more, well, *present* in his marriage from here on out.

And, in the end, what was so wrong about discovering an unconventional way to realize that you really, really love your wife? Wouldn't a lot of women, if they knew that this would be the outcome, be willing to go ahead and loosen the shackles on their husbands for a few short months? Owen was pretty sure they would.

He was proud of himself. He was proud of himself, and proud of Lucy, and proud of their marriage.

He decided he would bring up the subject with Lucy when he got home from work. Tell her he wanted to wrap it up, shut it down, pull the plug. The Arrangement had worked, better, really, than he'd expected, but Owen was ready to call it a day.

❧

"I have to bring Fang to church on Sunday," said Rocco.

"And why is that?" asked Gordon. He was reading Drudge on his iPad, something damning about Chelsea Clinton's little kid.

"Everyone is supposed to bring their pets to church. They're going to walk down the aisle. There's going to be horses and donkeys and a real live camel."

"What for?" asked Kelly.

"To be baptized by the priest," said Rocco.

"They're baptizing animals now?" Gordon turned to Kelly and asked, "Is that some sort of Catholic thing?"

"How should I know?" said Kelly.

"I thought you were raised Catholic."

Kelly froze, and then a look of complete disgust came over her face. "Are you being freakin'-the-freak serious right now, Gordon?"

Gordon realized he was in trouble. He did appreciate Kelly's use of the *freaks* in front of Rocco. He knew that took restraint on her part. Considerable restraint.

"Do you pay any attention to anything I say?" she asked him. "Anything? Ever?"

"Honestly, Kelly, I thought you said that once," said Gordon. "I have a lot of things I have to keep track of."

"I know, I know," said Kelly. "You're a very important man."

Rocco just watched as his parents talked, his head moving like he was at a tennis match, and when he found his opening he said, "We all have to go to church together, as a family, and we have to bring a pet."

"I can't go to church, Rocco," said Gordon. "I've got too much work to do."

"Maria can take you like she usually does, sweetie," said Kelly. "I have too much to do around here."

"Can I bring Fang?"

"Of course," said Gordon, going back to the baby Clinton story. "Just make sure to keep him on the leash."

❧

Owen didn't have a chance to talk to Lucy until they were getting into bed.

"I've been thinking," he started.

Lucy didn't say anything; she just reached for the tube of hand cream on her nightstand and squirted some into her hand.

"I think I'd like to stop it. The thing. The Arrangement thing."

"Really," said Lucy. "What brought this on?"

"Nothing. Just, you know." He pulled off his T-shirt and threw it across the room, missing the hamper. "Quit while we're ahead."

"This is what we agreed we wouldn't do," said Lucy. She

started rubbing lotion onto her elbows in a matter-of-fact, wifely way. "This is why we made the rules, Owen, so we wouldn't have to have conversations like this."

"I know, but I thought you might want to know that I'm ready to stop it."

"Well, I think we should stick to what we agreed to. Six months. That was pretty much the point of this whole thing."

Lucy wiped the lotion off her palms and popped open her laptop. She started clicking around the way she did every night, searching for a podcast that would lull her to sleep.

Owen got into bed and rolled onto his side and stared at the gray wall next to the bed.

What the hell? he thought. *What the fucking hell just happened?*

Eighteen

It's like my favorite T-shirt says: "No mud, no lotus."

—Constance Waverly
WaverlyRadio podcast #11

See that little kid right there?"

Sunny Bang gestured toward a little boy who was walking across the church parking lot toting a guinea pig in a plastic cage.

"Yeah?" said Lucy.

"Dick."

Sunny and Lucy were standing outside St. Andrews, watching as a few cars pulled in from the main road. The bulk of the traffic was being diverted to the school parking lot across the street by a local cop who was dressed for church except for a reflective orange vest. It was the Blessing of the Animals day, and it was starting to look like just about all of the good people of Beekman were going to show up for it.

"Total dick," Sunny said again.

"Sunny," said Lucy. "He's, like, four."

"You can tell by four," said Sunny.

The cop waved Edmund Chase's pickup truck into the church parking lot, undoubtedly because it was towing a horse trailer. Apparently, Claire had tracked down something big.

Lucy and Sunny watched as Edmund started to open the back of the trailer. A scraggly brown llama poked its head out the window and made a series of frantic, disturbing, high-pitched squawks, like a bagful of turkeys being hit with a baseball bat.

"Don't worry," Claire called out to nobody in particular. "The farmer told me he just does that when he's nervous."

Claire tried to coax the llama out of the trailer and down the ramp, finally pulling hard on a rope attached to its harness.

Just then, the Mulligan boys walked by, all three of them wearing identical button-down white oxford shirts over what had to be some of Louisa Chase's surplus white ballet tights.

Sunny Bang took in the scene and then said to Lucy in that way of hers, that way that sounded like she was taking a long, weary drag on her fourth cigarette of the hour, "Oh, this I can't miss."

❧

Lucy's Sunday morning had not started out well.

"I want to bring the chickens," said Wyatt.

"We're bringing Goldie," said Lucy. Wyatt had won Goldie at the Dutchess County fair. Lucy had expected it to die in two days, which was about the amount of bandwidth she had available for a fish at the time. It was two years later, and Goldie was still alive, swimming around in a murky old ten-gallon fish tank that was cleaned basically never. "Goldie wants to come. You can carry the bag."

"I want to bring the chickens!"

"We can't bring the chickens, Wyatt."

"I want to bring the chickens!" He slumped to the ground and butted his head against the bottom step of the staircase as hard as he could. Lucy grabbed him and wrapped her arms around him and held him to keep him from hitting his head again. He started to writhe, trying to get free.

"I want to bring the chickens!"

"We can't bring the chickens," said Lucy. "We've got too many chickens."

"I want to bring the chickens!"

"Okay, we can bring one chicken," said Lucy. "It can bring the blessing back to the rest of the flock."

"Five!"

"The priest will allow you to bring only one chicken," said Lucy. "It's the rule."

"Five!"

"One, Wyatt. One is all we can bring. It's the rule. We have to follow the rules."

"Five!" He arched his back and spit in Lucy's face.

"No spitting, Wyatt," said Lucy. "That hurts my feelings."

He spit at her again.

Owen walked down the stairs. He'd heard all of it, of course. It was impossible to miss.

"Hey, buddy," Owen said. "How about three chickens?"

Wyatt instantly relaxed. He stopped arching his back, he stopped spitting, even his face went from red back to normal, seemingly on a dime. He looked up at his dad and said, "Okay."

Lucy looked at Owen like she wanted to strangle him. "How are we going to get three chickens to the church and then down the aisle to be blessed?"

"I don't know." He shrugged.

"They can't just walk around, Owen," said Lucy. "There's going to be a million animals inside that place. It's going to be a madhouse."

"Wyatt and I will figure it out, right, Wyatt?" said Owen. "It can be like a science project."

Susan Howard was peeking out from the window in the church tower, having a moment.

She'd arrived at the church before seven to get everything arranged, had set out the programs she'd had printed up, put out the brand-new guest book she'd purchased for the event so they could have a record of who attended so the new members' committee could follow up with a phone call and a visit. The day promised to be unseasonably warm, which Susan thought was nice, a pop of Indian summer late in October after two and a half weeks of nonstop rain. It would be enough to coax some of the fence-sitters out of their homes, she thought. Snow was just around the corner.

Susan liked being a deacon at St. Andrews—she enjoyed teaching Sunday school, once she got the hang of it, and she liked having a base from which to launch her rockets of community enlightenment—but there was no getting around the fact that St. Andrews attracted a certain sort of person. A certain sort of family, actually.

Not the Jesus freaks, to be sure. The true believers went to Sunny Valley Community Church, which was a half-hour drive away and had an active youth group that drew families from all over. The people who ended up at St. Andrews weren't the believers, they were the behavers. Decent people who'd been forced to go to church as kids and now did the same to their offspring. Parents who viewed attending church as a way to uphold a certain kind of conventionality, a clean-your-plate-obey-your-parents-write-your-thank-you-notes mentality. Susan and Rowan Howard's kids didn't clean their plates, obey their parents, or write thank-you notes, and Susan was proud of those facts. When her daughter, Charlotte, showed a people-pleasing, girlish glee in filling out her Common Core worksheets, writing her numbers and letters neatly *inside the boxes,* Susan nearly pulled her out of Beekman's public school. She would have, too, if she and Rowan had had the money for private school—something Waldorf-y, filled with Weston Price moms still breastfeeding their six-year-olds—but they didn't. The only thing Susan's children lacked were rich grandparents.

Susan had been elected deacon of St. Andrews two years earlier. She chaired meetings of the garden committee—where five old ladies tangled with two moms fresh from Brooklyn over whether or not to pull out all of the nonnative species in the church gardens—and she policed the Friday-night sorting party for the annual tag sale, cracking down on women who seemed to think that volunteering to organize the donated items was their chance to cart off all the best stuff. No one could say that Susan Howard didn't pull her weight. She did her dharma to the staid, traditional God of St. Andrews, and she didn't complain.

But today's service was going to be different. It was progressive, it was community focused, it was decidedly non-speciesist. It was everything Susan wanted St. Andrews to be. She felt a little like she imagined a new pope must feel, the thrill of shaking up an ancient institution from the inside, from a position of power, but with humility and selflessness and grace.

Susan snapped out of her reverie and hurried down the stone steps. Rowan and the kids and the three baby goats would be arriving any minute.

It was time for her to pass out some skirts.

Lucy had solved the kids-in-white problem by putting Wyatt in one of Owen's white T-shirts, which drooped down nearly to his knees. Wyatt wouldn't even think about putting on the tights, and he refused to wear a belt, but he was all in white, at least, except for his light-up Spider-Man sneakers. He looked like a member of a doomsday cult.

Claire's wagon would have come in handy, Lucy found herself thinking as she watched Owen duct-tape Wyatt's rolling belly board to the bottom of a big cardboard box. Wyatt had traced three circles on the top of the box and looked on with hand-flapping excitement as Owen cut them out with a big serrated knife. ("It's *knife time!*") Lucy found some old rope in the garage, and Owen taped it all together so that Wyatt could walk in front of the box and pull it along behind him with, ideally, the chickens' heads poking out of the holes in the top. Lucy didn't think they'd pop their heads out of the box, but Owen and Wyatt were convinced they'd want to check out the excitement.

When they got to the church, Owen stuck the box of chickens next to a tombstone and then chased Wyatt around the graveyard for a bit. When they came back over to Lucy, their legs were splattered with mud.

"By the time I noticed the mud, it was too late, and he was off and running," Owen explained. "We've still got that old beach towel in the back of the car. I thought it was best for him to burn off some energy before all that sitting quietly inside a church."

"Fair enough," said Lucy.

Susan Howard walked over carrying a pile of skirts.

"Owen, the men are wearing skirts during the service as a show of solidarity with Colleen Lowell," she said.

"I'm not going to wear a skirt, Susan," said Owen.

"Please. For me. Just run into the bathroom and slip it on."

"Not gonna happen, Susan."

"You can wear it over your pants if you want. I won't object."

"I'll pass."

"Lucy?" Susan looked at Lucy with that fierce intenseness of hers, the intensity that made the mommies of Beekman move mountains on her behalf.

"I can't make my husband wear a skirt, Susan. That's not how our marriage works."

Susan sniffed the wind and headed off in search of her next prospect.

Claire had tied the llama to a lamppost and she was eyeballing the other animals, trying to see what sort of lineup would be the most dramatic, when she noticed the bees.

"Bees, Blake!" Claire shrieked. "Blake! Bees! *Bees!*"

Blake froze. Then he burst into tears.

"Get. Inside. The. Church!" Claire screamed. The llama started its battered-turkey wail again. "Walk slowly! Slowly,

Blake! I've got the EpiPens." She turned to her husband and said, "You need to go in there and sit with him. I've got to watch the llama."

"He's not going to want to stay inside when all the fun is out here," Edmund pointed out.

"Yeah, well, what do we do about the *bees*, Edmund? Have you noticed there are at least a million bees around here?" Claire said. "Do you want to spend the night with him in the ICU or shall I?"

"I'll keep him in the church," said Edmund. "Can I have your phone so he can play something on it?"

"Why can't you use yours?"

"I need mine," said Edmund.

"Right. To play something on," said Claire. She took her phone out of her bag. "Here. Take it."

Andrew Callahan, who had overheard the entire thing, said to Claire, "Those are Gordon Allen's bees."

"What?" asked Claire. "What are you talking about?"

"Gordon Allen put half a million honeybees on his land so he could qualify for an agricultural tax exemption. Those bees cost the town of Beekman tens of thousands of dollars in property taxes each year."

"Are you serious?" said Claire.

"It's in the town tax rolls," said Andrew. "They're public record."

"My son can die of a bee sting," said Claire. "I don't want half a million unnecessary bees around here because a fucking billionaire doesn't want to pay his fair share of the taxes."

"Well, you could sue him if your kid got stung."

Claire cocked her head and looked at Andrew with a plastered-on smile. "You mean if my child were dead? I could sue Gordon Allen? Does that sound like a good outcome to you?"

Susan walked over and said to Claire, "I just talked to Edmund. He says he won't wear a skirt."

Claire sighed a big wifely sigh. "Oh, just hand it to me," she said. "Keep an eye on the llama. I'll take care of it."

Between Claire's frantic bee freak-out, which sent at least three toddlers wailing into their moms' arms, and the Larkin twins screaming that they wanted to ride "the stupid pony or whatever it is" — not to mention the sullen, hungover husbands who exchanged grim glances to acknowledge they'd normally be teeing off on the back nine and cracking open their fifth IPA beer on any other Sunday as beautiful as this one was shaping up to be — the event was starting to look like a fiasco.

But just then, the opening chords of Bach's "Air on the G String" floated up from the church organ, out through the open stained-glass windows, and up through the trees, piercing the achingly blue sky. It was a piece of music that never failed to reach deep inside Lucy and evoke what she thought of as the purest, best part of herself. The fact that this sublime perfection was being played by the frumpy, never-married church organist Evelyn Bullard somehow added to Lucy's moment of gratitude.

The music was the signal for the adults to file into the church. Lucy and Owen got Wyatt and his box of chickens settled in his place in line and then took a seat on the aisle as close to the front as possible. The Reverend Elsbith stood at the altar and got things rolling as quickly as she could, without so much as an opening prayer, acknowledging that there was a long line of children and animals outside the church waiting to be blessed. Still, she invited Colleen and Arlen Lowell to come up and stand with her at the front of the church, "so the children can witness what it means to be an inclusive and welcoming community." Colleen and Arlen were clearly surprised, but pleased, and they walked to the altar together, holding hands.

Local supermom Gloria Mulligan had commandeered the Genslers' Jewish turtle for her triplets to pull in the procession, and she'd covered a Radio Flyer wagon so densely with home-made white-tissue-paper flowers you could barely tell it was actually red. It took at least two Mulligan boys to pull the fifty-pound reptile, so whichever one was left out walked alongside for a few steps and then slugged his nearest brother and took his turn pulling the wagon. Then came a line of sweet girls wearing white dresses and holding cats, and a redhead who was carrying a birdcage with two chattering parakeets. Terrence Long was next, wearing a white tuxedo and carrying a glass bowl housing what was surely the only surviving member of last year's second-grade nature-studies unit on crayfish. Tobias Bang shuffled along behind Terrence, palpably bored, carrying a nearly dead garter snake he'd found in his backyard four days earlier and stuck in a thirty-two-ounce mason jar just for this occasion. Then came the four-year-old dick with the guinea pig, which was out of its cage, tucked under the dick kid's arm like a furry football.

When Wyatt appeared at the end of the aisle, holding the rope, pulling his chickens behind him, Lucy found herself not merely teary, but on the brink of weeping. She took Owen's hand and squeezed it. Wyatt was walking on his tiptoes, with his eyes on the ground, completely focused on the task. The chickens weren't popping their heads out of the holes in the box as planned, but still, Wyatt was participating. *Just like a normal kid*, Lucy thought. *Exactly like all the other kids.*

Brannon Anderson was trailing along several feet behind Wyatt with his family's large yet gentle Italian Spinone hound by his side. Then came the three Howard kids, each with a baby Nubian goat that Susan had wrangled, not without difficulty, from Beekman's famous local goat-cheese lady/part-time chanteuse. Then came Rocco Allen, Gordon Allen's kid, with a large Doberman on one of those retractable leashes. A few more kids with dogs were clustered in the back of the church, waiting their turn, and Claire and Blake and the llama were tucked in the vestibule, clearly meant to be the big finish.

Wyatt had made it about halfway up the aisle when Cacciatore popped her head out of one of the holes and started to cluck. Cacciatore was a buff Polish chicken, and the elaborate feathers sticking out of the top of her head made her look like Kate Middleton at Ascot. Cacciatore clucked some more, and Wyatt looked back at his wheelie-cardboard-box contraption and smiled; the chicken-head holes worked! Wyatt stopped walking altogether, and Charlotte Howard's baby goat butted its head into the cardboard box and bleated while the rest of the procession came to a temporary halt.

Before anyone knew what was happening, the church echoed with the high-pitched *zip!* of a retractable dog leash rapidly unspooling. Rocco Allen's Doberman lunged past the three baby goats and the Italian hound and the startled children, pounced on top of the cardboard box, and set about shredding it with his nails and teeth.

The next few minutes were more or less a blur. Rocco dropped his end of Fang's leash and jumped on top of a pew near the back of the church, and the plastic part skipped halfway down the slate aisle, clicking and clacking as it quickly respooled itself. The goats froze, startled by either the dog attacking the chickens or the surprisingly loud plastic-on-slate clacking noise, and then ran in different directions through the pews, tripping over the feet of the stunned parishioners. "Grab the leash!" someone yelled, but no one was brave enough to try. Sunny Bang darted over and scooped up Wyatt, and the Howard kids ran down the aisle, away from the dog and the box.

Kiev and Cacciatore were both Polish chickens, which meant they could, in a pinch, fly about twelve feet in the air, which was what Kiev immediately did. Fang got a mouthful of Cacciatore's tail feathers and just enough flesh to draw blood before Cacciatore broke free and shot up into the air, flapping over the heads of the shrieking congregants. Fat Black, however, was an Australorp, a breed known for its large size and inability to fly. Fang sank his teeth into Fat Black's neck and shook her back and forth for what felt like an eternity, blood and feathers flying. Louisa of the many white tights had let go of her cat—actually, pretty much all of the girls had let go of their cats—and a few of them started clawing their way up the church's rustic burlap banners with the words *Spirit* and *Hope* and *Community* spelled out in green felt letters. Claire struggled to keep the llama under control, but it broke free and galloped up the center aisle, skirting the bloody chicken melee, then turned left at the altar, ran down the side aisle, raced past a stunned Claire, and shot out the main door.

Screams of kids and parents—it was hard to tell which—filled the church. Two husbands who were volunteer firefighters began evacuation procedures, leading the blood-spattered throng out through the wide doors.

Brannon Anderson had let go of his family's sixteen-hundred-dollar purebred hound and was jumping up and down with excitement, soaking in everything and yelling at the top of his lungs, "This is fucked up! This is so fucked up!"

Susan Howard stalked past him and said, "Oh, shut up, you little shit."

Lucy found Owen and Wyatt outside next to the car. Someone must have called 911 because a police car, sirens blaring, pulled into the parking lot. Meanwhile, Claire was frantically rushing up to each person, grabbing both arms, and yelling, "Have you seen the llama? Where is the fucking llama!" Apparently the police officers mistook Claire for an emotionally disturbed person—and the likely cause of the 911 call—because they were approaching her slowly from behind. Lucy noticed one of the officers had her hand on her Taser.

Just then the source of Claire's hysteria appeared, trotting madly toward the church graveyard, clearly panicked and making a shrill and very loud sound, louder even than the earlier bag-of-turkeys sound.

"Don't shoot it!" yelled Claire, having become aware of the police officers. "Don't you fucking shoot! It's borrowed!"

Claire charged into the graveyard, which caused the llama to bolt through a flower bed and run straight into the two-hundred-and-seventy-year-old headstone of the town's founder, Nelson Orion Beekman, cracking it in two.

"Fat Black is extinct!"

Wyatt was in the kitchen, flapping his hands frantically and pacing from one of his plastic grass sensory mats to the other, wearing a bloody T-shirt that hung down past his knees. If anyone had caught a glimpse of him, he would have been carted off by child protective services immediately.

"I watched him get killed!"

"Let me take your shirt off, buddy," said Owen.

"It's got blood all over it!"

"Yes," said Owen. "Yes, indeed, it does."

"My shirt is covered in *Fat Black's blood!*"

"Yes, let's take it off and I'll put it in the wash," said Lucy. She wasn't going to wash it, she was going to throw it in the trash immediately, but she didn't need to tell Wyatt that. He might protest. Wyatt protested the oddest things. "I'm really, really sorry you had to see that, Wyatt."

"I watched Fat Black get murdered! At church!"

"It was very sad. Are you feeling sad?"

"There was blood everywhere!"

"I'm gonna pull this shirt off over your head right now, buddy," said Owen. "It might feel a little sticky."

"It's sticky with blood!"

"Are you feeling sad, sweet boy?" said Lucy. "It's okay to feel sad, buddy. It's okay to feel sad about Fat Black."

"Fat Black is extinct!"

"Let's get you into the bathtub," said Lucy.

"No bath! No bath! I don't want to take a bath!"

Owen and Lucy looked at each other. It was like a million moments they'd had together with Wyatt and yet completely, utterly unique.

"Wyatt, you've got blood all over you," said Lucy. "You have to take a bath to wash it off. I'm going to take you upstairs."

And with that, Wyatt was off. He bolted into the playroom, screaming and now crying too, "No bath! No bath! I don't *like* baths! I don't *like* baths!"

"You do like baths, Wyatt. You love baths," said Lucy.

"I hate baths! I hate baths! I don't want to take a bath!"

"You can play with your bath guys. We'll just go play with your bath guys," Lucy said. Then she turned to Owen and said, "I can't handle this. He's covered in blood. It's going to get all over the house."

Owen walked calmly into the living room. "You don't have to take a bath, Wyatt. It's your choice. But I was thinking something."

"What?"

"What if I do something super-silly," said Owen.

"Like what?"

"What if I get into the bathtub with you with *all of my clothes still on!*"

Wyatt stopped running around the couch and looked at his dad.

"*All* of your clothes on?" Wyatt asked, flapping his hands.

"Yes, all of them."

"*All* of your clothes on?" He flapped harder, faster, higher.

"Yes," said Owen. "But only if you go take a bath with me. I'll only do it if you're in the bath with me."

Wyatt looked at his dad, seriously weighing this intriguing offer. "I'll go start the water!" he finally said, and he darted up the stairs.

Owen took his wallet out of his back pocket and pulled off his suede belt. He took his phone and spare change and his watch and heaped everything on the kitchen counter and then followed Wyatt upstairs.

"Thank you," Lucy said.

"It's what I do," said Owen, smiling back at her. "It's what we both do."

My husband is pretty great, thought Lucy, for the first time in a long time. There weren't a lot of men who could handle Wyatt. Certainly not many who could do it as kindly and creatively as Owen did. There was a statistic that floated around on the message boards online, about how many parents of special-needs kids end up divorced, and the percentage was truly staggering. Lucy didn't know if it was fair to blame it on the kids' fathers being assholes, but in her gut, well, she thought it was probably true. *Owen is sort of amazing,* Lucy thought. *So why did I let myself fall in love with somebody else?*

Gordon was upstairs in his office, lying on the couch with his eyes closed. He was listening to a live police-radio stream from his laptop. It was his newest hobby.

Gordon had to use a considerable amount of self-control to reserve his Simka-viewing for late nights only, during those all-too-frequent times when he couldn't fall asleep. He'd read about the police-radio feeds and was trying to use them as a substitute, and while they didn't give him goose bumps—quite the opposite, really—they were pretty interesting. He liked to listen to Phoenix and Chicago, depending on what sort of people he was in the mood to hear getting arrested. Sometimes he'd mix it up and listen to Los Angeles. Still, it was weak methadone compared to the heroin that was Simka.

Rocco grabbed his black-socked foot and squeezed it.

"What?" Gordon said. He pulled off his earphones.

"Maria wants to talk to someone."

"Go get your mom."

"Mom said she doesn't want to be disturbed."

"Well, I don't want to be disturbed either," said Gordon. He put his earphones back on. "Tell Maria your mother will talk to her later."

"Okay," said Rocco.

Rocco just stood at the foot of the couch, looking at his father.

"Fang ate a chicken."

Gordon pulled off his earphones again. "What?"

"Fang ate a chicken inside the church."

"Inside the—why was Fang inside a church?"

"You told me I could bring him to get baptized, remember?"

"Jesus Christ."

"That's a swear, Dad," said Rocco. "If it's not at church, it's a swear."

Gordon walked down the main staircase and found Maria standing in the entry hall and wringing her hands. The front door was wide open, and Fang was outside, tied to the antique lawn jockey Gordon had been given a few years back by a prominent senator from Alabama. Fang was hunched over and retching.

"Ees not a good dog," Maria said when she saw Gordon. "I tol' Miss Kelly, I can' control the dog."

"You told her you can or you can't?"

"I can' no. I can' no," said Maria, shaking her head emphatically. "So, no my faul'."

Gordon rubbed his forehead with his hand. "So, let me get this straight. Fang ate somebody's chicken?"

"Eet attack, Mr. Allen. Eet *attack* the chicken."

"Whose chicken was it?"

"A leetle boy. Kind of a"—and here Maria did some sort of spastic flapping movements with her hands to indicate… what? A disability of some sort? Epilepsy? Gordon couldn't really understand—"a boy weet som pro'lems. You know, som reel pro'lems."

Oh, wonderful, Gordon thought. *This is just great.*

It was dark before Susan was able to leave St. Andrews, and she was both physically and emotionally exhausted. She and Evelyn Bullard and a handful of old ladies from the garden committee had spent the afternoon cleaning up the feathers and the blood, along with some dog diarrhea and what Susan was convinced was a llama shit. The llama shit was on the brand-new red carpet in the vestibule, right in plain sight, an enormous dump that Claire had clearly ignored and left for someone else to deal with.

Colleen and Arlen Lowell had volunteered to catch the two surviving chickens, which were perched on the rafters, terrified. After two hours with a stepstool and a broomstick and one of those gentle green plastic rakes and an old sheet, they'd gotten them safely into a cat carrier. *The Lowells seem really happy together,* Susan found herself thinking as Colleen and Arlen laughed and joked and chased the two scared chickens around the church. *It would be nice to be that happy.*

Arlen told Susan they would drop the bloody chicken off at the vet ("The bill will be our treat"), and they'd bring the other one back to the McIntires' house the following day, once Wyatt was safely at school. They didn't want to retraumatize him.

"Do you think they're going to want the carcass?" Colleen asked Susan.

"Why on earth would they want the carcass?" Susan asked.

Colleen wrinkled her nose and said, "To bury it?"

"I don't know," said Susan. She sighed a huge sigh. "I don't understand people with chickens."

"Well, we'll put it in our trunk just in case," said Arlen.

Once everything was clean, and the church doors were

locked, and even poor Evelyn Bullard had gone home to her house filled with nobody, Susan remembered she still had to deal with the three baby Nubian goats.

The goats had spent the day behind the church, tied to a tree, gorging on the bushes and the grass, and they were covered in mud. Susan suspected they'd eaten too much, but she didn't have the energy to worry about it. She untied them and led them across the graveyard to the parking lot.

She and Rowan had traded cars. Rowan took Charlotte and the boys out for pizza and a movie in the minivan, and Susan had Rowan's Cherokee for the goats. She heaved the muddy goats into the back through the window one by one, wishing she had some help. Then she got behind the wheel, turned on her lights, and headed for the cheese lady's house.

Later, after Owen and Lucy dried their son off with towels warmed in the dryer, and let him watch an hour of *Pocoyo*, and gave him back scratches and sang him songs, and listened to the telling and retelling of what they would come to refer to as "The Tale of the Death of Fat Black" approximately three thousand times, Wyatt finally fell asleep.

Owen came into the bedroom. Lucy was sitting on the bed, brushing her hair.

"That," said Lucy, "is why I didn't want to bring three chickens to church."

"You foresaw this?" said Owen.

"I said one chicken. I'm just saying, I thought bringing more than one was going to cause a problem."

"So you're implying you foresaw this," said Owen. "You foresaw carnage, and Wyatt yelling *Fat Black* at the top of his lungs? While the entire town, including one of the four black people in Beekman, the only one who could conceivably be described as fat, looked on?"

Lucy smiled a small smile, the first one in what felt like days, and then she asked, "Just out of curiosity, why did you bring Fat Black?"

"He walked into the box first," said Owen. "Just out of curiosity, why did you name a chicken Fat Black?"

"I also named one Fat White and one Fat Red. It's not racist," said Lucy. "It might be fat-ist. You try naming nineteen chickens."

"I'm not sure bringing the chickens was a great idea," said Owen.

"Ya think?" said Lucy.

They both started to laugh.

"It was pretty fucking horrible," said Owen.

"It was completely insane," agreed Lucy.

"I'm not sure we can live in this town anymore," said Owen.

"We definitely can never go back to that church."

"Never, never."

"Which is unfortunate, because they have a nice tag sale every spring."

When Susan finally got home, she decided to do one last thing before she went inside. She pulled up the mats from the back of the car so she could hose them off. They snapped on and off, the mats in Rowan's car, so you could do things like haul goats. *I might as well do it now,* Susan thought. She was covered in blood and shit and feathers and mud, but if she didn't do it tonight, the car would never get cleaned. God knew Rowan would never do it. Tomorrow might be the last sunny day for a while. *If I hose the mats off now, they can dry tomorrow in the sun, and he'll have a nice clean car for the winter.*

She found them in the wheel well, tucked under an emergency tool kit nobody ever used. Copies of letters, in Rowan's handwriting, addressed to someone Susan had never heard of, some slut named Juliette.

Nineteen

We think we know who we are, particularly those of us who think we are committed to emotional and spiritual growth. But deep within us, just out of reach of our hard-won self-knowledge, is the cauldron of the dark unconscious. When it boils over—and it will—we find ourselves absolutely lost, groping for the familiar in an unfamiliar and terrifying universe.

—Constance Waverly
The Eros Manifesto

Gordon was thinking he wanted a snack and headed toward the fridge, hoping Gherardo had made those samosas with dipping sauce he liked. If not those, maybe he'd settle for a leg or two of Oprah's Unfried Chicken. Gordon had tasted it at a fund-raiser, and now Gherardo had standing orders to always have it waiting for him, any time of day or night. He licked his lips and had just opened the fridge when he heard the screams.

"Gordon! Gordon!"

It was Kelly, out on the back deck. Gordon sighed, let the fridge door close, and walked outside. Kelly was hopping from foot to foot and covering the right side of her face with her hand.

"It stung my eyeball! One of your fucking bees stung my eyeball!"

"Don't be ridiculous."

"It did. I swear. It stung my actual eyeball!"

"That's impossible. Maybe, *maybe* it stung your eyelid," said Gordon. "Maybe it stung near your eye. That's perfectly normal bee behavior."

Kelly took her hand away and shrieked, "Does *this* look normal to you?"

Gordon looked at her face. He suddenly felt hot and dizzy. Kelly's left eyeball was bulging out of its socket and the white was swimming in blood. It was like one of those special effects you see in a horror movie that make you think, *Okay, now that's taking things a little bit too far.*

Dirk, who'd been at work camouflaging Gordon's Hudson River golf-ball-driving hide—according to a friendly local cop, there had been complaints from some old-timers who had nothing better to do with their lives than hang out at the marina and stare out at the river all day—appeared on the deck just in time to take charge.

"Come on," said Dirk. "I'll drive."

❧

Dirk was at the wheel of Gordon's Range Rover, roaring down Route 9 at speeds approaching a hundred miles an hour, steering perfectly into the turns and accelerating out of them like a NASCAR champion. *For a guy who's basically a step up from a dirt farmer, the bastard can drive*, thought Gordon.

Gordon was in the backseat, holding an ice pack wrapped in a cream-colored Frette guest towel to Kelly's face with one hand and his phone with the other. He was talking to a golf buddy of his, the dean of Weill Cornell, and having him arrange for a helicopter to medevac Kelly to the city and for a top eye surgeon to meet them there. Gordon figured the local hospital could handle a sprained ankle, maybe a broken bone. A rapidly expanding eyeball? Highly unlikely. Meanwhile Kelly was slumped against him, moaning, tears streaming from her one good eye.

Kelly howled as Dirk made a sharp turn into the hospital entrance and pulled the Range Rover straight in the ambulance bay, leaning on the horn. Two orderlies rushed out, wrested the doors open, grabbed Kelly, and frog-marched her inside. Dirk leaned back in the driver's seat and exhaled. Gordon followed Kelly and the orderlies into the ER, where a doctor was calling out for a bed and an IV.

Just then Gordon's voice rose over everyone's like a crack of thunder. "Where is my fucking helicopter? Get her on a rolly thing, a whatchamacallit, and get her out, we're not staying here. You two"—he pointed at the ER doctor and an orderly—"help her and follow me."

"Sir, she needs treatment immediately," said the doctor.

"Not here, she doesn't, you idiot. She'll end up blind *and* dead. Where is my fucking helicopter?"

A nurse—whose nonchalance indicated years spent in the ER—gave the doctor a look that said, *Not worth the fight; let's just get this jackass out of here.*

As fast as Kelly was walked into the hospital, she was rolled back out. Gordon was blinking into the setting sun, scanning the sky, yelling at anyone in a hospital uniform, and barking into his phone. He heard a *thwop-thwop-thwop* sound and hung up his phone mid-tirade.

Once settled in the helicopter, with Kelly strapped in a gurney beside him and sedated with a shot of Ativan, Gordon felt back in his element. He'd summoned a helicopter with a phone call; they were on their way to one of the top hospitals in the world; they'd be met by the best eye guy in New York. His sense of well-being was confirmed when, after they'd landed on the helipad at Weill Cornell, the staff treated Kelly as Mrs. Gordon Allen. She was rushed into surgery and, afterward, given a room on the exclusive fourteenth floor, with its sweeping views and lobster dinners, the floor reserved for celebrities, Arab sheikhs, and shady foreign billionaires.

"Fat Black was attacked!"

Wyatt was lounging in the big red chair with his feet dangling over one of the arms, talking on Owen's cell phone. He looked like a teenager.

"We were in church and a dog ate his entire head off! Fang," Wyatt said into the phone. Then he started laughing and said, "Yeah, you shouldn't name your dog Fang! Fang is a *very* bad name for a dog!"

"Is he talking on your phone?" Lucy asked Owen. They were

sitting at the kitchen table, sorting through bills together, half listening to Wyatt's side of the conversation.

"If it's not yours, it's mine."

"Fat Black is dead as a doornail!" Wyatt said. "Yep, that is very dead! Dead as a doornail means totally, totally dead!"

"Who is he talking to?" Lucy asked.

"I have no idea," said Owen. "Maybe my mother?"

"It's good for him to talk about it," said Lucy. "He's going to have to process it somehow. I wish I could live inside his brain for a while and feel how it works."

"You're as close to the inside of his brain as anyone could be," said Owen.

"But you're better with him than I am," said Lucy. "Getting into the tub with him with your clothes on. I never think of things like that. I'm too busy being the bad guy."

It was one of those things that get said in a marriage, something that starts out as a genuine compliment but then turns into a criticism without either party noticing or caring all that much. It was true, though; among the various parts of her life that she was tired of, Lucy was tired of always being the bad guy. The one who got spit at and bitten and scratched till she bled, the one Wyatt said that he hated because she said no to the second bowl of ice cream, the seventh trip on the escalator, the iPad in bed.

One chicken, not three.

One chicken would have fit into the old plastic cat carrier, the one with the swinging mesh door. Lucy had woken up at two in the morning with that thought rattling around in her head. It took a lot for Lucy not to wake up Owen and point it out to him right then, point out how this entire situation could have been avoided if he had just listened to her in the first place. It took a lot for her not to say it to him now, but she didn't. Instead, she stared down wordlessly at their American Express bill, which was, as usual, surprisingly big. For people who didn't buy expensive things or go on fancy trips or eat at nice restaurants, they sure managed to spend a lot of money.

"Yes, it was pretty gross!" said Wyatt into the phone now. "Yes, it was super-gross and very bloody!

"Okay, I'll get him for you."

Wyatt bouncy-tiptoed over to the kitchen table and handed Owen the phone. "Izzy wants to talk to you," Wyatt said to his dad. "She says it's *very* important. Very, *very* important."

Owen took the phone from Wyatt and immediately powered it down. Lucy stared at her husband, completely enraged.

"Have you been spending time with this person *with our son?*"

"Of course not!"

"Then how does he know who she is?"

Owen took a deep breath. "He met her in the grocery store once. A long time ago. Before anything even happened between us. You know how good his memory is. And Izzy is an unusual name."

"So you knew Izzy before we started everything?"

"No! Absolutely not. I happened to meet her early on, but *after* we started this. I swear. And then I met her again in the grocery store, and Wyatt was with me. That's it. That's the whole story."

"And then you just started having sex with her? No, stop, don't tell me."

"I'll tell you anything you want to know," said Owen.

"I don't want to know anything."

"Well, if you change your mind, the offer stands. And I think it would be best to stop it all right now."

"You're free to do what you want, Owen."

"I'd like us both to stop it."

"You want me to stop it, you mean."

"I want it to be over. The Arrangement. Fight Club. All of it."

"What do you think I'm doing, exactly?" Lucy asked. "I'm curious."

"I have no idea. Probably nothing. I just want to end this whole thing now before things get any more out of hand."

"I see," said Lucy. "So I should stop doing 'probably nothing' because you picked a girlfriend who is unstable and erratic and more trouble than she's worth."

"She's not my girlfriend. She never was my girlfriend."

"Is this all the same person? Is Izzy the air-conditioner cat-hair lady? Or is she somebody new?"

"She's the air-conditioner cat-hair lady."

"You two have been at this for quite a while, wouldn't you say?"

"This, this thing, is not anything. And it's over," said Owen.

"She doesn't seem to think so."

"It's because I've stopped responding to her texts. She knows it's over, I've told her it's over, but she won't get the message and I don't know what to do."

"I really don't feel like giving you dating advice, Owen."

"I'm not asking for—I'm just telling you that this is the situation."

"We both realized a lot of things could happen. Maybe there's a reason I don't want to quit early."

"What?"

"Maybe something happened," Lucy said.

"Wait, what?" Owen asked. He looked genuinely confused. Like the conversation had taken a left turn somewhere back when he wasn't paying close attention, and now he was heading down a road he didn't want to be on.

"I don't know, Owen," Lucy said, her voice filled with disgust. She climbed up the stairs and said, "Maybe. Something. Happened."

What the hell happened?

Of course something happened. What had he thought? That Lucy wouldn't do anything? That was insane! She was a very attractive woman! And she had come up with the idea, now that he thought about it. Maybe she had tricked him! Maybe she'd had someone waiting in the wings!

The truth was, Owen had sort of thought that she wouldn't do anything. And now he was sure something had happened between Lucy and somebody.

But who?

An old boyfriend? Some guy in her French class? One of the husbands up here? Larry the handyman? Some dude she met online? The whole thing was harder for him to imagine than it should have been. He wished she hadn't said anything. There was a part of him that had thought the Arrangement should follow the script of the wives who say, "If you cheat on me, don't tell me. Don't try to clear your conscience by confessing. I don't want to know. Ever." Weren't there women like that? Women who said things like that, casually, dropped into a conversation on a car ride while the kids had their headphones on in the back?

He didn't like it. That was for sure. But he would let Lucy have her little bit of whatever it was with whoever he was and run out the clock. Never ask about it and never acknowledge it.

That was his plan.

Two days after her surgery, as Kelly drifted in a narcotic daze, Gordon clutched a glass of Laphroaig eighteen-year-old scotch—delivered without a whisper—and watched a freighter loaded with cargo cut through the chop of the East River. *Shipping*, he thought. *High risk, but still…*

Gordon's reverie was interrupted by a doctor poking his head into the room, followed by the rest of him. To Gordon, he looked about twenty. And Indian, which Gordon liked. He'd heard they sent their smartest students over here to become doctors, and the best and brightest of them never went back.

"How are we feeling!" the doctor chirped to the very

obviously zonked-out Kelly, half her face wrapped in bandages, the other half bruised beyond recognition, as he flipped open her chart.

"She's a little out of it," said Gordon.

"Yes, well, that's to be expected."

"How does it look?" Gordon asked, setting aside his glass of scotch out of a sense of decorum.

"We got some tests back," the doctor said. He flipped through the chart with an inscrutable look on his small brown face. "Well, um, this is not what I was hoping to see."

"Say more," said Gordon.

"It looks like she's going to lose it."

"What do you mean?" Gordon asked. "She's going to lose her sight?"

"Well, yes, on that side," the doctor said. "She'll have some trouble with depth perception, possibly get headaches while her brain adjusts to the new reality."

"That doesn't sound so bad," said Gordon. "A few headaches."

"And also the eye."

"What's that, now?"

"The eye," the doctor repeated. "Ball. She's going to lose the eyeball."

Years later, looking back, Gordon could never be sure who had first noticed Kelly was awake.

What he remembered perfectly was the *whoosh* of the Baccarat vase missing his face by mere inches, and then Kelly's voice, clear as a bell, saying, "I want a divorce!"

Twenty

The idea that one's marriage should be a primary arena for self-actualization can be profoundly destabilizing. The truth is that growing while married often means growing apart.

—Constance Waverly
The Eros Manifesto

T hree days after the Death of Fat Black, Owen and Lucy received an e-mail from Gordon Allen's attorney. He arranged to meet them at their house while Wyatt was off at school late the following week in order to discuss "the events that transpired inside the church."

"What does he mean by that, 'the events that transpired inside the church'?" Lucy said to Owen. "Gordon Allen's Doberman killed our son's chicken. Is he going to try to turn this into our fault?"

"I think that's just the way lawyers write e-mails."

The attorney introduced himself as Hugh Willix—Lucy remembered him from the school-board meeting; he had a very distinctive look, bald and birdlike, with a razor-sharp nose—and he accepted Lucy's offer of a cup of coffee and complimented them on their lovely home and asked about their experience with the local school system and basically chatted for a good ten minutes like this was a purely social visit.

It wasn't until Lucy topped off his cup of coffee that he brought things around to the matter at hand.

"I'm guessing you two realize why I asked to meet with you," he said. "Gordon Allen is very upset about what happened at the church. He wasn't there, as you know, and his son Rocco was in the charge of his nanny, but Gordon is very concerned about what took place and he would like to offer you compensation for the, uh, chicken and for any and all emotional toll that might, either now or at some unforeseen time in the future, spring from the events in question.

"Perhaps an education fund for your son," he continued.

"Or a trust to make sure he is taken care of in the event you are no longer able to care for him. Even some money to make your lives easier. I understand, and I hope I'm not out of line by mentioning this, well, I understand Wyatt has some special needs. Mr. Allen is truly sorry for what transpired in that church, and he wants to make sure your family and your son are well taken care of."

"We're not going to sue Gordon Allen," said Owen. "We're not those people."

"See, I appreciate that. And Mr. Allen appreciates that. But here's the problem. I'm an attorney. I get paid to worry. Right? That's what I do. I worry, I wake up in the middle of the night worrying, and in order to stop worrying, I have to do things a certain way to protect my clients. I have to dot my *i*'s and cross my *t*'s. And if I just walk away now, and we all agree nobody is suing anybody, and everything is fine, I will have to worry about this for the next forty years or so. I'm kindly asking you to save me from that."

"What do you want us to do?" asked Lucy.

"I want you to take a few days, a few weeks, even, talk about it with each other, and think about what you want. Mr. Allen is in a unique position to be generous, and he is deeply saddened by any distress he has caused your family and your son."

This is my blank check, Lucy thought.

It could all be so easy. Life had been so hard for so long, and now she could feel the tide turning, and she was floating on a raft down a stream with the sun on her face. She could feel problems falling down in front of her like dominoes, and this one, the last one, how to make it all work, had, by some miracle, been solved.

"Here's my card if you have any questions or concerns," he said on his way out the door. "And I'll get in touch with you before too long. Just give it some thought."

*　　*　　*

Later that night, after dinner, Lucy was loading the dishwasher when she said quietly, "I don't want to say no to the money."

"What?" said Owen. He looked up from his laptop. "You mean Gordon Allen's money? Are you serious?"

"Yes, I'm serious. I'm very serious."

"It was a chicken, Lucy."

"It might have been traumatic for Wyatt," she said. "We don't know if it was or not. There's no way to tell for sure."

Just then, Wyatt hurried down the stairs pulling his six-foot-long stuffed boa constrictor behind him like a tail. He walked through the kitchen on the balls of his feet.

"Heels down, Wyatt," said Lucy.

Wyatt put his heels down for two steps and then unthinkingly resumed his toe-walking into the playroom.

"Do you want to be that kind of people?"

"What kind of people, Owen? Rich, lucky people? Yes. Yes, I do want to be those people, Owen. I'm tired of everything being so hard."

"You want this to be the story of your life?" said Owen. "That you sued a billionaire over something that was truly nobody's fault? I mean it, Lucy, have a little integrity."

"We don't have to sue anyone," said Lucy. "You heard him. He'll give us whatever we want."

❧

Owen went into the downstairs bathroom with his cell phone.

He sat down on the toilet and powered it on. Ninety-eight texts, all from Izzy.

He scrolled through, not really reading them. This was not going to be easy, it seemed. No matter what he did, Izzy would not stop with the texting. It was getting to be a problem. He thought about changing his number. He really didn't want to, his entire work life was tied to that phone number, but it was starting to look like it might be his only option.

A slew of new texts started popping up on his screen while he was scrolling.

I know you're getting these

I can see you reading them

You're sitting on the fucking toilet

Come outside, please

I'd rather not have to knock on your door

I'm going to knock on the door in three minutes, Owen.

Owen quickly fired off a text that said, *Can we do this later? At your place?*

No.

Now.

Two minutes till I knock.

Owen walked into the kitchen and told Lucy he had to go outside for a bit.

"How come?" she asked.

"There's, um, kind of a situation I have to deal with."

Lucy just stared at him. "Is she here, Owen? Is she on our property? That is not okay. Tell her I'm going to call the police. No, actually, let me tell her."

"Let me handle it."

"You're not handling this well, Owen. You seem to have lost control of things," said Lucy.

"I'm taking care of it," he said. "That's what I'm going out-side to do."

"I don't like this," said Lucy.

"Neither do I," said Owen. "But do not call the police."

Owen slipped on his jacket and opened the door. Izzy was standing in the backyard, next to the trampoline, in the dark.

"Izzy, this is not cool," he said. "This is really not okay."

"I'm sorry, Owen. I just really needed to talk to you."

"No, Izzy. It doesn't work this way. You can't do this. You have to leave, now."

"I have cancer," she said.

"What?"

"I have cervical cancer," she said. "I went to the doctor today like you told me to."

"You don't have cancer. You have to wait for the results of the test. I know how this stuff works."

"They could see it, Owen."

"What do you mean?"

"They could see it."

"What. What could they see?"

"The cancer! It's, like, bad. Bad, bad. There was a medical student in there, this sweet Japanese girl, and she fainted."

"What are you talking about?"

"She looked at my cervix and she *fainted*."

"She's a student. That doesn't mean anything, Izzy."

"It's the worst my doctor has ever seen."

"Your doctor actually said those exact words?"

"Yes. And she started crying. And she got mad at me for skip-ping my Pap smears. She said her office had figured I'd moved out of state or something when I never returned their calls."

"Oh my God, Izzy. I'm so sorry."

"Damn you, Owen," Izzy said. She hit him on the chest.

"What?" Owen said. He was genuinely confused.

"I wish I didn't know."

"I'll help you through this," said Owen. "I'll help you get through this."

"I wish I didn't know."

"It's better to know. They can do something."

"They could see it," said Izzy. "They can't do something about it when you can see it."

Lucy watched the whole thing. She stood at the kitchen sink with a glass of wine in her hand and stared at them through the window the entire time. She knew Izzy and Owen both saw her staring at them, glowing in the lit-up kitchen window, and that's the way she wanted it.

Izzy's hair was in a real crazy-lady ponytail, sticking out of the very top of her head. She was wearing tight ripped jeans and a turtleneck sweater and a puffy silver vest.

She pounded him on the chest with both hands. He didn't kiss her or even try to touch her. She started to cry. She hit him some more.

I'm watching my husband break up with another woman, Lucy thought, taking a big sip of wine. *That's what this is.*

Lucy didn't notice when Wyatt dragged his stuffed snake out of the playroom and pulled it silently through the kitchen behind her. He spotted a set of red Mardi Gras beads on the floor and immediately forgot about whatever he had planned for the snake, dropping it in the middle of the floor.

He took the beads over to the bay window where he liked to do his bead flicking.

"Izzy and Owen!"

Oh, shit, Lucy thought. She looked over at Wyatt, who was smiling a big smile, staring out the window at the scene, and shaking his beads more and more furiously.

"Izzy and Owen!" Wyatt said again. "Izzy and Owen! Izzy and Owen! Izzy and Owen!"

*   *   *

"I don't believe her," said Lucy.

"Lucy."

"I don't. I think she is lying."

Wyatt was upstairs in bed with the iPad, watching God knows what. Owen and Lucy were in the living room, fighting.

"I don't think people lie about cancer," said Owen.

"People lie about cancer all the time. Especially crazy ones."

"Lucy—"

"I don't believe her. I'm sorry. You picked a crazy woman who lives in our town, you introduced her *to our son,* and you made it virtually impossible for us to keep any of this a secret from the people that we know. So, no, I don't think she has cancer. I think she's lying so she can keep you in her life. Which is fine with me. You've got a few more months, and if you want to spend your time shuttling that nutjob to imaginary chemotherapy appointments, be my guest."

"You sound like a horrible person right now, Lucy. Honestly, do you hear yourself?"

"I don't believe she has cancer, Owen! I think she's making it up!"

"She's not making it up."

"How can you possibly know that?"

"I know she hadn't been to the doctor in years, and I made her go, I told her I wouldn't see her again until she went. It's not like she just showed up and said she had cancer. There are parts of this you don't know."

"Well, then, yes, if she does have cancer, I feel bad. Cancer is bad. It would suck to have cancer. Cancer is a horrible disease. Is that what you want me to say?"

"I want you to be the woman I married," said Owen. "I want you to say what she would say."

"I don't think the woman you married would be in this situation, Owen. I think her head would never stop spinning. I think she'd think we were both completely out of our minds," said Lucy.

"We both did this," said Owen. "We agreed on the whole thing."

"I know we did!" Lucy practically shouted. "But you. Chose. Poorly!"

"Lucy—"

"And *if* that woman has cancer, then that's a bad thing for her. Cancer is a very bad thing. But that's about as far as I can go. And when you talk to her again, which I know you will, please tell her to stay away from my son or I will call the fucking police."

Twenty-One

What I find amazing is this: that two individuals who have zero genes in common can create a strong enough bond to stick together for a lifetime.

—Constance Waverly
The Waverly Report

Owen woke up late the next morning, in a quiet house, in an empty bed. It was strangely peaceful, alone in the cool soft sheets, and for a moment he tried his best to forget the high drama of the past few days, the fact that Izzy had cancer so bad it was visible to the naked eye, the fact that Lucy had more or less admitted she was doing something with somebody else.

She's having sex *with somebody else,* Owen found himself thinking, almost against his will. As his mother used to say, *They're not playing Parcheesi.*

When he finally went downstairs, he found Wyatt on the couch watching *Curious George.* His right arm was up to his armpit inside a box of Cheerios, but he wasn't eating them. It was like he had stopped eating them a while back and forgotten his arm was still inside the box. There were Cheerios everywhere, of course, on the couch and on the floor, and Owen let himself get a little bit mad at Lucy. Just a little bit.

"Are you buying episodes of *Curious George* with the Fire Stick?"

"Yes," said Wyatt.

"How many?"

"Six."

Six times $2.99. Eighteen dollars' worth of *Curious George.*

"We get it for free on Netflix," said Owen.

"I don't know how to Netflix."

For all of Wyatt's interest in tales of wide-scale death and destruction, he had recently discovered the innocent pleasures of *Curious George.* Owen sat down next to him and wished he were the man in the yellow hat.

"Hey, buddy, where's Mama?"

"She's in New York City!" said Wyatt. "She said she'd bring me a present from New York City!"

She's probably off on a sexcapade, Owen thought.

And this was the truth: He didn't like it. He didn't like it one bit.

⊱⊰

Lucy was climbing out of the subway station on her way to Ben's apartment when a flurry of texts from him came through all at once.

> I have to cancel. I have to go pick up the girls. The soccer game got rained out and Deborah is stuck in surgery.

> Are you there? Did you get this?

> I'm really sorry.

> Please let me know you got this.

> Can you do tomorrow afternoon? Or later this week? I know this blows.

Lucy just stood there, leaning against the subway railing, rain dripping down her neck, staring at her phone.

Of course she couldn't do tomorrow afternoon. Of course she couldn't! And she was mad that Ben didn't know that, that he didn't realize how hard it was for her to get from Beekman to Brooklyn, to extricate herself from the rest of her life to be with him. They had talked on the phone the night before, briefly, after the whole Izzy fiasco, and they'd figured out they could meet up today. Ben's girls had soccer, then a playdate at a friend's house, and then Deborah was picking them up, and Lucy figured she could leave Wyatt home with Owen.

She was mad that Ben didn't realize how much she needed to see him. She was mad at Deborah, a woman she'd never met, for being a very important surgeon and depending too much on her ex-husband to pick up the slack.

And this: *I know this blows*?

She texted him back: *Tomorrow won't work. Enjoy your girls. Talk soon.*

Lucy didn't know what to do with herself. It was raining. It was too cold to wander for any stretch of time, and she didn't want to go home, she didn't want to see Owen.

She was almost to Ben's building. At least that's what she told herself. She was six blocks away. She just wanted to take a look. And see what? What exactly did she expect to see?

She wanted to see if he was with another woman, she supposed, although Lucy knew life wasn't quite that simple. It wasn't like she was going to see Ben, what, step out of his apartment building holding hands with someone and head off to brunch? That was highly unlikely. If he was with somebody, well, it was raining, and they'd probably spend the morning in bed. Still, she wanted to see if there was something to see, if there was something she should know. Better to find out now. Before she fell any further. Before she ruined her life.

It was strange, really, that he had to cancel their entire day together because of a little rain. What about the girls' afternoon playdate? Couldn't he have moved that around, worked a little harder to figure things out? He was a divorced dad, for heaven's sake. Lucy knew that there were probably a dozen moms who would step in and help him out in a pinch, who would entertain his girls, feed them lunch, drop them off at the next house for him for the rest of the afternoon—women loved that shit, a chance to swoop in and help the hapless man who no longer had the benefits of a wife.

She found a little nook at the end of the street across from Ben's building. There was some green lattice supporting what turned out to be plastic foliage, hiding some garbage cans. She wedged herself in there, underneath an awning, and pretended to be checking her phone. She broke out in a sweat.

What if she saw something?

Lucy was driving herself more and more crazy with each passing minute. She was soaked to the bone. *Leave now,* she kept saying to herself. And then: *Just five more minutes. Now, Lucy.* And then, *Just a little bit longer.*

She had no idea how long she'd stood there, with her mind racing like a crazy person, before she saw him.

She recognized him by the way he walked. She didn't even know she *knew* how Ben walked, but apparently she did, because she spotted him from half a block away.

And he was with his girls.

Eliza was the older one. She was twelve but looked younger to Lucy's eyes, still a girl, still with a straight-up-and-down figure. When she got a little closer Lucy saw that the girl was covered in freckles, just like her mother. Peggy was ten and built like a young Teddy Kennedy. She already had her buds. They both had their soccer cleats tied together by their laces and dangling over their shoulders. Ben was holding a huge green-and-white umbrella and carrying a brown paper bag splotched with drops of rain. Bagels, probably.

They ducked into the apartment building, and the door closed behind them. Lucy took a few steps back and leaned against the brick building. She was shaking. She closed her eyes and tried to breathe.

"Lucy!"

Lucy's heart stopped.

"Victoria," said Lucy. "Wow. Hey. Hi."

It was Brooklyn Victoria, wife of hipster Thom, mother of the long-haired boy named Flannery. Lucy hadn't spoken to her since that drunken night on their deck back in July. The night that started everything, really.

"Oh my God, I thought that was you," said Victoria. "What are you doing here? You look like you're hiding from someone!"

"No, no. I'm just lost."

"I'd say," said Victoria. "What are you doing in this neighborhood?"

"Nothing, really. I had some time to myself and I wanted to see Brooklyn. I feel so out of it these days. I didn't realize it would be raining."

"Well, you picked the wrong part," said Victoria. "It's nothing but apartment buildings and dry cleaner's around here. You should have called me. I would have pointed you in the right direction."

"I should have."

"Do you have a few minutes for a cup of coffee?" asked Victoria.

Lucy checked the time on her phone to give herself a second to think. "Looks like I do," she said.

Owen was cruising slowly down Beekman's main street, searching for a parking space. Wyatt was in back, chattering away, happy to have his dad all to himself.

Owen hadn't wanted to involve Wyatt in this particular mission but he couldn't figure out a way around it. Lucy had disappeared into the city for the day, and Izzy had stopped responding to his texts and his e-mails. He felt like he should check on her. He wanted to see if she was okay.

He found a parking spot a few streets down from Izzy's house and was heading toward it when he saw Sunny Bang stepping off Izzy's front porch. He grabbed Wyatt by the shoulder and tried to spin him in another direction so they could avoid Sunny, but he wasn't quick enough.

"Sunny Bang!" Wyatt yelled when he spotted her. "Sunny Bang! Sunny Bang! Sunny Bang!"

"Wyatt!" said Sunny. "It's good to see you!"

Sunny knelt down to Wyatt's eye level and said, "Guess what? I've got an extra apple in my purse. Do you want it?"

"No," said Wyatt.

"No, *thank you*," said Sunny, correcting him.

"I hate apples."

"You can just say 'No, thank you.'"

"Apples are disgusting. They're completely, completely disgusting. They have worms in them!"

Owen just shrugged at Sunny as if to say, *What can you do?*

"Yo. Owen. Why are you here?"

"Me?" said Owen. "What do you mean?"

"I didn't know you knew Izzy Radford. This is her house."

"I, uh, know her."

"From where?"

"From her store."

"Oh my God," said Sunny Bang.

"What?"

"Do not tell me that what I think is happening is actually happening."

"I have no idea what you're talking about," said Owen.

"Oh my God! Oh my God, Owen!"

"What?"

"You and Izzy."

"Me and—what? No."

"Do not lie to me, Owen."

"I'm not lying, Sunny," said Owen.

"Stop lying, Owen."

"I'm not lying."

"Stop lying."

"I'm not—"

"Stop!"

Owen took a deep breath and then said, "Lucy knows about it."

"I know what Lucy knows. Lucy talks to me. I'm her friend."

"So you, uh, know the deal."

"I do know the deal. I think it's a stupid deal, but I do know about it. I probably know more than you do at this point."

"No doubt."

"Which isn't a problem, because I'm very good with secrets," said Sunny Bang.

"Thank you, Sunny. I appreciate it."

"You know who's not good with secrets? Izzy Radford," said Sunny. "And she has cancer."

"Yeah, I—she told me."

"It's bad. It's *bad* bad," said Sunny. "So you two can stop whatever shenanigans you've got going on right now. I'm serious, Owen. Right now!"

"It's stopped. We stopped already."

"Good.

"Right."

Sunny folded her arms across the front of her chest and cocked her head at him. "I'm arranging for people to bring her meals. I'll put you down for a week from Thursday. Grill some of those sausages you do so well. Throw in a side salad and a so-so bottle of chardonnay. Oh, and drop it off at my house, not here. I'll make sure she knows it's from you."

"Okay."

"Now go home," said Sunny. "I mean it, Owen. Go!"

Lucy and Victoria walked a few blocks west to a wine bar Victoria had been to before. *Coffee* for Victoria meant wine, of course, and Lucy was fine with that. It was barely noon, but drinking with Victoria was better than wandering around in the rain all by herself, and she wasn't in the mood to go home. And Ben was with his girls.

Ben was with his girls!

"You seem distracted," Victoria said once they sat down.

"I'm just cold," said Lucy. "My feet got wet."

"I'll go to the bar and get us something. God forbid anyone actually waits on a table in this place. What would you like?"

"A glass of sauvignon blanc, thanks."

Ben was with his girls! She had gone to such a dark place, and so quickly. *I love him,* Lucy thought. *I really do.*

"I can't believe we haven't talked since that night on our deck," Lucy said when Victoria came back with their drinks.

"That was a crazy night," said Victoria.

"It was."

"I can't remember being that drunk and still being able to function."

"Some crazy stuff was said," said Lucy. "*Crazy* crazy."

"Oh my God, I wish I could take everything back. You guys must have thought we were insane."

"We sort of did," said Lucy.

"Three weeks after we saw you, Frank and Jim split up."

"Really?"

"Yep. Frank filed for divorce out of the blue."

"Why? What happened?"

"He fell in love," Victoria said. She rolled her eyes when she said it, like love was an imaginary thing.

"With who?"

"With some stay-at-home dad whose wife is a managing director at Morgan Stanley. They're going for full custody of all of the kids, and it looks like they'll get it too. All five children. And neither of them will have to work another day of their lives."

"Yikes."

"It's really awful," said Victoria. She took a big sip of her wine. "Jim is devastated. Devastated."

"So you didn't go through with it?" Lucy finally asked Victoria after they'd ordered a cheese plate and olives. "The open-marriage thing?"

Victoria swirled the wine around in her glass for a moment and then said, "No, we did."

"You did?"

"Yep," said Victoria.

"And?"

"It was a total disaster."

Lucy couldn't hide her curiosity. "Really? What happened?"

"Let's see," Victoria said. "I became insanely jealous. Thom completely lost all perspective on his life. I begged him to stop. He asked for a divorce."

"Are you serious?"

"Yeah, it was a real shit-show there for a while."

"Why didn't you call me?" said Lucy.

"I was embarrassed. I couldn't face anything or anybody. I'm sorry I was so out of touch," said Victoria. "I think he had someone he wanted to sleep with and then sort of made this whole deal thing come up. And so he slept with her."

"And?"

"Apparently it was great," she said. "Apparently she was everything I'm not, in bed and otherwise."

"He told you that?"

"Yep. Apparently, I'm a bitch," she said. "And I'm cold and controlling and she is warm and sweet and kind."

"So you're getting divorced?"

"No," said Victoria. "Not at the moment, at least."

"What does that mean?"

"Well, after he promised to stop seeing her and yet kept right on seeing her, and then promised again and then kept seeing her anyway, I did that thing women have been doing since the beginning of time."

"What's that?"

"I decided to look the other way."

"Huh," said Lucy. "So, I don't get it; is he still seeing her?"

"Of course he is! But I've stopped asking. I've stopped

snooping. You know me, once I set my mind to something, I follow through."

"How do you do it?"

"Mostly I just play dumb. He comes home late from work? I pour him a drink and ask him how his day was. He has to go to Seattle for business? I send him a cheery e-mail around dinnertime saying I love him and I'm going to bed early and we can talk in the morning. Basically, I'm making staying with me easier than leaving me."

"Why?"

"Eventually he'll get as tired of her as he is of me. Eventually she'll turn into a bitch and a shrew and a nag and a bore. He'll come up for air, look around a bit, and see his son, our friends, his life, and our life together, and he'll decide it's easier to stay than it would be to go. And not just that it's easier. He'll see that he has a lot to lose, things that actually mean a great deal to him."

"Yeah, maybe," said Lucy, nodding slowly. "But how long do you think that's gonna take?"

"Three years."

"Three years?"

"All the marriages I've seen go through something like this, three years seems to be the number."

"Really?"

"I think sometime after the first year, the other woman starts to become demanding, maybe a bit of the sex haze begins to go away, and eventually the guy realizes that she isn't the magical solution to all of his problems the way he thought she'd be. And instead of one unhappy woman in his life, now he's got two."

"Three years is a long time to look the other way."

"I have this image in my mind when I do it," said Victoria. She leaned back and rested her head against the red leather at the top of their booth. "I think of a dignified, beautiful French woman. She lives in Avignon with her husband and her two adolescent children. And every time her husband goes to Paris, she knows in some part of the back of her mind that he visits his mistress. Just the way his father did and the way her father did. I'm not saying it doesn't upset her, but she accepts it as the way of the world. And she doesn't find it humiliating like an American woman would, because all the women in her circle are in the same boat. Or realize that they probably will be soon."

"You've really developed a philosophy about all this," said Lucy.

"Keep in mind, today is a good day. Not every day is a good one in my head, not by a long shot. And I do realize that after all of our high-minded plans, our 'new paradigm' and my feminist ideals, I've been reduced to a stereotype."

"What's that?"

"I'm economically dependent on a man and I'm too old to start over."

"You're not too old to start over," said Lucy. "Plenty of women do."

"I want to have Christmas with my son and my grandkids and not have to share them with Thom and his new wife. And I know this sounds bad, but I'm not interested in reducing my standard of living by sixty-five percent at this point in my life. I don't want to move into a condo next to a shopping center in Weehawken and go on Internet dates with seventy-year-old men. I just don't."

"Did you, um, did you ever…" Lucy made a hand gesture to indicate sex.

"Yes. A couple of times. All disasters. Not worth talking about."

"Where'd you find them?"

"The Internet. Plus one old boyfriend I tracked down on Facebook. None of it really worked for me."

"What do you mean?"

"Let's just say, the earth did not shake," said Victoria. She took a big sip of wine. "Who knows, maybe I'm just not that into sex. That's another thing I've had to deal with in all this. I don't think I'm really that sexual of a person. It just doesn't matter that much to me. And those years of fighting with Thom over what he called my low sex drive—well, turns out he was right."

"Maybe you're a lesbian," Lucy said.

"I've thought about it. I just don't think I am. And if I am, what difference does it make? Even in nature, any females, let's say female dogs—dogs my age, dogs who can barely still reproduce—are those dogs having sex all the time? Are they spending their energy trying to get laid, feeling bad about not getting laid, feeling jealous of the younger dogs who are getting laid instead of them? I don't think so. I think that would be considered extremely abnormal in the animal world."

"Couldn't he still leave you for her?"

"Sure he could. He almost did, twice, but both times he came back in less than a week."

"How come?" Lucy asked.

"I'm not sure. She's married and has three kids, and I get the sense she doesn't want to blow up her life any more than I do. But who knows? There's nothing I can do about it if that's what they want."

"But if he really, truly loves her—"

"It's not love, Lucy," said Victoria, cutting her off. "He's in a fog. He's temporarily lost his mind, and I refuse to sit back and let him ruin six innocent people's lives because of it. The fact that my life happens to be one of them is almost beside the point."

This is not a fog, thought Lucy. *What I'm feeling is not a fog. It's the opposite of a fog. It's the clearest I've been in a long, long time. Ben is with his girls. And I am in love with Ben.*

"Men and their pricks," Victoria said, signaling the bartender for another round. "Honestly, I don't think we can begin to understand them. I think if we really knew what went on with them, the strongest emotion we'd feel is pity."

It was getting dark by the time Lucy walked back to Ben's building. Her mind was spinning, and she was a little drunk. She and Victoria had spent the afternoon drinking, and through it all, the voice in Lucy's head wouldn't stop. *I am in love with Ben. Ben is with his girls, and I am in love with Ben.*

I'm here. Downstairs. Can you come down for one minute?

I've got my girls up here.

I know. I'm sorry. But please. I need to see you.

Be down in five.

When Ben came out, they stepped around the corner. He kissed her, and for a moment she forgot her plan, she forgot why she was there other than to kiss and be kissed, other than to spend five minutes with Ben.

"I just need to know if this is real," Lucy finally said.

"What do you mean?"

"Us. This," said Lucy. "I need to know if there is an us."

"There is an us," said Ben.

"Okay," said Lucy. "Tell me more."

"I want us to be together."

"You're going to have to be more specific," said Lucy. "I need specifics."

"Really?"

"Yes."

"Specifics aren't going to freak you out?"

"I need to know what your intentions are. What you want, I mean. With me."

Ben looked her in the eyes and said, "I want to spend the rest of my life with you."

Lucy stopped breathing.

The world stopped turning.

"I want to wake up with you every morning and go to bed with you every night," he said. "I want to figure out a way to blend our families. I want to get to know Wyatt and be the best stepdad any kid has ever had. And, yes, that means I want to marry you, Lucy, but I am not going to propose to a woman who is married to somebody else. That's just not something I'm prepared to do."

"Okay," said Lucy. "Go back up to your girls," she said. "I'll text you later."

Twenty-Two

There is such a thing as human limitation, whether by nature or by fate.

—Constance Waverly
The Eros Manifesto

Kelly was sitting at the midpoint of a long cherrywood conference table, flanked by her lawyers. She looked good, Gordon thought as he walked into the room and took his seat at the table, directly across from her. She was wearing huge Gucci sunglasses and a tight dress with a plunging neckline. She still looked pretty goddamn succulent, he thought, like the cocktail waitress he'd gone berserk for nearly seven years earlier. This was a first for Gordon, divorcing a wife who still looked young, and he remembered his other divorces, and how it had always seemed to him that he was still in the season of the rising sap while across from him sat some angry, bony old shrew who thought it was his moral duty to have sex with nobody but her for the rest of his time on this planet. Back when Gordon was forty-two, his thirty-seven-year-old wife looked old, and when he was fifty, his forty-year-old wife looked old, and when he was sixty-three, Elaine looked like a stringy plastic handbag, but now he was seventy. He finally felt old, and Kelly, well, Kelly was still young.

The eye, though. The missing-eye thing was unfortunate.

The sunglasses did a good job of hiding it, but Gordon knew that behind the left lens there was nothing but a flesh-colored patch. Of course, Kelly would get a prosthetic eye, the best prosthetic eye money could buy, but still—the woman was missing an eyeball. You don't bounce back from that, Gordon figured. There was no known cure for No Eyeball.

His lawyers did their best to put up a fight on his behalf but Gordon overruled them again and again. Kelly wanted the triplex on Park Avenue and planned to gut it. Done. She wanted the ranch they never went to in Sun Valley. Done. She asked for the place on St. John, and she undoubtedly expected Gordon to argue, since he'd managed to hold on to it through his three previous divorces. With a small, almost imperceptible gesture, Gordon indicated his wishes to his attorneys. The last time Gordon had been on St. John, he'd opened a drawer in the master suite and smelled a smell he hadn't encountered in years, a smell he could only think of as the Smell of Elaine. It wafted up from the drawer paper and nearly floored him. So, St. John, Kelly could have it. Done.

The dollar amount they began to circle around was truly astronomical, so high that Gordon's lawyers called for a short break and retired to a distant conference room to slow things down and to attempt to talk some sense into their overly accommodating client.

Lucy was out in the backyard, near the edge of the woods, watching Wyatt. It was snowing, and Wyatt was trying to build a shelter out of sticks. He was very excited about the snow, and he had it in his head that if he moved quickly enough, he could build a house that would keep out the snow.

"I'm going to sleep in the shelter," said Wyatt.

"You better get lots of sticks, then," said Lucy.

"You and me and Dada are going to sleep in the shelter."

"Then you really need lots and lots and lots of sticks."

Lucy pulled out her phone, but she couldn't get cell service. She wasn't sure if it was related to the snowstorm or something about the distance she was from the house, but she found it frustrating. She wanted to text Ben. Pretty much all Lucy wanted to do was see Ben, call Ben, text Ben, and think about Ben.

Susan Howard had filed for divorce. Lucy didn't know the whole story, but Claire told her Susan had found some letters, love letters apparently, hidden in the back of Rowan's Jeep. Secret love letters. It was a very old-fashioned way to break up. And according to that morning's *New York Post*, Gordon and Kelly Allen were getting a divorce. That one was less of a surprise, but still.

These things always come in waves, Lucy thought. And then: *They also come in threes.*

There had been a tarot card reader at one of the Beekman PTA fund-raisers the year before. It was a ladies-only event, with Moscow mules and mojitos and finger foods and a handful of "super-fun things" the ladies on the committee had dreamed up, like an old-fashioned photo booth and a decorate-your-own-gigantic-wineglass station (*You had me at merlot*), and three tables dedicated to bunco.

There was a tremendous amount of planning that went into these fund-raisers, committee meetings and e-mail chains and food-prepping parties and team trips to the discount wine emporium, which is why the tarot card reader showing up unannounced struck everyone as such a surprise. Susan Howard was the chairwoman of the committee, though, and the tarot card reader was one of her middle-of-the-night brainstorms and she hadn't bothered to run it past anyone else involved. The woman Susan found worked out of a storefront in New Paltz and she weighed about three hundred pounds and she either was or was not a genuine psychic.

The Good Christian Women of the town huddled in the corner of the room and whispered among themselves, oozing disapproval. There were only about twelve Good Christian Women in Beekman, but a lot more came out of the woodwork once you introduced the element of sorcery to a PTA fundraiser. There was talk about how *inappropriate* it was, how the PTA should *not* be involved with this, how it was a *community event*, and maybe they should go ahead and get the karaoke started early.

Susan got more and more frantic as the charges of

witchcraft and the dark arts began circling the local golf club's dilapidated ballroom. "It's just for fun! It doesn't mean anything! I'm a *Sunday-school* teacher, you guys, I mean, give me some credit!

"Are you hearing this?" Susan had said to Lucy. "Have these women all lost their minds?" Even Claire, relatively reasonable Claire, was overheard saying, "Well, I would have put a stop to it if I'd had the chance, but this is the first I heard of it."

"Please, just do it, Lucy," Susan said. "For me."

And of all the things Susan Howard was always pestering Lucy to do—judge the class scarecrow competition, make chili for the chili cook-off, man the Milk-a-Goat booth at the spring festival—this one seemed like the most painless. So Lucy paid her thirty-dollar donation and sat down across from the woman who either was or was not a psychic and watched as she shuffled cards and laid them out in the shape of a large cross and said a bunch of things Lucy could no longer recall. She remembered only one part of the reading, but it had stuck with her, and Lucy found herself thinking about it at the strangest times.

"You have a son," the woman had asked Lucy. Stated, really.

"I do."

"Just the one, right?"

"Yes."

The woman turned over three more cards, all in a row.

"Your son has very strong karma."

"What do you mean?" Lucy remembered asking. "Is that good or bad?"

"It's neither," the woman had said. "It's just very, very strong."

After Gordon and his team left the conference room, Kelly turned to one of her lawyers and said, "I want to hurt him."

"So far he's giving you everything you've asked for," said Lawyer Number One.

"I realize that," said Kelly. "What I'm asking you is, how can I hurt him?"

"He wants the child," said Lawyer Number Two.

"Yes, according to the postnup you brought us, all he really wants is physical custody of your son, with you being granted essentially unrestricted visitation rights," said Lawyer Number One. He flipped through the document and found the appropriate sections, running his finger down the text while he summarized it for her. "Not even *essentially*. You would have unrestricted visitation rights. He proposes purchasing an estate near the Eagle's Perch so that you can be with Rocco whenever you want. The assumption, it seems, is that you could reside wherever you chose and be able to spend time in Beekman with your son, as much as you want, and at your convenience."

"And I could fight that?"

"You never signed the postnup," said Lawyer Number Two. "You can fight for whatever you want."

Kelly took off her dark glasses and looked at her face in the bathroom mirror. It was strange, still, to see the patch where her left eye used to be. When she was fourteen, her creepy science teacher Mr. Skinner used to massage her shoulders during class and say, "You don't have to worry about science, sweetie. Your face is your fortune."

Well, now her fortune was her fortune.

Fuck you, Mr. Skinner.

Kelly knew her happiness wasn't to be found living full-time in Beekman, but she also knew this: Beekman was the best place for her son. It might be filled with boring old housewives who volunteered to be lunch ladies, but for a kid who stood to inherit billions, the chance to be a stone's throw from a normal childhood was priceless. Rocco's best friend, some kid named Theo, lived in a house that was smaller, square-footage-wise, than Rocco's playroom. Kelly knew this only because Gordon had found the school directory and looked up the kid's address on some real estate website and then told her about it. And just last week, Rocco had asked her if they could go to Hershey Park. A kid on his soccer team named Brannon—the same Brannon who had taught Rocco the word *titty*—told him it was the best place ever. Not Aspen, not Nantucket, not Gstaad. Not even Disneyland. Hershey Park.

And it was good for him, Kelly knew. All those things Gordon had wanted, the rock collections and the sledding and the little American flags, all of that was real. She might have been raised in a trailer park by a single mom with a weakness for bad boys and a taste for methamphetamine, but Kelly knew what childhood was supposed to be like. And Rocco had it.

But all of that didn't take away from the fact that Kelly wanted to cause Gordon some pain. She wanted the loss of her eye to cost him something, something more than just houses and stock portfolios and cold hard cash.

And so she sat alone in her lawyers' bathroom for a while and had herself a good long think.

Izzy had gone radio silent on Owen, so completely silent that he began to worry about her. No calls, no texts, no menacing emoticons—nothing. When he saw Sunny Bang at soccer practice that week, he pulled her aside and asked her if she'd talked to Izzy.

"She's gone," said Sunny Bang.

"What do you mean, gone?" Owen asked. *"She's dead?"*

"No, you idiot," said Sunny Bang. "She's gone. She disappeared. Nobody knows where she went."

"Someone has to know. She can't have just vanished."

"She did."

"What about her house? What about her store?"

"She hired a lawyer from Poughkeepsie to handle everything. He's selling her house, liquidating the inventory of her store, getting rid of all of her stuff. He won't say where she went or where she wants the money sent."

"That's crazy," said Owen.

"It's really unhealthy," said Sunny Bang. "She needs support. She needs the Sunny Bang meal-delivery treatment, at least. I would drive her to her chemo appointments. We weren't best friends or anything, but that's what I do."

"She told me she didn't want any treatment," said Owen. "She said she was too far gone. I figured she was upset and she'd change her mind."

"You're never too far gone. My uncle had stage-five colon cancer and the doctors said he had three months left. It's four years later and he's still alive."

"There's no such thing as stage-five cancer."

"There is in Korea," said Sunny Bang.

"Your uncle still lives in Korea?"

"No, he lives in Jersey. 'Every day is a gift,' he says. He has to crap in a bag but he seems pretty happy."

Conversations with Sunny Bang sometimes went like this, Owen thought. Half of you felt like you were talking to a wise woman from an esteemed and ancient culture, the other half left each conversation genuinely confused.

"Well, where do you think she'd go?" said Owen.

"I don't know. We weren't friends like that. I don't know her people. She's not even on Facebook under her real name."

"What about her ex-husband?"

"Christopher? He doesn't know anything," said Sunny Bang. "Not about the cancer, not about where she might be."

"Did he say anything? Anything at all?"

"Not really," Sunny said. "Just that he thought something was up when a delivery guy showed up at his front door and gave him his great-grandfather's desk."

When Kelly returned to the conference room, even her lawyers had no idea what she was planning to propose. They had been hanging out around the conference table, leaning way back in their chairs, billing their hours while they texted each other about how their client was the luckiest goddamn floozy on the planet. They joked about trying to seduce her and then marrying her and how they'd refuse to sign a prenup. They speculated about what she looked like without her dark glasses on and whether or not she'd be willing to wear them during sex and/or blow jobs.

Kelly settled down into her chair and looked across the table at Gordon.

"I want Gordon to get Mrs. Lowell her job back."

"And who is that?" asked Hugh Willix.

"The kindergarten teacher that Gordon got fired," said Kelly. "The one who turned into a woman."

"Mr. Allen can't do that. It falls under the jurisdiction of the local school-board officials. It's entirely beyond his control."

"I think Gordon can control anything he wants. And I'm not going to sign anything until it's done."

And with that, Kelly pushed her chair away from the conference table, hooked her elbow through her Dior bag, and made what she thought of as her Hollywood exit.

Twenty-Three

We all have a strong preference that life should be easy, comfortable, and pain-free, but that doesn't mean there's something wrong with life when it isn't those things. It's just life. It's just life and it's not how you would prefer it to be, but that doesn't mean there's something wrong with it.

—Constance Waverly
WaverlyRadio podcast #132

N o," said Owen.

"What do you mean, no?"

"I mean no, I don't want you to go to the city tomorrow. I don't want you to see whoever you see when you go there."

Lucy and Owen were in the living room, both on their laptops. Wyatt was asleep, early for once, and the house was quiet except for bursts of typing and clicking.

"The six months aren't up yet, Owen," said Lucy.

"I'm aware of that."

"I'm going to the city."

"No."

Lucy closed her laptop and looked at her husband. "Honestly, I don't know what you mean by no."

"I mean, I don't want you to go. I don't want you to go into the city to see the person you've been seeing there. We had an agreement. If things got too crazy and out of control, we would call it off."

"Is that on the paper, Owen? Because I don't remember that part."

"I'm going to go get the legal pad," he said.

"You're going to go get the legal pad?" Lucy started to laugh. It was a forced, angry laugh. "I love it!"

"What?"

"We are so far beyond any stupid list of rules. I love that you still think those are relevant."

"Why aren't they relevant?"

"The people who wrote those rules don't even exist anymore, Owen."

"That's not true. I'm still the person I was."

"Well, I'm not," she said. "The person I was when I wrote down those rules—that person doesn't exist anymore. That Lucy has left the building!"

"What are you talking about?"

"Do we really want to have this conversation?" Lucy asked. "Because I don't think we do."

Lucy went into the kitchen to get some wine. She poured herself a glass of sauvignon blanc and drank it quickly, and then instead of heading back into the living room, instead of talking to Owen, she put on her running shoes and a heavy jacket and an old scarf.

"I'm going to take a walk," she told Owen.

"It's pitch-dark outside."

"I'll bring a flashlight," she said. "I just need some air."

"Don't forget your phone," Owen called after her as she walked out the door. "You wouldn't want to forget your phone."

Lucy headed down the driveway and toward the dirt road. When she got out of sight of the house, she called Ben, but he didn't answer. She thought of calling her sister, but she didn't know what she would say. Mostly she hoped Owen would be asleep by the time she got home. And even though it was cold and dark, it felt good to be outside. She walked for a long time, and she didn't think to turn around until she was quite far from the house.

When she got back, all the lights in the house were out. She let herself in quietly and locked the door behind her. She was setting the alarm when she heard Owen's voice.

"I want you to stop, Lucy."

Owen was sitting at the kitchen table, in the dark. He was staring down at a glass of bourbon in his hand. "Whatever is going on, I want it to stop. We can talk about it or we can not talk about it."

Lucy walked over to the table and sat across from him.

"It was after you started, just so you know," she said. "I know how fast you found someone. And it wasn't because I was snooping."

"How did you know?"

"Because you were so happy all of a sudden. Slinking around, smiling all the time, showing up with cat hair all over you. I felt like I was living with a sixteen-year-old boy who'd just convinced his prom date to go all the way. And that was not fun for me, just so you know. That did not exactly renew my faith in our marriage."

"I'm sorry," said Owen.

"You know, it was one thing to be invisible to the world. To be yet another invisible mommy. I'd gotten used to that, actually. I'd gotten used to slipping on my Merrells and heading off into the world like a phantom of a person, being yes-ma'am'd if I wasn't ignored completely. But apparently I've been involved in a marriage where my husband doesn't even see me. What did you think? You thought I wouldn't do anything?"

"No! I tried to—I tried not to think about it. It's not the most pleasant thing to think about. I tried to put it out of my mind."

"You thought I just really, really needed French lessons," Lucy said. She put on a weird voice, like a dopey guy in a 1950s TV commercial. "'Those French lessons sure put a spring in my wife's step!'"

"Did you meet him in your class?"

"I didn't take French, Owen," said Lucy. "I never took a single class."

"So that was all just so you could—"

"Go see someone. Yes. Go see my person in the city. That's what French was for."

"Okay," he said. "Wow."

"We did this together, Owen. We did this to each other."

"Yes, we did a stupid thing, and we both did it. I should not have agreed to it, I should have shut it down the minute it came up, and obviously I didn't."

"You didn't shut it down," said Lucy. "Quite the opposite."

"Yes, right, I had fun. I enjoyed it. Guilty. Guilty as charged."

Lucy reached for Owen's glass and took a big sip of bourbon. And then another one. And another.

"Just tell your somebody that we decided to stop early," Owen finally said. "Say we agreed we made a mistake, and we decided to cut things short. We'll go to therapy and work on our marriage. Obviously all of this is a symptom of something bigger. Let's work on that."

"It's not that simple."

"Why not?"

For a moment, things could go one way or they could go the other.

"Because I'm in love with my somebody."

And then Lucy started to cry.

Lucy started to cry.

Lucy crawled into bed and got under the covers. After a bit, Owen climbed in next to her. They both stared up at the ceiling. Neither of them said anything. Owen finally reached over and took Lucy's hand, and held it in his. His hand was warm and big and soft and forgiving. Tears rolled down Lucy's face, slowly but continuously, but she did not sob.

"Do you still love me?" Owen eventually asked.

"Yes," Lucy said.

And it was true, she thought. She did love Owen.

"But I love him too."

"Okay," Owen said. He did not let go of her hand. "That's okay."

"You don't know him. He lives in Brooklyn."

"What? How did you—you think you're in love with him?"

"I didn't think it would happen. I wasn't looking for it to happen. But it did and it has and now this is what we've got."

It was late, three o'clock in the morning. Owen got up to go to the bathroom. When he got back into bed, Lucy sat up and turned on the light.

"I was thinking, no matter what happens, between you and me, I mean, the family part of us doesn't have to break up," she said.

"What are you talking about?"

"I mean, we'll always be a family. We'll always be his parents."

"Are my brother Greg and his ex-wife, Alexa, still a family? No. And do you know why? Because they got divorced and they're both married to other people. That's what happens when you get divorced. You stop being a family."

"I'm talking about something different than what your brother did."

"Like what?"

"Like, different. Amicable. Friendly."

"I honestly have no idea what sort of relationship you're talking about."

"I mean, we'll always be his parents. We can make it amicable. We can be those amazing divorced parents who are best friends and do holidays together and go to soccer games together and take, maybe, vacations together at some point."

"Okay, that thing you're talking about doesn't exist. And if it does, somewhere, it's because the parents are too selfish to go ahead and admit that they're ruining their kids' lives."

"It does exist, Owen. People do it. They stay friends."

Owen rolled over and stared at the wall, his back to his wife.

"I won't be your friend," he finally said.

"What?"

"I don't want to be your friend if you do this to us. If you do this, I'll never say two words to you again."

"You'll have to, Owen. We'll still be raising a child together."

"Correction," he said, "I'll never say two friendly words to you again."

"I feel sick," Lucy said. "I think I'm going to be sick."

Lucy ran to the bathroom and threw up.

The next several days were among the strangest of Lucy's life. It was a long weekend, thanks to teachers' conferences, and the dailiness of her world took hold again, almost imperceptibly. She shopped for groceries, she took Wyatt to Blake's Ninja Turtles birthday party, she dropped off the dry cleaning and then picked it up again. She texted Ben, and she called him every chance she got, but she didn't go into the city to see him, and things between her and Owen seemed to settle down. It almost felt like nothing was going to happen.

But then, late on an otherwise ordinary night, Lucy was straightening up the kitchen when Owen walked down the stairs and asked her, "What's his name?"

"What's whose name?"

"The guy," said Owen. "Your guy."

Lucy ran water over a sponge and squeezed it.

"Ben."

"Ben? What kind of a name is that?"

"It's a name, Owen. Ben is a name."

"Is he a Benjamin? A Bennet? What?"

"I don't know what it's short for."

"You don't know what it's *short* for? This man you're in love with? You don't even know his name?"

"I guess we haven't spent a ton of time talking."

"Nice," said Owen. "Thank you for that."

"I'm sorry, but I'm not sure what point you're trying to make."

"You don't think it's weird that you don't know this man's actual name?" asked Owen. "Has it occurred to you that you might be just a little less important to him than you think?"

Lucy reached for her phone, which was charging next to the coffeemaker. She was angry. She fired off a text.

"His first name is Benjamin," she said, reading her phone. "His middle name is Walter."

"Good to know," said Owen.

Lucy put the phone down. She started to wipe down the kitchen counters.

"So what is this, exactly?" Owen asked.

"What do you mean?"

"What is the scope of your relationship with this Benjamin Walter Somebody person as it pertains to our family? Why don't you ask him that? Send him a text and ask him that."

"He already told me."

"Oh yeah?" said Owen. "What did he say?"

"He said he wants to marry me."

Owen was motionless except for the fact that he was breathing fast and hard. Lucy could see his every breath.

"Get out," he finally said. "Get out of this house. I want you out now, Lucy."

❧❦❧

Owen went upstairs and climbed into bed with Wyatt, who had woken up and was jabbering away to himself, softly, rerunning things through his head, repeating sentences that had imprinted themselves on his brain. ("During a lockout we hide in the library behind a bookshelf, and if we can't get to the library we hide *behind* the yellow line, so the bad guy can't see us. We hide *behind* the yellow line, very, very quietly, so he'll move on to the next classroom." *My God*, Owen thought, *what the hell are they telling these kids in school?*)

Wyatt was talking in loops and fluttering his fingers in the air like butterflies. It was one of his ways of soothing himself, of making sense of his world, and the fact was, it worked pretty well.

Owen did not know how to soothe himself and could not make sense of his world, and so he'd crawled into bed with his son. His warm little body never failed to comfort. Someday, he would be too old for this. Someday, Wyatt would lose interest in snuggling his dad, he would balk, straight-arm him, or just say, "Dad." It was one of those truths about raising a child that was almost impossible to imagine. The fact that these things would disappear, the body-to-body connection that began that first day in the hospital would one day come to an end.

Wyatt's comforter felt like a lead blanket, probably because that's what it was. It was weighted — not with lead, presumably — designed to calm kids with sensory issues, with spectrum-y problems of every sort. It was a variation on Temple Grandin's squeeze machine.

It felt good, being under the blanket, like a full-body hug. *Maybe I should get one of these for the master bedroom,* Owen thought. He wondered if they made them in a California king, without the superhero design. Probably not.

"Dada, can I have your phone?"

Owen handed over his phone without resistance.

"Siri, show me videos of the *Hindenburg,*" said Wyatt.

"Okay, Owen, here are directions to Linden Road."

"Siri, you're stupid."

"I'm sorry you feel that way about me, Owen."

"Siri, show me videos. Of. The. *Hindenburg.*"

"Here are some videos of the *Hindenburg* I found for you online."

How did we end up at the Hindenburg? Owen wondered.

Well, you watch enough YouTube videos about the *Titanic,* pretty soon an algorithm kicked in and started suggesting *Hindenburg* videos. It's one of those natural progressions. What came after the *Hindenburg?* The *Challenger* explosion? The Twin Towers falling? Those South American soccer players who ate each other after their plane crashed in the Andes?

His wife was in love with somebody else. No, not "his wife" — Lucy. *Lucy* was in love with somebody else. Somehow that made it even worse. She loved him still, but she was "in love" with this other guy, this Ben character.

Falling in love was against the rules! He kept coming back to that. He felt as powerless as a kid on a school playground. No falling in love! No leaving! No falling in love and then leaving!

The *Hindenburg* was finally exploding. It had traveled from Frankfurt all the way across the Atlantic Ocean and exploded in New Jersey. *How come I never knew any of this?* Owen wondered. Like everyone, he'd heard about the *Hindenburg*, and as a kid he'd seen that black-and-white video with the news guy crying, "Oh, the humanity," but he never knew the whole story.

People were fleeing, jumping, screaming, dying. Owen felt the weight of Wyatt's special blanket, which failed to squeeze the terror from his chest, and tried to close his eyes. His last thought before sleep took him was that he was surprised only thirty-six people had died. It had felt like so many more, in that old video, as the flames engulfed the screen and the newsman cried.

Fifteen Months Later

Owen and Wyatt were heading up from the mailbox, sharing a big black umbrella. They were making plans to build a fire, and Wyatt was jumping in every puddle he could find. Owen flipped through the mail and saw an interesting envelope with unfamiliar handwriting. He read it while they walked.

Saturday was going to be the official opening ceremony for the Gordon and Simka Allen Center for Children with Special Needs. Wyatt was going to cut the ribbon, and he was very excited. He'd been practicing all week with a very big pair of scissors.

The center had a sensory gym, multiple therapy rooms, and a state-of-the-art PT gym, as well as an innovative program that would bring in graduate students from nearby universities to perform the kind of research that was difficult to do in a clinical setting. It wasn't a clinical setting, it was a school setting—it was connected to the Beekman public school by a winding, glass-enclosed walkway that took advantage of the view.

They'd even gotten a small school farm as part of the deal, the old Jenkins place, just out past the soccer field. The farm had been in the Jenkins family for over a hundred and fifty years, but it turned out the current generation was happy to sell it to the school, at a fair price, for the good of the community. The school farm would offer therapeutic horseback riding, as well as after-school programs in animal husbandry and organic gardening, permaculture and wilderness-survival skills, as a way for the neurotypical kids to interact meaningfully with the special-needs children in a structured yet nonacademic environment.

How it had happened was this.

Susan Howard had gotten wind of Gordon Allen's attorney's proposal to Owen and Lucy—the "whatever you want," the blank check—and Susan was not one to let such an opportunity go to waste. She was in the middle of her own divorce, Susan was, but the strange thing about her split with Rowan was that their shared custody arrangement left her with gobs of free time. When she realized that Owen and Lucy were too wrapped up in their own stuff to think about it clearly, she immediately grabbed the reins. She unleashed the full power of the Mommies of Beekman, gathering them over drinks, thinking about what made the most sense given who Owen and Lucy were, what Wyatt would benefit from, what kind of legacy they might want to leave, and what the community could use the most. First, they dreamed together. Then they narrowed it down—to their credit, the ladies nixed a lot of one another's pet ideas: the new auditorium, the state-of-the-art science lab, the indoor pool, the Maya Lin art installation—and then they did the research, they consulted specialists, they ran the numbers. Finally, they presented a plan to Owen and Lucy (separately, Susan had decided, after conferring with Sunny Bang) and, when they got their respective stamps of approval, they brought the whole thing before Gordon Allen and his attorneys. Claire had done the PowerPoint, Susan the artist renderings, and Sunny Bang the budget. *The women in this town could take over the world,* their husbands all thought as they sat on the sidelines, watching. *Thank goodness they're happy to raise our kids.*

The whole thing was a spectacular boondoggle in the end, but Gordon Allen didn't mind. All he asked for was that Dirk, his bee guy, be allowed to build a house on the farm property with zero interference from the town zoning board and that he be employed in perpetuity to develop whatever kind of cockamamie projects he wanted to do with the kids. ("If you want to build your house out of old tires and donkey dung, you can do it," Gordon said to Dirk as he watched one of his Titleist V1xs plop into the mighty Hudson River. "If you want to teach a class on how to make a tractor run on algae and old French-fry oil, go right ahead.")

All of it, the whole thing, was generously, perpetually endowed. With zero tax dollars involved.

Thank you, Fat Black.

Owen walked up the driveway, reading the letter as he went while he listened to Wyatt with half of one ear, the way a parent who spends a lot of time with his kid listens when the kid is talking about nothing much in particular. What was happening at school, who has a crush on who, what happened at recess, could he go camping with Brannon and Brannon's dad, were they going to go to Maine again in the summer. Sometimes the reality of Wyatt was a shock to Owen, but lately, more often than not, it was like this: It was no longer extraordinary for Wyatt to be just about ordinary. Not totally, not by any means—but just about. He was a quirky, unusual, challenging kid. He was an amazing, unique, wonderful kid.

"Who's that from?" asked Wyatt.

"What?" said Owen. He was lost, gone, deep in the letter.

"Who's that mail from?"

"Oh, this?" said Owen. "It's from an old friend."

Lucy was upstairs, looking out the window, watching Owen and Wyatt walk up the driveway.

Lucy had moved back home a few months ago. Or, rather, she and Owen had both moved back home, together. It turned out that Wyatt couldn't handle the shuttling-back-and-forth part of Lucy's original exit plan, and so Lucy and Owen each moved in and out of the house every few days while Wyatt stayed put. Owen lived in the Callahans' luxurious guesthouse when he wasn't at the house, and Lucy split her time away between Ben's place and the spare futon in Sunny Bang's dank basement.

Sunny Bang was completely beside herself over the whole situation. She took the blame herself, too much of it, surely, and she did everything she could to make things right, even when Lucy was swooning around like a love-struck teenager. Basically, Sunny Bang went to work. She made a few phone calls. She invited her sister up to Beekman for the weekend, poured tequila down her throat, and got her talking. Sunny collected as many unsavory tidbits about Ben as she possibly could—stuff from as far back as college, ugly details about his divorce—and she held on to them until the first hot heat of passion and escape and fantasy had begun to burn itself out of Lucy's system. And then? And then she oh so casually dropped them in Lucy's path, like ancient Asian coins or tiny hardened turds, whenever she sensed they would have the most impact.

"Ben cheated on Deborah during her residency, but she always said it wasn't really his fault," Sunny said to Lucy one night while they were cooking dinner. "She was pretty much gone all the time. They worked it out, though. Stayed together for eight more years."

"Why are you telling me this?" asked Lucy.

"To show that people can work things out," said Sunny. "Why else would I be telling you this?"

Victoria had claimed over drinks that rainy afternoon in Brooklyn that it took three years for something like this to fizzle out, but for Lucy it took less than half of that. There was a good six months of, well, bliss—there was no other word for it, and Lucy would not call it something else, it was bliss, falling in love with a new person, no matter how old you are or how complicated things were, falling in love is a thing like no other, and the fact that Lucy had fallen just as deeply and completely in love with Owen all those years earlier did nothing to detract from that fact. So, six months of bliss, five months of pretty horrible, and then four months of date nights and long walks and counseling twice a week with Owen.

"This is really fucked up," Lucy said to Owen when they met in the therapist's waiting room the first time.

"Yeah," said Owen.

"We really fucked up."

"We really, colossally fucked everything up," said Owen. And then he reached out for her hand.

Lucy found herself circling back again and again to something Ben had said to her on one of those very first nights she was on her own, right after Owen had asked her to leave the house. She was sleeping in a motel room two towns over, talking to Ben on the phone for hours every night, and driving home each morning in time to get Wyatt out of bed and off to school.

"I feel like I should tell you something," Ben had said to her.

"What?"

"Keep in mind, this is not a hidden message. This has nothing to do with you and me or our future together or anything like that. Do you understand?"

"I do," Lucy said. "At least, I think I do."

"I look at Eliza and Peggy when they're asleep sometimes, when it's one of my nights with them."

"Yeah?"

"And I can't shake it, the same thought just goes running through my head."

"What?" asked Lucy.

"It's, well…" Ben paused for a second, like he wasn't sure he should say this, but he forged ahead. "It's *What was I thinking?* It's *What in the world was I thinking?*"

Lucy heard the back door open. Owen and Wyatt were making a bit of a commotion, and the door kept opening and closing and then opening again. Lucy stood at the top of the stairs for a minute and listened to the two of them talking. They were hauling in firewood, and Wyatt wanted to carry each log one by one instead of using the canvas log carrier. Owen was telling him why the log carrier was better. "It's more efficient," Owen explained. "That means it's easier and faster and better."

"Okay," said Wyatt.

"We'll do it together," said Owen. "We'll each hold one handle. And then we'll make a great big fire for Mama."

Lucy slipped on her sweater and headed downstairs to her family.

"You want some wine?" she called.

"Yes, please," said Owen.

Lucy poured two glasses of wine and went into the living room. She sat in the big red chair and looked on as Owen and Wyatt set about building the fire.

"No fire starters!" said Wyatt.

"No fire starters," agreed Owen.

"And only one match," said Wyatt.

"Are you sure?" said Owen.

"Yes," said Wyatt. "We'll pretend we're in the woods and we've lost all our stuff and we only have one match left."

Owen turned to Lucy and said, "I've got something for you to read, if you want to read it."

"What is it?"

"A letter."

"Do I want to read it?" asked Lucy.

Owen thought about it for a moment and then said, "I think you do."

Dear Owen,

I'm writing to you from sunny Scottsdale, Arizona, where it's eighty-five degrees and the sky is blue and today, for some reason, there are about eighty hot-air balloons floating up in the sky. I'm still alive, just so you know. This isn't one of those letters people write when they're dying and then have someone mail for them after they've bit it. Well, let's just say it's March

Madness and I was alive when I put this in the mailbox. Real stationery too.

I'm sorry I disappeared on you. I left Beekman to go die at my sister Mona's house. I know, I know, I never said I had a sister. Mona and I both spent most of our adult lives trying to forget about each other and it turns out we did it more successfully than either of us ever imagined. When I called her to tell her I had cancer she laid out all of the reasons why I should stay in Beekman, but I got on a plane and showed up on her doorstep anyway. She didn't want me there. She really, really didn't want me there. I kept saying to her, "If the shoe were on the other foot"—but if the cancer shoe had been on her foot, I can't say I'd do for her what she did for me and offer to let me die on a rented hospital bed in her dining room because I was quickly going to be too weak to walk up the stairs.

I decided I would binge-watch The Sopranos *as I lay dying, while the docs from the Phoenix Mayo Clinic did some experimental last-ditch efforts on my failing form. The doctor stuff was a condition imposed by Mona if I wanted to go gentle into that good night shitting blood in her dining room while hiding my chardonnay in her breakfront. It's possible she thought it was experimental enough it just might speed the whole process along (okay, that's not fair—but I'm not crossing it out, just so you see that cancer didn't really soften me all that much).*

Where was I? Oh, The Sopranos. *Let me tell you, that show holds up. And I realized I missed about a third of the episodes on the original run so every few days I'd have this flicker of a good feeling, that hey-I-never-saw-this-one feeling, and when you're convinced you're dying it's nice to have a reliable source of good feelings.*

Christopher came to visit me, back when things were at their direst. Mona tracked him down and told him I was with her. I made him promise to keep it to himself, which it seems he did, unless you are <u>really</u> *over me (joking!). It was nice. Making peace with your ex-husband on your deathbed is not the worst thing to* do. He stayed at the Comfort Inn for a few days, played a little golf, and sat and talked with me when I was lucid. It's amazing how a slow and painful death looming over you makes all the other things shrink down to their proper size. So he put his dick into other women; so what? It really wasn't worth the amount of rage I carried around with me for all those years because of it. I mean it: it really wasn't worth it. And I don't like that Louise L. Hay stuff about rage causing cancer, it feels a little too blame-the-victim for me, but if rage DID cause cancer, then, well—I'm not going to finish that thought. Anyhow, talking to Christopher, I realized how nice it was to be friends again, and I remembered how he always could make me laugh. We were, in our own way, important to each other.

And I was completely ready to go down with this ship, I did not survive because of some inner strength or will to live or prayer or even a shred of New Age hope. There's only one reason I'm still alive: Because they caught it in the nick of time. The doctors said even three months the other way would have meant I'd be dead now for sure.

So what I'm saying is, basically you saved my life. Not even basically. YOU SAVED MY LIFE.

So, thank you. As Sunny Bang said to me after she figured out about the two of us, there's a pretty small overlap between the kind of men I sleep with and the kind of man who would force me to go to the gynecologist. I'm lucky it was you.

I thought Lucy should know too. I think, in a different life, in a parallel universe, the two of us would be friends. Tell her I apologize for putting the gravel in her gas tank. Better yet, ask her to read this letter if she's willing to. I'm sorry, Lucy. I hope you are well and happy. Truly I do.

I still stand by the statement that you two were idiots to do what you did to each other, what you did to your marriage, the peril you put your family in, and for what? One last taste of something you hadn't had since you were young? Passion? Freedom? Well, let me tell you something from this side of the cancer fence, and from this side of the divorce fence, let me go ahead and drop some wisdom on you. What you guys have is enough. It's a fuckload more than most people ever get, ever even dream of getting, and it is your job, it's your <u>duty</u> while you are alive on this planet, to be thankful for it. And to protect it too.

P.S. You're wondering how I know you and Lucy are back together. Please don't be mad at me. But I can read your e-mails and your texts. Other than The Sopranos, it was what kept me going for a while. It was sort of nice, like listening to a soap opera and rooting for the star-crossed lovers to figure their stuff out. Except you and Lucy aren't star-crossed, you're actually the opposite of star-crossed—you're truly and deeply meant to be together and just went a little crazy there for a while. Don't be too mad at Lucy for falling in love with Ben. I fell a little bit in love with you too—we're women, and where sex is involved, I'm starting to believe we can't help it. He seems like a quality person, from what I read. A stand-up guy, as my father would have said. In the end, he did the right thing, and so did Lucy, and so did you. What were the chances?

P.P.S. Lucy and Ben are really and truly 100 percent out of contact with each other in case you ever wake up in the middle of the night wondering.

P.P.P.S. You and Lucy should probably get new computers and new passwords and ditch your phones. Change e-mail providers, too, and maybe get a different phone carrier. I feel better with that off my chest. Oh, maybe drop a note to Ben to do it too.

P.P.P.P.S. I'm staying in Scottsdale. The women my age out here all have skin like beef jerky, they've had so much sun, so compared to them I feel pretty good about myself. I figure I've bought myself about ten more years in the forty-five-and-under dating pool if the terry-cloth-sun-visor crowd is my competition. I lost my hair, and then got it back again, but the texture changed, and it's been a whole learning curve for me. I have a pixie cut now, and people tell me I look like Mia Farrow—not a young Mia Farrow, just Mia Farrow, but hey, I'll take it.

Life is long. And it's getting longer for most of us. Most people in this country will have three or four marriages in their lifetime. Each one will challenge them and suit them in a different way. The lucky few, the ones who are willing to work at it, will have a handful of very different marriages, all with the same person.

— Constance Waverly
TED Talk

About the Author

Sarah Dunn is a novelist and television writer whose credits include *Spin City* (for which she cowrote Michael J. Fox's farewell episode) and the critical darling *Bunheads,* which you would have loved. Her debut novel, *The Big Love,* is available in nineteen languages. Dunn is also the creator and executive producer of the 2016 ABC series *American Housewife.* She lives outside New York City with her family and their seventeen chickens.